Elena
in
Exile

Gavin Boyter

First published by Sword Press 2023

An imprint of Gugnug Press

www.gavinboyter.com

A CIP record for this book is available from the British Library.

ISBN: 978-0-9571298-4-9

Set in Calibri 11pt (body text) and Corbel Light 16pt (headers)

In memory of
Henning Mankell

(a real inspiration)

Where you have gone,
I do not know,
Just that my soul is empty and hollow,
And so I go, and on I go.

"So Badly My Eyes Hurt, So Badly"
(traditional folk song,
translated from the Romanian by Elisa Hategan)

CHAPTER 1

It was a very casual nod of the head and hand gesture, but it was enough to throw Elena into disarray. Her first thought was of Ana, so she turned to her fourteen-year-old daughter, and asked softly, "Can you just wait here? I won't be long."

Ana began to protest but Elena flashed her one of those looks that brooked no contradiction, so the girl shuffled off in the direction of the chromium benches by the bathrooms. The airport was buzzing with more travellers than Elena had ever seen in one place, even in the terminal back in Cluj-Napoca. Somehow, she had been singled out by the short, squat, male Indian customs officer. That didn't bode well. Elena strolled over, trying to affect an air of bored indifference. Channelling Ana's primary mode, in fact.

"Spot check, Miss," the customs officer said. "We just need to take you aside, if that's okay?"

"I must agree?" Ana said, trying to make the question sound like one of casual curiosity, rather than burning necessity.

"No, but we do have the right to refuse you entry, if you won't comply."

So that's a yes then, Elena thought. Did they look too closely at our passports?

"Okay," Elena assented. *Is he going to search me?*

"If you would just follow me to our interview room, you'll just have a brief interview with two police officers. That's all. Won't take a minute."

The officer smiled thinly. He gives this spiel all the time, she thought. It could all be a bluff. But what choice do I have? Could Interpol have acted this quickly already?

It seemed unlikely. Elena turned to wave towards Ana, who was engrossed in her phone, as ever.

"Ana!" Elena called. "I'll be back in a minute. Routine check." She used Romanian to avoid anyone overhearing but at least two of her compatriots turned in response to her Latinate inflection.

Following the customs officer to the small, prefabricated office beside the customs booths, Elena felt her heart pounding furiously behind her ribs and tried to still it. They do spot checks, she thought, and they're not allowed to single people out by race or point of origin. At least that's what Frances had told her.

The office door blocked most, but not all, of the terminal's hubbub as two female officers rose to greet Elena. One was in her forties, black and well-built. The other was slender, white, pinched and barely five feet tall. Don't they have a height requirement for coppers? Elena wondered.

"I'm Sargent Mel Taylor, this is PC Joanne Renfrew. This is simply a routine stop and search procedure we do with randomly assigned arrivals. There's nothing to be afraid of."

Elena wasn't much reassured. It was exactly what she'd expect them to say if they were planning to search and arrest her. They have my passports, she thought. What else do they need?

"Your name is?" said PC Renfrew, consulting the passports the customs officer had handed her before he left, and a form on a wooden clipboard.

"Elena. Balanescu," she said, heart pounding again as she reinforced the lie.

"Take a seat, Mrs Balanescu."

How did they know she was married?

"Sorry, Mizz Balanescu. I misread," corrected PC Renfrew. Her Sargent wasn't saying much, perhaps overseeing the junior officer, perhaps observing Elena. Maybe both.

Elena sat on a hard plastic chair, which wobbled irritatingly. She put her hands together on the table, as if cradling a baby bird, so as not to fidget.

"You've come from Romania, is that right?" Renfrew continued.

Elena nodded, "from Cluj."

"And what's the purpose of your visit?"

"Visiting friend."

"Name?"

"Frances. Frances da Costa."

"And where are you staying? You and… Ana?"

Is she asking about Ana because she doesn't know she's my daughter? Elena wondered. That could be a good sign. No infodump from Interpol.

"Yes. My daughter. We stay at Frances, Soho."

Elena hoped they wouldn't insist on the full address. It was on a piece of paper in the front pocket of her suitcase, currently with Ana.

"Ok. Would you mind standing up and taking off your outer garments."

Even though Elena knew she had nothing to fear, she felt a rush of panic envelop her. Were they going to strip search her?

"Just the jacket and jumper will do," Renfrew said. These cops seemed to have a sixth sense for sources of anxiety. Then again, they'd probably done this a thousand times before.

She did as she was told, silently consenting to yet another woman's hands brushing against her breasts and the inside of her thighs. To be fair to PC Renfrew, the police officer patted her down with as little evident enthusiasm as possible. Meanwhile, Sargent Taylor took notes and examined the passports again. Shit, thought Elena. Are they convincing enough?

What would happen if this went badly? Would Ana be escorted to some holding place for family? Would she be sent on the first plane home? Would Elena be arrested here, or deported under guard? She should have gone through all this with Frances.

"That's fine. You can get dressed," said PC Renfrew and Elena realised that the pat down really was just a formality. Sargent Taylor shut her passports and passed them back across the table. In reaching for them, Elena spotted something unfortunate.

There was a dark arch of red under the unpainted forefinger nail of her right hand. Dried blood. Why hadn't she painted her nails on the plane? She'd meant to. She would at least have spotted the blood she'd missed during the clean-up.

The memory sent a spurt of bile into the back of Elena's throat. She gulped it down, though it burned. Tears began to prickle the corner of her eyes as she snatched back the passport. Was she about to break? Elena felt it was even possible she might blurt out her guilt to these two perfectly decent officers.

"Don't worry Ms Balan, we do this all day. Wish we didn't have to but... you know?"

Renfrew was trying to put her at ease. Neither officer had spotted a thing. She was in the clear.

"I can go?" she said, with an involuntary gulp. "My daughter..."

"Of course," Taylor nodded. "As we said, routine."

As she clicked shut the office door behind her and re-entered the buzzing arrivals lounge, Elena mulled over that word. Routine. Ana jumped to her feet and started pushing the suitcases over towards her. Eager to explore the big city.

Routine.

There would be nothing at all routine about this trip.

CHAPTER 2

So many people. The airport buzzed like a hive on a summer's afternoon. Music, voices in many languages, announcements she could only half understand. A rank of suited men stood, attentive, bored, or indifferent, holding paper signs. Mr Wellington. Colin McPherson. Siobahn. A young woman pulling an enormous purple suitcase rushed up to the taxi driver holding the last sign, pointed to it, shook her head, and laughed.

Half a pace behind her mother, yellow Minions-themed backpack hanging off her shoulder, Ana yawned dramatically.

"She's not here, is she? Of course."

"She'll be here. Be patient."

Elena felt a sinking dread in the pit of her stomach. They had been waiting for twenty-five minutes, their plane having been delayed by ten, plus the ten-minute customs check. Frances was already forty minutes late. It wasn't like her. Amongst the many things she liked about Frances was her punctuality. When they met at a bar or restaurant, Frances would be there fifteen minutes early to find a seat. Elena had never had a friend like that. A friend with occasional, inconclusive benefits.

"Mum, she's not coming", whined Ana.

Elena scowled at her daughter but had to admit that she felt the same way. Something was very wrong. She dialled Frances's number again, walking away from the throng of people at arrivals while the ringtones sounded, each offering less hope than the last. Midway through the eighth ring, a click, a buzz and then a continuous tone.

Number unobtainable.

Elena checked her daughter's whereabouts (Ana had found a branch of Accessorise and was entranced) and returned to the arrivals area. Another plane had spilled its variously happy, exhausted, or hopeful contents out through the terminal. A group of brightly clad African women embraced relatives with unselfconscious affection. Elena watched a young lesbian couple, one girl blue-haired and nose-pierced, the other boyish and gangly, kiss with shy enthusiasm. The feeling in her stomach roiled like she was being stirred with an invisible spoon.

Frances wasn't coming. This had all been a trick. She'd been duped. Elena tried not to think of all the money she'd wasted.

A full hour crawled by. Elena washed the last remnants of her crime from under her fingernails in the recently scrubbed restroom. Then, to mollify Ana, she squandered five pounds in the costume jewellery shop. A spiral, rainbow-patterned bangle that reminded Elena of a toy she'd had as a child. On Ana's slim wrist, the bangle looked garish and impractical. Nevertheless, her daughter loved it and her mood brightened as they shared an iced coffee at the café overlooking arrivals.

When Frances was an hour late, Elena would give up.

"Never trusted her," offered Ana, slurping on ice cubes through a straw. "She was lowkey shifty".

Elena chose not to remind Ana of the many times she'd played raucous board games with Frances or when the older woman had taught her daughter to paddleboard at Vama Veche. Ana had laughed like Elena had seldom seen before. Teenagers had selective memories.

"Five more minutes and then we go," Elena said.

Ana nodded, picking up an ice-cube by sucking hard on the straw then letting it tinkle back into the glass.

7

Fifteen minutes later, Elena and Ana squeezed onto a full Piccadilly line train at Terminal 4 and cast their eyes round a carriage full of bleary-eyed travellers. Elena noted all the different the various luggage tags. KRK, CDG, YYZ, ABB, CCU. She tried to guess the airports but, aside from JFK and ZAG, found herself stumped.

Ana sat on their suitcase and listened to music on the iPhone Frances had given her, second-hand, only a model 11, but generous, nonetheless. How could a woman capable of such kindness treat them both with such contempt?

Elena began to imagine the worst. Frances's car concertinaed against a motorway bridge. Frances curled foetal in an alleyway, beaten by thugs. A fallen stepladder and scattered tools.

Elena almost hoped it was true. Not that Frances would be injured or traumatised but that their off-on relationship would have a chance to weather this storm. They'd laugh at her catastrophising later, as Elena tended to France's surprisingly minor injuries – a fractured wrist, a purple bruise on her temple. Perhaps that was it. She'd been "unavoidably detained" (as she'd put it).

Elena wouldn't mention this weird hope to her daughter just yet. Ana didn't need an excuse to laugh at her mother's naiveté. They'd get to D'Arblay Street, find the hidden key (there had to be one), get into the flat and wait for news. Elena checked her phone. One text message – an alert from a package holiday company. She'd forgotten to opt out.

The tube train rattled out of a tunnel into fragile sunlight and ricocheted through the suburbs of Hounslow and Ealing.

"Mum, listen to this".

Anna, holding out her earbuds. Elena forced them into her own ears, listening to the sweet, fey innocent pop-song that swirled out. A catchy chorus, abominable lyrics, a swarm of electronica. The sound of youthful energy and hope. She smiled at her daughter, pulling a stray strand of hair from where it was stuck to Ana's forehead. Why was this train so swelteringly hot? Ana showed her the singer's album cover on her phone. An impossibly young man with a quiff struck a pose he'd probably have no idea was retro.

"He lives here. Maybe I'll meet him?"

Elena raised a sceptical eyebrow then laughed. Ana was at an age - fourteen, going on fifteen - where she shuttled between peer-learnt cynicism and childish optimism. Elena sometimes felt that she herself had never outgrown that knife-edge between hope and disappointment. Would Ana be the same?

The next station is... Earl's Court.

What was it with these Brits and their obsession with aristocracy? Knights, Barons, Earls... This one Underground line seemed obsessed with wealth and status. With a little over two hundred Euros left in her bank account, Elena felt the background hum of fear that she'd be penniless if this trip didn't work out. She should have insisted on a return ticket.

At Knightsbridge, a throng of shoppers poured into the carriage, filling every available space with Harrods bags and a heady cocktail of perfume that caught the back of her throat. Elena would never be seen dead wearing gold high heels with white trousers. The overdressed shopper caught her eye and smiled, seeing the protective arm Elena had instinctively thrown around Ana's shoulders. Elena immediately felt guilty for judging the woman.

Elena craned her head further into the carriage to study the schematic drawing of the Piccadilly Line. She knew D'Arblay Street was in Soho, but Soho didn't appear on the Underground map. A tall, afro-haired black man with enormous headphones caught her eye.

"Where are you going?"

His directness startled her. Then he smiled and she softened.

"I try to find Soho. I am on right line?"

He nodded.

"Depends where you're off to. Get out Piccadilly maybe?"

"Don't know. I'm going here."

Elena showed the young man her folded piece of paper containing the address from Frances's text message.

"D'Arblay Street? Think that's in Soho. Piccadilly or Leicester Square. Six or half a dozen."

"Sorry?"

"You can get off at either one."

She thanked him and he smiled again and went back to his music. London was not as unfriendly as some of her friends had told her it would be. Elena had suspected, at her send-off drinks, that they were jealous. She told them all to come and visit her. Perhaps she would regret that.

Elena decided to get off at Piccadilly. She'd heard of that place, and it would be nice to show Ana one of the sights.

Much confusion concerning station exits later, Elena and Anna bumped the suitcase up the steps and emerged in the chaotic vortex that was Piccadilly Circus. Ana marvelled at the huge, curved advertising displays and insisted on taking a selfie.

"Can we check out the fountain?" Ana asked.

"Later. We're close, I think. Let's find Frances's place. Dump this monster."

Elena gestured to the suitcase, an unnecessarily literal metaphor of rootlessness. As ever, Elena wanted to blend in, not stand out.

"Let's use English here," said Elena.

"Do we have to?" her daughter replied, predictably in Romanian. *Nu ne trebuie?*

An elderly lady at a kiosk selling t-shirts and trinkets grinned, wishing them well in Romanian. Elena nodded her gratitude.

"Don't you want to learn?"

"Not all the time," countered Ana.

"It's how you get better", pointed out Elena, negotiating a pedestrian crossing.

They zig-zagged slowly though pedestrians and sight-seeing tourists, found Windmill Street and headed towards Soho. Ana walked wide-eyed at the weird mix of stylish boutiques and restaurants and out-and-out pornography. Elena gave up trying to direct her away from the more lurid displays (a book of Robert Mapplethorpe photos in a shop window, neon 'Sex Shop' signs, transvestites in six-inch, size ten heels). Several consultations with shopkeepers and passers-by later, they turned off Poland Street into D'Arblay Street.

Number 19 seemed to be a drycleaner. Elena checked next door. A café at 21, a shuttered office for something called "Flagstone Films" at 17. Perhaps the flat was upstairs, and you had to enter through the shop?

Inside, a steamy chemical tang and a balding moon-faced elderly man with bifocals hanging bagged suits on a rack.

"Excuse me please. There are flats here?"

The man looked baffled.

"I'm trying to find Flat A, number nineteen."

The man scratched his earlobe, taking the piece of paper from Elena. In a room beyond, she could hear a radio and a woman singing along to a song from the 1960s. A perky melody with world-weary lyrics. The unseen woman had a pretty voice about an octave lower than the singer's. *Don't it always seem to go, that you don't know what you've got 'til it's gone.*

"No flats here, except ours. We been here thirty-six year."

"Thirty-seven!" came a voice from the back.

An angular woman in her mid-sixties appeared, carrying a pile of empty suit bags. Her husband handed her Elena's note.

"Some flats at number 16," offered the woman. "Try there."

Elena and Ana traipsed up and down the street for longer than was reasonable looking for Frances da Costa's flat. There were several doorways with name plates but all but one were numbered, not lettered. No-one answered at number 16 when Elena pushed buzzer A for the third time, holding down the button until the blood left the tip of her finger .

"Mum, give it up. She's gone and robbed us. This is embarrassing. Let's go."

Elena shook her head, though she felt the same fears. She pressed flat B's buzzer.

"Hello?" came a crackly, indistinct voice. Female but clearly not Frances.

"We just moved in, and my key won't turn – is broken. Could you open?"

Nothing for twenty seconds, then a buzz. Elena shouldered open the door. Ana waited outside while Elena walked up the musty, cold corridor to the first door. 16A, clearly labelled. She rapped the brass knocker.

No response. One more time... nothing.

Elena was about to try the opposite flat when she caught Ana's eye and saw pity on her face, part-silhouetted against the light from the street. Elena decided not to disturb the elderly person who had let her in. She found a pen and the back of a leaflet she'd picked up in the airport and scribbled a note which she pushed under the door of Flat A. *Frances – where are you? We are in town. Please call me.* No kiss, just an initial "E".

Ana pulled the door shut behind her mother, who had run out of ideas.

"Could ask a cop," Ana offered.

Across the road, a young, uniformed policeman was backing out of an off license, shaking hands with a middle-aged Indian man, evidently having trouble withdrawing from the encounter. The shopkeeper was smiling amiably, the policeman nodding.

The cop turned and caught Elena's eye, half-smiling awkwardly. He was handsome in an understated sort of way, his round helmet ill-suited to his angular face. He was wiry but not thin and his body language spoke of someone ready to flee (or give chase) at a moment's notice.

Elena remembered seeing an old black and white documentary film in which an elderly woman in trouble asked a jolly English policeman for directions. For some reason this gave her pause as the off-license's door shut with a tinkle. Perhaps he could be trusted? The policeman wrote something in a small notebook, then pocketed it. No, it was way too risky, given that she was—

"Excuse me!" called out Ana, as he was turning to walk away.

CHAPTER 3

PC Rob Yarmouth found himself staring at a livid purple bruise that had spread around a lump of hairy flesh like a half-submerged egg.

"You see? This where they strike me. I get headaches. I jump each time bell rings."

Mr Singh pulled his turban down over the injury and sat back on the stool behind the counter. The thin morning sunlight lit the jewel-like liqueurs behind his head. The shop had a sickly-sweet aroma. Incense, thought Rob, plus spilt alcohol.

"Can you tell me, from the start, what happened?"

Mr Singh cleared his throat and told the story in a breathless but studied manner. Rob suspected he'd told it to quite a few friends and relatives since nine o'clock.

"I open up. I put money cash tray under the counter while I unlock. These kids - they burst in, cloth round faces. One is holding knife. I remember—small blade like for peel potatoes. These are boys, not men, I think. Sharmila, my wife, upstairs doing laundry. One of them shout 'give us your cash'. I tell them I been to bank last night, I have only what's in till, but they don't listen."

"How much was in the float?" interrupted Rob.

"Usual for weekday. Hundred pounds maybe. So, listen, I reach for the cash. You know - they have knife, so of course I pay. Then they hit me in the head with bottle. Cointreau, I think. My clothes stink. Whole shop stinks."

"And you fell unconscious?"

"Yes. I wake up when Sharmila, she shouts for me and then I don't answer, she comes down".

"How much money did they take?"

15

"Took notes and a bag of pound coins. About seventy pound. Plus couple of bottles. Baileys and plum brandy".

"Baileys?"

"Maybe they panic. Grab anything."

"Why do you think they hit you?"

"Perhaps they think I have weapon."

"Did they take anything else at all?"

"The most important thing. Money – is nothing. They took Kirpan."

"What's that?"

The shopkeeper gestured to a space above the door where something rectangular had evidently been wrenched free.

"Ceremonial dagger. Don't worry, is blunt. Only for show."

"Is it valuable?"

"Not really. Very important for our religion. But you can't sell."

"Would you recognise it?"

"Certainly. In frame on black velvet."

"Like this?"

Rob scrolled through his smartphone, held up a photo. Mr Singh's eyes widened in recognition.

"That's it!" cried Mr Singh, eyes widening.

"Are you sure?"

"I swear", confirmed Mr Singh, nodding vigorously. "Can't believe. Did you catch?"

"Kid called Sidney tried to nick a scooter just round the corner from the station a half hour ago", answered Yarmouth. "Opposite the café where we get our lunches, would you believe? We didn't see an accomplice. Would you recognise them if you saw them again?"

16

A worried look from Mr Singh. "I don't know. Happened fast."

Rob held up another photo. A shadow flickered across Mr Singh's concentrating face. Could it be recognition?

"They cover faces. I'm not sure."

Rob sighed, gestured at a CCTV camera in the corner of the ceiling.

"That working?"

Mr Singh shook his head.

"Only for show. Not connected. Sorry."

So, this was how it was going to go. Mr Singh had recognised the boy, who had just turned fifteen. Rob was sure of it. But Soho, although a commercial district in the city centre, remained a close-knit community. And things work differently in communities.

"Will I get Kirpan back?"

"It's in evidence at the moment. We still need to catch the other boy."

"They're so young. Is necessary?"

Rob swallowed exasperation.

"You were assaulted with a glass bottle and robbed. It's a serious crime."

"They were terrified. Must be first time."

Rob counted to ten internally.

"You reported a crime, so we have to proceed. We'll need to keep the… kirpan… as evidence. You said plum brandy, didn't you, as well as the Baileys?"

"Yes? Was close to hand, like I say."

Rob had seen it all before. Although he had just turned 30 and had only been a qualified police officer for a little over four years, he already knew the drill here. Mr Singh probably knew the boy, albeit loosely. Perhaps the thief was his grandson's school friend or a known face in the

17

vicinity, perhaps a gang member. Whatever was the case, Mr Singh either felt threatened or, worse still, he felt some sympathy for his attacker. If Rob called him in for a line-up, his memory of the two boys would no doubt grow even hazier. Forensics was probably his best bet.

"I take it you cleaned up the shop after the attack?"

Mr Singh frowned, worried.

"Of course. Can't do business with broken glass and alcohol on floor."

"Where are the pieces of the bottle?"

"Bin in back yard. My wife…"

"Please don't touch them and do not throw them out."

Rob said this with a vehemence that surprised even him.

"Of course. Sorry. I thought…"

"We'll have a look at any CCTV footage from the street outside and a detective will be round to look at that bottle. We'll get the kirpan back to you as soon as we can. We may also have to call you to ID some suspects. Will that be okay?"

Mr Singh, looking chastened, nodded.

"I'm sorry I can't help more. Will I get something… for insurance?"

Mr Singh let the thought hang, looking worried, perhaps guilty for not seeming more helpful or grateful.

"Go online and list what was taken. You'll get a report number for the insurer."

Rob scribbled down the email address for reporting minor crimes and tore a page out of his pad. Mr Singh took it like it was a golden ticket.

"Appreciate. Thank you for coming so soon."

"Well, we're only ten minutes away. DC O'Leary will be round to talk to you a little later."

"Don't think I remember anything more."

"I know but it's protocol. I'm just a bobby on the beat. I'm not a detective."

"I see. I open shop? My regulars..."

"That should be fine. Goodbye now."

"So very grateful for return of kirpan… when you're able."

Rob began to back out of the shop as Mr Singh grasped his wrists.

"Very kind young man. So sorry…"

Mr Singh turned the 'Open' sign over and followed Rob out into the street, shaking his hand. He seemed to have dialled up the gratitude, perhaps again aware that he wasn't being as helpful as his civic duty required him to be.

Rob tried to disengage. Physical contact from strangers always made him feel on edge. The mistrust had persisted, ever since COVID-19 had upturned the world a couple of years ago.

He turned and caught the eye of a young girl and then a pretty woman of about his age leaning in a doorway to some flats opposite. He had the strangest sensation that they were both looking at him with unusual intensity. He had no idea why but flashed his most congenial yet business-like smile.

"Remember to call if you remember anything."

"I will, officer Yarmut, I will."

With relief, Mr Singh let him go. Rob turned on his heels towards Wardour Street.

"Excuse me!" came a perky voice from behind him.

CHAPTER 4

Damn her daughter for being such a mind-reader! Before Elena knew what was happening, Ana had trotted over the road to talk to the young policeman. Elena had to follow.

The officer, who seemed approximately Elena's age (32), listened attentively at first. Then, with a slightly pained expression explained that he wouldn't be able to report Frances as a missing person if she couldn't give him any more details of where Frances should be.

"She should be here," Elena insisted, handing over her crumpled piece of paper.

"And your friend gave you this address?", asked PC Yarmouth.

"I copy from text message."

"And it's the wrong address?"

"It seems wrong, yes."

"Then she gave you an incorrect address?"

Elena felt her face colour. It sounded absurd when spoken to a stranger. To her surprise she felt tears prickling the corners of her eyes. She shrugged, giving as non-committal an admission of defeat as possible. The officer just nodded and took a deep breath.

"I was going to get a coffee", he said. "Would you both like to join me? It'll be easier to talk there."

After some hesitation (was this normal procedure with British police?) Elena nodded gratefully.

PC Yarmouth, as the policeman had introduced himself, led them round a couple of corners of the maze-like centre of Soho to a café with the odd name of Chai Me. Elena ordered a green tea, Yarmouth a coffee. Ana wanted something sweet, as ever. For once, Elena relented. They took seats at the back of the cosy café, its furniture rustic and wooden. There were three other patrons, all concentrating intently on laptops or smartphones.

"I would normally interview you in your home or down at the station but if you don't mind talking here, it's a lot nicer," explained Yarmouth. "Plus, I'm knocking off in a bit. Early shift. I started at 4am."

"Really," said Elena, "how you stay awake?"

In response, Yarmouth tapped his coffee cup. Ana eyed them both over her hot chocolate with extra miniature marshmallows.

"I know. Coffee in a place with a thousand kinds of tea. I'm weird like that."

Yarmouth brushed a strand of his overlong hair away from his eyes. Elena had seen this expression on a man's face before. He was shyly sizing her up. Did he think they were on a date?

"Look, we're in UK for first time, supposed to meet our friend. She doesn't show up to collect, doesn't call. We can't get through..."

"And she gives you a false address."

Why must he keep harping on about that?

"But if you knew her..." Elena began.

She didn't finish the thought. After all, how well did she even know Frances? They'd met perhaps two dozen times, slept together just once. It had been her first gay experience since school, and the excitement of it hadn't yet dissipated. Something awaited clarification.

They had met in a bar. A 'gay friendly' place (although Elena hadn't known that at the time). Her friend Madeline was late, and Elena had cast her eye around the room looking for her, only to snag Frances's gaze.

She worked in IT, was a little older than her, perhaps forty. Elena was charmed by Frances's forthrightness. She had been tactile, placing a delicate hand in the small of Elena's back as Frances leaned in to make herself heard over the music.

When Elena said she had an ex-husband and a daughter, Frances didn't flinch or betray disappointment. Instead, she had showed Elena a photo of her own child – a son called Robbie, back home in London and currently staying with his father, whom Frances had amicably divorced two years ago. Frances had uttered the phrase "of course, I'm bisexual" as easily as you might admit to being left-handed. Elena had thrilled to the older woman's confidence.

Unlike some of her disastrous dates with men, Elena's sixth sense for untrustworthiness hadn't fired. Grudgingly, she felt herself opening up to the idea of having a girlfriend, rather than a boyfriend. That was just four months ago and here she was, in a foreign country, on forged papers. She had trusted Frances with her life. With two lives.

"I don't have much money. I don't know what we will do."

Elena caught Ana hiding her face behind her hand. She knew how pathetic this sounded but there was more than pride at stake. Elena could perhaps afford a coach and ferry fare home if it came to that, but she knew what awaited her back home, and she wasn't quite willing to admit defeat yet. Over their long, wine-fuelled conversations, Frances and Elena had planned a future in London. It had morphed from a pipe dream to a concrete plan to an absolute necessity, following the horror of ten days ago. When Elena ran to Frances, she didn't condemn her; she laid plans. And so here she was. But where was Frances?

PC Yarmouth exhaled pent-up breath.

"Did Frances ever show you any ID? Maybe a driver's license or passport?"

Elena frowned, suddenly feeling defensive.

"No—not exactly how one proceed in friendship."

"No, I just mean, maybe when you were planning your trip, you might have seen something. Don't take this the wrong way but how do you know she is who she says she is?"

"You think I've been duped? What could she possibly get from that?"

Elena knew what Frances could get. Approximately 35,000 Leu (around 8,000 Euros) from Elena for the forged passports for her and Ana. Perhaps she had pocketed a cut of that?

No, she trusted Frances. Besides, months and months of romancing her and getting through Ana's force-field of disdain, for a few thousand Euros? That would make her a very determined but low-ranking con artist. Of course, she couldn't reveal any of this backstory to PC Yarmouth.

"I don't know," he shrugged. "There are a lot of scammers out there. You didn't meet online or anything?"

"No! We met at bar. She was over on business. She works as IT consultant and her firm have office in Bucharest."

Yarmouth nodded and asked the next question with his eyes cast firmly down at a small, scruffy notepad he'd pulled from a pocket.

"Hope you don't mind me asking, but was this a romantic relationship?"

Romantic, Elena thought, blushing. The truth surprised her, as she blurted it out.

"I don't know. Maybe. Could be, yes."

She could almost hear Ana rolling her eyes. Sexuality was simultaneously so much easier, and yet more complicated for Ana's generation. Yarmouth looked up from his pad, unperturbed.

"And do you know for certain that she came home to Britain?"

"I saw her off from airport six weeks ago. We both did."

Ana nodded, looking intently at PC Yarmouth, who suddenly looked self-conscious. He folded his notepad away into a pocket.

"Do you have a photo of Frances?"

Elena realised with a jolt that Frances had never let her take a photo of them together. She had been camera shy, oddly, despite her outward confidence. Elena had assumed it was a precautionary measure. There were plenty of places in Bucharest where you could still be beaten for being openly gay.

The one time Elena tried to take a double selfie, Frances took the phone off her and fired off some photos of Elena instead, making her pose ridiculously by the Zodiac fountain. It had been a laugh... and perhaps a clever deflection?

She shook her head, decisively. "We didn't take many photos."

"I got one!" Ana piped up.

Elena stared at her daughter, surprised. Ana scrolled through her photos, found something, slid the phone over. Elena picked it up. The photo showed her and

24

Frances on her old sofa, both apparently asleep, Frances's head on Elena's shoulder, the older woman's long red hair curled across Elena's breast. Elena felt a tightening in her throat.

"When did you take this?" Elena asked, in Romanian.

"After that massive walk. You both fell asleep in front of some old film. I thought it was funny."

"I didn't know she took," Elena said to Yarmouth. "That's Frances."

Instinctively, the police officer smiled when he saw the photo.

"It's not ideal 'cause it's not square on. I suppose I could ask someone to run it through the system though, with her name. I'm not a detective but I can ask a favour. I wouldn't get your hopes up though. If we find her, she's likely a bad egg."

"Please do. I need to know I'm doing something. I will keep phone charged and hope she calls."

"I'm sure they'll let you plug it in here. They're decent sorts. I'm sorry I can't be more helpful, Miss Balan."

"Is okay. Can you direct me to cheap hotel? We're on tight budget."

"Em… There's a backpackers' hostel near Piccadilly. It's not fancy but…!"

"Fancy we don't need."

Elena looked at Yarmouth as he drained his coffee. He was more handsome than her ex-husband but unexpectedly shy for a police officer. Back home, Elena's family had had some dealings with the police. Her brother had run away several times and become involved with some rougher boys who hung out on an abandoned building site. The police officers who picked him up for truancy or smoking weed always looked like men you wouldn't cross, grim functionaries just doing their job. Yarmouth looked soft, caring, perhaps even a little out of his depth.

Ana messaged Yarmouth the photo and he paid for their drinks, despite Elena's protestations. Back out on the street, the wind had picked up and a light drizzle was falling. Ana shivered. Elena wanted to get them somewhere warm and freshen up. Then she would distract them both with a movie or something.

"The hostel is here," said Yarmouth, handing Elena a page from his notebook on which he'd drawn a crude map. "There's a fancy gym next door. The tube station is only two minutes away. It's always bustling – loads of kids. They'll know other places if it's full."

Elena thanked him profusely. She was certain he'd acted out of pity for her and that embarrassed her, but she was still glad she'd asked for help. As they parted company and Yarmouth promised to call her by the following afternoon, Ana surprised her mother by shaking his hand. Elena did likewise. His fingers were surprisingly soft and warm, his grim firmer than she would have expected.

As they walked away, following Yarmouth's map, Ana leaned in conspiratorially.

"He was hot! And he fancies you."

"Don't be stupid," replied Elena. "He was just doing his job."

CHAPTER 5

The Piccadilly Backpackers Hostel was run by a pair of professionally courteous men who had seen it all. Michael, the younger of the two, touched his colleague lightly on the shoulder, as he squeezed past to get to the room keys. That moment told Elena that they were a couple. It seems she had a better gaydar for men than for women.

It was evident that the place had a high turnover of both staff and clientele. It was run with military precision, as evidenced by the registration forms she was required to fill in.

Geoffrey, the greyer of the two concierges, talked them through the rules and regulations.

"You've got lucky today ladies. The female only dorms are full, but a couple just checked out of room 3, so I can give you that and it'll just be you and two German women."

"No private rooms?"

Geoffrey laughed, but not unkindly.

"We have six doubles, all booked for the foreseeable. We're not exactly the Ritz. But we are clean, efficient and..."

"Reasonably priced," completed Michael in a singsong voice, typing their details into the computer.

It was evidently something of a catchphrase.

"We have over seven thousand guests a year and many of them come back year after year, so we must be doing something right," added Geoffrey. "How long will you be staying?"

"I don't really know. That okay?"

"The limit is ten days, usually. We've had families basically trying to live here and we're not set up for that."

"It shouldn't be too long," reassured Elena.

Once they were booked in (for £30 per night, a little more than Elena expected) Michael took them up to the dorm, showed them how the key cards worked and left them in the empty room. Two metal-framed bunkbeds stood out against brightly patterned modern wallpaper. A small radiator, painted gold, was draped with drying t-shirts. One of the bunks had backpacks and clothes bundled upon it—the mystery Germans' things. The other was smartly made-up; Elena sniffed the pillow and sheets. Clean and fresh. It would do.

Ana bounded up onto the top bunk.

"I'm having this one!"

Elena had no desire to climb the spindly ladder each night, so shrugged her agreement. Ana lay back on the bed, thin arms folded behind her head, and closed her eyes. Her chest rose and fell under her light-blue top. They develop so young these days, thought Elena, and the thought sent a shiver of fear through her.

Ana already had the usual pubescent crushes on pop stars and actors but just before school had ended for the summer an older boy had been seen hanging around with Ana and her friends. Elena felt glad she'd taken her daughter away, regardless of the outcome of this trip. She knew she couldn't protect her from lustful boys forever but fourteen seemed a bit too young to be entering that particular battlefield.

"Can we go sightseeing? I want to see the palace!"

Ana rested on her elbow, looking down at Elena, who was digging through their suitcase for her phone charger. She was down to 11% on the iPhone.

"Sure. Don't you want to shower and rest first?"

"Rest? Mum, I'm not like eighty or something."

28

Elena had showered and changed, regardless of her daughter's irrepressible energy, when they walked out twenty minutes later. The water pressure had been a little weak, but the water was hot and the showers as clean as promised. Renewed, Elena decided to adopt a more positive outlook. Frances would get in touch and if she didn't, they would just have a little micro-holiday (on a budget) and then...

Nope, there was no use in trying to complete that thought. Elena needed to stay upbeat for Ana's sake. The future would take care of itself.

Reluctantly, she had left her phone on charge, hiding it under the mattress. She'd listened to the usual warnings about not leaving valuables in the rooms but there was no avoiding it. They'd come back in an hour or so and check messages.

Elena had grabbed a handful of leaflets from reception, including a basic map of central London. Michael had ringed a few sights – Trafalgar square and the National Gallery, St James Park, Buckingham Palace – and they'd settled on a basic itinerary. They were going to enjoy themselves despite Frances. Fuck Frances, she thought, refusing to feel guilty about her disloyalty.

Ana took her arm as they wormed their way through the crowds, past the fountain and statue of Eros, towards Trafalgar Square. Elena was struck once again by the variety of races and nationalities congregating in the large formal space with its imposing lions and the ridiculously tall column topped by the bird-bedecked statue of Admiral Nelson. The whole world is drawn here and welcomed here, she thought. Of course, the UK's recent and controversial exit from the EU gave Elena pause—would people look at her like an unwelcome interloper? Ana, ever-vigilant on social media, had informed her that London (and Scotland, apparently) had not so voted, so Elena decided to continue to feel welcomed by this place and its inhabitants.

Ana loved the fountains and the lions particularly and, before Elena could stop her, raced over to climb on top of one.

"You're not supposed to!" shouted Elena, futilely.

"Come on mum, take my picture."

Ana tossed down her phone, which Elena just caught in the jacket she'd brought in case of further rain.

"Ana! Make it quick then."

With her usual agility, Ana scrambled up onto the back of the massive, black metal lion. Elena scanned the square for police or officials. None were in evidence. Ana took a few furtive photos as her daughter struck dramatic poses.

"It's like that film with the talking lion who sacrifices himself."

"The Lion King?"

"No, not that one. Whatsisname… Aslan!"

"The Lion, the Witch, and the Wardrobe. Come down now, will you?"

Another mother restrained her son from following suit as Ana leapt down and grabbed her phone back to check the photos. Elena avoided eye contact with the disapproving woman.

"You're such a maniac", she said, experiencing a strange kind of pride. Ana was fearless.

They whiled away an hour wandering the National Gallery, until Ana could no longer feign interest in the old masters (and neither could Elena). They both loved Stubbs' horses and the Arnolfini portrait with its sneaky 'selfie' (as Ana put it) of the artist captured in a convex mirror in the background. But the society portraits and historical paintings left them cold, and they both soon felt the urge to get back outdoors again.

Having bought some provisions in a corner shop (chorizo, rolls, rather plastic cheese, juice, and apples), they made for St James Park, passing through the impressive Admiralty Arch and crossing the wide but strangely empty Mall. They walked around the duck-pond, Elena telling Ana her plans for staying in London should Frances ever surface.

They could stay at Frances's for a little while but, as a one-bedroom flat with a fold-out bed in the lounge, it wasn't ideal for anything long-term. Frances had said that once her salary hike kicked in, they could look for a two-bedroom place, somewhere reasonably central, perhaps even with a communal garden. To Elena, who had been brought up on a social housing project and had only ever managed to rent fairly substandard flats in unfashionable bits of Bucharest on her dressmaker's salary, the apartments he sent photos of looked palatial. London was a city of wealth and opportunity.

After finding their home, Elena would get herself a job, perhaps piecework, ideally something a little more creative but armed with a sewing machine, she could knock out anything up to thirty or forty garments a day at home. Frances's pay was good, but Elena wanted her own independent income; she'd let him know that that was non-negotiable.

"And what if Frances doesn't appear?" asked Ana, interrupting her train of thought.

Elena's first instinct was to scold Ana for her negativity, but it wasn't her fault. Her own father had absconded when she was a toddler. The pregnancy had been un-planned, and Karl had never bought into fatherhood. He'd been inconsistent, oscillating between acting like it hadn't happened and 'mucking in' but his participation in Ana's first three years had been perfunctory at best. It was nat-ural she had a cynical attitude about her mother's partners, male or female.

"Then it's Plan B, I suppose. We rent, maybe on the outskirts of town, I get work, we find you a school. We'll survive."

"Can't we just go back?"

"You know that's not an option."

"So you keep saying, mum, but why? You won't say."

They'd had this argument several times over the last ten days. Elena knew it was unfair to uproot her daughter from her network of friends without an explanation (alt-hough Ana had become expert in the perplexing array of social media connections kids had at their disposal these days). Still, there was no way she could tell her what they were running from. Not for a few years, at least.

"You just have to trust me, sweetheart. We can't go back."

Elena had a sudden flash of memory - a line of blood running between tiles, like a pointing finger. She'd never realised the kitchen floor had a slope in it, allowing gravity to create this macabre effect. How weird to have had that thought in the moment of aftermath.

A swan flapped its wings and hissed aggressively at a tourist who had stooped too close for a photo. Ana forgot her interrogation and laughed. Elena was for once grate-ful for her daughter's easily distracted brain.

They climbed a tiny railing and walked up a steep grassy bank to the shade of some tall trees. The sun had melted away the drizzle finally. Elena threw down her coat for them both to sit down, not caring if it got wet. They watched the unending parade of tourists, joggers and bird life skimming or bobbing on the placid lake. Apparently, there were pelicans but so far, they hadn't seen any.

Ana for once put her phone away (how on earth did she still have power on that thing?) and joined her mother in simply enjoying the day. They made up stories about the passers-by and pored over the map for the next port of call. Elena felt edgy though, thinking of her phone back in the hostel and the messages that might be pinging in from Frances or Yarmouth. She'd let Ana enjoy another hour of this 'holiday mode' and then they'd go back and check. Until Elena knew whether she was on this adventure on her own (daughter notwithstanding) she'd not be able to fully commit to London. A blank dread was filling her head, a background hum of anxiety.

Ana threw a piece of chorizo to a bravely curious squirrel, while Elena tried to dispel the growing feeling that she'd exchanged one trap for another.

CHAPTER 6

Yarmouth didn't know how much more hair metal he could take. Forget giving love a bad name, this place gave music a bad name. Guns and Roses had been replaced by Bon Jovi. Now Aerosmith took over the sonic assault. That said, the Temperance was the closest pub to Detective Fleischer's office and Yarmouth didn't want to set foot in there again. He could take jokes at his expense from one colleague. Running the gauntlet of the whole department was another matter.

He was eyeing the dregs of his pint of Director's and beginning to wonder if he should get another one when in bounced Tom Fleischer, in his rather affected manner. Yarmouth raised a hand to attract his attention, but Fleischer was already making a beeline for his corner table.

"Robin Redbreast! You look fighting fit. Punched out any superiors lately?"

Subtle, Yarmouth sighed. "No, I have managed to restrain myself."

Fleischer squeezed his rugby player's frame into the bench opposite. He pointed quizzically at Yarmouth's near-empty glass. He was not offering. Yarmouth downed the last mouthful.

"Okay Tommy, what can I get you?" Yarmouth said. "Pint?"

Fleisher mock-tutted.

"Now you know I can't drink on duty, mate. A coke will be fine."

Yarmouth squeezed out of the booth. Fleisher caught him with a hand as he edged around the fruit machine.

"Though if something crystal clear and Russian were to fall into the glass, well that would just be too bad."

"Message received."

"Oh, and try not to hit anyone on the way to the bar."

Yarmouth sighed. The oaf thought he was a comedian. Still, he was the closest thing Yarmouth had to a friend in the department. He headed for the bar.

Eight months ago, Yarmouth had been a junior detective, ten weeks into the job. His boss, Chief Inspector Robert McPherson was an unlikable bigot, small-minded and uncompromising. He got the convictions but treaded on a lot of fairly innocent toes in the process, especially if those toes were black or brown. The Met had long had a problem with institutional racism but had recently cleaned shop, edging out a few of the more obvious offenders.

McPherson was too good at covering his traces to put anything damning in writing or say anything dubious around his superiors though. Any witnesses to his excessively harsh interrogations and street intimidations were too afraid to rock the boat. He was painfully old school and if Yarmouth had had any sense, he would have waited out the eighteen months to McPherson's retirement and suffered in silence.

Yarmouth had not been sensible. He'd been dating a girl called Rupa, whose family ran an Indian sari stall in Southall. For the last few weeks, they had been intimidated by some local thugs who wanted to edge them off the marketplace and take over their spot, claiming it had been promised to them. Yarmouth had got involved as a favour, although Southall was not strictly speaking his patch. He'd been questioning Rupa's brother Amit away from the stall about the gang when one of them had turned up and started harassing Rupa.

Yarmouth, in plain clothes, had stepped in, flashing his badge. The would-be gangster, who looked scarcely out of his teens, seemingly wasn't alone. Within minutes a gaggle of youths were shouting at him and Rupa. Uniformed back-up appeared to calm things down. It didn't work. Tensions were high and weapons were brandished, scuffles finally breaking out. There were several arrests, including Rupa and Amit.

Back at the station, McPherson had got wind of the situation and inserted himself into the melee of shouting, angry Indians. Amit was the most wound-up, shouting loudly about the injustice of it all and the ignorance of the police. McPherson had not taken kindly to this and had whipped out his baton. At this point Rupa made the disastrous judgement call of stepping in between her brother and the exasperated Chief Inspector. Yarmouth tried to prevent her intercession, but Rupa held her ground, insisting that her family be set free. They were after all, the victims, not the perpetrators.

McPherson had simply barged her out of the way. Rupa had slipped on the recently mopped floor and gone down, hitting a moulded plastic chair with her shoulder as she fell. As Yarmouth went to her aid, McPherson had muttered the fateful line that had sealed his and Yarmouth's fate.

"That's right, go and help the Paki, fucking arsehole."

To this day, Yarmouth wasn't sure whether the insult to Rupa or himself had pushed his buttons most. He reacted instinctively, pushing his boss square in the chest. McPherson, glaring in disbelief, pushed back, bellowing. Yarmouth simply sidestepped and drove his fist into

McPherson's jaw, a glancing blow that caused no damage to anything but McPherson's pride, but one caught on two separate CCTV cameras, plus his chest-mount.

What wasn't caught on camera was what McPherson had said to prompt Yarmouth's rage (which was of a sudden ferocity that baffled even Yarmouth himself). It had been intended for Yarmouth's ears alone and none of the eight witnesses were able to repeat it when questioned. McPherson blamed the slick floor for his 'stumble' and Rupa's fall. He'd been let off with a verbal reprimand from his superior for acting 'without due care and attention'.

Yarmouth was demoted, booted back down to street detail, handed back the uniform he thought he'd relinquished mere months ago. A singular moment of madness he'd never experienced before or since had rocketed him back to square one.

Several of his colleagues, who hated McPherson as much as Yarmouth did, had applauded his actions, quite literally, in the pub that Friday night. Embarrassed and ashamed (but also with a hint of pride) Yarmouth had endured what would become a regular volley of piss-taking. A lengthy written warning was added to his HR file, and he was dropped from CID and reassigned to the city centre a month later. The government had bowed to public pressure to put more 'bobbies on the beat' and Yarmouth was to be part of the new vanguard of cops on foot patrol, an entirely ineffectual and pointless strategy, if you looked at the statistics but the new Commissioner always kowtowed to the Old Etonians, it seemed.

His relationship with Rupa lasted another few weeks, and then she announced she was going home to Kolkata to marry a neighbour's son, an old childhood friend she's never quite forgotten. She thanked him for his gallantry and his understanding.

"McPherson's retiring next year, you'll be glad to hear. We've all had a whip-round to buy him a gold knuckle-duster and a lifetime subscription to Leather Boyz dot com."

"I'll bet," said Yarmouth putting down the drinks.

"Might be good for you. Play your cards right, they might let you back."

"That'll be the day."

"Anyhow, I'm guessing you didn't call me here for a jolly," said Fleisher, sipping his Smirnoff. "Do I sense a favour coming on?"

Yarmouth rubbed his face, finalising his sales pitch.

"It's just a little thing, for a friend."

"Oh, a 'friend' is it? And is this friend of the female persuasion?"

"Yes, but that's irrelevant. Missing person. Her… friend."

"Is she hot? Maybe he should stay missing?"

Yarmouth glared at his ex-colleague.

"I'm kidding. So, tell me, why can't this just be reported the usual way?"

"It's complicated."

"It always is, bruiser, it always is."

Yarmouth slid the phone over, the photo of Elena and Frances onscreen. Fleisher drew in breath.

"Wow. Bit of lesbo action. Eastern European?"

"Romanian. The older one's English, or so Elena says. They've been dating a while. The older one, Frances da Costa, invited the Romanian and her daughter over to stay."

"Let me guess… Redhead never showed up?"

"Bingo. She's not called or texted and her phone rings 'number unobtainable'."

"You said 'them'."

"There's a daughter. She's fourteen, or thereabouts."

"Shit. You think she's a con artist?"

"Probably. Might be in our books."

"What was that name?"

"Frances da Costa. I know—sounds dubious. But maybe a mugshot?"

"Image is a bit shitty. This all you have?"

"Sadly, yes. So—can you run it for me?"

"No problem. So, what's your connection to all this?"

"I don't know. I just feel sorry for them."

"Always a sucker for a damsel in distress, Tommy Boy. Give me a couple of hours, I'll sneak it through."

Pocketing the piece of paper, Fleisher turned his attention to the TV screen where a European football fixture was playing, sound down, to a backdrop of Def Leppard. For the rest of their brief lunchtime 'catch up', Yarmouth would have to compete for attention with AC Milan and Barcelona.

CHAPTER 7

Elena found herself dashing up the stairs at the hostel two at a time, Ana rolling her eyes behind her. Elena had just had the strangest feeling that Frances had called. When she retrieved the phone from her hiding place under the mattress, there was indeed a message informing her of a missed call. It was not from Frances.

Elena played the voicemail on speaker. It was Elena's mother Constantia, Ana's grandmother. Her country-accented Romanian spilled out in a garbled stream. She sounded drunk; it was not an uncommon occurrence.

"Elena? Where are you? I went round your house – everything gone. The door was open. Are you on holiday? When are you coming back? My back hurts and I need my medicine. You need to come and visit me and bring me a new prescription from Dr Lazarescu. Oh, and Karl has disappeared too. Are you together? No – I don't think it's likely. I know you don't care, and I shouldn't too. That son of a bi..."

With comic timing, the phone's voicemail limit cut Constantia off. It was just as well, thought Elena. She didn't want Ana to start asking questions about Karl, her ex-husband.

Ana was rifling through her suitcase, tossing items of clothing onto her bed, looking for something. She turned from this task when the phone message cut off. Elena stood staring at the phone, feeling a clouding of indecision sweep over her.

"Aren't you going to call her back?"

Even though Elena was ambivalent at best about her mother's wants and needs, Ana had always liked the old woman, almost inexplicably as far as Elena was concerned. Constantia had been a more attentive grandparent than mother, it was true. She had developed a habit of handing Ana a handful of small coins and suggesting she buy herself an ice cream, even though Ana was in her teens and the cash amounted to less that the price of a postage stamp, let alone a toffee Big Milk. Ana found this endearing and funny and dutifully added the money to the piggy bank she'd had since she was five.

"Later, for sure. We have somewhere else to go, first."

"Where's that? I'm a bit tired. Wouldn't mind crashing out."

Elena was continually surprised how kids of her daughter's age got so drained of energy. Were their metabolisms in overdrive during puberty?

"I can't leave you here, so you're coming. It's only six o'clock. I'll get you an ice cream."

Ana's face lit up at the blatant bribery.

"Big Milk?"

"I don't think they have that here. Hurry up and find whatever you're looking for."

Twenty minutes later, Ana in a summery, patterned top and knee-length skirt, they weaved their way through Soho, following their crude tourist map. A few false turns and backtrackings later, Ana stopped and pointed dramatically, her mother almost stumbling into her.

"There!"

A neon sign containing a clock declared "Bar Italia". Frances had mentioned it as one of his favourite haunts. She'd once WhatsApped a photo of Frances with her arm around the proprietor, an elderly man with a boxer's face and a shock of white curly hair. Where had that photo gone?

Frances had said you could get a coffee and pastry at 4am here. Bar Italia had an eclectic clientele of Soho creatives, street-sweepers, tourists, and men taking a breather between the gay bars and nightclubs of Old Compton Street. If Frances had been seen anywhere in London recently it would be here.

At 6pm the place was half-empty. A well-dressed couple in their sixties sat at a table outside ignoring one another, engrossed in newspapers. Elena considered getting the photo of Frances out and accosting them but thought better of it and headed inside.

A much younger man than the one in France's photo stood polishing an impressive Gaggia machine while a woman with a narrow birdlike face took payment from a suited gentleman buying an espresso. There were a couple of lone customers at the long counter set along one wall.

"Can I help you?" The woman said, with a professionally thin smile. Her accent sounded Eastern European, perhaps Bulgarian.

"I'm not sure. Have you seen this lady here?"

The woman leaned in, shading the phone from the sunlight glancing in across the polished counters. She took a good look, then shook her head.

"I wouldn't really know. I only work Mondays to Thursdays. Maybe Luca?"

She gestured with her head towards her colleague, who had turned his attention to refilling a large glass jar with biscotti. Luca took a pair of reading glasses from a chain around his neck and studied the photo carefully. He shook his head gently, deflating Elena.

"Not recent."

His answer surprised Elena.

"So, you do recognise her?"

Luca rubbed a meaty hand across his face.

"I think. She came a few months ago. Used to meet people here. Name maybe... Fiona?"

"Frances. Her name Frances."

Luca looked sceptical.

"No. Wasn't that. Haven't seen her 'round lately."

Ignoring the conversation, Ana stood on tiptoes studying the old black and white photos of Soho in its seedier 50s incarnation. Careworn faces and trilbies, everyone smoking.

Elena thanked Luca, her emotions held firmly in check. Not firmly enough for Luca though, who took pity and poured them an espresso 'on the house'. It tasted wonderful and Elena told him so.

"Of course. Best damn coffee in whole city."

Outside, Ana reminded Elena of her promise of an ice cream. They headed for Leicester Square when Baskin Robbin's 35 flavours astonished them both.

Strolling around the square looking at the cinema marquee's promising epic thrills or heart-warming comedy, Ana took her mother's arm, a small gesture which moved Elena. Elena had chosen a small vanilla and pistachio cone, her daughter a triple chocolate creation that she ate too fast, and which gave her a headache.

"So, what's the plan?"

As ever, Ana's directness was hard to deflect.

"We could maybe see a film. There's supposed to be a discount cinema around here, somewhere. Prince Charles."

"No, I mean... generally. Are we going to wait for this loser like, forever?"

Occasional card games aside, Ana had never really warmed to Frances in the way that Elena had hoped she would. Perhaps because of their experiences with Ana's stepfather combined with her own inexperience, Ana mistrusted strangers and her mum's choice of friends. Elena couldn't really blame her for this. Had Ana known a single trustworthy adult in her life?

Suddenly, a face popped into Elena's mind, wearing a smile that couldn't be doubted. It wasn't Frances's face, it was that of PC Yarmouth, the young officer who had said he'd help them. Could he be trusted to be as good as his word?

"Look, Ana. We know Frances is in London or has been recently. Who's to say what's happened to her? We didn't come all this way to turn round and run back home again."

Elena couldn't tell Ana that running home was no longer an option. They were stuck here, with or without Frances. Travelling on a forged passport had been utterly terrifying. She didn't want to go through that shivering fear again. The face of the woman who had scrutinised their documents was imprinted on her memory. She'd shown a mild flickering of interest in the fake surname – Ceausescu – which had made Elena's heart pound so loudly she was sure it was audible. Then professional interest segued back to boredom before the immigration official handed the passports over and waved them through. The whole subterfuge had taken less than a minute but another few seconds would have finished Elena. She wasn't cut out for a life as a criminal.

She had to build a new way of living, here in Britain. If Frances could be found, so much the better, if only to explain herself so Elena would have some sort of closure. If she never turned up, at least Elena had Ana, and a new start, assuming she could find work.

Ana wiped her mouth with a tissue and pulled her mother into a throng of people surrounding a street performer. Skin spray-painted gold, with an orange robe protecting his modesty, the bald-headed man sat in a lotus position, Buddha-like, seemingly levitating several feet off the ground. He was playing a sinuous melody, eyes closed, upon a wooden flute. A swathe of cloth fell from his lap onto the chewing-gum spotted paving stones. Ana leaned in as they walked around the circle, saying a little too loudly,

"There's some sort of metal frame under his robe."

The performer's eyes flicked open. With a curl of his lip into a rather sinister smile, he said: "You cannot find what you seek by looking for it."

Elena laughed instinctively. The floating Buddhist's gaze seemed to range off into the middle-distance, over their shoulders as he began playing his flute once more. Something made Elena turn to see what he was looking at and in that precise moment, through a gap in the huddled bodies of tourists, she spotted a familiar flash of red hair, a recognisable gait.

"Frances!"

She couldn't help shouting out. The receding figure didn't stop or turn and the gap in the crowd closed. Elena pushed through impatiently, dragging Ana after her, drawing disapproving looks.

"Frances! Stop!"

The woman, dressed in a fitted black jacket and jeans, turned a corner down a side street. She was wearing outsized headphones. Frances wouldn't be able to hear Elena shouting at her.

"Come on, Ana!"

"Mum, I don't think that's her. Too tall."

"You can wait here if you can't move any faster."

The annoyance in Elena's voice masked a doubt. Were they chasing a phantom? They ducked and weaved through chattering groups of tourists, a rainbow of races. Ana vaulted a suitcase, Elena accidently elbowed an elderly lady, shouting an apology over her shoulder.

They tore down the alleyway, reaching a T-junction behind the National Gallery. Frustrated, Elena turned randomly right, then left again. There Frances was, turning onto Trafalgar square.

Ana ran ahead, leaping steps, Elena not far behind. They emerged onto the square and into a wall of sunshine and traffic noise. There, straight ahead, stood the woman, standing still, facing away from them, lighting a cigarette. Elena marched up to her.

"Frances! Hey!"

A little too loud.

The woman whirled on her heels. The same chin, straight nose, long wavy red hair falling to her collar. A cousin, a sister, almost a doppelgänger. Remarkably close. But not Frances.

"Can I help you?"

CHAPTER 8

"You'd better not be late, mum. This town is a maze."

Elena wrenched out a painful snag in her hair, standing in front of the small mirror that someone had leaned against the dormitory's sole window.

"I'm only popping out for an hour or so. That policeman might have news on Frances."

In truth, Elena no longer held out much hope of her lover ever showing up. It had been a mirage, a fantasy. But pursuing the mystery gave her something to do. A purpose.

"Can't he just tell you over the phone?" Ana whined.

"I guess not, otherwise he wouldn't have suggested dinner."

"I told you he fancies you."

"Don't be stupid. What time does the film end?"

Ana did a quick check on her phone.

"It's 93 minutes, so maybe add twenty for trailers and stuff. Can you come and get me at ten?"

"Don't worry. I'll be there. It's supposed to be funny, though. You'll enjoy it."

"Yeah, whatever. And you'll enjoy your date."

"Ana, it's not a date."

"Hmm… So why are you wearing that dress?"

Ana stepped closer to the mirror, squinting down to see how the floral-patterned strapless dress fitted. She had to admit, it was a little sexier than she'd imagined it might be.

"I didn't have time to try it on before we left home. Thought I'd give it an airing. How do I look?"

Ana sized her up.

"If I said way too sexy, would you change?"

"I haven't got time."

"Thought not. You look amazing. His eyes are going to fall out of his head."

Ana looked down at her cleavage, the low neckline making a bigger deal of her smallish breasts. Was this a terrible mistake? She'd wanted to dress up, to feel she was on holiday, not adrift and escape in a foreign land. And yes, Ana was perspicacious as ever – she wanted to impress Yarmouth. What harm could it do to get a police officer on her side?

Half an hour later, having dropped Ana off at the small repertory cinema for the Princess Bride screening, Elena took a deep breath and pushed open the door of Les Oiseaux on Wardour Street. The place was decorated with silvery-green wallpaper reminiscent of a Rousseau jungle painting, silver-wrapped tree branches decorated with stuffed parrots and red hanging lanterns. Somehow the effect was quite magical, rather than tacky.

Yarmouth had chosen a table near the back of the restaurant. Feeling a little chilly without a jacket, Elena was grateful. She also couldn't help having the thought that it would have been awkward if they'd sat by the window and Frances had walked by and seen them together. There were so many things wrong with that thought.

Charmingly, Yarmouth stood up as she approached and even pushed the chair back a little so she could sidle into it. The dress was a little too tight around her behind; she'd take it out a little before wearing it again. Yarmouth kissed her lightly on one cheek. He looked different out of uniform, a lot more relaxed and somehow loose-limbed, almost louche.

"You look amazing," he said.

48

"Um, thank you. I made dress herself."

Why had she said that? It seemed so boastful. Yarmouth raised his eyebrows as they took their seats.

"Really. Impressive. Is that what you do? I mean, are you in fashion?"

Fashion. She laughed a little.

"I work as seamstress, but I've had lot of jobs. Could never find right thing. Maybe here in London I will."

She was oversharing. And why did she feel so nervous? This wasn't a date, after all.

"I'm sure."

Yarmouth cleared his throat and slid a manila envelope out from under his menu.

"It's all I could find. Nothing definitive, I think."

Weirdly disappointed he had suddenly turned so business-like, Elena peeled open the envelope and pulled out a few sheets of paper. They contained a series of photos with accompanying names and dates of birth. The photos were all mugshots. A series of women, variously affecting boredom or nonchalance, a few looking genuinely upset. Quickly flicking through the pages, she could see that none of them was Frances. The names were wrong too – nothing closer than Frances de Silva (aged 52 and greying at the temples).

She shook her head, disappointed one more degree. Yarmouth leaned over, touching her left wrist lightly.

"It could be good news. It means she's not a known felon on our books."

"Or just too smart to have been caught."

Yarmouth pushed a strand of sandy hair away from his brow, sitting back in his chair again.

"Or she's not a criminal or con-artist at all. I'm sorry it's not more... helpful to you."

Elena forced a thin smile.

"Is fine. I don't know what I expect."

She pushed the papers back across to him and forced her attention to the menu. Her French wasn't good enough to translate more than half of the entrees and main courses. This caused another flicker of irritation and then she realised how ungrateful she must seem. Yarmouth had done her a favour outside of working hours and had now given up an evening for her. She made an effort to brighten up.

"Have you been here before? You recommend something?"

Fifteen minutes later, they were tucking into their starters – French onion soup for Elena, just garlic bread for Yarmouth. Elena was surprised to find herself enjoying the meal and Yarmouth's company. She also felt flattered he'd not cut the evening short and had committed to two courses. Pathetic. Of course he would stay.

She caught her reflection in a mirrored panel. The woman looking back at her did not look like a fugitive, she looked like smartly dressed thirtysomething enjoying a dinner date (it had to be admitted) with a handsome man who was paying her every attention. She realised her ego had suffered a bit of a bruising over the last few months and Frances had merely glued together a few of the pieces; a poor display of craftsmanship.

Yarmouth was good company. He talked a little about his work, how he'd joined the force after seeing a TV show called The Bill as a kid and deciding he wanted to do some good.

"Hopelessly naïve, I know. I still do believe in what the uniform represents. Even though I'd rather be out of it."

"What do you mean?"

"I used to be a detective. Until a few months ago."

"What happened?"

"I made a poor judgement call."

He hesitated, sizing up the wisdom of saying more. Elena held the moment in silence.

"I punched out a superior officer."

Elena's eyes widened.

"You did not!"

He nodded ruefully.

"The man was a complete arsehole. A racist arsehole, even."

"You didn't get fired?"

"A couple of colleagues backed me up in terms of what he said to provoke me. Plus, and this is a bit more embarrassing, I have uncle who works in the CPS. He pulled strings, apparently, though it happened behind closed doors and without my knowledge. I got demoted."

"You went back to street?"

"No choice really. I'm not sure I'm much use for a career change now."

"Well," Elena said, lowering her head, then flicking her eyes up at him. "You look very... dashing."

"Dashing, is it? Did you learn your English from PG Wodehouse novels?"

Elena frowned lightly. Yarmouth winced.

"Sorry, stupid joke. How's your soup?"

And like that, the evening segued easily into a good time shared between friends. Elena almost forgot the circumstances that had brought her there. Yarmouth appeared genuinely interested to hear about Romania, having never travelled further East than a week's package trip to Split with an ex-girlfriend. He asked about Ana, and said that Elena seemed very resilient and his first impression of Ana was that she took no prisoners. This made Elena laugh.

Yarmouth was thirty—two years younger than Elena—and had only had two long-term relationships, the longest of which had lasted six years and ended with an infidelity (hers, not his) and a broken engagement. He had no kids, an elderly father living in sheltered accommodation in a seaside village whom he visited once a month. Elena decided that he was a little too self-deprecatory for her liking, but she warmed to his sense of humour, nonetheless. She also decided that he was handsome, having at first thought he was a little too weak jawed. He was constantly looking around him, not in a paranoid or self-conscious way, just as if he was monitoring the environment. Training or personality? she wondered.

As their main courses arrived–both had opted for beef bourguignon–and the restaurant filled up, Elena had to lean in towards Yarmouth, whom she was trying to remember to think of as Robin, although the name felt too feminine. This made their knees touch under the table. Elena considered withdrawing but opted not to. Yarmouth–Robin–made no show of noticing and he too did nothing about it.

Elena laughed, thinking about how the evening was developing.

"What? What are you thinking?" he asked.

"Oh nothing. Just... This is funny."

"What's funny? I'm funny, am I? Funny how? Like I'm here to amuse you?"

Robin had gone into some sort of shtick and looked endearingly awkward until Elena recognised it.

"No, not funny like Joe Pesci funny. Just... I didn't expect... This."

She gestured about her, indicating the diners, the restaurant, her dress, finally pointing at Robin.

"Is nice." Elena felt herself grow serious. "Is really nice."

Now it was her turn to blush. She felt her face redden and pushed back her chair.

"Sorry, just have to go to... You know."

"Sure. It's behind you, between those feral-looking parrots."

Elena splashed water on her face in the small and dimly-lit bathroom. Its ceiling was decorated with tiny glowing constellations. They blurred against the dark blue painted tiles. Elena realised her eyes were moist with more than tap water. What was happening to her? She was such a sponge for emotion these days. She looked in the mirror, removing up a speck of mascara that had stuck to her cheekbone. The neckline of her dress was probably an inch too low for her liking but—fuck it—this was London, not Bucharest, and she could cope with the admiring glances.

Returning from the bathroom, a ruddy-faced man in a business suit brushed boozily past her in the hall and squeezed one of her breasts with a fleshy paw. For a split second, Elena could not process what had happened. Then the rage flooded in.

"What the fuck?"

She pushed the man violently away from her and, pleasingly, he slipped on a piece of tissue paper on the tiled floor and fell on his arse, knocking over a small pot plant in the process. He grunted animal-like and bewildered staff appeared, not knowing who they should help and how.

"She fucking assaulted me!" the idiot complained, picking himself up and batting away the hands of an over-eager waiter.

"Elena!"

The familiar voice and presence of Robin, back in charge as PC Yarmouth, burst upon the scene just as the man who had assaulted Elena began to gesticulate towards her. Elena backed away, into Yarmouth–into Robin's chest.

"He touch my breast! He attack me."

Minutes later, the idiot was being marched, hand-cuffed, from the restaurant, Yarmouth having called a few of his buddies in a passing patrol car. The restaurant had offered them a free dessert on the house, but their evening had been destroyed.

"What a total cunt," he said forcefully. "Sorry but I hate guys like that."

"Not exactly my favourite as well," she replied, wondering what would happen next.

In the street outside, Robin took out a pack of cigarettes and offered Elena one. She shook her head, taking a mental point off Robin's tally then adding several back on for his chivalry and resourcefulness, then shaking off the whole ridiculous score card. She was awful on dates. Dates? Was that really what they had had? Ana would rib her mercilessly.

"Shit!"

Elena looked at her phone for the time. Quarter past ten. The film would have ended almost half an hour ago.

"What's up?"

"I need to get to Prince Charles cinema. I'm super late. Can you direct me?"

"I can do better than that. Come on. It's about five minutes away and I know all the short-cuts."

He reached out a hand and she took it as they dashed across the street between cars. His hand was warm, and he grasped hers firmly. For perhaps the first time since arriving in London, Elena felt safe.

CHAPTER 9

Ana enjoyed The Princess Bride a lot more than she expected to. All mum had told her about it was that it was supposed to be some sort of classic funny fantasy film. It looked a bit juvenile at first. But as she relaxed with her pick and mix and let it wash over her, she found herself giving into to the silly jokes, questionable effects, and cameos from comedians that I guess you'd recognise if you were, like, eighty or something.

The cinema was only a third full, which oddly made her less self-conscious, and there were a lot of 'loners' there. Plus, the guy who had torn her ticket and shone his torch down the aisle for her had been cute. He looked mixed-race and had an impressive set of sideburns that made his ratty little moustache all the more absurd in comparison. Yet he'd had a friendly face, a gangly charm and Ana guessed he wasn't that much older than her—perhaps seventeen or eighteen.

When the end credits rolled and the lights went up, the gangly usher appeared, cleaning up spilt popcorn and drinks cups with a brush and a sort of shovel on a stick. He looked at Ana and grinned briefly and awkwardly.

"Enjoy the film?"

"It was all right," Ana shrugged. "I liked the tiny bald one who kept saying 'indubitably' a lot."

She'd decided to use the word 'indubitably' as soon as humanly possible, once she'd Googled its meaning.

"Wallace Shawn. Did you know he's also a playwright?"

"That funny guy with the lisp? Really?"

"Yep. You should check out My Dinner with Andre. He co-wrote that and stars. Two guys having lunch in New York. That's the whole film."

"Sounds great," she said, rolling her eyes.

Deadly boring more like, but Chris (as his name badge revealed) was reddening a little, so Ana decided to humour him.

"You know a lot about films."

"Well, I do work in a cinema. I mean, I love movies. I'm going to film school next year."

"Cool."

"What about you? You at college?"

College. She loved him a little bit already. He surely couldn't believe she was seventeen.

"Not yet. Summer holidays. I was thinking maybe I'd be a writer. Or a dancer. Maybe both."

A writer? Where had that come from?

"I'd better go," she said. "My mu.... My friend will be waiting."

Chris stepped aside with his brush and pan, clanging it loudly against the seats behind him. She almost made it to the door before he piped up again.

"Look, if you want to come again, I can get you a cheaper ticket."

There was no way she could tell him she was there on a child discount already.

"Why?"

The question came out a lot more aggressively than she'd intended.

"We're building customer loyalty."

Chris seemed proud of his reply, so she let it hang.

"Thanks. Maybe. See you."

Then she stepped back out into the half-light of the foyer with the little snack kiosk and a view of the back of another, much grander, cinema. Why were they all clustered together? she wondered.

Elena was nowhere to be seen. Ana hung around the foyer for a few minutes, feeling awkward. She'd said goodbye to Chris as coolly as she'd been able to. Having to say hello again while waiting for her mum to collect her would just be too embarrassing. She kept one eye on the street outside, another on the corridor leading down to the screens.

After fifteen minutes it was too much to bear. Ana stepped outside, looked up and down the street, saw no sign of her mum. She looked at her phone, which she'd kept on silent in the cinema. No missed calls. Elena was twenty minutes late.

"You okay?"

Ana spun round—Chris was leaning against the wall behind her, taking out a packet of cigarettes. He seemed to fight a small inner battle within himself then held out the packet towards her. Marlboro Lights. She was sorely tempted, but shook her head.

"My friend's late. She texted me, said she was at Bar Italia. Can you direct me?"

She could easily have looked it up herself on Google Maps, were she really going there, but she wanted him to show her. Chris was a good six inches taller than her as he hunched over her phone and began describing how what she saw on the tiny screen related to reality. He smelled of cigarettes, hair gel and, very faintly of sweat. She liked it.

"So, just past the Eastern side of Chinatown, Gerrard Street, can't miss it, lots of lanterns, stinks a bit. Then up past the fire station…"

She didn't want to tell him she was staying in a back-packers' hostel or that she was new to the UK, though he probably guessed by her accent.

"So where are you from?"

And there was the question.

"Bucharest. Well, just outside. Romania."

"I see. Economic migrant."

"Oh sure, reduce me to label, why not?"

Her vehemence surprised them both.

"Sorry, I'm a bit touchy about the whole anti-immigrant bullshit," she said.

"Brexit? Yeah, well, we're not to blame in London. We wanted you guys. London's a melting pot, innit? Look at me. Mum's from Mozambique, dad's half French and they met in Morocco, went travelling together, landed here and stayed."

"Sweet. Well, I'd better go. Coffee calling."

She grinned, spun on her heels, and gave him a little wave as she headed up towards the restaurants and paper lanterns. He waved back, affecting a casual drag on his cigarette. She could see right through his artless posing.

On the other hand—coffee calling? Jeez.

Elena and Robin reached the cinema at a jog. He'd let go of her hand after crossing Shaftesbury Avenue, but the memory of that touch lingered. She shook the confusing associations off and yanked open the cinema doors. There were a few couples loitering in the foyer between screenings, plus one gangly youth with an unconvincing moustache but no sign of Ana.

Elena approached the youth, who was eyeing them both with curiosity.

"Have you seen young girl waiting by herself? She was in eight o'clock screening. My daughter Ana."

The kid looked a little dazed as he processed the question.

"Em, yes. I sent her to Bar Italia."

"You did what?"

"We must have just missed her," said Yarmouth.

"Sorry miss, she said she was meeting…. friends."

Elena groaned.

"When did she leave?"

"About fifteen minutes ago. I'm sure she'll still be there?"

Elena dashed back outside, heading back the way they had come, Robin in tow.

Back at the hostel, Ana clumped back upstairs, preparing the devastating expression of hurt and world-weariness with which she would flatten her mother. How the fuck could she have forgotten her own daughter? Out drinking with a police officer, supposedly because of some random woman who'd stood them up. What a loser Elena was.

So distracted was Ana by these thoughts that she didn't question the additional resistance behind the dormitory door after the light clicked green and the spare card the night manager had given her let her in. She forced back what turned out to be a chair piled with bags and clothes, causing one of the German women kneeling between her friend's thighs to turn fearfully, hair rumpled, face sweaty.

The woman underneath her shrieked and grabbed for some clothing. Ana backed out of the room, embarrassment flushing her face. On the way down the stairs, her embarrassment turned into anger.

She stormed into the foyer and accosted Michael.

"There's a pair of weird women up there, doing sex!"

"Sorry?"

"I said, there's Germans doing stuff in our room. Is allowed?"

"It's not… recommended. I'm really sorry."

"Well, make them stop. I need to have a shower and my stuff's in there."

"Of course. I mean, you absolutely shouldn't feel you can't access your room."

"No shit. Are you going to do anything? Go up and make them stop."

Michael looked decidedly awkward.

"As I'm sure you're aware, this is a LGBT-friendly environment."

"What?" Ana exploded. "I don't care what they do with each other, I just want to get my stuff!"

"I don't really think I'd feel comfortable…"

In that moment, a flustered Elena and stony-faced Robin burst into the foyer. A three-way argument ensued, with Michael in mollifying mode and Robin as out-of-his-depth mediator. Eventually, free soft drinks and two free night's accommodation in a private room notwithstanding, three things were clear (at least to Ana, who held all the cards).

Elena was a neglectful mother, Ana an abused child and they couldn't possibly stay in the hostel another night.

CHAPTER 10

Elena had been grateful for nearly fifteen hours now and was finding it exhausting. The suspicious part of her felt the need to question just where all this kindness was coming from. Her inner pragmatist told the cynic inside to just shut up. Robin really wanted to help her and Ana and that was that. A third voice then interjected, a needling voice that resented yet another lover 'rescuing' her from a difficult situation. Plus, the men in Elena and Ana's lives had always been the problem; it felt weird for one now to provide a solution.

Still, it was only one night at Robin's place and then she would pay her own way. It had been a busy and hopefully lucrative morning. Robin lived in Ealing, which meant shuttling back West on the same line she'd taken from the airport, albeit in the opposite direction. They had arrived at almost midnight, an exhausted Ana falling asleep on Elena's shoulder in a way she hadn't done since she was about eight. The familiar warmth and pressure against her breastbone made Elena nostalgic for the carefree, charming child her daughter had once been.

Parenthood was a constant state of grieving as a bigger, more angular and awkward child replaced each simpler, younger version. She was just getting used to Ana version 14 and OS 15.0 was waiting just around the corner.

"Nearly there," Robin said, watching Elena's eyes begin to close involuntarily.

The next station is South Ealing, announced the tannoy, perkily.

As they'd stumbled out into the quiet Ealing suburbs, there had been little to see. A few restaurants and pubs letting their last customers out, Saturday night kids wandering home in small but noisy groups. The streets were noticeably greener and leafier, Elena noticed as Ana stumbled along, arm in arm with her. Robin got out his keys between a Polish delicatessen and a solicitors' office, rattled a door open and they clumped up to his small bachelor flat on the second floor.

Somehow Elena had expected more. Robin had one front room, one small bedroom, a kitchenette, and a separate bathroom with shower cubicle but no actual bath. The shower curtain was mouldy at its base. The bedroom was littered with papers and clothes, the lounge noticeably tidier. Elena got the impression Robin spent as little time here as possible.

"Mi casa es su casa," Robin announced, immediately seeming to regret the faux-Spanish. "Make yourself at home."

After much argument, Elena and Ana agreed to take the bedroom while Robin took a sleeping bag to the sofa. Before they went to bed, Robin made them all a cup of tea, a pre-sleep ritual he maintained helped him sleep. Then he found them fresh bedding, another kind gesture Elena tried to protest against (but not too strongly, there was a bit of a "single man" odour about Robin's bedclothes). Ana was wandering idly, picking things up and putting them back down. Elena was too tired to tell her off for this small impertinence and Robin didn't seem to mind. Ana examined a photo of Robin, out of uniform, with his arm around a diminutive Indian girl, taken in a sunlit park.

"Me and the ex. Don't ask."

Elena had no idea what he meant, and didn't.

When Robin had said his goodnights and Elena and Ana had thanked him once more, Ana slumped down on the side of the bed near the window. Since childhood she had liked sleeping with a slight breeze blowing in from an open window.

"This side's mine."

Elena didn't argue. She slid open a drawer, looking for somewhere to put her glasses.

A paperback, some cufflinks, business cards for 'DC Yarmouth', strips of chewing gum, two miniature in-flight bottles of gin and an open packet of condoms, ribbed, half-full. She shut the drawer rapidly. She had forgotten that there were lives as lonely as her own.

The following morning, a Sunday, brought thin sunlight and an autumnal chill. Elena woke unusually early, at just after 7am, and decided to make breakfast as a more tangible thank you to PC Yarmouth.

Half an hour later, having found the Polish deli already open downstairs, Elena had found the pots and pans in Robin's kitchen and was frying thinly sliced Kielbasa sausage, eggs, and buttering rolls. She'd retrieved a dusty cafetiere from the back of Robin's Spartan cupboards and brewed a potful of Italian coffee. Plates and glasses of fresh orange juice plus Ana's favourite cereal stood in place on the small side-table she'd wiped clean in the lounge. Making breakfast was a little presumptuous and Elena felt her heart flutter a little as Robin, patting down a tuft of hair, entered the kitchen.

"Smell's amazing. What is it?"

She tried to pronounce the name of the sausage, got it on the second attempt.

"This is really nice of you. Thanks."

Slightly stiffly, Robin leaned in and brushed his lips against Elena's cheek. He stepped back into the doorway, awkward in the narrow frame.

"Is the least I could do. Plus, I might have found job while I was downstairs."

Oh really?

"There was a card in window of the deli. Wanting Eastern European translation services for a charity. All I need is mobile phone and I can work from anywhere. I'm going to call them tomorrow."

"That's brilliant. You're English is nearly perfect, so I'm sure they'll want you."

"Nearly perfect?" She teased.

"Totally perfect. What I meant to say."

"Why don't you take coffee to table?" she said with a smile.

Robin grabbed the cafetiere and three mugs and almost bumped into Ana in the doorway.

"Well, this is… domestic," Ana said, in Romanian.

Elena rolled her eyes at her daughter as Robin edged past her.

"Cheeky. And English, remember. I'm amazed you're up."

"Me too. It's so quiet here. Birds woke me."

"Go sit down. Your cereal's on the table."

"Cool."

It did feel surreally natural to be sitting down with Robin and Ana to their basic Sunday breakfast. Robin introduced her to the joys of HP sauce and his mother's gooseberry preserve and, midway through his second cup of coffee, dropped his bombshell.

"I think I might have found you a flat."

"A what?" Said Elena, almost choking on her mouthful.

"A place to stay. Rent-free, well, for the first six months at least. It's no big deal; the guy owes me a favour. It's a bit of a dump but maybe better than nothing?"

She could have hugged him. The inner voices began to niggle away at her again, but she decided to go with the flow.

Ana did the washing up. She even offered, which heightened the odd feeling Elena had that this was some sort of dream. Then they took their showers, made themselves presentable and headed back to the underground, looking for all the world like a family unit out for a Sunday stroll.

She hadn't thought of Frances all morning.

CHAPTER 11

Yarmouth had thought of Malcolm Carver's place when Elena had first asked about a cheap hostel, but had of course immediately discounted it. Carver was his confidential informant (or had been) and he wasn't yet ready to sour that arrangement. Perhaps it was because Yarmouth still harboured hopes of one day being invited back to join DI Fleischer and his buddies at the West End.

Nevertheless, he felt himself compelled to help and not just because he found Elena strangely alluring (or "hot stuff" as McPherson would have put it). In the tenacious Romanian and her daughter, he saw echoes of his own family's story. His mother had been a single parent since Yarmouth had been eight years old, his father having been killed in an accident on one of the North Sea rigs. Juggling the responsibilities of raising Robin and his big sister Maisie in that unforgivingly small seaside town in Fife while holding down a succession of thankless jobs had been Karen Yarmouth's struggle. An Englishwoman abroad, raising two wild fatherless kids, mum had fought many of the same fights Elena would now face. Since Robin could so easily alleviate some of this difficulty for her, why wouldn't he?

And so, he had gone, cap in hand, to a man he despised. A verminous but very well-connected ex-pimp turned slum landlord who had amassed, through crime, intimidation and, Yarmouth had to grudgingly admit, some business nous, a large slice of Soho real estate. Much of the area had been gentrified and sold upmarket for flats and restaurants in the last twenty years and Carver had been one of the chief beneficiaries. However, it had proved hard for the old lag to entirely leave behind his shady ways, despite an armful of prison tattoos that should have reminded him of his earlier poor choices.

One of Carver's warrens of tiny bedsits that had once housed 'models' plying their ancient and horizontal trade had been the site of a drugs killing some months back and forensics had just finished with it. It was between tenants and Carver had been agitating for the boys in blue to clear out and let "an honest man do an honest day's business", a phrase that had made Yarmouth snort Starbucks latte through his nose. Carver still owed him one, though and now it was time to collect.

Two floors up behind an anonymous-looking Dean Street doorway, Yarmouth located the bijou office of Carver Holdings and, out of uniform for obvious reasons, flung open the front door. A bored-looking receptionist put away her Harry Potter book and cast a baleful eye over him.

"Have you got an appointment?"

"Just tell him Yarmouth's here. He'll find a slot in his schedule for me."

"Mr Carver's out in meetings until four."

"No, he's not. I can hear him ranting behind that door."

This was true. A shadow crossed the frosted pane in the door on the far wall, between a thriving pot plant that was beginning to flirt with the light fittings and a less thriving tank of languorous terrapins. A raised voice declaimed in an East End accent; there were strong suggestions of fist-waving.

"Take a seat. When he's off the phone, I'll tell him you're there."

The receptionist, Janine, offered up a plush white sofa beneath some ugly art and behind a coffee table stacked with style magazines.

Yarmouth considered it, but not for long. Carver was not a fellow who respected those who waited, and Yarmouth needed to show a strong hand. In five strides he was invading Carver's inner sanctum and making the big man pause and re-adjust mid-flow.

"...Well tell the fucker that if he doesn't have the deposit, he can sling his hook. I'm not waiting another day for that pair of cunts to hum and haw! I've got a family of chink... of Chinese who are gagging for it. I don't have to provide any furniture either as they don't use any where they're from. Or is that the Japs? I can never remember."

Carver threw an exasperated look Yarmouth's way, seeming not to object to the intrusion as much as the phone call he was having.

"Debbie, dearest, either they sign the contract and hand over the cash by five, or they can fuck off back to Poland. And no, they cannot have a fridge-bloody-freezer. Goodbye."

The last word was delivered in a sort of singsong as Carver slammed the phone receiver back down (or would have if it hadn't been a sliver-shaped designer artefact that required careful slotting into a base module).

"Fucksake Robbo, can't I just go back to running hookers and dope, instead of dealing with these knobheads? At least you know where you stand with sex-deviants and junkies."

Yarmouth couldn't help but laugh. Horrible person though Carver was, he could be entertaining.

"What can I do you for, son? Hear you're back in the zoot suit. Not today though, which I'm guessing makes this not exactly an official visit."

Damn. Carver had just played the first hand and it was a good one.

"Had a bit of an altercation with a superior, as I'm sure you heard. They put me back on the beat. Good news though: I got the Soho detail, so you'll probably see a lot more of me from now on."

"Always nice to see a familiar face, my son. Now what can I do for the boys in blue?"

"It's more of a personal favour."

"Oh really? Now I'm intrigued. Look, take a seat, will you? You're wearing out the Axminster."

Yarmouth flumped down on an armchair while Carver sat down behind his desk, hands positioned into a little tent on the varnished wood. Don Corleone couldn't have looked more poised.

"You've been a reliable CHIS, Carver. I'll say that for you."

Carver winced.

"Hey, less of the confidential informant stuff round here, if you don't mind. I'm legit now but there's folk might hold grudges if they knew about my little tip offs."

"That's kind of what I'm counting on."

A darker cloud passed across Carver's face now.

"Look Robbo…"

"PC Yarmouth if you don't mind."

"Okay, PC, whatever. We had a relationship of trust and honour."

"The operative word being 'had'. My responsibility to you ended when they bumped me off the detective desk.

And Fleischer tells me you've been pretty uncooperative with my replacement."

"That nonce Kendall? I can't trust him. A man with my kind of... associations... has to be cautious."

"Point taken. Anyway, I have no intention of accidentally mentioning your collusion in, for example, our busting that burly gentleman from Ukraine with his six pituitary case brothers."

"Smirnov? Why the fuck would you...?

"Well, I wouldn't. That's what I'm saying. I just need a little favour from you to, I don't know, reinforce my sense of trust and honour."

Carver sighed and sat back in his chair, no longer so amiable–or so confident.

"Spill. What do you want?"

Fifteen minutes later, Carver's receptionist was handing Yarmouth a packet of keys while Carver tapped disconsolately at his terrapin tank.

"Janine, did you feed these lazy fuckers? I think this one's dead."

Janine threw Carver a surprisingly confrontational look.

"Course I did. Just as you told me. One half spoonful each morning and at four o'clock."

"Should've got fish like everyone else round here."

Yarmouth smiled at Janice and stuffed the envelope into a side pocket.

"Well, it's been a pleasure as ever, Carver."

Carver didn't look up from the murky water of the tank, as he dipped a fountain pen below the surface to prod a terrapin. Gratifyingly it shrank into its shell.

"Three months, that's all. Then I'll want rent," he muttered.

"That seems perfectly fair to me."

"Fair? It's fucking thievery. You should arrest yourself."

Carver laughed bronchially and loudly, as if this were a bon mot worthy of Wilde.

"And Carver," said Yarmouth. "Needless to say, don't go mentioning this arrangement to Kendall, Fleischer or anyone at the Met."

Carver harrumphed a grudging agreement and started wiping his pen with a handkerchief.

"She'd better be worth it."

Yarmouth hesitated at the door. He hadn't said anything about who the keys were for. And now by stopping, he'd just validated Carver's guess. He was about to turn and reiterate his warnings but thought better of it. Cool was the way to play it.

"See you later."

"No doubt, Robbo, no doubt."

Back in the street, Yarmouth took a deep lungful of Soho morning air. A sickly-sweet odour wafted across the road from a Chinese restaurant gearing up for lunch. A whiff of hot tar accompanied by an undercurrent of leaky drains added to the heady stench.

It was time to make Elena smile.

CHAPTER 12

Robin had to elbow open the door, behind which lay a pile of unopened mail, alongside a fragment of something he snatched up and stuffed into his pocket. Elena felt a flicker of suspicion that something was wrong, but quashed it.

A tiny vestibule containing only a forlorn side table and a round mirror with a crack across it opened into two rooms—a compact lounge with a tiny kitchenette off it and a sparsely-furnished bedroom whose wall was still adorned with a single left-behind poster. It displayed the imposing image of a frowning rapper with massive, tattooed arms cradling an Uzi in an inner-city backstreet. The juxtaposition was at once bizarre and strangely-fitting.

"Nice," Ana couldn't help but drawl.

Elena shot her a warning glance.

"Yeah, it's a bit shitty but it is rent free, for the first three months at least," Robin said.

"Why free?" Said Elena, trying to make the question sound as casual as possible.

"All I can say is the landlord owes me one."

"Has it got Wi-Fi?" Ana asked.

Yarmouth scouted around the front room, locating a router behind a faded curtain. Its lights still blinked optimistically.

"Oddly enough, I think it does. Password is on the base."

Elena walked around, feeling ungrateful even as she opened chipboard-fronted cupboards in the kitchenette and located the bathroom—a door in the hall she'd assumed was a closet led to a miniscule space into which a shower cubicle, toilet and Lilliputian hand basin had somehow all been crammed. Yarmouth had gone out of his way to help, and she appreciated more than she could adequately convey but this place stank—literally—of desperation. The lives lived here had not been easy. Bolthole was the English word that sprang to mind. Elena had read it in a novel recently. A place of refuge or escape.

"It's just what we need. It's perfect."

"It's a place to start, that's what it is," said Yarmouth, ruefully. "Look, I can show you Freecycle and how to get some cheap furniture if you like but I've got to get to my shift. Let's meet soon, eh?"

Yarmouth stood hovering in the doorway from the lounge to the vestibule. Elena could just let him go if she wanted.

"Look, why don't you come back after shift. I'll cook. Something traditional. You like meatballs? I got a great dish my mother taught me."

"I don't know. I don't finish until nine. I'd get here maybe nine thirty. That's pretty late."

"It's not like we're going anywhere," Ana muttered.

Elena was grateful for the unexpected support and grabbed her daughter round the shoulder in an embrace that made both of them a little awkward.

"We eat late anyway. Come over."

"Okay then. You're on. I'll bring wine. Assuming you drink, I mean."

"I'm Romanian. I drink," laughed Elena, knowing in that moment that she'd made a friend.

"See you later then. I'll be in uniform, hope that's okay."

"Are you kidding? That's essential," said Ana.

Was her daughter flirting with Robin for her own sake or her mother's? thought Elena fleetingly.

After Yarmouth left, Elena and Ana made a wish-list to-gether. It was a thing they liked to do, both being pragmatic and idealistic at the same time. It began:

New curtains
Sofa
TV
Coffee table
Coffee pot
Teaspoons
Proper plates
Saucepans (3)
Kettle
Iron and Ironing board
and ended, somewhat optimistically:
PS5 (Ana)
Record player (Elena)
Fridge-Freezer

The list made them both feel better, like they had already transformed the blank canvas of their drab flat into a de-signer pad for a modern single parent and daughter.

A little later, Elena stood in the bedroom, having un-packed her suitcase and the small backpack she'd used as a carry-on. Her clothes lay folded in piles on the bed, de-pressingly small piles. Was this all she amounted to at thirty-two years of age? She quickly put them away, grat-ified that there were old hangers left in the walk-in cupboard. She felt a little more optimistic once her things were safely hidden away and she had showered and changed into what she was trying not to think of as her 'date night' outfit.

Torn away from Snapchat for a moment, Ana laughed when she saw what her mother had chosen, commenting on its low neckline and the jewellery she had added as a grace note. Elena asked her to help by chopping some vegetables and, for once, Ana complied without complaint.

Robin arrived a little early, around 9:15 and caught Elena having a steadying glass of wine as she compacted and rolled the meatballs and dropped them into the hot oil. He kissed her on the cheek rather more wetly than she was expecting while Ana watched from the doorway. The cooking smells and candles Ana had lit already made the place feel more home-like and inviting. As promised, Robin was in uniform, and Ana goggled at the paraphernalia of policing. Around the base of his jacket, which had four deep pockets, Robin wore handcuffs, a baton, a can of pepper spray, a torch and, most fascinatingly, a Taser.

"Can I have a shot of that?" Ana asked, eagerly.

Robin raised an eyebrow.

"That's not going to happen. You don't want to be on the receiving end of one of these, believe me. The CS spray's pretty horrible too, unless you enjoy rubbing hot chillies in your eyes."

"What about the cuffs? Will you be using them on mum later?"

"Ana!" objected Elena, coming at her daughter with a meaty spoon.

Pursued by Elena, Ana leapt over the sofa and hid behind the curtain. Elena returned to her cooking.

"Sorry about my daughter," she said, "Embarrassing mum is one of her all-time favourites."

"There's always the cuffs," Robin said, dangling them at Ana from one finger.

"Don't worry. I'm on my best behaviour with a cop in the house."

"We have house," Elena thought aloud.

The moment of silence that followed required something. Elena walked up to Robin and, heart beating unreasonably loudly, squeezed his upper arm, feeling a taut and lean muscle beneath the cloth. She whispered in his ear simply:

"Thank you."

Robin relaxed into the evening more than he had at the restaurant and Ana, true to her word, was on her best behaviour, lively and funny but letting the adults have their time too. On cue, as Robin leaned back in his chair with a satisfied expression, having finished the last mouthful of cheesecake, Ana excused herself and went into her room to continue catching up with her friends online.

"Do you ever worry what she's looking at? Who she's talking to?" Robin asked.

"No, not really, she knows not to be stupid."

"It's just... I guess in my profession you suspect the worst. The things we see."

"Should I worry? I put parental locks on her internet?"

"Kids can get around those, if they're clever."

"Why you say this? Now you got me worried."

"Forget it. She seems a sensible kid."

But Elena couldn't forget what Robin was suggesting and felt irritated that he'd injected a note of darkness into the evening.

"Maybe it's habit for you," she suggested, partly to herself. "You know how ugly the world is so you're always looking for it".

"Perhaps. I can also recognise when it's beautiful too. Like this meal, the way you've transformed this place with a few candles and your things. And you."

Elena was surprised to see Robin swallow and pause before he finished his thought.

"You're beautiful Elena. Sorry, that's a daft thing to say."

"Shut up."

Elena put a finger over his lips and Robin let it linger there before grasping it and pulling her towards him over the table. They kissed, tentative at first, then deeply and hungrily. Elena could taste the food on his breath, an aftertaste of the beer he'd preferred to wine.

They broke apart, both suddenly a little shy. Robin looked about to say something, then evidently thought better of it. Elena broke the silence.

"Will you do me huge favour?"

Robin looked up expectantly at Elena as she cleared the plates from the table.

"As long as you don't ask me to kill a man."

It was evidently a daft joke, but it resonated in ways Robin couldn't have guessed.

"I was thinking more like you do the washing up," Elena said.

"Of course!"

Robin hurriedly pushed his chair back and took the plates from their hands. Elena went in for another kiss and this one felt easier, more natural. Looking a little dazed, Robin followed Elena into the kitchen, where he turned on a tap that made a weird repetitive clunk as it poured surprisingly hot water.

While Robin did the washing up, Elena tidied up the lounge and lit a couple of candles. Her heart was pounding. Was this a good idea? She decided not to think too hard about it, moving Robin's jacket from the sofa to a hook behind the door. Robin was whistling a song she half recognised—something about surprises—as she found herself slipping a hand inside his jacket pocket.

The thing he'd tried to conceal was still there—a fragment of police tape. Of course. That's how he'd known this place was vacant. She was living in a crime scene. A chill ran through her, one she tried to dispel with another glug of wine. It almost worked. She put her smile back in place and went into the kitchen to help Robin with the drying.

They could have slept together. Elena knew he wanted to; she had too, before finding what was concealed in Robin's pocket. Now it felt too risky, too soon. There were still secrets between them. Instead, they spent an hour on the sofa talking, cuddling, and kissing like teenagers, facing an empty, painted-over fireplace into which Elena had placed a single white church candle. Then, with a theatrical yawn and stretch, Robin announced that he had an early shift the next morning and the spell was broken. Elena felt a weird mix of disappointment and relief.

A final kiss in the doorway and he was gone, handcuffs rattling as he descended the creaky stairwell. Elena blew out the candles and looked in on Ana, who had fallen asleep in her pyjamas cradling her iPhone, her head resting against Edmundo, a stuffed elephant toy she'd kept as the only remnant of childhood. Elena wondered when she'd know that her little girl was an actual woman. She already had the athletic frame and subtle curves of her mother and a little of her father's jawline, an unhappier resemblance. Fifteen next year. In Latin America that would make her a woman.

This though was England and Ana was still young enough to be tucked in by her mother. Ana stirred a little as Elena pulled the cut-price duvet out from under her and laid it over her. Then she plugged in the phone for Ana, for whom having a powerless phone was akin to being rendered mute.

Elena could still feel the warmth of Robin's embrace, the strangely comical sensation of his baton pushing into her hip (he'd made the obvious joke) as she made sure the front door was properly shut. What was she doing? A flame of guilt flickered through her; what if Frances returned?

The very thought was absurd. Clearly Frances had absconded, taking her money and her fantasies of a new life. She'd have to build new fantasies now.

What was that? A crash of glass, then female laughter. Ana opened the door, looked out into the hall. Light was gleaming in the frosted glass panel above the door opposite. Flat D.

A latch turned and Elena almost retreated but curiosity got the better of her. Two men in their forties or fifties emerged from the flat opposite, evidently drunk, wearing rumpled business suits. One turned and leered at Elena, winking a lazy eyelid.

"Fucksake, its hottie central, this place," he muttered in a drunk's approximation of a whisper.

"Quietly, gentlemen please!" came a stern but teasing voice from within. "The neighbours."

"No worries. Next week eh, love?"

"Text me. We'll see."

As the men stumbled down the stairwell, a svelte black woman, Somali possibly, appeared in the doorway as Elena pretended to examine the letterbox of her front door.

"Is the music too loud? I'm really sorry," said the woman, who was heavily made up, her silk dressing down gaping at the neckline to reveal an impressive bosom.

The make-up and dramatically spiralling hair falling across her face made it hard to tell but Elena guessed she was perhaps twenty-five. She seemed a little tipsy.

"No, not at all. I just moved here. Elena."

Elena offered a hand. The Somalian ignored it and planted a kiss on her cheek.

"Don't be so formal. We're sisters. I'm Qamar. Carver just set you up, did he?"

"I'm sorry."

"Mr Carver. That's his flat you're in."

"Er, not exactly."

"I'm sorry, I thought you were working."

"Working?"

"Fuck, this is embarrassing. Forget I said anything. Just let me know if the music's too loud. We'll chat soon."

With an awkward smile, Qamar shut the door, a swirl of dance music replaced by a low bass thud, darkness filling the hallway once again.

It took Elena a couple of minutes to register what her neighbour had probably meant by 'working'.

CHAPTER 13

Elena had a dilemma—she had a job interview with the translation agency she'd seen advertising in the deli window. There was nobody to leave Ana with and, although her daughter was a pretty savvy fourteen-year-old, Elena was wary of leaving her up to her own devices. It was pouring with rain, a cold, slashing downpour that rendered umbrellas futile. There was little chance that Ana would venture out in that, but Elena worried about the implications of what she'd found in Robin's pocket as well as her neighbour's likely profession. Was she really a sex worker, or had Elena got the wrong end of the stick? How would you even ask?

Until Elena was sure that whatever had happened in her flat was not a threat and that her neighbour was a benign as she'd seemed, she couldn't leave Ana there. Which presented two problems. She couldn't really tell her daughter why she was insisting she come out into the filthy weather with her. Nor could she really leave her with anyone. Robin was at work and, in any case, had done her enough favours. She knew nobody else to turn to.

"I'm not a baby mum. Just leave me here and I'll read or something. Or watch the imaginary TV."

"I can't do that Elena. Not until I know the neighbourhood is safe."

"You do remember where we come from? Compared to Glina, this place is heaven. It's all posh restaurants and cafes."

"And Robin told me it had a bit of a seedy past. Strip clubs, stuff like that. Just let me be sure before I leave my only child alone, eh?"

"Okay. Tell you what. I liked that cinema you took me to. Despite you totally forgetting me and everything. It was cool. Can I go there?"

"Well... I don't know. Is there anything on?"

"Romeo and Juliet. It's got Leo di Caprio in it when he was young and hot. Two o'clock."

"Shakespeare? You want to see a Shakespeare play? Are you ill?"

Elena put the back of her hand against Ana's head, affecting concern.

"Very funny. It's a modern version. Hawaiian shirts and stuff. Can you take me?"

It did solve her problem and the film was long enough that she could maybe meet Robin for coffee too – he'd texted her that he'd be on patrol and due a break around three.

"Fine, let's go. Sensible coat though. It's foul out there."

A little later, Elena felt a tugging of doubt when Ana stopped at the top of the street upon which the little cinema hid. Ana dismissed her with a gesture.

"You can go. Give me the cash and I'll get my own ticket."

"Okay Miss Independent, if it's important to you. Will ten do? I'm still getting the hang of this money."

"Twenty, more like."

Elena paid up without protest, watching her daughter trot off down the road, weaving between tourists and Chinese delivery men servicing the local restaurants. Again, she was struck by the speed with which Ana was growing up. Was it sensible to let her loose in London? Elena made sure Ana went into the Prince Charles then stood outside for ten minutes, until she was almost late for her interview. She wouldn't put it past Ana to have sneaked out and gone roaming once her mother was safely away. It's exactly what Elena would have done in the same circumstances.

Ana felt her heart beating vividly under her coat as she approached the kiosk. Chris was there, serving a couple of twentysomething arty types, bearded and plaid-shirted. He flicked his eyes up to see Ana and smiled. That smile melted her thin pretence at reserve, and she beamed back.

"Hey you! Back already? You're becoming a right cineaste."

"A what-ass?"

"It means you love film."

"Whatever. I just need to get out of the rain."

"It's pretty grim out there, isn't it? You can put that away."

He spoke this last sentence sotto voce and Ana took a moment to realise he meant the £20 note she was brandishing.

"Your money's no good here miss."

"What?"

Was that him blushing?

"I mean, jeez, I'll get you in for nothing."

"Really?"

"Just be cool, though. I'm tearing the tickets in a moment anyway, when Ludo takes over. Spend it on popcorn or something. I'd recommend the salt and sweet mixed."

"Wow. Thanks! What did I do to deserve this?"

"I dunno. You brightened up my day a little."

Again, the shy turn. God, he really fancied her, didn't he? Ana realised she had absolutely no idea what to do with that information. She bought the recommended popcorn and a Coke and took a seat in the foyer while Chris served the people behind her. She opened Snapchat and began updating her friend Sophia on her new home and 'the hot guy in the cinema'. After a bit of banter, Sophia dropped that some news that sent a strange cold thrill through her.

Sophia had had sex.

She'd broken the pact. Ana and Sophia had been best friends since they were six and nine months ago, they'd agreed they'd talk to one another before making the decision to sleep with a boy. What was worse was that Sophia was six months younger than her, having only just turned 14. What was even worse is that Ana had never even heard of this boy Petru.

"It all happened really fast. His family only moved here last month. He's so amazing. Plays the guitar. And he's fifteen", Sophia said, breathlessly, her face half in shade as she walked through a Bucharest market.

Ana went text only. She didn't want to see her friend's face right now.

—*sorry, can't do video. bad signal. what happened?*

—*we drank loads of cider and were snogging. in his parents' place when they were out. we knew we had hours alone. it just kind of happened.*

—*you make it sound like an accident. his dick just fell into you by mistake?*

—*are you pissed off?*

Ana took a moment before replying. Counting internally to ten the way her grandmother had once advised.

—no. i'm not exactly thrilled though. we said we would wait until we were 16.

—i know but it just felt right. i love him and i think he feels the same.

—how did it feel?

This time it was Sophia who took a while to respond.

—i was scared at first. he was all over me, then his hand went in my pants. it felt amazing, much better than when i do it myself. i meant to say no but i kind of didn't. then when he went in me it was sore at first but then it felt awesome.

"You can come in now."

Chris's voice startled Ana, who was feeling hot and agitated, with a familiar moistness and tingling starting down below that she had no way to satisfy. He stood before her, one hand rubbing the tight, shiny curls over his small skull nervously. Instinctively she thrust the phone into an inside pocket.

"Top secret?"

"Em. Totally. Girl stuff."

Ana tried to laugh but her hotly flushing face made it feel forced.

"You can go into the cinema now. It's a bit cooler than here. Air-con's broken in the foyer."

He was being kind, reading her flustered skin as overheated. For a moment she wondered what it would be like if he took her into the cinema and pushed down onto her and…

"Sure. Same place?"

"It's the only screen we got. Turn left at the bottom."

His hand brushed the small of her back as she started on the steps. A moment's boldness made her turn.

"What do you think of it? The film?"

He affected a scholarly pause for thought.

"Bit like all Luhrmann's films, totally mental and OTT. Not much subtlety. But it's got some power too. Di Caprio's as good as ever, Danes is hot. It's passionate, a bit crazy, like teenage love."

Teenage love. How old was he, exactly?

"Cool. See you later, then."

With that, she trotted happily down the carpeted steps into the musty auditorium, just knowing his eyes were on her all the way down.

CHAPTER 14

At the end of the briefing, Sergeant Brompton injected a note of unusual urgency into his Monday morning drawl. Urgency was hard to do in a thick Dudley accent.

"You want to be keeping a particular eye out for two chancers who have been lifting mobile phones and iPads on a scooter. Well, on several scooters actually. In fact, it might be more than two lads, they're always helmeted and masked up, so the CCTV is not telling us much."

"Helpful," muttered Constable Gibran, a wryly skinny veteran officer of twenty-two years serving.

"They've taken about forty devices at last count and keep moving about, making it hard to keep up with them. We've sent bikes out but they're wary little buggers," added Brompton.

"Age? Race?" piped up Dave 'Pikey' Threave (so called because his dad owned a field of static caravans in Margate).

"Unknown. They keep themselves well-wrapped up. Brown skin though, from the few glimpses people have had."

"Oi oi! No racial profiling sir," quipped Thomson from a corner of the room, exaggerating his natural Jamaican burr. "Black lives matter, innit?"

"I'm just telling it like it is, smartarse. Anyway, you see these guys, call it in. We'll have bikes with you ASAP. Do not try to apprehend them alone."

Various nods, grumbles and noises approximating agreement. The men and women of West Central headed out to their bikes, squad cars and vans for drop-offs.

When Yarmouth had been 'moved sideways' from DC to plain old C, he'd angled for a car patrol, but it hadn't been forthcoming. Instead, he found himself grinding down the shoe-leather on foot patrol, something communities wanted but management begrudged as a painfully old-fashioned and impractical way of policing a city as huge as London.

Technically, he was window-dressing, a PR exercise in 'community policing', forever condemned to taking reports of stolen bicycles and broken shop windows. On an especially exciting day there might be a fight in Berwick Street market, or a pharmacy might be broken into. Soho, however, was a fairly cushy detail, it had to be said, much quieter in reality than its sleazy past might suggest.

It came as something of a shock therefore when the afternoon suddenly turned into something like an episode of The Sweeney. Yarmouth had been paired that morning with a new recruit, a wide-eyed young man called Jamie Conover. PC Conover wore the self-conscious look of someone new to the uniform, ultra-aware of the effect it had on people.

Although many folks were blasé about uniformed police officers on the street (and a tiny minority were actually appreciative) there did seem to be a sizable group who, without being felons in any way (probably) seemed to avoid eye-contact, stiffen slightly, or affect a forced nonchalance when passing officers on the street. It was unsettling at first but something Conover would quickly grow used to. As Yarmouth had told the 25-year-old that morning "it's called respect and it's actually a good thing."

Yarmouth was quite enjoying being the 'old timer' for once, pointing out the alleyway haunts of drug-dealers, nightclubs where trouble had taken place and market stalls raided for stolen merchandise.

"This young Syrian guy came up to me a couple of weeks ago, bold as brass, with a kit-bag full of dodgy Blu-Rays. Tried to sell me a copy of Cop Land, would you believe. Didn't even seem to think it was a crime."

"Did you nick him?"

"Didn't seem worth the paperwork. Gave him a caution and told him we'd not be so generous next time round. He seemed genuinely shocked that you can't sell iffy bootlegs of the new Marvel movie while it's still in the cinema."

"But he was openly committing a crime. Shouldn't you have acted anyway?"

"Well, technically, yes, of course. But look at this guy's life. He's probably spent months stuck in a shanty town in Calais, paid all he owns to be sneaked over on a container ship or gone the legit route and spend months applying for asylum, his whole life destroyed."

"Isn't it the court's job to make those calls?"

"Again, technically, yes. But clogging up the courts with countless petty cases where people are just trying to make ends meet. Refugees, seriously poor people. I don't see the point."

Yarmouth suddenly remembered he was talking to an impressionable stranger.

"You do realise this is entirely between you and me, all this?"

"Sure. I'm just not clear on…"

"Oof!"

Yarmouth was jerked round by the impact of a small scooter, whose pillion passenger had clonked his shoulder with a rucksack. Neither driver nor passenger reacted as they sped up the street and cut down a pedestrian alleyway.

"Hey! He took my phone! Officer!"

A middle-aged woman, executively dressed, had rushed breathlessly up to them, waving like a drowning person signalling to shore. Reacting physically before he knew entirely why, Yarmouth belted up the road and down the alleyway, bellowing behind him.

"Stay there!"

The bike had been negotiating a group of tourists snapping photos of each other and was only now crossing leaving the lane and cutting across another road, causing a taxi to screech to a stop, horn blaring.

Yarmouth, who had gone through a marathon-running phase in his late twenties, pounded past the startled Koreans and vaulted a pile of litter sacks, before dodging through the cars and entering the next lane.

He knew he should already have called for back-up and hoped Conover had done just that, though he knew the rookie had probably forgotten protocol already. Yarmouth also knew the small lane had been fenced off at its other end by the massive perimeter of the Crossrail development. The riders had made a big mistake.

Yarmouth heard the roar of an idling bike at the end of the alley, its riders skittish as squirrels, trying to decide whether to try to scale the eight-foot-high metal fence into the building site beyond or try something even more desperate.

"Stop where you are!"

Taser in one hand, baton in the other, Yarmouth faced off against his nemeses, who levelled off the bike and revved menacingly.

"Don't even think about it! Switch off the bike and step aside," Yarmouth said, trying to maintain the level, authoritative tone he'd been taught.

Nothing from the men at the end of the street.

"I'll use this if I have to," warned Yarmouth, feeling a quaver entering his voice.

Nothing from the thieves. The rider revved and Yarmouth raised his Taser.

Then, with a brief wheelie, the bike roared towards him. From only twenty feet away, it was on him in seconds, the leather-clad and masked riders holding on tightly. Yarmouth fired his weapon, the wires leaping out with a buzzing twang. Simultaneously, he saw the flash of a blade and side-stepped as the driver slashed at his stomach with something that resembled a Stanley knife.

Too shocked to react quickly, Yarmouth watched the electrified wires rip off the pillion rider's shoulder, jerking him to one side, enough to cause the rider to wobble but regain his balance and continue tearing down the alleyway towards Conover, who had ignored Yarmouth's warning—of course.

"Stop right there!" Conover shouted shrilly, baton raised.

Yarmouth would not easily forget the way Conover's skull cracked against the pavement as the bike seemed to drive straight up his falling body and launch itself into the street, where it bounced off a passing white van, scattering rider, passenger, and contraband over the wet Soho streets.

Conover lay as prone as roadkill as passers-by gathered. Yarmouth looked down, feeling a wetness spreading between his fingers. The knife had cut through canvas and cotton layers and just pierced the skin, creating a gash about three inches long.

Yarmouth limped his way to the end of the alley in time to see a panda car pull up and a member of the public attempting CPR on his colleague. Then he too found himself surrounded by concerned citizens.

"Has anyone called an ambulance?" he heard himself shout as sound and vision seemed to recede.

It was if a succession of veils were being pulled across his consciousness. Before he blacked out, he saw one of the riders trying to stagger to his feet, getting as far as his knees before collapsing again. One last thought flitted across his shutting-down mind: why attack two police officers—attempt to kill one of them even—for a bag of phones?

CHAPTER 15

Elena sat as primly as the schoolmistress in a period drama, awaiting the sound of her name. It came just as she was starting to count the blooms in a dried floral display on the receptionist's desk.

"Elena Balan!"

The receptionist said it a little like "Milan", rather than the version that rhymed with "Alan" the way Elena herself pronounced it. Elena smiled at the woman seated next to her, a fellow Romanian who might be one of the charity's clients or a fellow interviewee. They'd exchanged a few friendly words, but Elena hadn't felt like asking.

"You can go through now. Straight through there, third door on the right."

Beyond the double fire doors, Elena passed down a hallway with several rooms on the right and tall windows to her left offering an eclectic street view. The doors were all open, leading to, respectively, a library with two computer terminals, a small canteen, and a lounge. Reclining in the latter, clipboards in hand were a turbaned Sikh man in his fifties and a much younger, blonde woman with sharp Eastern European features. The woman stood up first, offering her hand.

"I'm Aldona Petrovska, this is Tony Singh. Tony heads the translation team and I'm in HR. Actually, I pretty much am HR. We're a small organisation."

"Elena Balan," she said unnecessarily.

They sat down and Aldona and Tony explained the aims and work of the charity. Voices Unlimited was set up by Tony and two colleagues to provide free spoken and written translation services for refugees and immigrants in their first six months of UK residence. Tony, a journalist and former Labour party speechwriter, had been angered by the rising tide of anti-immigrant sentiment he'd seen during his time in both journalism and politics and had managed to put together, on a volunteer basis at first, a group of likeminded individuals to help give newcomers to Britain "back their own voices" as he put it. As Elena listened to their pitch, she felt immediate warmth for both her interviewers. She'd anticipated a lot more antagonism; interviews she'd had back home had always felt adversarial.

Partly she knew, the low wage and zero hours contract under which she'd be working meant that VU (as they self-abbreviated) would be lucky to have her. She shouldn't be surprised they were being so accommodating. She wondered if she would have been as welcome if they'd known what she'd been fleeing. The temptation was strong to tell her own story.

"Just arrived in Britain myself and I am still finding my feet," she began tentatively, being methodical in her tenses. "I'd love to do something to help Romanian community here though. I feel they are not much respected?"

"We hear a lot of sad stories," began Tony. "Just the other day we had a woman in here—mother of two small kids—who was pushed over on the tube for putting down one of those little packets of hankies with a message tied to it. Most people, if they don't donate, just ignore it. These idiots decided to take exception. That said, we don't condone begging, in any form."

"People do what they have to," said Elena. "Especially when there's kids."

"This poor woman spoke hardly any English," Aldona added. "Her brother had brought her over but was alcoholic and not working. Without the language skills it's difficult to get work. That's where you'd come in. Help with applications, CVs, a bit of interview coaching, translation of letters, forms, and other documents."

"I'd love to help," said Elena.

She really meant it, which surprised her a little. The job was only supposed to be a stop-gap, but this could actually be fulfilling. Half an hour later, after a cup of tea (Tony had mistakenly added sugar but Elena let it pass) and what seemed more like a friendly chat than a job interview, she left, feeling optimistic. They said they were keen to fill the position quickly and would let her know by the end of the week.

Elena delayed heading to the cinema, opting for a wander through Soho and into Covent Garden. She watched the matinee crowds heading from restaurants and bars into the big theatres where shows like Wicked and Avenue Q seemed to alternate with grittier fare starring well-known Hollywood actors. She'd heard that Matthew McConaughey was in town, acting in something by Tennessee Williams (or was it Eugene O'Neill)? She daydreamed that she might spot him, emerging from a limo, entourage in tow.

Without really planning it, Elena found herself back outside Bar Italia and decided to pop in for a quick coffee. Ana's film still had twenty minutes or so to run, she reckoned. A different waitress stood behind the counter, making coffees but Luca was also there, immaculately dressed, clearing tables. Elena was gratified that when he saw her, he broke off what he was doing to greet her.

"Bella bella! How are you? I hope you are not getting your coffee elsewhere?"

Elena laughed.

"I wouldn't dare. Anyway, yours is unimpeachable."

96

"Unimpeachable, is it? What a word. Sit down, please. I bring you something on the house?"

He said these last three words behind a hand, in a stage whisper. Elena suspected Luca was flirting with her but probably without intent, as some elderly Lotharios are wont to do. She was in a mood to humour him. When he brought her a giant cappuccino and two biscotti, she insisted on paying, and he made a show of protesting until they settled on her paying for the coffee only. She suspected the biscotti were always complimentary and Luca was just a good salesman, but it was entertaining, nonetheless.

"And how is your beautiful daughter?"

"Still beautiful," Elena said. "Is enjoying a bit of Shakespeare. Well, Shakespeare with guns."

"Cultured too. Just like her mama."

A little later, when Elena was halfway down her coffee, Luca surprised her again by pulling up a chair and sitting on it backwards, his hairy arms crossed over its back.

"And now my dear (again the stage whisper) we must get serious. I saw your woman."

"My woman?"

Luca frowned.

"Your red-haired friend. The one who you were looking for."

"Frances?"

Elena was so stunned she almost choked on her drink.

"You saw Frances. When?"

"Just yesterday. But I couldn't call you. The number seemed wrong or something."

Luca ferreted about in his apron pocket, producing the piece of paper with Elena's number on it. She was touched that he'd kept it. Looking more closely, she saw that she'd flipped two of the digits. How stupid!

"She was in here, had usual espresso, talking to two men. I was in the back doing stock-take. I didn't see her until she was leaving and couldn't stop her, but I swear it was this Frances woman."

Elena hardly knew how to react. Her feelings seemed to include joy, trepidation, resentment and even a weird kind of disappointment. She was already folding away her memories of Frances and storing them in the attic of her subconscious. Robin had appeared from nowhere and supplanted Frances, fulfilling the hope she still seemed to need to attach to another person. What was she to do with this news now?

"Okay," she said. "I give you my address and right number. Please, please, if you see her again, get her to call me."

Elena carefully wrote out the information this time, on a flier for a local open mic music night. Luca took it with all the ceremony of a deed or contract.

"I promise you, I will. Now... have you tried our wonderful lemon cakes? I bake them myself, fresh this morning."

Somehow, head and heart thumping, Elena left a few minutes later, with a bag of lemon cakes. Six for the price of four, of course. She made her way to the cinema by memory this time, which would have pleased her, if she hadn't been focused on the miracle that had just occurred.

Ana sat in the foyer, sitting next to a tall, thin, mixed-race boy with unruly hair. Elena could see her through the glass as she approached. Something made her pause and not go straight in.

Ana was engrossed, holding an iPhone earbud to her ear while he boy, who looked very young but still much older than her daughter, wore the other. Ana was nodding her head in time with the music, her shoulder touching the boy's. He too was nodding along. They shared a joke and Ana, passed back the earbud and touched his arm lightly. Elena felt odd watching this. She felt another cocktail of emotions, largely worry and irritation, but with a hint of pride.

Ana's eyes flicked up and her smile fell as she saw her mother waiting, bag of cakes dangling. She said a hasty goodbye to the boy and dashed out into the lane.

"Mum! Were you spying on me?"

"Who's that boy? Does he know how old you are?"

"How long have you been here?"

"Did you even see the film?"

It often began that way, their arguments. They'd both interrogate one another's motives with questions both treated as rhetorical. None of the questions would be answered until both felt equally betrayed and unhappy. Elena, who should probably let it slide, given how well her day had been going so far, found she couldn't. First the unpredictable insertion of Frances back into their lives, and now this?

"You are fourteen years old, Ana. He's practically got a moustache."

"He's only eighteen and a film student and he's really, really nice to me."

"Listen, sweetheart, you have no idea what he's after."

"Oh, I have a good idea, mum. I'm not an idiot. We haven't even held hands or anything. He's just a friend. Why do you have to interfere in everything?"

Elena let the question hang for a while.

"Because I'm your mother. I'm responsible for you."

"And I'm responsible for myself. I'm not some sort of slut, like Sophia."

Who was Sophia? It didn't matter; Elena was glad her daughter had someone to compare herself favourably to. That meant she had a moral compass, painfully skewed by hormones though it might be. She decided not to press the matter, although Ana sulked on the short walk home and slammed her bedroom door shut in the time-honoured manner of frustrated teenagers everywhere.

It'd blow over. It always did. Maybe knowing Frances was coming back would ground her a little more. Was Frances coming back? Why did she assume that? Her one-time lover was nearby but hadn't been in touch. That had to be a bad sign, didn't it? She should forget her and move on. Elena almost already had. How typical it was of this woman to wait until Elena no longer needed her or especially cared for her whereabouts and then pop back up.

On second thoughts, Elena had better not tell Ana anything about Frances. Let her come crawling back, ideally with a craven apology and a watertight explanation for her behaviour. Or let her really vanish this time, leave the city, never appear again.

Elena decided not to be too harsh on Ana and popped out to buy some groceries for her daughter's favourite meal—sausages, mashed sweet potato and peas. Her shouted goodbye at the door was met with deafening silence. Elena headed down to the Polish delicatessen nearby and came back moments later to see her neighbour letting herself into the flat.

"Qamar! How are you?"

The Somali flashed her beacon of a smile.

"I am wonderful, my dear. Just about to get my drink on. Client cancelled tonight but I'm bushed anyway."

Then Qamar's eyed narrowed in momentary appraisal of what she'd said.

"I'm a masseuse. Got my own cards made and everything."

Qamar passed an ornately lettered card with a swirly purple and red pattern on the back.

LADY QAMAR – massuse

Did she know about the misspelling? Elena thought it best not to mention it.

"Listen. You should some around later. I have an epic Bordeaux in there. Present from a client."

Qamar pointed into her open flat, which was redolent with warmth, colour, and an aromatic joss-stick of some sort. It looked tempting.

"I've got to cook dinner for my daughter. We're having fight. Boys."

Qamar rolled her eyes.

"The old story. Well, bring her along. Later I mean, after your meal."

"We'll see. We're both tired."

Qamar tutted.

"Ridiculous. You're both young and gorgeous. Like me. We don't get tired. Come. When you're ready."

Turning down Qamar was evidently something few found easy. Elena thought her neighbour would probably forget the invitation the moment her door was closed. She'd make it up to her another time. Elena and Ana had talking to do.

As it happened, the talking was less problematic than Elena had expected. Ana told her about her friend Sophia's revelation about sleeping with a boy. Ana's dismayed reaction to this turn of events gave Elena a bit of confidence that she wouldn't go out and do anything stupid in a spirit of competition. Chris, it turned out, sounded more like a protective older brother than a threat. Elena decided to extend her newfound spirit of trust to her daughter's friend, despite her misgivings.

"He gets me free tickets too," Ana said, as she stuffed sausage and mash into her cheeks with the urgency of a hibernating squirrel.

"I want you paying next time. He might lose his job."

"Aw, you're concerned for my friend. That's sweet."

"Don't patronise me, sweetie. Be safe, be sensible."

Ana nodded, chasing rogue peas around her plate.

After Ana had surprised her mother again, this time pleasantly, by doing the dishes, they sat drinking tea and eating the delicious little lemon cakes Luca had given her. Elena noted the slight contradiction of her accepting freebies from Luca while chiding her daughter for Chris's cinema tickets. Parents were allowed to be hypocrites though.

She turned her attention from her daughter's excited babbling about some developments on a Netflix show she was watching on her phone to the remaining three cakes.

Ana, would you like to meet the neighbour?

Qamar answered her door a few moments after the second round of knocking. Her music, a lilting ringing guitar-driven raga, rang out into the stairwell, explaining the delay.

"My friend Kelife's new album. I just can't get enough of it!"

"I hope I'm not disturbing," began Elena, somewhat ironically.

"Not at all. I invited you, remember. Come in, come in. And who is this lovely young woman?"

Ana smiled, despite her misgivings about tagging along.

"I'm Ana."

Ana found herself enfolded in an impetuous hug, her hand, proffered in a handshake, limp at her side. Elena wondered if she was on something. She would take a good look at Qamar's pupils when they got inside.

Qamar led them into her lounge, a sumptuously furnished and decorated place midway between an exotic bazaar and a boudoir. Elena was beginning to think her first instincts about Qamar's profession had been correct. She couldn't gracefully back out now, so slumped down beside Ana in a low sofa while Qamar sat cross-legged back down onto a beanbag that already bore her generous imprint. A joss-stick was burning in the corner and the room was lit exclusively with candles and a couple of strings of fairly lights, one surrounding an impressively ornate antique mirror.

Elena had to admit the place had a seductively soothing aesthetic, particularly once Qamar had turned the music down to a reasonable volume and opened a bottle of wine. It appeared she had already finished one, along with a visitor who had left lipstick around the rim of a half-empty glass. The wine glugged out into two giant, thin glasses. A third stood ready.

"Can I have some?" asked Ana, in as reasonable a tone as she could muster.

"I don't think..." began Elena, before she was waved into silence by her host.

"Of course she can, Elena. Look at this young woman."

"She's still a child. I don't want her getting drunk."

"Mum!"

"Not so much a child anymore, I think," Qamar suggested. "Already turning many men's heads, no?"

Was that Ana blushing?

"Just look at her," said Qamar.

Elena looked. She tried to see her daughter with the eyes of a stranger and was startled to see that there had been a change from the shy child Elena still held in her mind's eye, as if she'd been denying the evidence of her senses. Ana's body was widening, developing curves. Her face had lost its chubby childishness, developing cheekbones and a tiny chin dimple. She was no longer the flat-chested, wiry tomboy who had practically leapt up trees and raced through cornfields while her mother struggled to capture her on camera. Soon enough, Ana's independence would be unchallengeable. She must make her own mistakes, as Elena had. Within reasonable boundaries, of course.

"Go on then. But just one small glass."

Ana rubbed her hands together and accepted the glass, its contents the colour of dried blood. She took a sip and Elena could see she was pretending to enjoy it more than she probably did. Good.

"So, what do you do?" Ana asked.

Shit. Elena looked at Qamar, who hardly missed a beat, her eyes only as dilated (Elena decided) as the low light of the candles required.

"I'm a model and a masseuse. I'm starting my own business soon with two... colleagues. It's called MMM. We got a logo designed—a fancy font and three dots like mmm..."

Qamar tossed over a piece of card upon which the logo had been printed. Like everything else in Qamar's world, it looked seductive.

"The first M is for massage... of course. The second is for meditation. My pal Rajesh will cover that. The third one is music, which is where Kelife comes in. He's a music therapist as well as a musician and DJ. I sing with him sometimes. It's very relaxing."

"Sounds great. When are you launching?" asked Elena, a little confused now.

Was this a cover story for what Qamar really did, or the truth?

"We did a pop-up in Shoreditch a few weeks ago, in this weird box-park place. It was amazing—really popular. Some of the girls... some girls I know... are volunteering to be trained up in one of the skills so we can offer after-hours and do it seven days a week. One of my clients is getting us a start-up loan. He works in finance. It's all so..."

Here, Qamar remembered to pause for breath.

"...very exciting."

Elena couldn't help but be impressed. If this was a cover story, it was convincingly delivered. After staying long enough to convey her mixed feelings about London (there was so much to see but no friends to see it with) Ana began yawning and Elena took the half-finished glass of wine off her and let her back into the flat. She then returned to Qamar's. This woman intrigued her and besides, Ana wasn't the only one who lacked friends. And although Qamar was beautiful, Elena was oddly relieved to realise she didn't fancy her.

"So, what is it you do?" Qamar asked, adding slyly, "or rather, tell me what you'd really like to be doing. Nobody in London is doing what they really want to be doing."

"I'm going to be working as a translator. Is quite a cool job, actually."

Elena told her about Tony and Aldona and the charity's mission and activities. Qamar seemed genuinely interested, as she nibbled politely at a lemon cake and refilled their glasses with the fruity Bordeaux. Elena began to warm to her, suspicious no longer, even if she did sell her body for sex. Who was Elena to judge? Elena had endured an abusive relationship with her ex, before meeting Frances. That was a kind of prostitution of the soul (or so Elena thought in her most self-recriminatory moments).

The conversation flowed and Qamar disappeared briefly to change out of her dramatically short skirt and cleavage-enhancing silk shirt into a demure, though brightly patterned, silk kimono. She began to tell her own story, in a strange mixture of self-deprecation and self-aggrandizement. Both were defence mechanisms, Elena guessed. Qamar had had a hard life.

"You've heard of FGM? Where they cut you down below, to stop you enjoying sex. And all in the name of Allah. It's bullshit. It's male control. Me and a couple of friends ran away at fifteen, before my father and uncle could have it done to us. We fell in with a charming, but very dangerous man who uses girls to rob rich men. We'd hang out at the bars of fancy hotels in Edinburgh, Newcastle, Manchester, go upstairs with the men we'd meet.

Once we got in their rooms, we'd insist they shower before we sleep with them. While the Johns were in the en suite—bang! We run away with their wallets, watches and gold-plated crap. Things got a bit hot when one of them turned out to be a local celebrity. Police got a little too lively. Our spotter made himself scarce and we went our separate ways. I landed in London, dancing in some clubs. One night, Mr Carver, who part-owned the club, asked me if I wanted to meet with one of his photographer friends, take some photos, maybe think about joining Girl Oasis."

"What's that? Sound like tribute band."

"I wish. It was, still is, a camgirl site. You know, bored looking girls in skimpy outfits chatting to guys and trying to take them into private rooms for sex shows. Easy money, if you can cope with the boredom and the morons.

"Anyway, this photographer took some pictures and I really enjoyed the session. He was good-looking in a scruffy sort of way and towards the end of the session he just came right out and said he'd love to sleep with me. I was kind of flattered, kind of creeped out and tried to laugh it off. Then he got out his wallet and pulled out two hundred quid. I was broke back then, desperate. I was taking a bit of coke to get by, to pull all-nighters at the club and the cams. I said I wouldn't sleep with him, but I would suck him off. He gave me the £200 anyway. That's how it started."

Qamar was no longer making eye contact now and her story had taken on the mood of a confessional. Elena wasn't sure she wanted to hear much more but didn't want to seem prudish or stand-offish either. Despite her misgivings, she liked this young woman.

"It was easier than I thought. I kind of pulled away from my body and focused on what I'd spend the money on. Mostly crystal or coke, as it happened but that's another story. I'm off all that shit now. So, I started on the cams and I took in a few clients. Mr Carver popped round every so often and he would bring clients or sometimes he'd bring me dresses to wear, special outfits that guys had requested. I guess he was a pimp, but he was pretty low-key. He rented me this place and I paid him a quarter of my take on top of the rent. But it's changed recently."

"What do you mean?"

"Clients are getting, how can I say this? Low class. They don't pay as much, and they demand more. Sometimes they get rough. I reported this one guy for trying to beat me with his belt buckle. The next week he was back with a chain, as if nothing had happened. I had to threaten him with a knife to make him leave. He spat on me and threw a tenner on the floor 'for my trouble'. What a bastard. I'm sick of it all now and I'm getting out."

"The triple-M business?"

"Exactly. We're getting ready to launch, it's going to be great."

With that, Qamar lifted her eyes to Elena's and smiled her thousand-watt smile and Elena couldn't but believe her. This woman, who had experienced so much adversity, was a kindred spirit. They were both fighters, disappointed by life but determined to persevere on their own terms.

Elena left, more than a little unsteady with a warm and fuzzy wine haze dulling her sense, three hours later. She let herself back into the flat with exaggerated and not entirely successful care. Dropping her keys on the floor in the hallway, Elena looked up into the sleep-dulled features of her daughter.

"Have you been over there all this time? It's nearly one thirty," queried Ana.

"I've been... I've just been with my friend," Elena muttered, before heading into her room to fall asleep, fully clothed, on the bed.

CHAPTER 16

Qamar had been dead for two days when the police broke down her door, the coroner estimated. At some point in the small hours of the 9th of September she had evidently decided to end her life, taken one of her four kitchen chairs into the lounge, wrapped an internet router cable around her neck and tied it to the faux-antique electric chandelier that was the room's centrepiece. Then she must have kicked the chair away and hanged herself. One of her shoes was found several feet away, the other dangling from her foot, evidence of the spasms that must have wracked her body as animal instinct took over from the terrible act of will that had finished her.

A suicide note, of sorts, was found pinned to a cork board in the kitchen. Written in biro in a spidery hand it read, simply 'I am ashamed. I do not want to live.' A scrawled signature beneath.

Elena found out about her friend (she did not hesitate now to designate her as such) when, returning from her first day at the translation agency, she saw a police officer taping off Qamar's door. The POLICE tape was of the same variety Robin had once concealed from her. Perhaps it was time to broach that act of subterfuge.

"What's happened?" Elena had asked, her voice quavering.

The policeman, fortysomething, balding, shrugged. "Woman who lives here offed herself."

Offed herself. The casualness of the term hit like a hammer-blow.

"She was my friend. And she would never do that."

A gratifying flicker of shame crossed the man's features, concealed swiftly behind bland professionalism.

"We'll send someone over to talk to you, offer support. We may have a few questions, if that's okay. Just routine."

Elena nodded, stunned. She entered her flat, slumped down on the cheap sofa she had recently decorated with throws and cushions from a local discount store. She could hear the loud voices of police officers outside as well as heavy footsteps traipsing in and out of Qamar's flat. She found herself worrying about Qamar's immaculate cream-coloured carpet.

Could Qamar have killed herself? It seemed hardly credible. She had seemed so full of possibilities, so vibrant with excitement about the future. Elena had taken heart herself from her friend's example. Over the last two days, during which she had simply assumed Qamar was away visiting someone (or with a client?) she had taken her neighbour's advice on several points.

Firstly, she had decided to be more trusting and sympathetic towards her daughter, who was going through a difficult and confusing life change. Secondly, she had decided to treat her poky apartment as if it was palatial and, in addition to the throws and cushions, had stretched her credit card balance a little further by purchasing candles, a few small rugs, some things for the kitchen and even a wine rack, though it currently stood empty. She had been looking forward to having Qamar round.

A warm wetness on her cheeks informed Elena that she was crying. Fortunately, Ana was out—Elena had said she could go clothes shopping and had given her thirty pounds. Elena knew it wouldn't stretch far but it was a nod towards giving her daughter a little more freedom. Elena had also got around to making her phone work here and had insisted Ana text her regularly. She needn't have feared. A series of changing room selfies had already arrived during the day, taken from a place called Top Shop. Elena had given a thumbs up emoji to a salmon-coloured top and white jeans.

The day at Voices Unlimited had gone really well too. After all the usual induction stuff, Elena had been set to work translating some CVs and a lawyer's letter for some clients. Hearing the old tongue again and rolling those syllables round her mouth while she turned them into functional English had made her a little homesick, but not in an unpleasant way.

She'd gone for lunch at Bar Italia (where Luca shook his head to her perfunctory question about Frances) and the busyness and noise of the place had cheered her too. She ended the day reassuring a worried mother that the letter from her daughter's university about her bursary was merely bureaucratic and not disastrous. She'd felt useful and helpful and thought she was probably going to enjoy the job, although it was only for three days per week at the moment. Everything had been going so well. And now this.

Then she felt bad focusing on how Qamar's death affected her, rather than how Qamar must have felt when Elena left, and she had perhaps sunk into depression. Had she been bipolar? Certainly, the energy and wildness of her neighbour had seemed a little forced, possibly even manic. Perhaps Elena wasn't such a good judge of other people's mental states, after all.

She had to find out more. Robin would be able to help. He was supposed to come round after his shift to play Scrabble (Elena's idea—she wanted to test her English).

She would ask him then. Her instinct told her that something was just not right about what the officer outside had told her.

Could Qamar have been murdered?

She let the possibility sink in. Could it be true? Her friend must have had some insalubrious clients and colleagues in her oldest of professions. Could one of them have killed her, either in a pre-planned way, or accidentally, and made it look like suicide?

She said nothing of this to the pretty blonde Detective Constable Milner, who knocked on her door about an hour later. She merely listened, asked a few tentative questions, and answered those directed at her as practically as possible. Milner had clearly been tasked with tying up loose ends in a case that the police considered self-evidently suicide.

"How well did you know Ms Liibaan?"

"I just met her. She invited me and my daughter for tea."

"Your daughter Ana you mentioned. How old is she?"

Why was that relevant?

"Fourteen. She's out shopping."

"I hope you didn't give her your credit card!"

It was a gauche attempt at humour. Elena smiled thinly.

"She has pocket money. She's a good girl. I don't want her to know about this... yet. I mean, I want to tell her."

"Of course. That's your prerogative. How did Miss Liibaan seem when you last spoke? And what time was that?"

"She seemed in good mood, she had plans. Full of hope. It's so hard to believe."

"It's commoner than you think," said the officer, with a rueful head shake.

Elena both wanted and didn't want to know the answer to her next question. She shuffled uncomfortably amongst the new cushions.

"Can I ask, how did she do?"

"Are you sure you want to know? If you were friends..."

"I only met her a couple of times."

Elena blurted out this truth and then felt guilty and wanted to retract it.

"I mean, I like her, but we also just met."

"Okay. Well... I shouldn't really say but you might as well know. She hanged herself. With some sort of electrical cord."

"No!"

"It was probably fairly quick. I mean compared with, well, with other methods. Look, I want to give you my card. Just in case you want to talk to anyone about this."

"It's just so sad. Why couldn't she just knock on my door?"

The young office shrugged, but not callously.

"I can only tell you that people can be really unreadable. And you mustn't blame yourself."

"Oh, I don't."

The thought hadn't really occurred to her. It was true that she hadn't seen Qamar in a couple of days and hadn't rung her buzzer, but there had been no reason to. There was a rattle of keys in the lock and Ana blustered in.

"Mum, what's going on out there? There's police and... oh, hi."

Ana's face had hardened into the front with which teenagers face down authority.

"Ana," Elena began. "I've got some sad news to tell you."

CHAPTER 17

"Aggravated fucking assault!"

Yarmouth stared down at the charge sheet in disbelief.

"Those bastards stab me and run over my colleague, putting him in intensive care and we go for aggravated assault. I don't get it."

Sergeant Brompton closed the office door gingerly and sidled round the room, putting two feet of sturdy wooden desk between him and his angry officer.

"Look, Yarmouth, the CPS don't think there's enough evidence of a serious attempt to kill..."

"They fucking ran over Conover with a motorbike."

"When he jumped out in front of them, yes. I don't like this any more than you do."

"Then fight it! Take it upstairs. Aren't we supposed to look after our own?"

"You know we do. Only these were two young lads..."

"Let me guess, from a sinkhole estate, poorly educated..."

"That's about the size of it. We can't be seen to be over-punitive."

"That's a description of the background of half the Met. Only we don't go around nicking fifty mobile phones and slashing at policemen with Stanley knives."

Brompton sat down in his chair, swivelling left and right in the habitual manner that told you he was uncomfortable.

"How is it?" asked Brompton tentatively.

"I still have my kidneys, if that's what you're asking, and a sexy little scar like a smile under my belly button. I won't be breakdancing any time soon."

Brompton's awkward smile sat somewhere between sympathy and professionalism. It wound Yarmouth up.

"I want to complain," decided Yarmouth aloud. "I want to talk to Purvis."

"You can't do that."

"Oh really? Watch me."

Yarmouth pushed his chair back and stormed out of Brompton's fishbowl and straight up the metal stairs to the 3rd Floor. Ordinary PCs like him seldom made it up this far, unless they were receiving a commendation... or facing a disciplinary. Yarmouth had been here once before and it hadn't involved smiles, handshakes and souvenir photos.

He made a beeline for DCI Purvis's street-facing office. Through the glass panel, he could see the deputy chief inspector on the phone, hunched over with both elbows on his desk. A rank of colourful daubs by his two small children decorated the wall behind him. When he saw Yarmouth approaching, Purvis raised a hand as if to say 'wait just a moment'.

Yarmouth piled straight in, leaving the door provocatively open.

"Even unmassaged, the quarterlies are looking pretty good. Look, I have to go. Someone's here to see me. I'll have the reports over by end of play. Thanks."

Purvis hung up, took a moment to collect himself and fixed a resolute stare at Yarmouth.

"What the hell are you doing, constable?"

"Aggravated assault. Are you fucking serious?"

"Less of the profanity, PC Yarmouth. The Crown Prosecution is serious, if that's what you mean. In any case, its assault plus possession of a deadly weapon, multiple counts of theft, evading arrest..."

"By riding over an officer's head."

"That's not what the witness saw."

"I'm sorry?"

A dangerous silence spread between the two men, one standing shaking, one seated and defensive.

"The one witness who stopped. The theft victim."

"What did she say?"

"She said they snatched her phone and you both cornered them in an alley."

"So far so true..."

"And then your colleague, Officer..."

Purvis rummaged around the papers on his desk.

"Conover," interjected Yarmouth. "Constable Angus Conover."

"Constable Conover jumped in front of the bike as it was exiting the alleyway, endangering his own life and ignoring protocol."

A tidal fury swelled up in Yarmouth's chest. He had to stop himself from speaking for a moment—nothing good could come of him expressing the way he actually felt in this moment. He was already on his second disciplinary for punching out McPherson.

"I'll be submitting my report tomorrow morning. It'll tell a different story, I suspect."

"That's your prerogative," sighed Purvis. "I'll look over it carefully, in case there's anything the investigating team missed."

Again, Yarmouth had to calm himself. He turned and was about to leave when he couldn't stop himself from asking one more thing.

"The blade. The Stanley knife. The SOCO team retrieved it?"

"I'm afraid not. If you say one of the kids had one, that's good enough for me, but I'm guessing some passer-by had it away before we could secure the scene."

"CCTV?"

"Nothing helpful. Look, San is on it. Liaise with her. Don't waste time on it though. You should be recuperating. Take another week."

"I'm taking a couple of days."

"Whatever, just... Tread carefully."

Yarmouth mulled over that phrase as he trudged lethargically downstairs. Tread carefully. It sounded like a warning.

"Bunch of wankers," was Fleischer's pithy response to Yarmouth's tale of woe.

They sat in the same booth in the Temperance, comparing the merits of Cornish Doom Bar ale and a local Fuller's bitter.

"I'm telling you," Fleischer went on, "the department's gone to pot since Purvis has been in charge. We're stifled in bureaucracy, everything's by the book, none of the usual harmless corner-cutting we used to get up to. He's really taken the joy out of putting a bunch of gormless fuckers behind bars."

"I guess they are only kids," mused Yarmouth. "Maybe I'm over-reacting."

"Yeah and a half-inch closer and you'd be over-reacting your guts all over Dean Street. Whatever the fuck happened to protecting our own?"

"Committees, focus groups and Defund the Police."

"Too right. Policing by social media. Can't twist a wrist without some oik uploading it to YouTube."

So the conversation went on, the usual round of off-loading and bitching. It helped. Plus, Yarmouth later got the satisfaction of hammering Fleischer in five games of pool (one pint per game) before he looked at his watch and realised he was likely to be late for meeting Elena.

Fleischer caught Yarmouth's panic-stricken glance at his iPhone.

"Late for the girlfriend, are we?"

"What makes you think...?"

"I am a bloody detective, don't you know? You went into the loo thirty minutes ago smelling like a copper and came out doused in that poncey stuff you spray on."

"Calvin Klein."

"If you say so. Suppose you don't want to make it best of seven then?"

"Mate, you're four games down," laughed Yarmouth as he slipped his jacket back on.

"Am I? Huh. Arithmetic was never my strong suit. Tell you what, though... nor is it O'Leary's."

Yarmouth was only half-listening, reaching unsteadily behind him for his backpack.

"What are you on about?"

"Those stolen phones. First there was 48, then it went back down to 47, then back to 48."

"The ones the scooter lads nicked?"

"Yeah. O'Leary logged them as 48. Then a change was requested and then he did a re-count and, now it's back to 48 again. I reckon he's on the sauce back there. Boring as fuck, that job. I'd drink myself silly too."

Yarmouth didn't doubt it. O'Leary was probably a functioning alcoholic. He hadn't smelt booze on his breath during working hours, but he wouldn't put it past him.

"Right then. See you around."

"Indubitably, old bean."

This was delivered with a thespian burr. Indubitably. Where had he heard that word before?

CHAPTER 18

Elena looked at the inebriated man facing her in her little kitchen, watching him trying to focus on what she was saying, trying to appear considerably less drunk than he was.

"Your neighbour? Which neighbour?" he asked, frowning.

"Across the landing. Somali girl. Very beautiful. Qamar."

"Okay. And you're saying she was murdered? When did this happen?"

"Three nights ago. I came home from work. My first day. Went very well, thanks for asking."

Elena didn't know why she was taking it out on Yarmouth. Sure, he had turned up a little drunk and almost an hour late. But he was here, and Frances wasn't. And that made him the only punching bag she had available. Against her better judgement, she'd allowed Ana to go and visit her new friend Chris, who was DJing at a trendy café-bar South of the river. She had strict controls to come home, with no alcohol in her bloodstream, by nine o'clock.

"I'm sorry," began Robin, feebly.

"Doesn't matter. Anyway, there were officers going in and out and tape over her door. You know, like you hid from me when we first arrive."

Robin's eyes widened visibly.

"I know something bad happened here. This is a dangerous place you've put us."

Now he coughed in surprise and began to protest.

"Put you? I got you three months rent-free accommodation in Central London. Do you have any idea...?"

"They found her hanging," Elena interrupted. "As if she would do. I talk to her for several hours. No way she was that depressed."

Even in his inebriated state, Robin had the sense to shut up and let her tell her story. Elena did, leaving out only some of the intimacies she had shared with Qamar about Frances, after Ana had gone to bed. Robin stopped leaning so nonchalantly against the kitchen counter, sat Elena down in the lounge and, gratifyingly, got out his police notebook and began writing.

It took half an hour for Elena to disburden herself, not without a few tears and a gruff hug from Robin. Then he read over his notes, shut his book, sat back on his side of the sofa and looked seriously at Elena.

"You told all this to PC Milner?"

"Most of it. I left out most of my crazy notions. I don't want them to think I'm some paranoid Eastern European woman who's delusional or something. Can we go there?"

"To the station?"

"No, dummy. To Qamar's flat."

Robin rubbed his chin, uneasily.

"We shouldn't. I'm not a detective and I'm not assigned. Plus, we don't have a key."

"Oh really? Come."

Elena led Robin out into the hall, holding his hand like a child about to get either a treat or a talking to. She located the pipe in the corner of the hallway that Qamar had shown her with the simple but touching words *because I trust you*. She slid her hands up and down the pipe, finally locating the strip of gaffer tape, behind which Qamar's spare key was taped.

"It's still a crime scene, at least until the inquest returns a verdict," began Robin.

"You're a police officer. I'm a witness helping you. So, either come with me or arrest me."

Her tone was jocular, but Elena felt this was a turning point. Robin took a deep breath, exhaled slowly, and walked towards the door.

"Touch nothing, okay? We should be wearing gloves..."

Moments later, after Elena wiggled the key in the specific way Qamar showed her to make the ancient lock function, they were in. A musty remainder of incense and perfume hit Elena's nose as they peered into the gloom. Robin hit a light switch with his hand wrapped in his shirt cuff.

They turned from the tiny hallway into the lounge and Elena steeled herself for... something that would shock her.

But there was nothing but an overturned chair and a cheap chandelier whose fitting had pulled out from the plaster ceiling rose, pieces of fallen plaster dotting the carpet beneath. Folded and numbered pieces of card adorned the scene, which Elena felt resembled a stage set. A drab, off-West End stage set, tawdry without the illuminating personality of Qamar.

"Evidence numbers," explained Robin, indicating the cards. "The photographer records everything and it all gets logged. They'll take it seriously."

"Really? Prostitute kills herself, leaves a note. She has history of using drugs, few friends, no relatives who still talk to her."

"Forensics will still do their job."

"To back-up their suicide theory. I'm telling you, I don't believe."

The overturned chair Qamar had presumably stood on to end it all was a high-backed, wooden one with lathe-turned legs. Qamar had painted it red. Elena took out her phone and began to take photos.

"Is that a good idea?" Robin said, quietly.

"I don't know," Elena admitted. "I just feel I have to."

They wandered slowly around Qamar's place, taking stock. Nothing indicated a struggle or fight of any kind. A single wine glass by the sink held the dried remainders of red wine and the brighter red of Qamar's lipstick. The glass had been numbered '8'.

"They didn't take it for fingerprints?" Elena wondered aloud.

"They sometimes do it on site. Only if there's a need will they take it to the lab."

"I told you. They didn't bother."

"I guess she would have had a fair few... guests. Fingerprints might not be very helpful, even if she was killed."

"They still should have done."

Robin kept his opinions to himself, which Elena appreciated. She was beginning to come round to admit that she might have been mistaken. Without Qamar's energy, this apartment did look like a rather lonely little nest. Who knows what darkness might have descended after Elena had left her neighbour.

"What was she like?" Robin asked, quietly.

Elena took a moment.

"She was explosion of energy and ideas. A great hostess. Bringing plates of snacks—cheese and... I don't know what you call... *castraveciori*, pickle cucumbers..."

"Gherkins," Robin explained.

"Sure, gherkin, biscuit, even fried chicken wings that were amazing. My glass was never empty. I had to stop her topping up Ana."

"Ana was drinking?"

"Okay Mr Policeman... half a glass. I got impression her work, the sex she was selling, was just like another act of generosity. Sure, she got paid, but she had so many regulars, guys who brought her flowers and gifts. She was proud, not ashamed. She had absolutely no sense of shame and I mean in good way."

"Quite a lady."

"Really she was. I thought she might be a... friend."

Elena's last word was choked in a sob that surprised her as much as Robin. It had taken the intrusion and then removal of Qamar from her life to make her realise how lonely she really was.

Robin took her face in his hands and kissed her. He pushed her back against the kitchen counter, his kisses hot and hungry. She reciprocated, then pushed him gently away, keeping hold of his left hand.

"Not here. Is weird."

They went back to her flat and wordlessly Elena led him to the bedroom. Ana would be back in about half an hour. There was time. She ran her hands down his chest to the waistband of his trousers, and beyond. His penis was hard and taut behind his zipper. Robin unbuttoned her blouse with unsteady fingers as she stood with her back to the wardrobe, feeling the handle digging in to the small of her back. The discomfort was not unpleasant. He kissed her breasts, freed one from her bra, took her nipple between his teeth as she pulled down his zipper and slipped a hand inside.

They made it to the bed a little later, half undressed, laughing, suddenly cut free from their sources of guilt, shame and fear, adrift in the moment. Elena was surprised to find how wet Robin's kisses had made her as he pulled off her panties with one hand and touched her where nobody but Frances had in almost a year. When he slipped inside her, she felt the shock and relief of his entry and the last fragments of self-consciousness and worry dissipate as he moved upon her, bringing her quickly to an orgasm that made her spasm beneath him, frightening Robin until she reassured him her climax was "normal". Normal! Nothing was normal. Perhaps nothing would be, ever again.

A little later they lay on top of the duvet, tousled, sweaty, Elena's head cradled against Robin's chest. Elena felt so relaxed she almost wanted to purr like a contented cat. It had been too long since she'd felt the protective comfort of a warm body. The tension and fear and the sadness she'd been bottling up had dispersed like mist. She was so comfortable in fact that she completely forgot about Ana, until the front door crashed open and her daughter's shuffling gait announced her return.

Elena bolted from the bed as if electrocuted. Robin began to search the floor for his underwear.

"Mum! Where are you?"

The bedroom door opened fractionally as Elena pulled on her dressing gown on and jabbed a foot against it. Hilariously, Robin had pressed himself out of sight against the wall, trousers held in a bunch at his groin, like a character from a questionable French farce.

Ana's face peered through the gap in the door.

"Mum? Have you gone to bed? Didn't we have some ice cream left? I'm starving. What's blocking the door?"

Elena slipped out into the hall and shut the door behind her. Ana looked at the robe then down at the floor where Robin's shoes sat side by side with Elena's own.

"Are you...? Is he...?"

The last two words were delivered sotto voce. Ana's face wore an expression mingling delight and disapproval.

"Mum! You're terrible. Can't believe I'm the sensible one. Look, I'm back on time. Nearly."

Ana proffered her phone. It read 9:28pm.

"Good girl. Look, we... kind of finished the ice cream but the shop's still open downstairs. Take some cash from the drawer."

Elena hadn't yet got around to opening a bank account, her remaining cash hidden under a phone book in a kitchen drawer.

"Cool."

Ana was about to breeze back out when she stopped in the doorway.

"I hope you at least used protection."

With a grin, she trotted off downstairs. Elena let the door swing shut with a rattle.

She hadn't used protection. Robin hadn't brought anything. They hadn't discussed it either, which was doubly bad.

Two hours later she was receiving the morning after pill from a pretty young Indian pharmacist who gave her the compulsory lecture about it not being a form of contraception. Did the girl think she was a wayward teenager or something?

Back at the flat, she swallowed the tablet with a glass of tap water and watched Robin frying eggs in her kitchen. Things were changing, quicker than she'd ever imagined they could.

127

CHAPTER 19

Yarmouth knew he most definitely shouldn't be here, but he had made Elena a promise. The last thing he had said to her as he'd left that morning to begin his last week of 'compassionate leave'.

"I'll talk to the owner, see if he knows anything."

An innocent sounding proposal but Yarmouth was out of uniform, asking a confidential informant about an open case that he had no business investigating. If word of this got back to Purvis it could potentially end his career and just when he was getting himself back to a point where he could reapply for a transfer to CID.

So why was he here, waiting patiently in Carver's musty antechamber while Janine roundly ignored him and finished booking her package holiday to Kos?

Because he believed Elena. She had been so unswervingly sure that Qamar had not been suicidal that night that it warranted more than a cursory once-over. Carver's world remained a murky one, even if the police had decided to ignore its darker corners to take advantage of the titbits Carver threw them. He had once run a dozen girls out of Elena's apartment block, subdividing rooms into fragrant little dens of sex and drug-taking. There were probably still regulars from those days prowling the remnants of Soho's sleazy past. If Qamar had been murdered by some sicko, or accidentally killed, Carver might have some names.

"No fucking way!"

Carver's response to the news of his tenant's death surprised Yarmouth. It was about the only genuine shock reaction he'd seen from the old rogue in several years.

"I gave that girl a decent place, replaced the water pump and the boiler. Even gave her a new fridge freezer. Well, new-ish. What has she got to go and kill herself about?"

"Your compassion humbles me, Bill. And that's exactly my point."

"What?"

Carver stood open-mouthed, like one of the gaping terrapins in his tanks.

"I'm not at all sure she did kill herself. It's all too neat. And there are witnesses who say she was anything but suicidal."

"What witnesses? Your girlfriend?"

Carver might look dumb but in truth he was anything but.

"Her neighbours. Look, I'm just covering all the angles."

"Yeah, why are you? You 'ain't Detective Constable anymore."

"Never mind. Just tell me—any Johns you know of who might've been around and who like it a bit rough? Anyone with a grudge... any real perverts?"

To give him a modicum of credit, Carver sat on the edge of his desk and rubbed his chin in at least the semblance of thought.

"I usually had those fuckers dealt with, if you know what I mean. Most of them don't come back for seconds."

"You're a veritable emancipator of women, Carver. Just tell me about the bad eggs who might have been around."

"I don't just sit here wanking off, you know. I have an empire to run."

129

Empire. Did Carver have any self-awareness of how pompous and absurd he was? He belonged behind bars and someday Yarmouth would enjoy visiting him there to ask him how his 'empire' was doing.

"Plus, I've got another room to let, apparently. When will your boys be done with it? Guess I'm going to have to get the place deep-cleaned or something."

Yarmouth took a deep breath.

"You'll have to contact the office about that. I'm sure they'll be in touch soon anyway. As will Mr Smirnov and his delightful brothers if you don't sit down and write me out some names."

He knew he could only use this bluff a couple of times before Carver saw through it. Yarmouth could do nothing to compromise Carver, but his fear of the genuinely lunatic Ukrainians (who had once fed a competitor his own fingers, with barbeque sauce) was a strong motivator.

"Fine. Christ, you're no fun at all anymore, Robbo. I'll email you some names. Can I just have an hour or two to think about it?"

Yarmouth could bend that much. He left the office satisfied that he'd get at least one lead out of the would-be property mogul. That should satisfy Elena, although Yarmouth was beginning to think that lip-service wouldn't do here. Elena was tenacious.

Edina Mulligan, the bifocal-wearing coroner, tightened the collar of her overall and peered at Constable Yarmouth's ID for what seemed to him an unreasonable length of time.

"And your role in this is?"

"Just following up something a witness said, for DCI Purvis."

"Really? Nobody told me you'd becoming down. I was heading out to lunch. There's a place with the amusing name of 'Mo Pho' I wanted to try. If it's decent, I might not even mention it's pronounced fa."

Of course. Mulligan was a massive foodie. And a massive pedant.

"If you can answer a couple of quick questions, just to tie up a couple of loose ends, I'll but you lunch, even though I have no idea what pho is."

"Vietnamese noodle soup. I'm obsessed with it. So... what's up?"

Mulligan brushed a strand of red hair over her ear, pushed her glasses back up on her nose and walked Yarmouth over to the metal table upon which, under disposable white sheets, the body of the Somalian woman lay. In repose, this lively force of nature turned out to be a little over five feet five inches tall.

Mulligan pulled back the sheet with what seemed almost a flourish.

The naked body of Qamar gave Yarmouth an odd jolt of guilt. It was both beautiful and awful, a perfect form from which all the life had drained. He had never lost the creeping dread of looking at dead bodies, although his four years in CID had meant he'd seen over a dozen, many in more pathetic stages of mortification than this one.

Qamar's painted finger and toenails stood out, a splash of colour against her midnight-black skin.

"You can see the ligature marks round the neck, that big bruise at the side is the knot."

"At the side? Isn't that a bit unusual?"

Mulligan shrugged.

"I doubt suicides have your sense of symmetry. The noose worked, however she chose to tie it."

"You're certain its suicide?"

"I have no reason to draw any other conclusion."

The coroner was something of a politician. A function quite deliberately distinct from the police, the coroner's office had the ability to return only a handful of specific verdicts. However, those verdicts had the power to stymie an investigation, if the powers that be decided that the bureaucratic burden of conflict with the coroner was simply not worth fighting.

Qamar's long elegant neck was circled with a repeated indentation, darker ridges of flesh occurring at half-inch intervals.

"What's that from?" asked Yarmouth.

"The router cord was partially-coiled, leaving that patterning."

"Any signs of violence?"

"Age-old scars, some bruising in the inner thighs and finger-marks on the arms, congruent with vigorous sex. No evidence of forced penetration though. Those scars on her legs are from adolescence. Self-harm. Nothing especially recent. She had drunk about a bottle and a half of wine and taken a couple of paracetamols."

"Really? Only a couple?"

"Period-pain, possibly. It was her time. Maybe just a headache."

"Or to stave off a hangover? The old 'head it off at the pass' technique?"

He'd forgotten Mulligan was teetotal.

"Never mind. Suicide, cut and dried, you reckon?"

Mulligan nodded. "One slightly odd thing, though."

"Oh yes?"

"Look at the toenails on her left foot."

Yarmouth looked. Qamar had painted all five toes on her left foot but only three on the right. The middle toe was only half-painted.

"That's weird. Something interrupted her?" guessed Yarmouth.

"Or she got distracted. The phone rang, maybe."

"Maybe. Look, can we take a rain check, as the yanks say, on that pho?"

Mulligan gave a theatrical sigh.

"Why did I know you were going to say that? Fine. You know where to find me."

On another day, Yarmouth might have suspected she was flirting with him.

CHAPTER 20

Elena too was somewhere she shouldn't be, namely back at Qamar's. Something had been bothering her, something about that chair.

She had just about persuaded herself that Qamar might have been erratic enough to seem full of joy and hope one moment only to fall into a pit of despair hours later. Then, as she sat translating some letters for an elderly man from Brasov in the offices of Voices Unlimited, a recurring image took hold.

Qamar stepping onto the red chair in her room, tying a cable around her neck, tightening it against her flesh, all the while teetering on tiptoes. Then kicking back the chair and dropping...

Something was wrong. Elena felt an old instinct kick in, an instinct she'd had whenever Franes told her he'd always be there for her. The last time she said it, Frances had broken Elena's gaze as she looked into the older woman's eyes for evidence of honesty. Elena had chosen to ignore her instincts, the insistent and irritating feeling that all was not as it should be. It had been a mistake not to listen to that sensation.

She let herself back in to Qamar's place, steeling herself against the stale smell of incense and the irrepressible layering of dust. Elena focused her attention upon the chair. It still lay face down, all four of its legs tilted upwards as the top of the backrest and front edge of its seat touched the floor. Elena had a notion that this was mathematically suspect. Of all the positions for a chair to tumble into when kicked backwards, this looked the least likely. But how unlikely? There was only one way to find out.

After some thought, Elena realised that the only way to enact her experiment was to get all the variables as precisely correct as possible. She wasn't going to get drunk to simulate Qamar's possible mental state, but the physical set-up of the trial had to be precise.

Elena found a coiled electrical cable belonging to some long-lost device in a cupboard in Qamar's tiny hall. Tying the cord securely to the dislodged light fitting in the ceiling proved more of a challenge. Qamar had been shorter than her and wearing only slippers too. Still, it was not beyond the realms of possibility and, as Elena stretched up towards the faux-chandelier, a dark chill began to descend upon her. Her heart began to pound as she stood upon the wobbly red chair, knotting the cable with a loop big enough to hook under her armpits.

Then, letting the cable take her weight, she was gratified (almost guiltily so) to find that her heels could now only just reach the chair. The next bit would make or break the experiment. Rocking on the balls of her feet, Elena worked up a little momentum and then lifted her feet off the chair for a split second and kicked out as hard as possible. The chair fell away and bounced a little towards one side, before finishing on its backrest.

Elena hung there, not knowing whether to laugh at the absurdity of what she was doing or cry at the pathos of her reconstruction. A few seconds later, she dropped from the cable to the ground. This could end here, she thought. I am being ridiculous.

The second and third attempts ended the same way. On the fourth kick, the chair bounced onto its side. Three more times it fell onto its back, then twice in a row onto its side and then, finally, she managed to give it a massive belt and it bounced away, coming to rest face down, but lying on its front legs, backrest parallel with the ground.

Aching under her arms, Elena got an old bill from a drawer and a stub of pencil and began to make tallies. Twenty minutes later, during one vigorous kick, the ceiling rose seemed to explode in a shower of plaster and Elena dropped onto the carpet, just managing to get one foot under her in time to soften the impact, as the cheap chandelier crashed down onto her arms and head. She felt a throbbing impact in her coccyx and knew a healthy bump would raise on the back of her skull.

Still, she felt triumphant as she extricated herself from the wreckage and hobbled over to the sink to look at the piece of paper she'd marked up. Twenty-five times the chair had fallen on its back. It had ended up on one side or another thirty-three times and thrice it had finished face down, backrest parallel to the floor. It had never landed as Robin and Elena had found it the other night, balanced on a diagonal between backrest and seat. Instinctively she knew that this was not impossible; just very, very unlikely. Almost like it had been positioned without enough thought.

Robin was sceptical. Elena had told him the whole story, which she recounted with a mixture of pride and mild embarrassment. He'd scratched his head and paused before responding.

"You do know that even if you're right, it could never be admitted as evidence."

"I know, I know..."

"Not least because you gained entry illegally and there were no witnesses. Even if we reconstructed the experiment... hell, even if we re-enacted it in court, it's just statistics. However odd that chair looked, it only had to happen once."

"I know all this. I study statistics at school. Unlikely events, coincidences, they happen all the time. It's more how it made me feel."

"What do you mean?"

They were sitting, with wine, on the sofa while Ana was curled catlike and asleep on the armchair, the television turned down low. Elena should probably wake her up and send her to bed. Not an easy task with a fourteen-year-old who sleeps up to twelve hours a day.

Elena refilled their glasses.

"The more you told me about police report, suicide note, everything. And the more I thought about the life Qamar must have led and how I knew her so little, the more I begin to doubt my instincts."

"Which say?"

"That this was… murder. There. I said it. She was killed, maybe accident. They had to cover it up, so they make it look like just another sad sex worker ending it."

Robin was rubbing a wetted finger round the rim of his glass while Elena spoke, making a high-pitched ringing tone. Elena stopped his hand with hers.

"Are they looking into it? What did coroner say?"

"Suicide. Plain and simple. Just…"

"What?" Elena's eyes lit up, eagerly.

"The ligature marks looked odd to me."

"The what?"

"Marks round her neck."

Robin explained, in his patient policeman's manner, about the spacing of the marks on Qamar's neck, which

137

he felt didn't quite match the cable she was found hanging from. He also mentioned the knot-mark, found on the side of her neck.

"Sounds like you have doubts as well," Elena said, hopefully.

"I don't know. It's beginning to add up to something that worries me. Did you see a laptop in there?"

Elena cast her mind back.

"Not when we visited, or today. But, yes, I think was small MacBook when I first went over."

"It's not in the evidence log, nor is it in there now," Robin said. "Maybe someone took it. Or she gave it away, I suppose."

Elena frowned.

"I doubt it. She had screensaver showing photos of her and her friends. And her sister. Happier days. Has anyone told her family?"

"We're having trouble tracing them."

"Can you take me with when you do?"

Robin looked awkward.

"It's not my case and I wouldn't normally..."

He looked at her, saw her disappointment, changed tack. "I can have a word with the investigating officer. She's a... friend."

"You hesitate. An ex maybe?"

Robin looked away, turned back with a grin.

"Christmas party last year. She was separated from hubbie, I was newly single. We have little in common bar the uniform. But we were drunk... it was a one-nighter we both regretted."

"These things happen. So... you can ask her if you can call on next of kin?"

"I can try. She'll probably be relieved."

DI Sanchita Shah ('San' to her colleagues) lifted her head from her Daily Mirror, apple turnover poised halfway to her mouth.

"Are you kidding? I'd totally love that. If I have to listen to another mopey set of parents, who totally neglect their kid for years and then act all amazed when she turns up dead..."

"I get it. I'll take it off your hands," said Yarmouth. "You can assign me to the case?"

"What case? We're tying up loose ends. But it you want to help... be my guest."

"Great."

Robin grinned and was about to go when San stopped him with a hand.

"What did I do to deserve this favour? You're not secretly in love with me or anything, after our little tryst, are you?"

"I can barely sleep a wink without thinking of it. But seriously... I'm doing a favour from a friend."

"A friend is it?" smirked San, returning to her newspaper. "The hottie in flat 11 perchance?"

Robin sighed. "Does everyone know my personal business?"

"Everyone that matters. Oh, I just remembered, can you pop by the office and see Fleischer. He wants to talk to you about missing phones or something."

"Gotcha. Thanks San."

"You can do my dirty work anytime, lover-boy. Tread carefully."

"I will."

Tread carefully. There was that phrase again. A person more paranoid or precious than Yarmouth might begin to suspect that 'they' were out to get him.

CHAPTER 21

Yarmouth settled back into their familiar booth at the Temperance, watching Fleischer return from the bar with two pints of inscrutably named hipster beer.

"Dark and Stormy, that's yours. Mine's the Fiddler's Elbow. Jeez, remember when pints were called things like "Special" and "Best Bitter"?"

"Nope. I'm far too young. It's been Gandalf's Sleeve and Rubberneck as long as I can remember."

"Shurrup! You're less than a decade younger than me, pal. Get that down your neck. I need to pick your underappreciated brains."

Flattery. And from Fleischer. Clearly, he wanted something substantial.

Fleischer adjusted himself on the uncomfortable-looking pub stool. He'd had testicular surgery to remove a malignancy a couple of years ago and had taken perverse delight in detailing the whole grisly process. Inwardly, Yarmouth winced in sympathy.

"You know I've been as pissed off as you about this thing with the two scooter kids who knifed you...?"

"Well, not quite as much as me."

"Okay, fair enough. Still, it's fucked up when two young twats can attack one of ours with a Stanley knife and knock another over and them upstairs roll over when CPS says assault is all we can charge."

"Fucked up is right. If I hadn't worn a belt that day..."

"You'd have your trousers and your intestines round your knees."

Yarmouth laughed a blob of froth off the top of his pint. It landed on the table and they both watched the tiny bubbles begin to pop into nothingness against the wood grain.

Fleischer leaned in, conspiratorially.

"I was able to sit in on the interrogations. DC Kendall, McPherson's man, kept asking questions about the phones they took. Were there any others? Did anyone ask them to take them? Were they planning to use a fence? If so, who? That sort of thing. Way more detail on the thefts than we'd normally bother with, given how many witnesses we had, CCTV..."

"Plus, you had all the stolen goods."

"Well, that's the thing. Did we? That discrepancy with the count... I did a bit of digging. It seems the change was authorised by McPherson."

"Really? Why would he be involved?"

"Nobody seems to know. Suddenly 48 phones became 47."

Yarmouth had a brainwave, stopped mid-gulp.

"One of the phones was his?"

"That's what I was thinking. You know he likes to storm about outside making his calls. I checked and he was at a retirement do a couple of days before we nabbed the kids, in the very area where they'd been stealing phones."

"Bloody hell."

"Sure, it would be embarrassing for a high-ranking officer to have his own phone pinched in the high street, but why would it warrant him tampering with evidence?

"Maybe there was something embarrassing on that phone?" Yarmouth offered. "Saucy snaps from his mistress?"

"Could be. It might explain why he's so keen to have this just disappear."

"We need to find out if he got his phone back. If it was amongst those taken. Were they logged with serial numbers?"

"Should have been. You'd have to get his serial number, of course."

"Is it police issue?"

"I don't think he has one. Private most likely."

Yarmouth sighed.

"We should probably leave it alone. Anyway, why is it me who has to grab his phone?"

"Cause you're the one you started all this mate. You might get a chance when you go to see Purvis."

"What are you talking about?"

"Do you not read your emails?"

Yarmouth quickly got his own phone out, logged onto the server and read his messages. There was one from DCI Brian Purvis.

Please see me in my office at 12 on Wednesday. It's concerning the scooter thefts.

Your duty officer will excuse you. Brian.

Fleischer laughed at the message.

"When he calls himself Brian, you know you're in trouble."

Yarmouth mulled over what Fleischer was asking him to do. It sounded like the latest in a series of attempts at career suicide. Probably the very last thing he should risk doing right now.

"I'll need a distraction at a key moment."

Now it was Fleischer's turn to sigh at the inevitable.

"You can count on me, pal. Especially if you get a round in."

Once more, Elena was in Qamar's place. This time though, she was with Ana. She felt a little guilty enlisting her daughter in this subterfuge, but it was in a good cause and, besides, Ana was brilliant at hiding things (Elena had only found her daughter's love letters from a boy at school when she'd taken her cushion covers off to wash them).

"Can I take the bedroom?" Ana asked.

"Good idea," answered Elena as they turned into the lounge/kitchen.

"Shit!"

Ana had seen the pile of plaster and smashed metal and crystal that had once been a chandelier.

"The police," said Elena. "It happened when they took her down."

"Such a shame," answered Ana gruffly, sadness deepening her voice.

Elena hugged her briefly.

"Go – bring back any paperwork you find."

Ana trotted off while Elena turned her attention to the kitchen drawers.

Half an hour later, every scrap of paper, from bills to letters to wrapping paper, lay piled up on the kitchen counter. Elena and Ana sat side by side raking through it all, looking for names, numbers, addresses, anything that might lead them to Qamar's family.

A further forty minutes later, all they had unearthed was the tag from a gift bearing a feminine-looking handwriting, in Somali and three red kisses. The handwriting was a little shaky and joined-together in a very learnt manner. Elena instinctively knew it was an older woman's handwriting. Not Qamar's sister then, her mother's. But

Qamar had claimed she'd had no contact with them for years.

Ana had found he tag, inside an old slipper, under Qamar's bed. Hidden away but not forgotten.

CHAPTER 22

Elena shaded her eyes from the early evening sunlight as she looked up at the upper storey of the small semi-detached house where Qamar's parents and sister lived, just off Kingstanding Road a mile or so North of Birmingham proper. A dark face appeared briefly between lace curtains, then vanished. Sunlight flashed between wintry trees in the gardens behind the long row of boxy houses.

Robin squeezed her hand encouragingly. Evidently, she wasn't hiding her nervousness as well as she'd hoped.

"Let me do the talking to begin with. I've done a few of these. Plus, you're a civilian. You shouldn't really be here."

Elena looked at him. Robin wasn't criticising her; he was just reminding her of the delicate emotional protocols involved in telling two fragile people their eldest daughter had taken her own life (or so it was officially thought).

They'd discussed at length how to approach this moment. The official verdict was suicide and the evidence overwhelmingly supported that verdict, so that's the way they would have to play it. As a mother, Elena wasn't sure what would be worse: thinking your daughter had killed herself or had been brutally murdered. Both were unimaginable to her; if she even came close to playing a thought experiment with Ana in place of Qamar, an inner wall came down, blocking off the thought process.

The door opened on its chain. A wide pair of eyes in an oval face, surrounded by chaotic, tight curls. Qamar's mother looked tiny and birdlike and yet strangely youthful. Elena recognised the high, almost regal cheekbones immediately.

"Mrs Liibaan," began Robin, his voice low and serious.

"Yes?"

Robin held his ID up to the gap in the door.

"PC Robin Yarmouth. I need to talk to you and your husband about your daughter."

"What? My daughter... she is at work... has something happened?"

"We mean your daughter Qamar."

For a moment Waris Liibaan's face froze and she frowned slightly as if she'd forgotten she had another daughter.

"Qamar.... But I haven't heard from her in years."

"We've got some bad news, I'm afraid. May we come inside?"

As Mrs Liibaan let them through into a chintzy front room, it's long lace curtains mysteriously closed, Qamar's mother seemed to crumple before she reached the three-piece suite where she'd gestured for them to sit. Elena ran to her aid, grabbing an elbow and leading the distressed mother to a chair.

"Please don't tell me.... Please, no. No."

She'd guessed the worst. From then on, the conversation was largely one-sided, Robin relaying what was known of the suicide, Waris sobbing into a handkerchief, answering only yes/no questions with a nod or shake of her head. Yarmouth had introduced Elena as a "close friend" of Qamar and finally, the bewildered woman turned to Elena, as if she'd suddenly thought of something.

"You were her friend. I didn't know about you. We didn't speak much, not in the end. Not after she ran. Abdullahi wouldn't let me."

Elena looked to Robin for approval and was gratified when he nodded.

"I hadn't known Qamar for long. Only a few months."

A little white lie, necessary to explain her presence.

"She was so kind to me," Elena continued. "So gracious and full of life. I still can't imagine why... it happened."

Elena had been about to say "why she did it" but that seemed a falsehood too far. Mrs Liibaan got up and walked unsteadily over to the windows, where she drew the curtains.

"I get migraines. It helps to keep out the light. We shouldn't be sitting here in the dark."

"No, no," Elena protested. "It's absolutely fine."

Instinct, however, kept her in her seat as the tiny woman turned and shook her head.

"I haven't offered you any tea or coffee. I'm so sorry."

Robin leapt to his feet.

"Allow me. Please, do sit down. Is the kitchen through there?"

Mrs Liibaan looked confused, then nodded. Any other day she would have objected to this lapse in etiquette but now, her reflexive offer of hospitality had vanished by the time she sat back down in her armchair.

Elena could hear Robin bumbling around the small kitchenette next door as she took a deep breath and ran over in her mind what they had discussed last night. Elena had insisted she be the one to ask the questions that had been troubling her. After some negotiation, Robin had assented. He would write up her findings as his own, if this ever became a legitimate investigation.

"Do you know what your daughter was doing when she died? What her work was?"

Elena had objected to this line of questioning vehemently when Robin had brought it up in the car, but he'd pointed out that if a parent is going to have their heart broken, the blow was better delivered all at once. Elena has insisted she tell the mother the awful truth.

A head shake. Elena cleared her throat.

"She was working in modelling for, various websites and she also saw paying clients. She was sex worker."

Waris Liibaan's head tilted slowly up from her sodden handful of tissues.

"A what?"

"Qamar worked as prostitute. She had done for a few years but was planning to stop and start a business with some friends. I'm really sorry to tell you."

Elena could see that this news was even more baffling to Mrs Liibaan than the news of her daughter's death, and possibly harder to hear.

"That can't be. I knew she was modelling but... no, no. Our faith forbids it. She wouldn't."

"I'm really sorry. She told me herself."

Just then, Elena's attention was drawn by a shadow at the door and two things happened at once. Yarmouth appeared from the kitchen, holding a wooden tray with three cups of tea in China saucers and the front door rattled open. As Mrs Liibaan leapt to her feet, a man with the roundest, largest belly Elena had ever seen walked in and stopped stock still in the middle of the room, dropping a doctor's bag on the carpet.

"What is this?"

Qamar's father, Abdullahi. His eyes were fiery with mistrust and confusion. Yarmouth put down the tea-tray as Waris whispered in Somali into her husband's ears. He stepped away from her as if stung.

149

"In English, woman. We have guests. What are you telling me?"

"Qamar is dead," Waris stated, baldly. "The daughter you banished murdered herself."

Things escalated rapidly after that moment. Later, Elena couldn't quite recall the sequence of events, but the following occurred:

Abdullahi pushed Waris away violently. Waris stumbled over the carpet and fell into Elena's arms. Abdullahi roared like an injured bull and punched a framed photograph on the wall, shattering the glass. He then stepped towards his wife as Robin interposed his body, hands held placatingly open. Seeming to notice Robin's uniform for the first time, Abdullahi stopped short of attacking him. The father's shoulders seemed to slump as he looked into Robin's eyes.

"Tell me she's lying, officer."

Robin shook his head.

"I'm very sorry sir."

The remainder of the afternoon (they stayed for almost two hours) was spent teasing the whole sorry family history out of the couple, whilst saying as little as possible about their own suspicions. Elena had initially wanted to tell them her doubts about the suicide verdict, but Robin had reminded her that, as well as being poor protocol, most murder victims were killed by members of their own family or circle of friends.

Honour-killing amongst Somali Muslim families was not unknown, and Qamar had done plenty to provoke family shame, as unthinkable as such a conclusion might be to Elena. Nobody was beyond suspicion in a murder enquiry, Robin had said. Elena could well believe him. Her own recent family history bore testament to the truth of that assertion.

Aged eight, Qamar had read a leaflet about FGM (female genital mutilation) that had been handed out at her school and it had terrified her to the core. She had known that her sister Taifa was approaching the age when it would be done to her. She had brought it up at the dinner table and Taifa had started crying. Her father had banished her to her room. Qamar's mother had gone to talk to her daughter, attempting to reassure her that the procedure was ordained by God and therefore couldn't be as dangerous, painful, and damaging as the propaganda made out. After all, she had had it done to her too, when she was much younger than Qamar or Taifa. Qamar had seemingly quietly asserted. The following day, however, the girl had left school between classes, taken her bag and books, and run away.

The family had found her at an aunt's house a week later, brought her home where Abdullahi had slapped her and locked her in her room (Abdullahi appeared truculently unapologetic when his wife alleged this abuse). Three days later, a seemingly cowed Qamar had emerged, meek and dressed immaculately for school. She never made it there, stealing a bicycle from the neighbours' yard and leaving a note reading 'mothers who love their daughters don't cut them'.

Waris's sorrow turned to anger when she had revealed this part of the story, and she flung a volley of abuse at her husband in Somali, which he took, arms folded, in silence. On best behaviour for the police, Elena thought.

"It wasn't my decision. I would have changed my mind, but he wouldn't listen. It was his way, or she can go to hell."

"She's already there," came the growled response.

Qamar had called her mother two weeks later from her grandmother's house and Waris attempted a reconciliation, saying that her husband would come round. No, he won't, Qamar had insisted. She'd always been as stubborn as her father but was afraid to return home. He had effectively banished her.

"Don't talk rubbish," interjected Abdullahi. "I would have listened."

"And then done whatever you wanted. I know you." Waris pointed an accusatory finger.

Over the following eight years, Qamar was brought up by her grandmother, who stubbornly refused to let Qamar be circumcised (she herself had almost died from an infection following her procedure in early childhood). Taifa was given the 'operation' and when Qamar found out, she turned up at the house, banging on the door to be let in.

Abdullahi refused to have Qamar back in the house and never spoke to her again for defying his religion (and his rule). Aged nineteen, Qamar ran away to London and all but vanished from family life.

Qamar's mother had kept in intermittent communication, always by means of the daughter calling her mother when she was sure her father was out at work. Finally, just a few months ago, Qamar had given an address, making her mother promise she wouldn't tell her father. On Qamar's 25th birthday her mother had sent her a card and a gift, an embroidered top in real lace and silk. She'd been meaning to follow up with a surprise visit but hadn't been able to figure out a way of getting away from her husband.

"Anyone would think I was a monster," laughed Abdullahi bitterly. "I always wanted what was good and godly for my daughters."

To that, Waris gave only an equally sarcastic snort.

CHAPTER 23

Elena and Robin sat in his car, a silver BMW that had seen better days, at the Newport Pagnall services eating their bacon and egg rolls and drinking the milky substances that passed for coffee at the chain outlet behind them. A rain shower was giving way to patches of blue sky and Elena could see miniature distorted versions of them reflected in the water droplets that gradually ran down the windscreen onto the bonnet of Robin's VW.

"They took it very differently, didn't they?"

Elena laughed at Robin's understatement.

"Just a little. She was crushed, totally shocked. He seemed, yes, damaged and angry but there was one thing I didn't see in his eyes."

Robin turned to face her. "And what was that?"

"Surprise. He almost reacted like was inevitable. Like was something he expected to happen. At the very least."

"Do you think he know more about her life than he was letting on?"

"Probably. If I was being kind, I'd say he was protecting wife."

"And if you weren't being kind?"

"Then, he was ashamed. Admitting what his daughter had become, in his eyes, to anyone else – is unthinkable."

"But she was the one who kept in touch. The wife."

"I didn't say he kept in touch," corrected Elena. "Maybe he just knew – had spies or something. We must speak to sister, I think. Qamar's mum gave me her work number. She's nearby. I guess you should call, officially?"

Robin screwed up his face.

"I don't really think I can. I've probably interfered enough. Plus, I'm technically on compassionate leave. For one more week. If it can wait until I'm back?"

"Sure. I guess it's not exactly urgent. Maybe is better we leave them time to talk about it as a family."

Robin looked unsure.

"It's not always a good idea. Families stick together. If you want an honest reaction, now would be the time…"

Elena was dialling.

"Well, I didn't mean this minute…"

Elena raised a hand. On the third ring, the phone was answered.

Taifa Asad Liibaan stood in frozen horror looking at the pile of masonry and mangled metal in the middle of the carpet that had once supported her sister's weight. She began muttering something under her breath in Somali. A prayer?

"Did she fall?"

It took Elena a moment to understand what Qamar's sister was asking. Early evening light slanted between the thick, colourful curtains and lit up the despairing scene with an inappropriately "Hollywood" glamour.

"Actually, I did that. Testing theory."

"What theory?"

Taifa, every bit as powerful a character as her sister, but much more serious in aspect (probably unsurprising, given the circumstances) whirled and locked her huge brown eyes into Elena's. Elena decided not to look away.

"I don't think she killed herself," Elena admitted.

"Elena!" interjected Robin, leaning in the doorway.

"Let her hear," Elena insisted. "Taifa, you must understand that this is not official story. But I was one of last people to talk to your sister. I don't buy official line."

Robin sighed, but didn't interrupt as Elena led Taifa, over to the sofa to explain. Taifa sat rigid against the lush velveteen material as if afraid to relax into it, or perhaps in case it tainted her in some way. She wore smart woollen trousers and a fitted jacket as well as her Islamic headscarf. Elena thought it unlikely that this immaculate and intelligent young woman might submit to something as horrific as female circumcision but then she had been scarcely out of girlhood when it had been done to her. Perhaps in part her defiance was rooted in that early, barbaric betrayal.

Elena unfolded her theory gradually, telling Taifa about Qamar's business plans, her enthusiasm, her optimism, then mentioning the missing laptop, the unusual ligature marks on Qamar's neck (Taifa flinched, hearing this) and finally, the question of the overturned chair. She was careful to say that the latter factor was very much a speculation on her part. Taifa asked a few brief questions then lapsed into brief silence, wiping away a single tear with a paper handkerchief.

"Qamar was always a little crazy and impulsive but she would not do this."

Robin maintained what he thought was a poker face throughout the women's exchange but Elena already knew how to read him. He scratched the side of his face when uncomfortable.

"Did she leave a note?" Taifa asked.

Robin nodded, getting his phone out. Taifa's question took Elena aback. Robin had told her the contents of Qamar's brief note, but she had never actually seen it.

"DI Shah emailed me a scan. Let me see…"

Robin located the file, opened it and showed the hand-written note to Elena and Taifa. If possible, Taifa's eyes opened even wider and she began to shake.

"What's wrong? Did she write it?" Elena couldn't help but ask.

Taifa only nodded.

"Is that her signature?" Elena pressed, once more worried that she'd made a dreadful mistake.

"No. It's her handwriting and it looks a bit like a signature, yes, but it's not."

Elena and Robin exchanged looks. There was nothing in evidence about the signature being unusual. Stupidly, they had not thought to show it to Qamar's parents.

When she'd been taken to identify the body, Taifa had apparently had a similar response to her mother at home, DC Shah had told them. The Somali's body simply collapsed under her. Edina Mulligan been quick with a chair as the young woman's reserve had crumbled entirely away.

This response was different. As Elena put her arm around the young Somali girl (she seemed instantly more a girl than a woman since seeing the note) she realised this was not grief or shock. This was fear. She was staring fixedly at Robin's phone, expanding the signature with two fingers so that it filled the screen.

DIL. Those were the cleverly entangled letters that resembled initials. They'd assumed the D and I were a Q.

"It means murder," said Taifa softly, as her shoulders continued to quake.

CHAPTER 24

It was fifteen minutes past nine and Yarmouth had pretty much exhausted the potential of the Newton's Cradle executive toy that adorned DCI Brian Purvis's desk. He's been summoned by urgent email and had no idea why. This was the last day of his compassionate leave, however, so perhaps it was just a formality. Purvis did have a tendency to make everything seem urgent.

The door opened with a crash, interrupting Yarmouth's thoughts and Purvis stormed in.

"Sorry to keep you waiting, Robin. Emergency 8:30 over-ran. Right, let's get down to it."

Purvis crashed down into his chair, which swivelled and creaked in protest. His expression mingled, oddly, conviviality and grim determination.

"DI Shah wants you back onside and I've been told, in no uncertain terms, to give her what she wants, since her clear-up record is, frankly, stellar."

Yarmouth was dumbfounded. So much so, it seemed, that he failed to formulae a reply before Purvis felt obliged to intercede.

"I know. It's a shock. But what with the incident with PC Conover and the fact that you've toed the line, it seems only fair."

"Sorry, did you say San requested me?"

"Yes, that's right. Seems the family of this... Qamar Liibaan... have insisted on an inquest and there's some evidence come to light that we have to clear up. It's still overwhelmingly a suicide verdict but there's a modicum of doubt, apparently."

"Really?"

Yarmouth hoped his feigned surprise was convincing. After some discussion, Elena and he had called Qamar's parents and told them Taifa's bombshell about their daughter's signature. In part, the idea had been to see whether they pursued an inquest or not, and thereby rule them out. It appeared they could strike immediate family off the suspect list.

"So, I'll be DC again?"

"Yes. You'll get your ID back and will be officially reinstated as of Monday. However—and let us be absolutely clear about this—you are very much on probation and are absolutely, definitively not to punch any superiors if you disagree with them."

Yarmouth took a while to realise that Purvis was attempting levity.

"I will bear that in mind, sir. Thank you. That's... wonderful news."

"Well then, I'm glad. You can bring in your uniform next week."

A hand had been proffered, which Yarmouth shook unsteadily. This was not what he'd expected from this meeting.

"How's the battle scar? Won you any bragging rights in the Temperance?"

"Oh—this?" Yarmouth lifted his shirt to show the line of fine stiches above his navel. "It looks just like an appendectomy scar, unfortunately. Won't stand up at all against Kendall's metal plate. He claims to pick up Capital Radio on it."

Purvis's booming laugh bounced around the room as he rose from his chair, signalling the meeting was over.

On the way down the hall, Yarmouth looked in on Bob McPherson's department. No-one was in but DI Sanchita Shah and a couple of younger DCs he didn't recognise.

Shah didn't notice him enter; she was preoccupied pouring over the statements made by Qamar's family in support of their inquest enquiry.

"San! My new favourite person."

Yarmouth walked over and gave her a deliberately chummy shoulder squeeze. San smiled thinly.

"You're not mine. You offer a favour and come back with a murder case. I'm having to push all my other work onto the back burner for this... hunch of the sister."

"I think it's a bit more than that. I saw her face—a Somali person can't exactly go white with fear, but she was terrified."

"You showed her the suicide note. What made you do that?"

"She asked. I couldn't withhold it. You still think it's suicide?"

San took a deep breath.

"I have a theory. The girl signs off with 'murder'. But think of it this way - she's been a prostitute for years, and a drug-user. She's been abused by men many times over, either hitting her or taking advantage of her or selling her stuff that will kill her. All of which sends her into a spiral of despair one night. She feels the world is against her, conspiring to finish her off—murdering her."

"You think she signed her suicide note with a metaphor?"

"It seems likelier than this 'perfect crime' nonsense. Have you seen the forensic report? They found nothing to indicate a struggle."

"There's the ligature marks on her neck," offered Yarmouth. "They don't seem like a good fit for the cable she hanged herself from."

"Then it slipped, or she tried once with something else."

"Nothing else has been found. Are you going to take this seriously?"

Yarmouth found himself becoming riled up by San's dismissiveness, took a moment to consciously swallow the anger. San looked a little chastened, nonetheless.

"Absolutely, Robbo. But I'd like you to lead on it, if you don't mind. Unofficially, of course."

"Fine. Have you set up an incident room and assembled a team?"

"You and me and Tom Fleischer – that's your team. You can get to work on that room on Monday. I've got three gang-related teenage stabbings to deal with already, but I will monitor your progress and feed in now and again."

"Suits me. Oh, is Bob McPherson around?"

San frowned. "I doubt he'll want to be on your team."

Yarmouth laughed. San did a great line in deadpan.

"Just looking to smooth the waters, if I'm coming back and everything."

"I think he's out on a case. Try him tomorrow. Boy, I hope I'm here for that reunion."

Yarmouth smiled and made no further comment. It looked like getting hold of McPherson's phone would have to wait, if it happened at all.

On any other murder investigation, Yarmouth might have felt inclined to argue for more resources, but the case was fragile enough as it stood and it might be good to have a little more freedom than usual, especially as Elena was not going to quietly bow out. In fact, he'd found her input useful, her instincts strong and she seemed to have a nose for a witness not telling the whole truth, invaluable in a detective.

Yarmouth found himself entertaining a strange fantasy in which Elena was his partner in detection (as well as in the bedroom). Was he making a mistake in becoming so involved with her? What did he really know about her? She'd hinted strongly at something traumatic in her background. Should he press her on that or allow her to reveal it in her own time?

Probably the latter, he concluded, before saying his goodbye and walking out into a brisk, bracing late Soho afternoon.

Elena had some important thinking to do and that entailed one thing—strong coffee. She'd walked with Ana as far as Bar Italia and then let her daughter go her own way, not without more than a flicker of worry. She was still not used to letting her roam the city streets but there didn't seem too much harm in it, now that they were both forming a virtual map of the neighbourhood in their heads (and once Elena had made sure Ana's phone was with her and charged).

Part of the thinking Elena had to do was focused on Ana, as it happened. There were two local schools with availability for new students in the next semester, both comprehensives but with good enough Ofsted reports and positive comments from parents online. To get Ana in to one of those, Elena had to reach a decision soon. But that meant admitting that they were both going to stay. Which in turn, hinged on the importance in their lives of two people—Robin and Frances.

Frances at least she could pretty much write off—she'd proven herself untrustworthy and little more than a criminal (although she had at least got Elena out of Romania under her assumed name). She now realised she'd probably paid over the odds for Frances's services but at least now she felt safe. Notch up another lesson in trust and move on, she thought decisively, as she sat at the counter with her newspapers (The Guardian and a day old Jurnalul, which she'd been impressed to find in a nearby newsagent).

Robin's presence in her life, however, was another thing entirely. A policeman, no less. Who could ever have seen that coming, given her past? He both calmed her and agitated her. The former feeling was there each morning when they cuddled in bed before rising, or when he washed her hair in the shower, which he loved to do and which she found strangely arousing. The agitation came only when she remembered the secrets she harboured and what they might mean to a man in Robin's profession. Still, Elena knew that most men would panic if they found themselves dating someone with Elena's recent past.

She had to focus! What was she doing drinking Italian coffee, with newspapers, idly daydreaming about her boyfriend when there were high schools to consider? Then there was poor abused, forgotten Qamar...

"Benvenuto, miss Elena!"

The cheery tones of Luca breezed through her consciousness as he appeared at her elbow, bearing a tray of small tomato and broccoli tartlets.

"You must try one of these. New recipe. You like, I put them on the menu."

Elena beamed and tried one, finding it delicious (and saying so). And at once, her worries scuttled away to their dark corners and left her with a mouthful of puff pastry and Luca's relentless conviviality.

"I miss you when you come in. Stock-taking day. Very boring but very important. Oh! Wait a minute."

Luca seemed to remember something and ferreted about for a piece of paper in his apron.

"Your woman. Frances. She come in and I told her you were looking. She wrote here her number. You can call her now?"

Luca's smile invited a grateful response, but all Elena could manage was a thin smile and a quiet thank you' as she took the paper napkin from the Italian's fingers and watched as he was swept away by a wave from his colleague at the counter. A small queue of businessmen demanding takeaways had formed.

Elena looked at the napkin. There was Frances's handwriting – the bold loops and angled S's. A number and then just the words 'Call me—F'. No kisses, nothing apologetic. She should probably throw it away.

Instead, she pushed back her chair, asked a friendly-looking woman nearby to mind her bag and walked outside into the cold sunlight with her mobile phone.

Frances's voice, answering on the seventh ring was terse, her apology perfunctory and hurried. Elena wanted to hang up, to demand answers, to tell her to fuck off. Instead, she made a tentative agreement to meet in a week's time. Making Frances come to her at Bar Italia was her one concession to the anger she suddenly felt rising within her.

Why was it that whenever she attained a kind of fragile equilibrium, the ripples finally fading away, life would toss a stone into the waters?

CHAPTER 25

When he first kissed her, Ana thought her head would explode from the excitement of it. She had gone to meet Chris after his matinee shift at the Prince Charles ended and they had wandered through Covent Garden, where he had surprised her by taking her hand to cross the road at the Seven Dials. They'd spent some time in the various clothing shops (Chris picked up a hoodie in Fatface and Ana bought another bracelet to add to her ever-growing collection). Then they wandered down to Embankment and crossed the bridge to the South Bank.

On the way, Chris had popped into a shop by Charing Cross station and bought them a couple of bottles— Corona for him, an unpronounceable Swedish cider for her. He made her swear not to tell her mother and Ana rolled her eyes as if this were the most obvious thing in the world.

They made it as far as some benches by Gabriel's Wharf and sat down to watch the river traffic and dying late afternoon light. Ana was a little chilly and hoped she'd not start shivering or embarrass herself in some other way. Chris talked about movies (something he did a lot) and music (he was DJing at a friend's pop-up club in a box-park in a place with the unlikely name of Elephant and Castle.

"Do you want to come? I mean, it's not a big deal or anything. It might be fun, and you'll meet loads of people. Maybe make some new friends."

It was as if Chris could read her mind. New friends were what Ana most wanted in the world. She missed Sofia and her gang from school back in Bucharest, despite their stupid fight. She would text Sofia later and make up.

Ana nodded a quiet assent to Chris's plan. That was when he leaned in and kissed her. She had kissed some of her friends before, just fooling around but this felt different—more forceful and full of risk. Ana felt a sudden flash of guilt, which pointed in two directions: towards her mother and also towards Chris, who thought she was sixteen. At least, she hoped he did.

The kiss lasted less than a minute but for Ana it felt like something epic. Their lips parted wetly, and Ana thought she would try more tongue next time. She felt a hot flush fill her cheeks and buried her head in his neck and shoulder to hide it. She finally felt something she'd been missing for so long. She felt at home.

"I can't believe you bought a whiteboard."

Elena knew that Robin was teasing her, but she felt a little defensive anyway.

"It helps me think. I use one in my old job, for presentations. I like how you just wipe everything clean and start over."

"And that's not Freudian at all. Okay, Detective Balan, let's list the suspects."

They talked through the suspects and ranked them on the left side of the board from the likely candidates (Qamar's father, a client from the shortlist Carver had given him) to the least likely (Qamar's sister, another prostitute). Robin told Elena about his misgivings about Carver and they placed the crooked landlord and sometime pimp in the middle.

On the right-hand side, they listed the evidence for the murder as well as avenues of forensic investigation. Robin wanted to look more into the ligature marks on Qamar's neck. If the electrical cable didn't make them, then what did and what happened to it?

Where was Qamar's laptop and why had it been taken? How had the killer induced Qamar to write a suicide note? Was this a thrill kill or was there some more mundane motive?

Robin had checked the HOLMES database for MOs related to strangulation—there were no outstanding warrants for serial stranglers, so this was either a one-off killing or the start of something. The sad cliché about psychopaths murdering prostitutes was unfortunately based upon truth. These women tended to be the most vulnerable in society and by definition, they invited men into private liaisons that nobody else would know about. Lonely, sexually dysfunctional men and vulnerable women made a dangerous combination.

Elena wasn't convinced as Robin painted this picture. Again, she had little but her instinct and the brief meetings she'd had with her neighbour to go on, but it felt wrong.

"Qamar wasn't vulnerable. Not like you mean. She wasn't using drugs anymore, she had friends, savings, business plan. She told me she only accept new clients as referral from existing ones she trust. And she kept her list small. She had regular."

"We'll need to speak to those regulars as well as Carver's list," Robin suggested. "I wonder if Qamar kept a diary? I'll check with Fleischer. We might get lucky and there'll be some names."

"Do sex-workers keep appointment books?" asked Elena, innocently.

"You'd be surprised. The names are usually coded, but it's a start."

Elena told Robin she'd check out the friends that Qamar was working with on her triple-M business. They were low on the list of suspects and Robin agreed that the risk was minimal.

"You find anything out, let me know and I'll go visit them for the official bit."

"Get me the details from diary, if you find one," Elena countered.

Robin looked concerned.

"Are you sure you want to get into this? It might get... kind of depressing. The things people do to one another... sometimes it's better not to know."

One day Elena would tell him just how much she already knew about that.

"I need to do this. For Qamar. For the women we ignore, forget about, or look down on. Is important."

"Then it's important to me too."

He kissed her, gently taking the whiteboard marker from her hand and pressing her against it, against the wall. Elena entirely lost her train of thought, just happy to be with someone who would seemingly do anything for her. Anything legal, of course.

Forty minutes later, Elena went to put her blouse back on and found the word 'Suspect' imprinted there in smudgy black writing, back to front so that it only made sense in a mirror. It would come out in the wash.

Robin left Elena's bed at the eighth ring of his mobile, which he was charging in the living room. It was seven pm and when he saw Fleischer's name, he wondered why his colleague was calling two hours after he was supposed to knock off. It had to be important.

"Robbo! You are not going to believe this."

"Believe what? Are you still working?"

"I'm looking at CCTV footage from outside the Somali girl's flat. Been at it for five hours. Mostly commis chefs having fag breaks and drunks pissing most nights but then I hit the jackpot. The jackpot of jackpots actually. Seriously mate, you are going to jump for joy."

"Dammit man, spit it out."

"Oh no, Robin Redbreast. You can come and check it out yourself."

Robin sighed and grabbed his coat.

"I'll be there in half an hour. I might bring someone, if that's okay."

"Is it who I think it is?"

"A material witness, yes."

Fleischer's laugh echoed raucously down the line before developing into a smoker's cough.

"Whatever mate. Just get your arses down here."

CHAPTER 26

Fleischer, Elena and Yarmouth huddled in semi-darkness around a bank of monitors as a rather harried operative called Ben, who looked all of twenty years old (although he claimed to be closer to thirty) shuttled back and forth between clips from the two cameras that had a view of sections of the street opposite Elena's apartment block.

Elena wondered if Fleischer had seen shots of Robin coming in and out of her place. Come to think of it, she had no idea if her boyfriend (as she was beginning to think of him) had mentioned her at all. Maybe so - he was probably required to declare an interest in her, given her status as a witness. The thought made her want to giggle, or perhaps run away. She wasn't sure which response was least appropriate.

"Show them again, both angles," asked Fleischer, excitedly.

Ben clicked his mouse a few times then rolled it across a timeline while two screens cycled between 2:23am and 2:27am on Saturday 23rd July. A timestamp on both screens identified the time and date.

In the leftmost screen, Elena's street stood empty, save for a fox tearing at a bin bag in the upper right corner. Moments later, the fox scurried away as Elena's door opened and a tall, angular figure in a long coat emerged. He stopped to light a cigarette and his face caught the lamplight.

Ben froze the image, enlarged the face.

"That's Bob McPherson!"

Fleisher made a whooping sound.

"Bingo! And it gets better. Ben, take it forward to 2:32."

Ben did as he was told, scrolling forward so that both screens fast-forwarded. McPherson took out his phone and wandered around the side-street in random patterns, talking to someone. Elena thought it was a shame there was no sound. There was something about the man's face. Something oddly familiar—what was it?

Eventually, as the seconds flashed by, McPherson wandered out onto the main road, vanishing from one screen and appearing on another. This view was much wider, taking in a length of much busier Soho street.

"That's Wardour Street. See that."

Fleisher pointed to where a scooter was idling about two hundred yards from where McPherson stood, back turned, still engrossed in his call. The scooter had two helmeted figures on it. Yarmouth drew a sharp breath.

"It's the kids that assaulted me."

The scooter raced towards McPherson, mounting the pavement as he turned. An arm stretched out from the back of the bike, deftly grabbing the phone, as the thieves sped off. McPherson ran a few steps up the Road, arm raised and evidently furious. Then he stopped dead still, leaning against the wall of a shop, hunched in thought.

"He just stands there for twelve minutes," marvelled Fleischer.

Ben cycled through the next quarter of an hour and Elena and Yarmouth watched in fascination as McPherson stood rock steady, moving only to light another cigarette or rub his face in evident panic. He then walked back towards the door of Elena's apartment, re-entering the other screen.

Now that he was bigger in frame, they could see McPherson's agitation as he repeatedly pressed the buzzer to Elena and Qamar's building.

"I remember," said Elena in an excited voice. "Woke me up. The buzzing."

"Did you hear him say anything?" Yarmouth asked.

Elena shook her head. "I was half-asleep. Was just a noise. That's the night after I went over to Qamar's. The night before she was killed. Is what the coroner said?"

"It's not a certainty but it probably wasn't this night that she died," admitted Yarmouth. "The skin hadn't discoloured enough. Rigor mortis hadn't set in sufficiently and there were other indicators too. Were you able to hear where the buzzer was sounding?"

"I think Qamar's. Is the only one I can hear, apart from my own," said Elena. "Ben, can you pause his face again?"

"No worries," said Ben, deftly flicking back to the optimum freeze-frame.

Elena gasped.

"I know him. I mean, I've seen him. He left Qamar's flat the night I spent with her. He was one of her... customers."

"You're certain?" Yarmouth asked.

This was almost too good to be true. Elena nodded.

"I'm certain. Was with a younger man, who looked a bit like him."

"His nephew," Fleischer prompted. "He's only about eight years younger and they're thick as thieves. Was the other guy kind of heavy-set and much shorter?"

"Yes. I remember his face too. He had a kind of droopy eye."

Yarmouth turned to Fleischer.

"Dan McPherson's got a lazy right eyelid, hasn't he? Bob calls him Rocky."

"Rocky Raccoon, more like," replied Fleischer. "Guy's not much of a fighter."

Yarmouth turned to Elena. "We've got a lot of explaining to do. Pub?"

Elena looked at her watch. She had about forty minutes before she said she'd be back home to talk to Ana about schools.

"Sure. Just quick one."

The Temperance was quiet for a change. A few men in suits stood around the bar talking about electric cars (a couple of them still wearing conference name badges). A young couple huddled in a booth, talking in conspiratorial tones over pints of craft lager.

Elena, Fleischer, and Yarmouth talked in equally hushed tones as the two men relayed all they knew of McPherson's evidence tampering and the stolen mobile phones. Elena nodded thoughtfully, taking it all in.

"You have grievance against this guy?" she asked.

"He's the one I lamped," Yarmouth said. "I never told you the whole story, did I?"

Fleischer laughed, relishing the story before Yarmouth re-told it. Elena felt an impulse to kiss him when he came to the dramatic dénouement, the disciplinary action and the list of nicknames Robin's colleagues had called him. Bruiser, Tyson, Raging Bull.

"I have theory," Elena said tentatively. "I mean, if you don't mind."

"Go on," Robin said reassuringly, his colleague nodding assent.

Elena cleared her throat. She couldn't believe she was here with two seasoned detectives, yet she was the one proposing a theorem. She rather liked it.

"Well... we know McPherson and nephew were clients of Qamar. Something in their manner says it wasn't their first time, either. Qamar was really organised, she had wall-planner for her social events and future plans, all books were in alphabetical order by author. I thought only my dad did that."

"OCD?" interjected Fleischer.

"I don't think. She was just determined to better herself. Part was getting back in control of life. I think she might have given clients a number to call to book… appointments. Or maybe email address. Maybe this McPherson had some… incriminating messages on that phone, linking him to Qamar."

"Which is why he was terrified of not getting the phone back, added Robin. In case we hacked it for contact details and got more than we bargained for."

"Who knows? Maybe just paranoid about wife finding out," Elena concluded. "He's got something to hide, for sure."

Fleischer looked sceptical, swirling the dregs of his pint around in the glass.

"I can totally buy that knob McPherson getting his end away with a prozzie. What I have a harder time accepting is that he might have done her in."

"I'm not saying that," Elena explained. "Just that he's tied to Qamar and it could come out in investigation and that would ruin him."

"Of course. It's a dismissible offence and anti-corruption would probably press for prosecution too, if they could prove he was a client," admitted Fleischer. "It's got a bit draconian lately, after the Everard case, and that bellend Carrack. A guy in our office was investigated for three months for unpaid speeding and parking fines."

Yarmouth turned to Fleischer.

"We could get him in. I mean, he's a material witness to potentially two crimes. Roast him a little about the phones."

Fleischer looked pained.

"I'm sure you'd like that, but he's got friends high up. It'll get buried, he'll clam up. They protect their own when they can. You know your life won't be worth living if you're the guy who brings in IA against one of the most popular CIs in the division."

"There's another way," Elena said quietly.

She was waiting for permission to speak only to realise, looking up, that both men were already hanging on her next word.

"We get phone, hack it, pull off data."

Fleischer whistled appreciatively whilst Yarmouth winced.

"Great minds think alike," Fleisher said.

"He'll have wiped it by now," Yarmouth countered.

Fleisher shook his head.

"Bob's the least tech-savvy person I've ever met. He can't even work the office microwave. He might have deleted his messages and emails, but I bet he's not emptied his trash."

Robin began to smile. Elena felt a thrill of validation.

"Even if he did that, I'll bet there's still a way to retrieve data. Don't most modern phones back up to the Cloud, or something?"

"Good call," said Fleischer. "There's just one snag."

"What's that?"

"How do we steal the phone of a guy who hates you, doesn't respect me, is twitchy as hell and has had his phone nicked recently?"

The silence that followed was the sound of three brains working overtime. Once again, Elena was surprised to be the first to speak.

"Apologise."

"What?" Robin said, baffled.

"Say you're sorry. Invite him out for drink."

Both men collapsed into laughter.

"Can you imagine it?" Fleischer said.

"Maybe I can," Robin answered, becoming serious. "The guy's got an ego the size of a house. He'd love to see me eating humble pie. It's not exactly how I want to spend one of my evenings, but it could be worth a shot."

"I see a problem," Fleischer interjected. "We don't want him to know his phone's been stolen, do we? I mean that will really put him on his guard."

Elena smiled, waving her hand to draw Fleischer's attention.

"He won't have clue. Trust me."

And just like that, once again, Elena Balan took the floor. It was a position in which she was beginning to feel comfortable.

CHAPTER 27

Ana and Chris had been playing TikTok videos to one another on the bus to his box-park gig and her phone was dangerously low on power.

"One of the guys will charge it for you there, don't worry," said Chris casually.

Ana decided not to ask this favour. She knew she should probably text her mum just in case but didn't want to. It was hard to explain, even to herself, but she wanted to let the phone's battery die and, for once, be unreachable and doing her own thing.

Chris's arm was stretched out behind her, along the bar of the seat-back. She couldn't be entirely sure if this was an attempt to touch her or not. She took his hand and rested it on her knee, feeling powerful and also terrified at the same time. He squeezed her knee, smiled at her and then gave her a reassuring kiss, which became a deep and lingering one. Ana relaxed into it. She had a boyfriend! And not some sleazy one-nighter like Sofia had thrown in her face. This felt real and lasting.

They got off the bus at the chaos that was the Elephant and Castle roundabout and market. Ana was a little disappointed by the strangely small statue that gave the place its name. She was felt a little tense as they threaded their way past the crowded bus stops and marketplace to find the box park. Ten minutes later, they passed under an archway, trains rumbling overhead, and located the colourful jumble of metal crates and pulsating noise that Chris had told her about.

"It's partly an album launch for this small record label a friend of mine started. Mostly though it's just us fucking around for the hell of it."

Ana liked his modesty and his fearless use of the F-word in public. "Fuck" was so much more dramatic a sound than *futu-i*, its Romanian equivalent.

There was a crowd of about forty people variously sitting, standing, or wandering around a space between various cafes and bars. It was decorated with giant graffiti panels, all of them reading 'Wax Effigies' (apparently the name of the label). Chris waved to a Rastafarian in a badge-strewn khaki suit who was behind a set of record decks playing actual vinyl.

"Kelife is well old-school. Half those records are his dad's."

Kelife heard this and mock-frowned, waving them over. Chris called out "Kel! My man."

Chris and Kelife did a complicated handshake thing while Ana shyly offered hers in a fist bump.

"This is Ana, I'm showing her round. She's from Transylvania, you know... when the vampires came from."

Ana couldn't be bothered correcting Chris's geographical or historical errors, instead opting for pulling a scary "vampire face" then immediately regretting it. Still, it made both Kelife and Chris laugh and that was surely a good thing. Her heart was beating so loud she was surprised it couldn't be heard over the music.

She didn't really calm down until half an hour later, when Chris took up the decks and Ana could slide into an anonymous corner and watch, enjoying the music and the fact that her boyfriend was so good at this, even making people dance, outside and in daylight hours.

That said, the light was gradually fading as evening wore on and Ana began to worry that she hadn't contacted her mum. Perhaps she should just ask someone to charge her phone.

"Hey there! These seats taken?"

Ana's thoughts were interrupted by Kelife and a tall, elegant Indian girl sliding into the spare chairs beside her with an easy familiarity Ana found flattering. They were treating her as one of the gang, and it was comforting. The girl, Pushpa, started raving about Ana's hair, though her own was far more impressive, piled up on her head in an intricate whirl, streaked with red and purple. Kelife passed her something surreptitiously under the table. It was a cigarette. Actually, no—it was better than that. It was a joint.

Very quickly, the concept of charging her iPhone became a complete irrelevance to Ana.

Elena knocked on the door of flat 8, the one directly above Qamar's, preparing her opening line in her head. In the end it didn't quite come out as expected.

"Hi. I'm your neighbour. Downstairs neighbour... and over the corridor. I knew Qamar and I wanted to ask you..."

The dishevelled blonde woman who had answered the door abruptly, jerking it open on its chain, had slammed it just as quickly. A puff of stale air blew back Elena's hair.

She stood there a few seconds, listening. The woman hadn't yet walked away from the door.

"Susan Rae?"

A shuffling of feet behind the door.

"I'm not police. I'm just a friend."

A moment of silence. Congested breathing.

"You're no the pigs?"

Elena presumed this was a derogatory term for the police.

"No. And I don't believe their story. I don't believe was suicide."

The door burst open and the thin, pale hands of Qamar's neighbour all but pulled her into the musty, under-furnished flat.

"Shh. Ye dinnae want to be saying that around here. It's no safe."

"Not safe? What do you mean?"

The Scottish woman took her arm and led her through to a room containing a filthy mattress, a beanbag leaking polystyrene beads and a wooden chair, of the same sort Qamar had stood upon in her final moments. The window was open, letting in a little air into a room that otherwise stank of a desperate life lived from hour to hour.

Susan had track-marks up both arms and her hair was matted. She started smoothing out an old, stained duvet over the mattress and gave the beanbag a whack with her foot, in something close to a parody of house-proudness. A flurry of beads scattered like snow. Elena felt repelled but also desperately sad for this poor woman.

"Ahm sorry it's such a state. I've no been maesel' lately."

"It's okay. I just want to talk to you."

Elena sat down stiffly in the chair.

"That's mair comfortable," said Susan, pointing at the beanbag.

"I'm fine. Really, don't worry."

"Wan' some tea?"

"No, I'm okay."

It took a while for her host to settle. Finally, Susan looked up at Elena from under her fringe and said, with appalling certainty:

"They kilt her, sure enough."

Elena exhaled a breath she hadn't realised she'd been holding. She began to probe a little deeper as Susan's mixture of sad truth, paranoia and suspicion poured out.

Susan and Qamar were the last two of the sex workers once employed directly by Carver who now officially paid him inflated rents. Except Susan hadn't paid the rent for two months due to her heroin habit and had received an eviction notice. She was terrified, expecting Carver's heavies to appear at any moment. She said if she left, they'd throw her stuff out on the street and change the locks. Elena wondered what 'stuff' Susan was referring to—the room was depressingly empty.

"Qamar was paying rent, wasn't she?"

"Aye, mebbe. But she refused to move oot too."

"Move out?"

"Carver wants tae sell this place tae developers. They've offered a ton of cash. But we have contracts fur 12 months and we jist signed in June. He has to go through due process and gie three months' notice and aw. I'll probably go and stay wi' my nan, if she'll hae me. I'm sick o' this place. London's a shithole."

"You think he killed her for that? Because she wouldn't leave?"

"That an' getting aff the game. He gets kickbacks oan that tae."

"Prostitution?"

Here Susan did a scathing impersonation of Elena's last word and then looked like she regretted it.

"Sorry, dear. But the guy's a bloodsucker. He'll take whatever he can get. Qamar was working on her wee business idea, getting other girls intae it. Was going tae employ girls aff the street. Carver wasnae exactly chuffed."

"But to kill her? A bit extreme."

Susan laughed but the sound carried no humour.

"Ah've seen a girl had her throat cut 'cause she stole some cash and a bit of coke aff her pimp. She hud aboot seventy quid. Told ye. This place is a shithole."

Elena could believe this. She heard those kinds of stories too, had lived one once. After declining a cup of tea but tentatively accepting water in a lipstick-tinged glass, Elena probed a little deeper. Susan had overheard a man in Qamar's apartment the night she was killed, shouting in an Eastern European accent. Elena was surprised this hadn't woken either her or her daughter.

"You wanna speak to Carver, he's got some dodgy blokes whit dae his dirty work. I'll bet it was wan o' them greasy fuckers."

"Thanks. I will. If you think of anything else, I'm just down below. Flat 11."

"Aye. Ah will. You feel free tae come up for a wee cuppa anytime you fancy. No after five though as ah've usually got clients."

Clients, there was that word again. As if the transactions Qamar and Susan had provided were somehow just straightforward business dealings. Even as she nodded her assent to Susan's invitation, Elena knew she would probably not be popping in for tea any time soon. The thought made her feel guilty as she headed back downstairs.

Ana felt herself bump back into consciousness. Where was she? It took her a moment to find her bearings.

She was in a taxi. A minicab, sitting between two boys. Chris, reassuringly sat to her right, fast asleep, head tucked back into the corner between the seat and the door. She'd evidently been asleep on his shoulder—there was a small damp patch where she must have drooled. Nice.

Less happily, she also found a hand wandering up her thigh under her skirt. It belonged to a guy in his late twenties with a crew cut and red-flecked stubble. She didn't recognise him at all. He smelled of stale beer and marijuana. As she turned to look at him, he leered at her, revealing a gold front tooth.

"What the fuck? Get away from me!"

Ana slapped he hand back, but it returned, this time squeezing her left breast urgently. The stranger's face was hot with alcoholic desire.

"Come on. You were eyeing me, earlier. You so want it."

She so did not, and aimed a slap that landed clumsily, making its point but inflicting no real pain. Still, he flinched back, as if stung. Ana turned to shake Chris violently by the shoulders.

"Wake up! Your friend is touching me, the disgusting pig."

Chris, rising from sleep, then did something that tipped Ana over the edge. He laughed, lightly, nervously. Ana screamed.

"Stop the car! Fucking stop, will you!"

She banged as hard as she could on the back of the driver's seat. The Sikh driver jammed on the brake and turned to face Ana alarmed as she clambered over her crew-cutted molester to grab for the door handle. A moment later, she was out, the driver having released the locking mechanism.

"Ana! Where are you going? I'm sure it was just a joke," cried Chris, starting to follow her, then turning back to shout abuse at his friend.

Ana ignored everything and ran along an anonymous high street, tears streaming down her face. How could she have been so stupid? She had no idea where she was but knew she didn't want to face Chris now. She felt woozy and sick and ducked inside a pub where she ignored the questioning faces and raced to the loo down a flight of rickety stairs.

After throwing up copiously in the cubicle, Ana felt a little better. She rinsed her mouth out with icy tap-water and when a girl in her early twenties stood gawping at her, she fired back:

"What the fuck are you looking at?"

After about fifteen minutes of wandering very dull and similar-looking suburban streets later Ana realised she could have asked the girl where on earth she was.

It could be anywhere. It could even be a suburb back home.

CHAPTER 28

Yarmouth couldn't quite believe what he was doing until he knocked on McPherson's door and it swung open to reveal his arch enemy (comical phrase but true enough) scowling at him as if he'd just trodden dogshit into the carpet.

"What the hell are you doing here? Haven't you got homeless people to move along or drunken pikeys to lock up?"

Several cutting one-liners sprang to mind but Yarmouth swallowed his pride as McPherson stood aside the least possible amount to let his visitor squeeze by.

"Nice one. Believe it or not, I'm back on the team. Albeit seconded to help out with an investigation under Sanchita Shah."

"Really? I'd better have a word then. I thought I made it clear when you assaulted me..."

"I wouldn't bother. The super has approved it and that's kind of why I'm here. I guess I never really apologised."

On hearing this last word, McPherson's face attempted a serious of expressions ranging from astonishment to disbelief to irritation, before settling on wry scepticism.

"I'll believe it when I hear it, Sonny Jim."

"Well, you're hearing it now."

"No, I'm not."

McPherson stood with arms folded, waiting with an expression of mock truculence. Did he ever express anything without a layer of cynical irony, Yarmouth wondered? He took a deep breath.

"I am sincerely sorry I slapped you..."

"You bloody well broke my nose. A lucky one, if you ask me. I was unprepared..."

"Sorry, punched you in the face. I was a bit emotional. Things weren't going well with me and..."

"The Muslim girl? Forgotten her name already, have we?"

"Rupa. Hindu, actually. Anyway, it doesn't matter. I'm burying the hatchet because we'll be around one another and it doesn't help any of us for there to be bad blood between us."

McPherson Let this settle in. Then raised a meaty paw. They shook hands, Yarmouth refusing to acknowledge the knuckle-crushing squeeze McPherson applied.

"And to show I'm sincere," Yarmouth said, "let me get you drink after work tomorrow."

This at last broke through McPherson's protective layers—he now wore an expression of genuine discomfort.

"I've got loads on. I doubt I'll get out of here until late."

"Same here. The Temperance's open until midnight and there's half price burgers on a Thursday night. Come on, it's on me."

Yarmouth could tell McPherson was now considering the burgers. McPherson's thought processes were so transparent, Yarmouth was surprised they didn't come with an accompaniment of grinding gears. McPherson was also probably also thinking about how he'd tell his cronies that Robin Yarmouth had come grovelling, wanting to be his friend and buy him dinner. It would be worth the discomfort for the warped kudos this would give McPherson.

"All right then. Swing by around nine. I'll be ready to knock it on the head by then."

"Will do."

With a tight-lipped smile, Yarmouth turned on his heel and fled. That was quite possibly the least pleasant encounter he'd had since the Stanley knife-wielding scooter thieves. But it was necessary. During the time he'd been in McPherson's den, he'd spotted his iPhone, reliably clad in its faux-leather case, sitting on the table. Yarmouth knew just where to get such a case—there was a stall on Berwick Street market selling them for a fiver.

The next part of the plan would be the tricky bit though. And for that he would need Elena's help.

Right on cue, she called. Yarmouth fumbled his own phone trying to get it to his ear in time but just managed it before it went to voicemail.

"Robin. She's missing."

"Who's missing?"

Elena sounded tearful.

"Ana! She's not home. There's no message. Her phone goes to voicemail. I might know where she might be, but can you bring your car?"

Robin winced. Elena sounded really scared but his BMW was in a local garage for its MOT and borrowing a patrol car was out of the question.

"Give me a moment. I'll call someone. Call you straight back."

Having walked around for almost an hour in somewhere called Camberwell, trying to find a tube station (South London seemed distinctly lacking in them) Ana had flagged down the first black cab she'd seen, knowing she could get the cash off Elena at the other end of the trip. She didn't tell the driver this, of course. She would break the bad news when she was at least within walking distance. Stupidly, she couldn't remember the address of their flat so she said Bar Italia instead. It was the first land-mark she could remember. Perhaps that kind-looking old Italian guy would help her out.

To make matters worse, her phone was completely dead now. As the taxi jostled at reassuring yet alarming speed through the darkened streets, Ana jabbed futilely at the power button, hoping that the battery might have recovered enough power to fire off a text. No such luck, unfortunately. Ana felt the hot, burning sensation of tears forming in the corner of her eyes and wiped them away surreptitiously. She felt like such a child, overly trusting and naïve. Chris had let his friend get away with touching her. What an asshole.

Her mood was lifted a little by the rapidly warming taxi interior and by the strange Middle-Eastern music issuing from the taxi's speakers. Ana leaned forward.

"Excuse me. What's that music?"

The driver twisted in his seat, idling at a traffic light.

"Amr Diab. Should I turn it down?"

"No, no. I like it."

It would help with the awkward payment part later on if she befriended the moustached, balding man in the driver's seat. But Ana did also like the music. It wasn't as antiseptic as a lot of modern music (Ana loathed Cardi B and Ariana Grande) and made her think of a bazaar or a foreign musical, handsome movie idols dancing across a giant screen.

They crossed the river at Vauxhall and Ana looked down at the dark, gleaming river below and at the skyline, glittering like a necklace of coloured light. She felt she could grow to love this city if she could just figure it out. For the first time in her life, she longed for school: the rou-tine, the friendships, the harmless flirtations. She wondered what Sofia was doing right now. Pprobably sucking off her boyfriend down some side street. Ana knew she was doing her friend and injustice with this image, but she relished it anyhow.

For once, London traffic was relatively light, and Ana found herself coming out of the spiral of despair she had fallen into. She was looking forward to getting into her room, putting on her pyjamas and giant fluffy slippers and getting into bed with her newly charged phone. She would Skype Sofia first.

"Can you turn left after Bar Italia? I can't remember the street name, but I know where it is."

The driver shrugged.

"Is no problem. Just direct me."

It was a little bit more of a problem when Ana stopped the taxi outside her house and told the driver she had to go upstairs for the money. His kindness turned to suspicion in a way that made it clear he was used to dealing with fare dodgers.

"You are joking?"

Ana shook her head. Ahmed (as his ID revealed) rubbed his tired face, then nodded curtly and gestured towards the street. Ana thanked him and jumped out, slamming the door behind her.

Elena was nowhere to be found. Ana was sure she'd said she would be home tonight but perhaps something had come up. She pushed away the fleeting thought that her mother might be out looking for her and began to search the living room for the stash of money Elena had hidden.

It was missing. Shit. Ana had forgotten that Elena had opened a bank account—she'd had to in order to be paid by the translation agency. There had to be something somewhere though. Elena was nothing if not cautious.

The lounge and kitchen quickly exhausted, Ana opened the window and called to Ahmed, who was standing outside his cab, smoking, saying she'd be there "in a minute". She went into Elena's room. A chair in the corner was piled with clothes, a suitcase open on the floor. Nothing in either. She looked on the shelves, in between the pages of books, even inside a vase filled with dying flowers. Her heart began to thump in her breast in panic as she traipsed back into the living room. Then she saw the loose floorboard.

Just beyond the limit of the cheap, brightly patterned rug Elena had bought (Ana had chosen it) was a plank that didn't quite reach the skirting board. Ana threw back the rug and prised the foot-long board up. Underneath, already covered by a thin layer of dust, were two passports and a roll of cash, held by an elastic band. Ana opened the passports first, out of curiosity. Mum had never shown her their photos.

Elena's serious face stared back behind the transparent plastic. Ana was about to put them back and unwrap the roll of cash when she saw the name. Elena Ceausescu.

That wasn't her mother's name. Ana flipped open the second passport. Ana Ceausescu.

Now it all made sense. Why Elena had insisted on keeping hold of both their passports, giving the excuse that her daughter was always losing things (partly true). Why Elena hadn't even let Ana see the passport to check if the photo was mortifyingly ugly or not (it wasn't). They were travelling on false names!

Ana's heart was still racing but now she had two conflicting things to panic about. She bent down to stare into the space beneath the floorboards, hands grasping amongst the grime for more secrets.

BANG!

The sound of the front door closing downstairs. Ana jumped up, replacing the floorboard, just in time to catch Elena and Robin entering, her mother putting her purse back in her handbag, somehow looking relieved and furious at the same time. Had she seen Ana rummaging in her hiding place?

It didn't matter. Ana still had the passports in her hand.

"What the fuck are these, mum?" Ana pre-empted.

CHAPTER 29

Two hours previously, Elena had collapsed gratefully into the back seat of Tom Fleischer's battered Volvo estate, too emotionally wracked to brush away the dog hairs or remove the toys that rolled around beneath her feet. Fleisher turned and flashed a reassuring smile while Robin did the introductions. Elena could only manage a weak smile in response as they pulled away.

"Thank you so much. I'm really worried. It's not like her. With everything happened in neighbourhood..."

Robin twisted round in the passenger seat, placing a hand firmly on her forearm.

"It's totally fine. I'm sure she's just out having fun and she's forgotten to tell you she's late."

"I know, it's probably stupid. I just have such bad feeling."

She did, although she had no rational reason for it. Ana was in trouble—she felt certain of this, a sympathy pain running down both forearms when she thought of the melodramatic possibilities. After all, there was a killer out there somewhere. A killer who had struck just yards from their front door. One who might know she was helping with the investigation. She shouldn't dwell on it.

"Where to?" Fleischer asked, like he was just their taxi driver and not an experienced police detective.

Elena had thought through all the possibilities and could think of only one option that made sense.

"Prince Charles cinema."

Half an hour later, Elena was back in the car, with the information that Ana had met Chris after work and they were going to some event at Elephant and Castle, which was presumably some eccentrically-named part of London. Fleischer nodded and turned on a blue flashing light to speed them on their way.

Elena was surprised by how busy London's traffic was, even at almost eleven in the evening. She was gratified (and, she had to admit, a little bit excited) by how people pulled out of the way, one driver even mounting the pavement, to let them pass. They made it to Elephant and Castle in fifteen minutes flat.

Fleischer seemed content to remain their driver as Robin and Elena marched over to some outdoor tables between the converted shipping containers, where a few twenty-somethings drank and smoked to percussive sounds blasting out from two large speakers. There was no DJ in evidence behind the decks and it looked like the party was winding down.

One blue-dreadlocked black woman remembered a young girl getting into a car with a mixed-race boy and a tall, Irish graffiti artist apparently called Spider. When Elena asked if they were drunk, the woman just shrugged and returned to her can of Red Stripe. Elena could have punched her.

"Any idea where they went, my underage daughter and your drunken friends?"

The woman looked chastened.

"Probably to Spider's gaff. He's got a studio down in Camberwell. Does these massive canvases in circular format, they're..."

"I don't care a fuck," spat Elena, her English slipping as it did when she was stressed. "What's address?"

Robin placed a cautionary hand on her arm as he took down what little information the group could give them.

Then it was back into the car and on with the blue light again.

Elena found herself becoming tearful in the car and leaned into Robin's shoulder (she liked the fact that he'd been sensitive enough to get into the back seat with her).

"Don't worry, she's a sensible girl. I'm sure she's okay."

Elena sighed. "I know. I over-react. I know what I was like at fourteen. She's better behaved than me, to be honest. That's why I'm worried. She would usually call."

"Might be her phone battery has died," offered Robin softly.

Elena nodded, hoping he could feel the affirmative as her head moved on his shoulder. She feared the worst. She couldn't tell Robin specifically why she was so distraught. Her thoughts tumbled chaotically to Frances, who she was supposed to be meeting in a couple of days. This couldn't have anything to do with her, surely?

Robin probably thought she was just a hysterical mother. She wondered how long he would stick around.

"This is the place," said Fleischer, executing a dramatic right turn in front of a white van which had the temerity to honk as they rattled down a potholed alleyway into a dark yard enclosed by warehouses. Loud music was blaring from one of them, sparks flying out of the darkness, a sound of spinning metal on metal.

They dashed inside, eyes adjusting slowly to the gloom. It was evidently the workshop of a sculptor. Various, weird, vaguely vegetable-looking pyramids of welded together car-parts dominated the room, leaving a small circle of space where three figures were intent on their tasks.

Chis was there, tapping intently at his mobile phone while nearby, a diminutive young Chinese man wearing goggles held a circular saw as it buzzed against a piece of metal piping, throwing out shards of light. Beside him stood a gangling, shaven-headed white man, also wearing safety glasses, and shouting in his friend's ear.

"Not so hard. You want to go slowly, or you'll break the blade!"

Robin waved his arms to silence the activity and then flashed his ID badge.

"Police. I'm PC Yarmouth. We need a word."

Chris looked up from his phone and his face fell from an expression of childlike joy to shock when he recognised Ana's mother.

"Oh my god, Mrs Balan, I am so sorry. I was just texting her."

The Chinese man handed the circular saw back to his friend as its blade slowly stopped rotating. There was a smell of iron filings and oil in the air. Now that the circular saw had stopped its harsh drone, frothy pop music could be heard playing from unseen speakers.

Chris seemed to be oscillating between the hangdog expression of a pet that knows it's about to be scolded and the defensiveness of a defiant youth.

"I tried to call her like nine times but she's not answering," he continued.

Elena sighed. It didn't seem worth throwing her paternal weight around but for form's sake she walked uncomfortably close to the teenager. He smelled of stale beer, cheap perfume and weed.

"I was just texting her when you arrived," he continued. "She just ran off..."

"What you mean ran off?"

"We was in a taxi coming here. This idiot tried to put his arm round her or something. I was asleep."

The shaven-headed man looked at Elena, sheepishly.

"I was just fooling around," he added.

Elena directed her fury at the pale, tall redhead, though he dwarfed her.

"If either of you come near my daughter again, I swear I fucking end you!"

The threat echoed in the cavernous space as Elena stared at the penitent group of boys. Robin got out his notebook and began asking questions and a few minutes later they left the warehouse with the conclusion that Ana's phone was almost certainly out of power and that she'd be making her own way home.

They arrived at the flat and Elena immediately saw a light in a second-floor window—hers. Relief flooded her. She took the steps two at a time, Robin just behind her. Fleischer had blithely accepted their thanks for the loan of his car and time and had driven off to his bowling match.

Rounding the top of the stairs, they saw an elderly Middle Eastern man standing outside the flat door, fist poised as if about to knock.

"Who the hell are you?" Elena asked.

The man shrugged, as if it should seem obvious.

"Am taxi driver. This girl has not paid me. She say wait, I wait outside. Nothing. Is cold. I come upstairs."

Robin asked to see his ID and the man grumbled and waddled off downstairs to get it. Elena counted out some cash and they paid him after he huffed back upstairs, complaining about passengers taking advantage of him. Elena dropped her keys trying to get into the flat. She realised her hands were shaking, her relief now having progressed to anger. Ana had kept Elena in a state of panic for almost four hours.

Robin picked up the keys and opened the door for Elena. She thanked him and shut it behind them, unnecessarily firmly, so that it slammed. Elena stormed into the lounge, wondering if her daughter would even know what she had done wrong. She was prepared for truculence or for sullen silence (the two modes Ana favoured when she was in trouble and didn't want to admit it was her fault). What Elena hadn't counted on was the sight of Ana, hand on hip, holding out the two passports she'd so carefully hidden.

"What the fuck are these mum?"

Elena turned to Robin.

"Please can you give a bit of privacy?"

In the heat of the moment, Elena realised how rude this sounded, but she couldn't have the police around if she was going to explain things to her enraged daughter.

"You want me to wait outside?"

"I want you to go. Thanks, for everything, but I have to talk to Ana alone."

Robin looked hurt and confused but just shook his head and walked to the door.

"I'll call you tomorrow," Elena pleaded. "I'll explain."

"Fine. Bye."

With that, he left, closing the door with almost exaggerated care. Elena turned to Ana.

"We need to talk."

CHAPTER 30

Ana sat back in the corner of the sofa, legs tucked under her, arms folded.

"Go on then."

Elena took a deep breath. This wasn't going to be easy.

"You must remember everything I've done has been to protect us. To protect you."

Ana remained unmoved. Elena began her story, a tragic tale whose inciting episode began before Ana was even conceived.

Elena had been nineteen, working in a clothing retailer during the day, taking night classes in fashion design, with the encouragement of her mother, who had harboured ambitions of being a dressmaker as a girl which she had never been fulfilled. The family had recently moved to Bucharest from the small town of Focşani and Elena found it both an exciting and daunting place. She hadn't yet made many friends when she met Karl.

He worked in a bank, was smartly dressed, and conducted himself with poise and (to her teenage eyes) maturity. He was buying a winter coat for his quite elderly mother and Elena had rushed to help the handsome, quiet young man in a way she rarely did with most customers (it's always the good-looking ones you're nice to, her boss had pointed out).

"Can I help you?" she had asked, a catch in her voice.

"I sincerely hope so," he had replied with a smile.

That was their first exchange, and she would never forget it. He turned out to be 28—a little too old for her, she would normally have thought. He was well-groomed, with close-cropped hair, a dark, pinstripe suit and a single, mysterious ear stud. Karl had flunked a degree in computing and turned his aptitude for numbers into a more mundane but lucrative career as an investment banker. He didn't talk about his work that much at first, which Elena appreciated (she had always been dreadful with money; too much of it seemed to turn into shoes and the plum brandy *pálinka*, for which she had latterly discovered a liking).

After helping Karl select a faux-fur coat for his mother, he impressed her even more by asking her out with straightforward confidence. She finished work within the hour, and he remained in the shop, browsing through ties and shirts while Elena's colleagues embarrassed her with questions.

They went for a walk through the Old Town, where Karl showed her his favourite haunts, even boldly stating "I'll take you there one day," whilst passing a stylish-looking restaurant. They visited the eternal flame by the imposing war monument in Carol park, and dashed down the steps to the Fântâna Zodiac, where Karl kissed her, bending her back so far over the lip of the fountain that Elena was worried she might fall in, had Karl not gripped her shoulders so firmly.

The relationship blossomed with speed that might have alarmed an older Elena but felt just like how true love was supposed to be to an infatuated teen. The pregnancy, of course, was unplanned, the result of one too many 'spontaneous' nights of sex in strange places—the back of his car, the offices of a small IT start-up Karl's firm were bankrolling, under a pile of coats at a debauched party. Condoms are mood-killers, Karl had said. So are abortions, Elena had replied, but they'd gone ahead anyway.

Before long, Elena was three weeks late. She bought a testing kit from the pharmacy and spent a couple of hours weeping at the result. Then, as the realisation sunk in, her thoughts on having the baby changed from 'no way' to 'maybe'. She'd stopped to study a poster in her doctor's surgery waiting room—a cross-section of pregnant women's bellies at different trimesters. The mothers' heads were callously cut off, while the metamorphosing forms inside them were detailed in painstaking precision: first something like a tadpole, then a kidney bean, a foetus, finally a recognisable child, vacuum-sealed but perfectly new.

Although she knew intellectually that what was inside her at the moment was little more than a blob of undifferentiated matter, Elena's eyes couldn't help but be drawn to the images at the bottom right of the poster, where the growing baby was depicted with fingernails and eyelashes. She was having one of those. Suddenly abortion was off the table.

To give Karl some credit, once the initial shock and defensive fear of fatherhood had broken over him, he had at least grudgingly accepted his destiny and his girlfriend's choice. He had thrown himself into his work—Elena suspected as much to avoid some of the heavy lifting of being a new parent as to pay for the seemingly endless array of baby gear that parenthood required. At times, Elena felt alone and unsupported, although her mother mucked in where and when she could, surprisingly accepting of her daughter's situation, since it didn't conflict with her Catholic belief that the spark of human life was somehow divine and inviolable.

At other times, Karl came home with flowers and gifts for the new baby and spent a half hour cooing over his daughter, who seemed determined to scream the neighbourhood down only when her father wasn't around.

Then, as Ana began to develop a nascent personality—cheeky, insistent, very bright but almost cruel at times—Karl began to withdraw a little. Although he had proposed marriage when Ana began to show, as much to appease her mother as anything more romantic, Karl wasn't in a hurry to actually tie the knot, it seemed. He argued that marriage was "just a construct, a legal arrangement" and said that his love for her didn't require "a piece of paper" to prove it. Elena countered that she just wanted to symbolically celebrate their little household with all their friends and family. A wedding was just a big party, in a sense—what was so scary about that?

Thinking back, Elena couldn't really remember seeing many clues to what was really wrong with her relationship with Karl. Certainly, he wasn't the most avid of lovers, after their crazy first couple of months. He seemed content to make love to her on a roughly fortnightly basis, usually claiming he was just too exhausted from work to be amorous (in the latter months he was working up to 70 hours a week).

That wasn't enough for Elena, who masturbated furiously in his absence, usually with an attendant feeling of guilt and sadness. Once she used a courgette and then washed and served it to Karl in a salad—a kind of secret symbolic revenge. He said it was "delicious" and then went out to spend an evening with a new group of work-friends he'd seen a lot of lately. Perhaps she shouldn't have washed it.

Then one day, Elena had taken a half-day from work to visit her mother, but Constantia had texted her to tell her not to come. Constantia had the flu and didn't want to give it to Ana. Elena struggled with the moral calculus of this, before realising her mother was probably right. Ana had suffered a spate of viruses recently and was still sniffy from a cold. Instead, Elena wheeled Ana around a park, bought some pastries and headed home.

She'd assumed Karl would be at work but it appeared he had better things to do.

She caught him with his trousers and underwear around his ankles, sitting on a wooden chair in the small spare room he called his 'study', wanking wildly to something that involved a ten-year-old girl, a vibrator and a man in his fifties. The girl was crying, softly, the camera operator cruel enough to offer a brief close-up. This seemed to arouse Karl more, so much so that he didn't notice Elena had entered the room until a gust of wind blew the door shut.

Then the scene became a farce as Karl tried to close the laptop and pull up his trousers in one move, succeeding only in knocking the latter off the desk and tripping over his underwear, hopping towards the bed like a character caught in flagrante delicto in some 1970's blue movie. Yet there was nothing funny about the scene.

Elena couldn't remember what she shouted but she remembered how raw her throat was while she gathered Ana's things together, put her back in the pushchair and left the flat, jabbing viciously at the lift's control panel while a half-dressed Karl pleaded with her across the landing.

"It's not what it looks like", he'd had the temerity to offer in his defence. "I can't help it, it's not something I chose". She ignored him, relieved when the lift doors clanged open, and she was able to escape this horror. She felt her mind creating a wall between her memory and the substance of what she'd seen. She'd give it a name later. For now, she had only one thought—to run to her mother, influenza be damned.

One more detail from what she'd seen on the screen that day. Karl had a chat window open while he was masturbating. With whom was he speaking? What awful confessions was he sharing? She couldn't think about it; her defensive wall grew thicker. She arrived at mum's place within the hour and Constantia did not need to know anything more about what had happened beyond "Mum—he's a monster!" before she did what was required and brought her hot, sugary tea, switched on the radio (Simon and Garfunkel's America was mid-chorus) and took Ana away to change her.

The next few days constituted a gradual process of eradication as Karl came to accept that he was to leave their lives immediately and never return. "I have a problem, I just need help!" he pleaded, as Elena kicked his suitcase down the stairs and threatened him with the police.

She never called them though. Something in his eyes really did look terrified and she'd heard stories about paedophiles killing themselves. She didn't want that on her hands, no matter what he'd been doing in their spare room. She instinctively knew he wasn't lying when he said he's never touch a child, and that his thrill was purely voyeuristic. Elena also knew that this was no excuse and that his perversion was feeding a whole disgusting industry of abuse but still she couldn't quite bring himself to ruin his life.

"Get some help then!" she'd screamed, slamming the door on him for the last time. Or so she'd thought.

Karl emailed her a couple of years later, when Ana was in her first week at primary school and Elena was planning her dressmaking business. A familiar icon pinged onscreen and Elena's instinct was to erase it without reading. Yet she couldn't. She kept seeing Ana's face, with its subtle traces of Karl's own. Sick and depraved he might be, but he was her father. For Ana's sake, she ought to be able to answer the inevitable question that might come one day—what happened to my daddy?

Dearest Elena and sweet Ana, the email began. *You probably know that I moved out of Bucharest. I'm now with a bank in Brussels. Forgive me if I can't be more specific. I'm also in this treatment programme for people with my condition. They told me it would be a mistake to try and reconnect with you. That it would stop me from properly beginning anew. But I had to say again how sorry I am for what happened. For what I was doing to those girls. I know I wasn't touching them or anything, but the counsellors have made me admit that I was an abuser just by viewing those images and sharing them, even though it felt like I had no control over it. I had plenty of control, but I did nothing for so long. Your seeing me was the best thing that could have happened (and also the worst). I'm not pleading forgiveness, I'm not going to ask to see Ana (but how is she? Please reply on her account if you can bear it). I just want to you know I'm sorry and I'm doing something about it. I hope you are both well and thriving. Send me a picture of Ana Banana if you can. I'll leave you in peace now. I hope to hear from you though. It's lonely hear and work is mundane and demanding (I got promoted though I've nobody to spend the extra cash on). Perhaps we'll speak soon. Love, K.*

There were so many things that angered Elena about the email. The weird mix of apology and self-justification. The almost offhand way he mentioned Ana, whilst insisting she was somehow important to him, the lack of questions about their lives, the use of Ana's infant nickname (she was over her love of bananas now). Even the typos (*It's lonely hear*) infuriated her. Didn't he have a spell-checker? The veiled boast about his income. Even with the last initial, Karl angered her. 'K'—the pretentiousness and offhand familiarity of it. Love but no kisses. Perfunctory, box-ticking. She was well rid of him. They both were.

And so it went for another nine years. Elena built up her business, selling patterned summer dresses online (and scarves in the winter), then expanding to sell the sewing patterns themselves. It didn't bring in a fortune but that, plus the couple of days a week she worked in Ana's old nursery, watching over a pinball-machine of three- and four-year-olds, was enough to scrape by. There were relationships – Bartek lasted three years then left her for a younger, child-free woman. Stephen was fun (a double first for her - a black man and significantly older, at 46) but he was separated from his wife and child and eventually, tearfully, went back to them.

Then finally, as Ana approached her fourteenth birthday, intelligent, headstrong but not as obnoxious as many of her peers, she met Frances in that bar and allowed herself to open up to something different, something new. Four months into that, Elena answered her door to a knock she thought was Frances's (had she lost the spare keys Elena gave her) and there was Karl.

Elena was so staggered that she just stepped back and let him in. It was mid-afternoon and Ana was at school.

Elena was just about to unload the dishwasher (she'd bought it on an instalment plan, but it had made her life so much simpler). Into this domestic scene strode Karl, the deviant sex fiend, looking around Elena's new flat's hallway like a safety inspector.

"Hi Elena. You're a hard woman to track down."

Elena regained her composure and interposed herself between Karl and the lounge.

"What the fuck are you doing here? I thought you were someone else."

Karl smiled broadly and then, in a rare moment of self-awareness, turned down its wattage.

"I'm sorry. I tried to call but the number was disconnected."

"I changed it. To avoid this."

"I said I was sorry, and I meant it. I've done a lot of soul-searching these last few years, in therapy and out of it. The main thing is, I'm still Ana's dad."

"Biologically yes. In any way that's meaningful no."

"Come on, Elena..."

Elena's memory of what happened next always seemed to play out in slow motion, but not completely smoothly. There were little jumps and breaks in the timeline, flickers of uncertainty.

Karl followed Elena into the kitchen as she tried to return to her work as a way of warding him off. His entreaties would fall on deaf ears. She'd been mopping the floor and had then remembered the full dishwasher. She should have done her chores the other way around, but she had a lot on her mind. How to afford the dance classes Ana had signed up to, whether to book a holiday with Frances (was it too soon?), how best to grow her business. She was wearing slippers to avoid dirtying the floor as she turned her back on him. His feet were on her pristine, bleached tiles.

"Just talk to me at least. She's my daughter too, whatever you say."

Elena span round, the dishwasher drawer a protective barrier between them.

"I don't give a fuck. You're not seeing her. Now get the hell out!"

"What, do you think I'm going to touch her?"

"I'll kill you if you ever came close."

"You're being ridiculous." Then Karl dropped even the pretence of remorse. "To be honest, she's a little too old for me."

That's when she lashed out. It was only meant to be a slap—a bit of non-verbal communication that would get her point across incontrovertibly. But it knocked him off-balance, and he slipped on the wet floor.

They'd made kebabs for dinner the previous evening—it wasn't even something Elena much liked, but Ana had asked about the long, sharp skewers she'd found at the back of a drawer, and it had been a spur of the moment decision to make use of them. Elena had put them spike-up in the cutlery rack part of the lower washer drawer.

Karl instinctively twisted like a cat as he fell, putting his hands out on either side of the drawer but his right hand slipped on the wet tiles. Elena believed in a good clean kitchen floor. Karls' head and neck slammed down on the claw of skewers. One must have caught a major vein as blood began to gush vividly as Karl struggled to rise. Another pierced an eyeball, from which more blood, and a strange clear fluid ran.

His screams were the most terrible thing—animalistic at first but quickly ebbing to a low moan as what seemed like litres of blood poured out of Karl's neck. Elena stood frozen to the spot, unable to react (or perhaps unwilling to?) Even months later, she couldn't really decide whether she had let him die or not. Her memory kept throwing up different, contradictory versions of what she did next.

In one version, she'd tried to catch him as he fell, and had definitely tried to pull his body off the skewers. In another, she just slumped into a chair and watched his life ebb away. Then she decided to call an ambulance... and then somehow didn't. She'd definitely checked his pulse at one point—or rather, the lack of a pulse.

Elena did remember taking ages to unlock her phone with bloody fingers and surprising herself by phoning, not the police, but Frances. Her female lover had reacted as if this horror were just a routine calamity, as if it was something she'd dealt with before.

Frances told her to get undressed, shower and shut the kitchen door. Elena did so, curling up on the sofa in her dressing gown, rigid with fear. Frances, meanwhile, arranged for Ana to go home with one of her school-friends. She said the boiler at home had malfunctioned and there was no hot water. Frances and Elena would wait in for an engineer. Ana shrugged assent at this suggestion—a visual 'whatever'.

Frances arrived forty minutes later, put the TV on as a distraction for Elena while she unloaded the car and brought up a selection of cleaning products, plastic wrap and a large cardboard box. An hour later, Frances left the flat, dragging the cardboard box with surprising ease. Karl had been a rather slight man.

Elena was still too frozen to manage more than a murmured thanks as Frances dashed back up to say goodbye and check that she was okay.

"I'll call you later on with the plan for what happens next."

"Will you call the police?"

Frances winced. "That wouldn't be a good idea."

With that phrase, she cemented their criminal pact. Frances would remove all traces of Karl from the apartment, then set in motion a plan to get Elena out of the country. They'd been talking about visiting Frances on her next London trip and now fate had forced their hand.

"You'll need fake passports though."

"Why?" Elena asked as she whispered down the phone to her from the sofa she'd hardly risen from since Frances left.

"I'm not a forensic expert so I can't guarantee I've not missed anything. I've checked around the neighbourhood and I don't think there are any CCTV cameras that could have caught him entering the flat but there will be ones that caught his number plate."

"He didn't park outside, did he?" asked Elena, stirring to alertness.

"Fortunately not. Several blocks away. I don't think we should touch his car. Do you think he might have told anyone where he was going?"

"I doubt it."

"Still, we can't take chances. If the cops figure out he was here, well... You've got motive, means and opportunity. You'd be the prime suspect. A freak accident like that? Would anyone believe you?"

"Oh great. Thanks for the reassurance."

"I'm just telling it like it is, sweetie. Plus, his family has money, and they can hire the best lawyers in the country. You and Ana had better run. I'm leaving in five days for London. Come and join me."

"And the passports?"

"I have a friend. Trouble is, he's not cheap..."

In the version Elena told Ana, she skipped the worst of what she'd seen Karl doing. She glossed over the full horror of his death too. In this version, he just banged his head and Elena found she couldn't wake him. It didn't stop Ana's eyes from widening and filling with tears in a way that demanded a huge hug, one that would certainly have been rejected. Ana was still furious.

"You killed him! My father—you as good as murdered him."

Only the "as good as" gave Elena hope that Ana might come to understand.

"He died. It was an accident."

"So why did you run like a guilty person?"

"Who would have believed me? I'd be in jail, and you'd be in care if it wasn't for Frances."

"And you're saying my dad was a... paedo?"

Ana sobbed the last word. Elena had dropped an immense weight on those narrow shoulders. She felt immediately guilty, but it was no good. The truth had to come out sooner or later. Ana had found the passports— nothing but the truth would have satisfied her agile mind. Even if she'd not found them, Elena would have had to make something up to explain why she was registering Ana with her new school under an assumed name. It was better like this. It would hurt now but in time... hell, what did Elena really know? There was no precedent for this situation, no 'handy hint' in a parenting manual.

She tentatively sat down beside her daughter and put a hand on her knee, in sympathy. Immediately, Ana jerked her leg away, as if scalded.

"You're such a liar. Why should I trust you with anything?"

Ana got up and marched out of the room. Moments later aggressive guitar music from her room made it clear Elena was not required to give chase.

Elena sighed, poured herself the last glass from a bottle of Pinot Grigio and sat down in front of some idiotic television (she'd rented one to appease her daughter) to have a think. What were the risks and dangers ahead and was it all worth it? Perhaps it was good that she was meeting Frances soon. She could perhaps get some much-needed closure.

There were too many dysfunctional partners—alive or dead—controlling her destiny right now. She had to draw a line in the sand.

CHAPTER 31

When the moon hits your eye, like a big pizza pie, that's amore.

On the morning of their appointment, when Elena called Frances to check she'd actually turn up, Frances pretended to be busy at work—clearly a falsehood. Since when did investment firms blast Dean Martin as background music? That and the whirr of the bean-grinder told Elena where Frances really was.

"You're at Bar Italia, aren't you? Fran, just drop bullshit for one minute".

"I came early to get some work done. Look, I'm here aren't I? Where are you? I've been worried sick."

"Stop it! I'll be there in ten minutes, and I want answers."

She could imagine Frances rolling her eyes as she hung up, grabbed her coat and dashed round the busy Soho streets, arriving at Bar Italia in time to see Frances order her a coffee. A skinny mocha latte—her favourite. She took her seat opposite her lover without comment.

The silence grew between them, expanding like dough in a hot oven.

"What is it Elena? You want me to go through everything I texted you? We shouldn't be meeting in public."

Frances spoke in hushed Romanian but Elena's response came in no-nonsense English.

"You can cut the bullshit," Elena said, enjoying Frances's expression at her use of American vernacular. "Ana knows."

"She knows…. What exactly?" Frances asked, warily, arranging her red locks over the back of her chair.

The way she leaned back in her chair with studied non-chalance annoyed Elena. Hell, everything about Frances annoyed Elena.

"The whole deal. Well, most. I had to tell her."

Frances now leaned forward, visibly shaken.

"That was a bad idea."

"Perhaps, but how was I going to explain to a fourteen-year-old she must use an assumed name whenever she leaves country? She's not an idiot you know. So…"

Now it was Elena's turn to lean back in her chair.

"What?" Frances asked, stirring her espresso unnecessarily.

A young waitress breezed over with their coffees and Elena flashed her a smile before turning a cold stare towards Frances. Elena felt her English begin to slip again but held onto it like a life raft in a storm.

"What was crisis that means you leave us stranded at airport, give non-existent address for accommodation, ignore all my calls and texts and, in fact, completely fail to get in touch for weeks? All this whilst supposedly my…" here Elena couldn't help lowering her voice. "My girl-friend. You've had month to come up with something, so go ahead. I'm listening."

Frances sighed.

"I know I behaved badly. I was terrified. I helped you without really thinking through the consequences to my-self if it all went tits up."

"So you ran?"

"Well, I needed to get away until I felt it was safe. I couldn't contact you until I was certain. There couldn't be anything from my side—no calls, emails, or texts."

"But you could still meet us. I don't know—in disguise or something."

"Elena, airports are full of cameras. They have technology now that can identify a person wearing a bloody balaclava."

"Wearing what?"

"Balaclava. It's a kind of woollen facemask."

"The false address?"

"That was to get you through customs. For the visa, they need to know where you are staying but they don't check it's legit. I couldn't give my real address."

It was all beginning to sound superficially convincing, but Frances seemed even more wary of prolonged eye contact than usual. When Elena asked her a question, she had an odd habit of looking up to the right, as if seeking inspiration from an invisible autocue. Frances was the very definition of untrustworthy, but Elena decided to play along.

"So, what now? What happens to us?"

Frances made a show of looking emotionally wrought.

"Elena, as much as I love and care for you and Ana, with everything that's going on in my life, my job. And the risk attached to...."

Here, she lowered her voice and leaned across the table. "You know what... it's all a bit much. I think we need some time apart."

Take all the time in the world, thought Elena. She nodded thoughtfully.

"It's probably for best. We're pretty settled anyway, without your help."

"I'm glad. And again, I'm sorry."

The chair-legs groaned against the flooring as Frances stood up abruptly.

"I'll be in touch."

Frances kissed Elena on the cheek. Unlike the long, lingering kisses they had shared what seemed a lifetime ago, this touch was perfunctory. She was in such a hurry to leave that Frances jerked her chair over whilst taking her coat off it. Elena saw what her former lover was trying to gloss over—Frances was significantly afraid. Of what or whom? Elena wondered. Frances's eyes flicked around the crowded, narrow café before she hurried outside.

It had gone pretty much as Elena had expected, with nothing tangible to hold onto. Frances was essentially untrustworthy, and she should push the older woman to the back of her mind.

Elena sat stirring the dregs at the bottom of her cup as he planned the rest of her day. She had meetings at Voices Unlimited and translation work to take home. But at home there was an angry, confused daughter to deal with (who should have been reading through her coursework before her first week at the new school).

In addition, he had received three texts from Robin so far today:

You seemed distressed yesterday – what's up? xxx
Elena, I'm here for you. Please call me back. R x
Getting off my shift in half an hour. I'll call you. R.

Elena tried not to read too much into the gradual reduction in kisses at the bottom of these messages. She had sent him away when Ana had accosted her with the fake passports. She'd panicked and over-reacted. Robin was no doubt hurt by her sudden and inexplicable dismissal of him, especially given their ongoing investigation.

She had to think of a cover story—there was no way she could trust a police officer, no matter how lovely, with the awful truth. Perhaps a version of the truth would do. Elena and Ana were fleeing an abusive partner.

Ah, but Robin already knew about Frances—she couldn't be running from one lover to another. That just sounded pathetic, even though it had been kind of true. Perhaps she was escaping an abusive relative—an uncle. That would probably do. And yet...

For some reason it seemed important to Elena that Robin know the emotional truth of her situation, even if he didn't have the actual facts. She wanted him to know she was running away from an abusive, controlling man who had re-entered her life without her consent, that she had briefly taken refuge in Frances, another manipulator. Elena needed him to know that she was looking for something utterly different—a real partnership of equals. If equality could co-exist with her own necessary lies, that is.

She called Robin from the street outside, dodging tourists and media types on their way to expense lunches.

"Hi, Robin—it's me."

"I'm glad you called. I was so worried."

Elena apologised for her abruptness the previous evening, reassured him, did her best to deliver the falsehood she'd prepared as convincingly as possible. It was easier to do without him standing before her. Elena even found she broke down a little when she mentioned the abuse, which she characterised as physical and emotional but not sexual. She did not mention Frances. A moment's silence on the end of the line meant Robin was considering her explanations.

"Okay. I knew you were running from something. Why didn't you just tell me?"

"Was embarrassed. First one man abuses me, then another partner vanishes. So pathetic, so fucking predictable."

"It's just bad luck, Elena. I've come across women who attract abusive types, ones who move from one foul relationship to another. You're not one of them, believe me."

"Sometimes I just need some time to explain things to Ana."

"Elena, its fine. We've only been seeing one another for a few weeks. I know when I'm not required. Just don't hide anything more from me, will you."

"I'll try not to."

Although she said it with conviction in her voice, it was a promise Elena knew she couldn't keep.

CHAPTER 32

Ana really ought to be reading through her 'welcome pack' for the school she was supposed to be starting at in four days' time, but her mind kept slipping to the horrible story her mother had just told her. She had just learnt that the hazy image she had of Karl—the man who was supposedly her father—was hazier still, since he existed now only in the past. Karl was dead.

She didn't think Elena was lying to her about her father's tendencies or about the terrible accident that had resulted in his death. She just wished Elena had been honest with her when it happened. She remembered the depression her mother had sunk into in the week before they left to meet Frances in England. She always assumed this was something to do with Frances and her mum's confused feelings towards the redhead. Mum was of a generation for whom bisexual wasn't really a thing.

Ana had been unsure about Frances, at best. Nevertheless, she had even spent an evening reassuring her mum that she would be okay with the move and that she was looking forward to seeing the United Kingdom.

Now it seemed Frances was only a means to the end of escape. No wonder she hadn't come to meet them at the airport and had disappeared. Her mum had just used Frances to escape the police. Ana couldn't blame her mum for running. She'd probably have done the same thing. To involve someone like Frances seemed risky and selfish though. Flying to London to start a new life, with a lesbian lover—what a crock of shit that had been. This wasn't a new life, this was exile.

A pile of papers and a glossy brochure lay open opposite her on the bed. Happy, carefully multi-ethnic faces smiled back in their well-pressed uniform in the kind of glorious summer's day that Ana had seen little evidence of so far in London. St Bartholomew's. Even the name suggested prestige, although apparently it was just a regular comprehensive school. Ana both envied and hated these images of smug, high-achieving happiness. What contentment could there be for an international fugitive and her daughter? By her actions, Elena had doomed them both to a life of looking over their shoulders. How could Ana ever trust her again?

Ana folded the suggested reading and lists of elective subjects back into the brochure and tossed it on top of her wardrobe, where, gratifyingly, she heard it drop and slither down into the spider-infested gloom between wall and furniture. School could wait. Ana looked at her phone. Two missed calls from Chris and five messages. The last message ended with eight kisses and an emoticon of a rabbit with a black eye.

Perhaps she should forgive him. He'd run after her when she jumped out of the taxi, had done nothing but apologise since and, supposedly, had told his friend with the wandering hands to go fuck himself. He wasn't perfect, for sure but what boy was? They were all a bit rubbish at emotional stuff. Chris was more sensitive than most – his favourite film was something called Picnic at Hanging Rock. Some old Australian mystical film and about as far from superhero movies as you could get. Ana wanted his arms around him right now. She thought about figuring out the buses to get to Chris's place in Streatham (a house he shared with three boisterous Australians) and decided on a better course of action. She'd take a taxi.

Elena had moved the TV table over the 'secret' floorboard, but the furniture slid aside easy enough when Ana attacked it with her shoulder. She prised open the board and peered into musty darkness. Was the money still there? Ana's hand connected with an indeterminate ball of fluff which made her recoil in disgust as she reached further in.

No roll of cash anymore but... what was that? Something snagged around her thumb and Ana pulled her hand out to discover a small necklace – a string of tiny white skulls with miniature pink and black dice between them, open at the clasp. Ana fastened it and blew off some dust. It was cute, in a gothic kind of way.

She hadn't found any money though so, wearing her new find, she grudgingly replaced the board and shunted the TV table back into place. It would be buses after all.

Ana was applying her make-up and adjusting her top and push-up bra into some semblance of cleavage when there was a thumping knock at the door. The thumping mirrored her own heartbeat as it grew more forceful. Then silence, the shuffling of feet, deep male voices... and keys. One turned in the Yale lock. Ana rushed into her room and shut the door. Something told her nothing good could come of being discovered so she grabbed the handle of the door and held it tightly. There was a keyhole beneath the handle. Perhaps the intruder might think it was locked.

"We should come back when she's home. If she catches us..."

"What? She rents from Carver, he gave us keys, simple as."

"Agencies call ahead, or leave a note."

"Don't be such a wuss. Just get searching, will you?"

"I still don't think she took it."

"I don't either, but we gotta be sure. You take the bedrooms."

Ana felt panicky. None of the male voices were Robin's but one of them sounded familiar, nevertheless. She could peer through the keyhole, or she could make her escape—there was a fire escape just outside her window leading down from the upper floors.

Ana ducked down to squint through the hold in the door in time to see a heavy-set man approaching her bedroom door. She couldn't catch his face and instinctively stood up and grabbed the handle, wishing desperately that she'd opted for the window instead. She pulled at it with all her might, standing on tiptoes and trying desperately not to breathe too loud.

The handle moved a little under her fingers, but she held it in place.

"Think this one's locked."

"Shouldn't be. Try the bathroom will you and we'll come back to it."

The pressure on the handle fell away and as the intruder's footsteps receded, Ana exhaled. Then she skipped lightly over to the window, slid it open as quietly as she could, grabbed her trainers and climbed out through the foot-high gap. Heart pounding furiously, she tiptoed down the metal steps and ran around the corner, before wedging her shoes on and getting her phone out.

Ana had almost dialled her mum's number when she hesitated. Not yet. She didn't want her mum to stop her doing what she planned to do next. She phoned Chris. He answered after seven rings, just as Ana was about to give up.

"Chris. It's me."

Ana was gratified by the brightness in Chris's voice as he again apologised.

"It's fine. I need to come and see you. Want your advice about something."

They arranged for Chris to meet her at Streatham Hill station in an hour. She'd call her mum on the way there.

Or text her... probably.

CHAPTER 33

"Baked potato with chilli?" the young nose-pierced barman asked the room, as if he were posing some sort of existential dilemma.

"That's mine!" Robin waved, rescuing the quizzical South African.

"How can you eat that crap?" asked Elena, genuinely concerned as Robin began to wolf down the overcooked, steaming platter.

A pallid lettuce leaf acted as a miniature boat for half a radish. Elena guessed that this constituted a garnish to the chef of the Temperance.

"When I'm hungry I'll eat anything put in front of me... or anything I can basically reach," grunted Robin, between mouthfuls.

It had been surprisingly straightforward for Elena to reassure Robin that her dismissal of him the previous evening had been nothing more than a parent not wanting to make a scene in front of an outsider. Robin had only bridled slightly at being called an outsider. Elena had reminded him that, as he'd already pointed out, they had known one another for just six weeks, whereas she'd known Ana for over fourteen years.

"Fair enough," he'd said, then changed the topic to the investigation.

Robin had just spent five fruitless hours interviewing sex workers who had known Qamar. The few who even knew the victim/suicide's name denied knowing whether she had any enemies, unusual visitors or had complained of any especially abusive clients. To be honest, Robin hadn't expected to find much out by talking to the variously damaged or abused women who still worked the

223

Soho hotel bars, the streets or offered online 'escort services'. It wasn't just the old cliché (which bore some truth) about them being too afraid to talk. Partly, Robin realised, it was how depressingly circumspect and limited these women's lives were—they had conditioned themselves to ask no questions and make no judgements. That strategy worked best for themselves, their clients, and their employers. The less they knew and shared, the less exposed they felt.

Only one woman had let anything much slip—a voluptuous Nigerian girl called Sadie, who admitted she was planning to help Qamar with the administration of her massage, music, and meditation business. Sadie had said that, in recent months, Qamar had become more withdrawn and secretive than usual, more concerned about the security of her flat and her money. Sadie had said she thought Qamar was constantly "looking over her shoulder". When asked if she had any idea who Qamar might be afraid of, Sadie hadn't said anything but had mouthed a word. Carver.

Robin wasn't surprised. He's suspected the old lag was playing both sides, informing on his rivals whilst moving his core business—girls—more underground to evade the police. How he thought he could get away with it with Fleischer and Yarmouth on his heels, was anyone's guess. If Carver was threatening the girls in some way, he was probably using a heavy of some sort, but Sadie had no idea who this might be. Yarmouth felt this was vita— get to the foot-soldier, throw the book at him and he might well flip on Carver.

Their current endeavour, the one Yarmouth was fortifying himself for while Elena did her make-up and viewed his lunch with distaste, was probably a wild goose chase.

Still, Yarmouth had offered McPherson a drink and had to follow-up the stolen phone lead, as much to rule his nemesis out as anything else. Plus, viewed from a certain angle, hoodwinking his own adversary might be fun, especially if there was something salacious or compromising in the old bigot's phone.

They had an hour before McPherson arrived to get everything set. Yarmouth had taped the decoy phone under the table. He'd also enlisted the help of a young colleague from Digital Forensics called Nigel. The junior officer owed him a favour or two (Robin had listened to Nigel's lengthy tales of relationship break-up more times than was reasonable in Tom Fleischer's opinion).

Nigel sat in the corner of the pub tapping away at his laptop—apparently writing a science fiction novel—looking the very definition of the Soho 'remote worker'. He had iTunes loaded up, logged in to McPherson's account. Getting the password had been a little tricky—Yarmouth had to do some nifty work to persuade McPherson to log-in, supposedly to look up a playlist for a colleague's wedding reception (McPherson considered himself a bit of an expert on northern soul). Yarmouth had seen him type "Lou..." and then some numbers and, after a number of tries, had figured out that this equated to his wife's first name and birth year. Police officers were just as rubbish as everyone else at creating uncrackable passwords.

Fleischer was round the corner in a smutty bookshop, awaiting a text message. He'd just sent Yarmouth a photo of the front cover of a Robert Mapplethorpe book—two heavily oiled muscular nude men with the caption 'your boyfriends'. Fleischer was only a slightly more sophisticated a wit than McPherson.

Yarmouth pushed aside his plate and took a deep swig of his beer. Elena adjusted her cleavage, noticing that Robin had flicked a few longing glances her way throughout his meal. Teasing him was fun and if everything went well, Elena knew she'd invite him back later to make good on the promise of her slutty outfit. She'd hidden the miniskirt, tight white blouse missing a few buttons and red La Perla bra under a long, black coat this morning to evade her daughter's inquisitive glances. What she was about to do would be hard to explain.

Elena felt her pulse racing as a heavy-set, partially balding man in a suit two sizes too small for him marched over to their table, extending a bone-crushing handshake to Robin and a slobbery kiss to Elena.

"Robbo said he might be inviting his missus. Didn't do you justice love."

McPherson drew in breath, leaning back to assess Elena's figure. His gaze made her feel queasy, but she flashed him a toothy, lipsticked smile.

"I'm here to make sure he doesn't smash you in the face again."

McPherson looked uncertain, Elena's best deadpan expression wrong-footing him. Then he decided her response was hilarious and gave a baritone guffaw.

"Caught me on the back foot, he did. Won't happen again, that's for sure. Pint?"

This last word was aimed at Yarmouth, who merely waved his nearly empty glass in agreement.

"And for the lady?"

"What he's having," Elena said, thumbing Yarmouth.

With a raised eyebrow, McPherson gave a mock-bow.

"A modern woman I see, fair enough. Couple of largers it is, then."

Robin stopped him with a hand.

"My round. Least I can do."

McPherson didn't argue.

"Fair enough. Mine's a Stella. I'm off for a slash."

Then the bearlike Scotsman lumbered off to the loo, unfortunately still wearing his jacket, where his phone no doubt resided. As McPherson left, Elena leaned to whisper across the table:

"He's completely loathsome."

Yarmouth snorted into his last swallow of warm Kronenburg before heading to the bar.

"You're not wrong. So, let's befriend him quickly, run the switch and get the hell out of here."

Elena and Yarmouth put the plan into action in the middle of the second pint, when they'd both heard all the lairy anecdotes they could stand. First Yarmouth fired off a text under the table and excused himself, heading for the gents. Fleischer picked up the message and dialled, stepping out from the bookshop into the street. Eyes drilling deep into Elena's cleavage, McPherson answered on the seventh ring.

"This better be good, Tom, I'm out on the lash. You'll never guess with who. Nope. Try again. You're wide of the mark. It's only bloody Robbo Yarmouth… and his unexpectedly hot Bulgarian girlfriend…"

Here McPherson winked and cupped the receiver with one hand, feigning tact.

"Didn't catch the name, sweetheart."

"Elena. And I'm Romanian. Not bloody Bulgarian."

McPherson laughed, then listened.

"Yeah, come and join us. The more folk witness your mate's craven apology the better. He's even getting the drinks in. I know. Will wonders ever cease? Righty-ho. See you in five."

Shaking his head at how his evening was going, McPherson was about to slip his phone back in his pocket when Elena grabbed his hand. McPherson visibly gulped as she leaned closer.

"Nice case. Can I see it?"

McPherson was momentarily confused, then realised what she meant.

"This? Five ninety-nine from the market. Nothing special."

He passed it to her, and Elena made a show of looking the faux-leather case over before putting it back on the table, timing her action to give Robin enough time to return from the bar, carrying three pints with apparent (but faked) difficulty. McPherson looked like he was about to stand up and relieve Robin of one of the pints, then evidently thought better of it, preferring to watch him struggle.

Robin put the pints down on the table, pushing McPherson's phone off the table in the process. It fell to the carpeted floor and McPherson grunted and reached down for it. Elena stopped him.

"I'll get it."

"Sorry mate. I'm still a bit wobbly since I got stabbed," Robin interceded while Elena swapped McPherson's iPhone for their duplicate.

Elena hoped McPherson wouldn't hear the gaffer tape tearing from the bottom of the table or notice that the cover they had bought was very slightly darker than his own. She needn't have worried. Their mark was too busy teasing Robin for his effeminate pint-handling skills. McPherson pocketed the phone without comment.

Robin then excused himself to head to the gents, palming McPherson's phone and flicking it to mute before it could ring and give the game away. On the way to the loo, he passed Nigel and dropped the phone, minus case, into his hands. Nigel plugged the phone into his laptop and began to run a piece of cracking software, getting the phone's passcode in seconds, and uploading its contents. By the time Robin returned from the bathroom, Nigel was able to drop the phone back into Robin's jacket pocket.

The next bit was a little fiddly. Prompted with another text, Fleischer called Robin (on his iPhone). Robin frowned, listening to his colleague.

"I'm kind of two sheets to the wind. Can't it wait? Okay, give me a second, I'll go outside where it's less noisy."

Robin held up a hand to the others in apology and wandered outside, but not before dropping McPherson's phone into Elena's handbag. Elena now launched the operation's trickiest phase.

Leaning forward once more, her breasts squashed against the edge of the high table, she mock-whispered:

"He's always on that bloody phone. I'd mute it if I knew how."

McPherson rose to the bait.

"What's he got? An iPhone?"

"Yeah. I've never had one. Is that what you've got?"

"Yep, and it's dead easy to mute. Look."

McPherson showed her his phone's mute switch and Elena took it from him, flicking it up and down.

"McPherson, you massive twat!"

Fleischer's voice called from the doorway, distracting him and giving Elena the moment she needed to swap the phones back. She did it in such a panic that she fumbled

McPherson's over the edge of the table; he jammed a shoe under it as it fell to the carpet again.

"Just as well I got that bloody case," he muttered, putting it away and rising to give Fleischer a massive bear hug.

Elena tried not to break into a triumphant grin as Robin walked back in, as casually as possible, announcing that he had to head back to the office. To Elena, it felt like the triumphant denouement of a heist movie. She could even cope with the twenty minutes or so of McPherson and Fleisher's company it would take to down her pint and make her own excuses. Mission accomplished.

Cue credits and sassy music.

CHAPTER 34

They reconvened at Yarmouth's place, Elena having sent a message to Ana to tell her she would be home by nine pm. Ten minutes later, Ana hadn't replied but Elena realised that she'd better cut her daughter a little slack, given the scale of what Ana was dealing with, emotionally. It would be easier when she was at her new school; Elena suspected she missed her friends more than she was letting on. Having someone to bitch to about her mother was a teenage girl's inalienable right.

They stood hunched over Nigel's laptop, the room illuminated by a desk lamp and the dim blue glow of the computer, as Nigel clicked through endless photos of holidays, McPherson's family and (to Fleischer's amusement) downloaded photos of Chihuahuas wearing Mexican sombreros as well as a multitude of tedious or unhelpful text messages. All they had learned in their first hour of illicit snooping was that McPherson had a rather one-sided flirtatious text message 'thing' going with the female receptionist Cynthia at Scotland Yard and that he was surprisingly sentimental about his nephews and nieces.

Then appeared a folder called 'fun and games', which McPherson had managed to password protect. Badly, as it happens - Nigel had it open in seconds. They clicked through a series of photos and videos, whose lurid content reduced Yarmouth to a giggling mess and made Elena variously frown, laugh, and hide behind her hands.

In the first few photos, McPherson was undressing, apparently whilst wearing a disturbingly coy expression. Caught in a full-length mirror in one of the shots, it was clear the photographer was Qamar. In the next photos, the police detective lay named on the bed, in an attitude

231

of babyish helplessness, while Qamar talcum-powdered his genitals and bottom, dressed him in an adult-sized nappy (where do you buy such things? Elena wondered) and stuck a dummy in his mouth. There was a short video of McPherson's huge semi-naked bulk drooling over Qamar's shoulder while she grappled the immense 'infant' in an armchair, then another video of McPherson being changed – this one produced universal disgust in its unintended audience.

Both videos were evidently filmed from a fixed webcam, presumably on Qamar's laptop. McPherson did not acknowledge the camera.

"He doesn't know he's being filmed," Elena said.

Yarmouth nodded.

"But he did know about the photos."

"Taken on his phone. I guess he trusted her. But she filmed him secretly. I wonder why?"

"Insurance?" Yarmouth guessed.

"Blackmail material," snorted Fleischer. "If the boys at the station saw this, he'd never live it down."

"I don't think so," Elena said, "I think it's a game. Something they shared. She liked him, understood him. He trusted her. Look."

Again, they watched the shot where Qamar was rocking McPherson to sleep. A skein of milky drool ran across the shoulder of her black dress. McPherson's face was blissful, Qamar's expression surprisingly peaceful.

"She likes her job," Elena said. "Strange as it may seem, she's happy."

Fleischer shook his head.

"She's a good whore. Doesn't step out of character."

The vehemence of Fleisher's reply seemed to surprise even him.

"I mean, she's just good at her job. I'll bet there's more where that came from. Have a look."

Yarmouth rubbed the side of his face. Elena already knew him well enough to recognise this 'tell'. He wasn't comfortable.

"I don't know. There's nothing actually illegal in this video. There's no sexual touching. Sure, I can see how he might be mortified if this got out and there's a part of me would love if this leaked, but I don't buy it as a motivation for murder."

Fleischer nudged Nigel impatiently, looking like he wanted to grab the mouse and take over.

"Do a search or something."

Nigel looked over his shoulder incredulously.

"You want me to put 'homicidal rage' into a search field and see if anything pops up? That's not really how this works, you know."

Elena had a realisation.

"Put 'Qamar' in."

With a shrug that extended throughout his whole body, Nigel complied.

"Four years of computer science and a PhD in crypto-analysis for this. Hang on..."

Nigel had typed the murdered girl's name into the search field in Windows and hit "search everywhere". The laptop had whirred away for a few seconds without effect and then highlighted several messages within a folder in McPherson's email app. They were directed to QamarL@MMMtherapeutics.com and told a concise story of escalating rage.

Why are you sending me this? Is this supposed to be funny?

Don't you fucking dare. I'm not kidding.

I'm serious. This gets out, you're dead.

Elena and Yarmouth exchanged looks of astonishment.

"And there's your smoking gun," cried Fleischer triumphantly. "We've got him. Nice one mate."

He slapped Nigel on the back, heartily. Nigel shrank away.

"I didn't actually do anything an eight-year-old couldn't have."

The others ignored him, planning their strategy for arresting a senior police detective within their own force, despite having found the incriminating evidence illegally. After a few minutes' head-scratching Yarmouth came up with the answer.

"We get a warrant to search Qamar's email history, trace back the messages from there."

"Now that I can help you with," said Nigel, finally smiling. "The IP trail, that is."

"Well, great. Let's do it", Fleischer said. "For fuck's sake. You two look about as enthusiastic as a monk in a brothel."

Yarmouth and Elena were troubled each in their own way, for reasons that, for now at least, neither could quite put into words.

Driving back to Elena's, Robin placed a hand on Elena's knee, caressing her through her thin tights. At first reassuring, the pressure of his fingers grew more urgent as Robin's hand slipped under the hemline of her skirt, seeking somewhere warm to rest. Elena opened her legs slightly, finding herself suddenly wet, allowing him access. She leaned over, straining against the seatbelt and quietly murmured:

"Pull over. Somewhere quiet. Now, please."

They made logistically awkward love in the backseat of Robin's car, finally finding a position that worked—Elena's legs wrapped around Robin's back, his left hand cradling her head to stop it banging against the door, his other hand finding purchase on her exposed neck and shoulder. Elena's right hand gripped, absurdly, the handbrake as he thrust deeply into her. With each push, Elena lost a little more of herself but the feeling of everything slipping away felt good. That was what she was after. Robin was fervent, almost aggressive this time as his thumb pushed up under her chin.

"Ow!" Elena winced, feeling an incipient cramp building up.

Robin quickly finished, pulling out just in time to decorate the back seat and her stomach with his ejaculation. He reached down to touch her between her legs, but she gently pushed his hand away.

"It's okay. I can't in this position. Ouch."

Robin looked concerned as Elena rubbed the arch of her foot. His expression made her laugh.

"Looks, it's totally fine. It was crazy and I enjoyed it. Don't be so damn serious."

She took out some tissues from her bag and wiped herself and the seat down. She was kissing his frown away when her phone vibrated in her bag. Apparently, she had missed two calls already. It was Ana.

You coming home soon?

Elena sighed.

"I know is a drag, but I think I'll need some alone time with Ana tonight. Is that okay? We can meet tomorrow."

Robin nodded. "Whatever you need."

Then he insisted on driving her home anyway.

As the sound of Robin's BMW receded and Elena let herself into the flat, she was greeted by two perplexing sights. The first was Chris, sitting drinking tea with Ana and watching The Walking Dead on an iPad. The second was a subtly ransacked room. Cushions lay on the floor, paintings had been left hanging askew, the sofa pushed away from the wall. Nothing was actually damaged or torn but everything was substantially out of place. If this was Ana 'acting up' she had a weirdly avant-garde way of doing it.

"Ana, what the hell?"

"It wasn't me mum! I've got a hell of a story to tell you. It's why Chris is here..."

"Sorry, Miss Bal...," Chris began, sheepishly.

"Be quiet!" Elena said, with more force than she'd intended. "You are on probation, mister. At best. Now—Ana?"

Ana poured out the story of the two men who had let themselves into the flat, searched it thoroughly and apparently left, while she waited on a Soho Square bench for Chris. Chris had brought his older brother's cricket bat, in lieu of something more traditional, and they had crept back into the apartment a couple of hours after the strangers' intrusion.

"Why didn't you call me, for Christ's sake?" Elena interjected at this point.

"You were busy... and anyway, they knocked first... and they had a key. Maybe they were from the landlord or something."

"Then why did you hide?"

"I dunno. I had this weird feeling about them. They were looking for something."

"So I see," said Elena, scanning the room.

She walked around the flat and saw that the situation was the same everywhere—drawers were left open in the kitchen, the contents of cupboards scattered on the counters. In the bathroom the mat was crumpled up in the bath and toothbrushes and moisturiser discarded in the sink.

Then Elena panicked. She raced through to the living room and prised up the loose board behind the sofa. When she got it open, Chris piped up, unnecessarily:

"Cool!"

Elena shot him a withering glance as she reached into the darkness and withdrew the roll of money, not bothering to hide it from her daughter's boyfriend.

"They didn't take the cash?" Said Elena, half to herself.

"Maybe they didn't find it," suggested Ana.

"You did," countered Elena.

The sofa, whose leg had stood firmly over the secret hiding place, had been moved out. It seemed unlikely the mystery men had failed to spot the one loose board underneath. What had they been looking for?

Elena got as full a description of the men as she could (from the chest down, since that's all Ana saw), including their voices, how old they sounded, their clothing and posture. She'd need this to relay to Robin...eventually. She had an idea who the men might be; or rather, who they might be employed by. First thing in the morning she'd check out her intuition. She wouldn't involve Robin just yet. This one was just for her.

CHAPTER 35

Janine Clarke was used to angry customers. Her employer wasn't the most generous of providers towards his growing list of tenants. It seemed that every other day someone's boiler was on the blink, or a couple's flat had been flooded, or a family three months behind on rent had mysteriously had all their crappy furniture tossed out onto the street with 'Take me: I'm yours' signs pinned to them. What she wasn't used to, was a perfectly calm but utterly immovable eastern European woman refusing to leave the waiting area until she'd seen the boss.

"He may be some time. There's a big deal in process. Wouldn't it be better if I called you when he does have time to see you?"

"I can wait. Either he see me, or his police friends. I think he prefer to talk to me. Oh, and by the way, I hear you whisper, 'I think she's Hungarian or something' and, for your information, I am Romanian. There's a world of difference."

With that, Elena turned back to her paper and Janine finally had to admit that she was defeated. She knew Carver wanted to leave for one of his long, boozy Friday lunches but the only way out of his office, apart from a window and drainpipe getaway, was through his frosted glass door. Elena had him trapped.

Twelve minutes later, the door opened and Carver, in heavy raincoat and trilby stormed out and almost made it to the office front door before Elena interceded.

"I need to talk to you."

"I'm sure you do, but as my girl here told you, I'm a busy man. Things to see, people to do, maybe another time."

Carver attempted to side-step Elena, but she was too nimble for him and darted sideways in tandem.

"I know your men were round my place."

There it was. The frown. An instinctive response, hard to conceal.

"Don't know what you're talking about love. Which place?"

"Flat 11—Robin Yarmouth arranged. You know this, so stop playing dumb. Anyway. Two men were in my flat, ransacking, last night. I have fourteen-year-old daughter! The only reason I've not informed the police is…"

"Wait a minute. What are you on about?" wheedled Carver. "Come inside."

He made a faux-magnanimous gesture towards his open office door and Elena followed him in where, she noted, he carefully closed the door, took off his trilby, and lowered his voice.

"What did these men look like, exactly?"

"You know what they looked like. They mentioned your name."

"They what? Back it up a bit. Tell me what happened from the start."

Now Carver seemed to be playing the role of concerned uncle, sitting with fingertips touching, elbows on the desk, as if channelling don Corleone (or at the very least, Ray Winstone).

Elena sighed and decided to play along. She told him all that Ana had told her. She felt certain she would know if Carver was lying. For all his would-be gangsterisms, he was easy to read and lacking in subtlety. Carver took it all in, then nodded sagely.

"The fucking little weasels."

He let that hang in the air for a moment.

"Bent coppers. Lowest of the low. They've got all my keys and warrants mean fuck all to them. Probably got wind of you having a little money or something."

Now it was Elena's time to feel baffled.

"These men were police?"

"Most likely. They came to see you, after that Qamar girl topped herself, didn't they? Probably noticed you're not exactly established, foreign, probably don't have a bank account yet or, like me, you don't trust banks at all. Bankers are down there with bent coppers, if you ask me—ninth circle of hell. Anyways, you said they were looking for something?"

Elena nodded.

"But it sounded like a specific thing, not the off-chance of some hidden cash."

Elena of course couldn't tell him that he was spot-on about her concealing money. Nor should she reveal that these supposedly crooked policemen hadn't found the cash, or hadn't taken it.

"One of them said "I don't think she took it", meaning me, I guess, or maybe Qamar. The point is, they had your keys."

"Darling, they're the police. I gave them my spare set of keys when that—thing—happened in your place. Our little arrangement is going to have to come to an end soon, you know that, don't you?"

Was he changing the subject deliberately? Elena wouldn't bite.

"So you didn't send them?"

"Why the hell would I? I'm trying to lay low, avoid trouble. And your building's scheduled for redevelopment. I've got money in that place. I'm trying to encourage people to leave but not by ransacking their flats."

"No, by putting their rent up to the point where they have to invite creeps in to abuse and murder them."

The vehemence of this came out of nowhere and surprised even Elena.

"Murder? What are you on about?"

"Qamar. She was killed."

"I thought she hanged herself and left a note."

"She was found hanged and there was a note, yes. But she was murdered, believe me."

Elena leaned back and watched Carver. His usually impassive, boxer's face was betraying a thought process—he was either considering how to lie to her or he was considering whether to tell her the truth.

"That girl had no enemies. She was a peach. A really classy lady."

Was that a catch in his voice?

"I know," Elena said. "Spent an evening with her. She was full of life, full of ideas. She want to get away from you and your sleaze."

Carver laughed, meaner now.

"My sleaze paid her rent, darling. Just as it pays yours. I got the girls on the site, to get them off the street. They make good money, work from home. If they decide to see customers at their place, that's their lookout. I advise against it."

"What are you talking about? What site?"

"PhantasyGirls dot tv. Camgirl site. Qamar was a star attraction. They don't even have to go fully nude or use toys or anything—it's all up to them."

Elena remembered Qamar saying something about a website she 'posed' for. Carver seemed genuinely upset that Elena might think he had something to do with her death.

"Look, sweetheart. I've been a pimp, a dealer, I've fenced, I've done all sorts, but I am not a murderer and whoever is rooting around your stuff, it isn't anything to do with me. Tell, you what though. You might want to ask your boy Yarmouth what he knows. Or DI Fleischer. I told them both about those boys but apparently confidential informants 'aint meant to squeal on the coppers, just the crims."

"What are their names?"

"Fleischer has them. He's my main contact."

Carver rubbed his neck and sighed as Elena sat with fingers poised over her phone on its 'notes' application.

"Barnett and O'Neill," he said decisively. "No... O'Reilly. O'Leary! That's it—some dumb paddy."

Carver affected an Oxbridge accent.

"Would you mind terribly if I had my lunch now, dearie?"

"Fine. Thank you."

Elena put her phone away and walked to the door. Carver grabbed his hat.

"Say what you like about Frances. She certainly had a good eye for the talent."

Elena stopped, frozen in surprise. She turned, affecting nonchalance.

"Frances? You mean Frances da Costa? You know her?"

"Known her for years. She recruited Qamar. And you."

"Me?" Elena laughed outright. "What are you saying? Recruited me?"

"What exactly do you think you're doing here?"

Elena felt blood flooding to her face as Carver breezed by her and left the office. Maybe Carver did know

Frances—perhaps that's where the forged papers had come from. But why 'recruited'?

A bizarre idea formed unbidden. Frances was a Ghislaine Maxwell type. A procurer. Elena had been chosen to… no, the very notion was absurd. Carver was just trying to spook her, divert her from digging any further into his business. It was unthinkable that Frances might have seen in her the kind of vulnerability that Qamar and her upstairs neighbour had.

So why was she thinking it?

CHAPTER 36

McPherson was in his dressing gown eating Coco Pops and watching Saturday Kitchen when his colleagues came from him, two discreetly chosen constables noted for their tact and muscularity, plus DI Shah. All three prepared expressions of professional blandness as they knocked on the front door of McPherson's three-bed semi in New Malden, disturbing the homeowner's appreciation of Antonio Banderas preparing a Spanish omelette whilst being interviewed about the new Almodovar movie. Funnily enough, when he answered at the third knock, McPherson led his colleagues into the lounge and turned off the TV as if he'd been caught watching hardcore pornography.

"What's this all about, lady and gents? On me day off, too. Just as well I wasn't having a Tommy tank, isn't it?"

Shah swept aside the banter with a hand gesture and cut to the chase.

"CI Robert McPherson, we would like you to come down to the Yard and answer a few questions for us."

McPherson framed a laugh, then killed it.

"You're joking, love? About what, exactly? I paid my parking fines. Is this that arse Yarmouth having a laugh?"

O'Leary, one of the constables, shook his head, eyes downcast. Seeing his colleague's embarrassment, McPherson stiffened.

"Are you arresting me?"

"We're questioning you. Under caution," Shah clarified. "You do not have to say anything. But it may harm your defence if..."

"Yeah, yeah, I know the rigamarole. What case?"

"Qamar Liibaan," Shah said.

244

"Never heard of him."

Shah sighed. This was going to be as awkward as she'd imagined.

"Just come down to the station and we'll clear it up, then. We assumed suicide. It now looks like murder. The evidence is strong. You've come up on a CCTV feed and it's possible someone has been hacking your email account. We just need to clarify a few things."

"Bloody Nora! I'm a suspect?"

"You were in Soho at about the right time. We have CCTV and witnesses. But we shouldn't do this here. Is your wife out with the twins?"

"Swimming lessons. I don't want her to know anything about this."

"Fine. Make an excuse. We need you to come with us now though."

"Really? Or what?"

McPherson didn't quite square up to Shah, but the implication hung in the air. DI Shah tapped the handcuffs at her belt and nodded to her well-built colleagues.

"You don't want to go that way, Bob."

Neither Yarmouth nor Fleischer could question their colleague, for reasons DCI Purvis described vaguely as "conflicts of interest". What he meant, of course, was that Yarmouth had once belted the suspect in the face, whilst Fleischer had been on one too many drunken benders with him. Yarmouth thought Fleischer seemed subdued but was a little surprised by how little he seemed to be defending his sometime partner.

"Do you really think he did it?" Yarmouth asked, as they looked through the one-way glass into Interrogation

Room 2 where Bob McPherson sat slumped in a metal chair like a very confused sack of potatoes.

Against usual protocol for a murder suspect, McPherson had not been hand-cuffed to the table. He was trying his best to look bored, thought Yarmouth, rather than tense or fearful. Yarmouth wished he could be the one trying to catch his ex-boss in a lie, rather than DI Shah, but it was her case, her problem if McPherson was guilty. Yarmouth almost wished it wasn't true. If anti-corruption were called in, the department would find itself under a lot of unhelpful scrutiny. Shah had been instructed by Purvis to "clear Bob as soon as possible", as if McPherson's innocence were a foregone conclusion.

"I don't know. He's always had a temper and his relationships with women have been, it has to be said, pretty fucked up. But I don't see him as a killer."

"Maybe he lost it in a moment of rage, covered it up?"

"The suicide note?" Said Fleischer with a sceptical look.

"Of course."

The note showed premeditation, thought Yarmouth. The killer made Qamar write the note. She knew her fate, because she left the word "murder" encoded there. This was a crime committed in cold blood. Was McPherson the type? It seemed a stretch.

DI Shah entered the room, dressed immaculately, carefully poised. She sat down in the chair opposite the suspect. The furniture was bolted to the floor to minimise the potential for violence (for some suspects, the CCTV cameras and microphones weren't enough of a deterrent). Behind her entered DC O'Leary, flicking a wave to the darkened glass behind which Yarmouth and Fleischer waited. Yarmouth almost waved back, stopping himself. Why did he feel so distracted, so exhausted?

"For the record, entering the room is DI Sanchita Shah and DC Adam O'Leary. Interview with Robert Hugh McPherson starts at 11:35am."

Shah turned to Bob, flashing a brief, disarming smile. Yarmouth had forgotten how beautiful she could be when she smiled. It had happened all too rarely when they had dated.

"Bob. You don't mind if I call you that, do you?"

McPherson shrugged.

"Can we get this over with? I told the missus I'd be back to take them all out for a Harvester. Place gets a bit packed by 12:30."

"I think that's unlikely to happen, Bob. Can you take a look at these photos and tell me if that's you, entering the stairwell at Carlisle Street? The frame grabs are from the camera at the end of the street, taken at 1:25am."

Bob's eyes involuntarily widened as he looked at three glossy printouts of the blurry image of him leaving Qamar's flat and then having his phone stolen.

"Might be."

"And what were you doing there?" Continued Shah.

"I'm pretty sure you already know. You've got my phone data, right?"

Shah's mouth betrayed the ghost of a smile.

"I'm going to have to ask you to confirm it. For the recording."

Bob rubbed his face with both hands and spoke in a low, steady voice.

"Sure. I used to visit this woman, Qamar. For the odd massage, and some other services."

"Prostitution?"

"No. Not really. We never had sex or nothing. I'm not stupid."

Bob looked challengingly at Shah. He thinks he's clever, thought Yarmouth.

"It's only soliciting if sex takes place and money changes hands, 'aint it?"

"We just need to know what you were doing, Bob."

"Look, you've got the photos. They're probably all round the department by now. Fucking Robbo and that cunt Flasher."

There was something oddly endearing in McPherson still using nicknames, even for men he actively loathed.

"You seem angry Bob. Did Qamar make you angry too?"

"What? No, of course not."

"Then how did she make you feel?"

Shah had him with that question. The suspect's bottom lip began to quiver.

The word came out of Robert McPherson almost as a sob. He suddenly seemed much smaller, as if he were crumpling in upon himself.

"Safe. She made me feel safe."

CHAPTER 37

Elena sat opposite from Chris and Ana, watching her daughter fidget with a strand of her hair and the mixed-race boy looking at anything other than Elena's face. They sat with lattes and, in Ana's case, a hot chocolate on top of which Luca had heaped a pile of miniature marshmallows, with a wink at the sullen girl.

Elena cleared her throat. She hated this stuff, trying to negotiate the thorny territory between discipline and understanding.

"So, Chris. I want to thank you for coming to help my daughter, first. She should have called her mother, of course. But you came to help, and that's good."

"Here it comes," mumbled Ana, examining her nails. "The but."

Elena looked at her daughter, flashing her the trademark stare that usually silenced her.

"Chris. My daughter is fourteen."

"Nearly fifteen!" Ana interjected then, receiving the look again, quietened.

"She is underage. In terms of, well, you know. And you are much older."

"I'm eighteen, sure. I know. I'd be wary in your position too."

The nerve of this lad!

"Yes, thanks for that," Elena said with barely controlled sarcasm. "Is time for mother to talk and her daughter's boyfriend to listen."

At that, Ana looked up from her nails, something like awe in her eyes.

"I'm not naïve and I'm not stupid. I know kids grow up fast these days. If you have had sex, I'm not going to report you."

"Mum!"

Now it was Chris's turn to squirm. He looked like he wanted to slip quietly under the table and run for the door. Except he didn't. Instead, he nodded gravely, almost a parody of how he thought a responsible person would respond to this excruciating interrogation.

"My intentions are pure, swear down."

At this both Elena and her daughter laughed in unison.

"Whatever," Elena said, struggling to maintain an appropriately adult demeanour. "I just want to know that you're sensible and careful and respectful."

"Always, Mrs B. Always."

And with that, Chris turned to look at Ana and she gripped his forearm supportively. It was enough to send a prickle of moisture to Elena's eyes. She had made that very gesture herself, not long before, when Robin had been recounting the trauma of his knife assault. Ana was growing up—an obvious truism it was no longer wise to ignore.

Little more needed to be said and both Chris and Ana seemed to get the message. They surprised Elena by saying they were heading off to the V&A museum. Chris had bought tickets to an exhibition about the 1960s—fashion, music, and revolution. He even showed them to Elena, as if providing his homework to a teacher. Chris was a lot younger than the plain fact of his years.

Ana kissed her mother on the cheek and headed out, hand in hand with Chris, passing Robin in the doorway. Robin greeted Ana with a hand on her shoulder and Elena could see Ana introducing Chris. Robin shook the boy's hand and watched the kids wander off down Frith Street. Then Robin paused in the doorway for a moment, looking for Elena. He looked older in plain clothes, more at home. His smile made Elena instantly relax, as she rose to kiss him.

"Did the suspects give you what you needed?" Robin said.

"They did," laughed Elena. "He's good boy. Ana's crazy about him. First love. It won't last."

"A scary moment, for any parent," remarked Robin.

Then his expression changed. Elena recognised this change—he was moving into business mode.

"Shah called me. McPherson's admitting visiting Qamar on the night in question, and falsifying the evidence record so he could take his phone back. That's a suspension right there. He's adamantly refusing to admit anything relating to Qamar's murder. And he's just lawyered up, so I wouldn't count on getting anything more from him."

"But the evidence?"

"Compelling but circumstantial. That's the word from the CPD. We need DNA—not in Qamar's apartment but somewhere on her person. We know McPherson was a regular so we would expect to see prints, hair et cetera. What we need is something linking his presence explicitly to the killing."

"What about the cord she was strangled with, or suicide note?"

"Forensics are giving them the works. Should have the results in the next few days."

"And the text messages?"

"We got his phone easy enough, which suggests someone else might have too."

"Come on!" Elena said, exasperated.

"It's really hard to prove provenance of electronic messages. These days, even your twelve-year-old nephew can hack phones. I'm convinced those messages are his, but a jury might not be."

"If we had the laptop..."

"You're right," Robin sighed, miming to Luca that he wanted an espresso. "It could all hinge on that. We got a warrant for McPherson's house and for his mum's place in Clapham, just in case. He visits her every weekend. I think he might have a lock-up somewhere too."

"He's got many friends in the police, hasn't he?" Elena asked, delicately.

"I guess. Where are you going with this?"

The way Robin asked the question, it seemed more like he was challenging her than accusing her. He wanted to know if she understood what they were facing.

"Can you trust the officers searching his place? Not to... misplace anything?"

"I'm with you on that. I'll be attending all three searches. And McPherson's on suspension and under surveillance. We haven't arrested him just yet but that'll come the moment we get a bit of positive DNA."

Elena leaned back in her chair, digesting it all. "Why though?"

"Why what?"

"Why did he do it? You said he was racist, a total asshole. But killer?"

"I don't know. Maybe she told him their mother and baby sessions were going to end. He couldn't handle it, wanted her to commit to more. She refused. His temper flared up..."

Now Robin sat back, and they sized one another up across the table. Neither looked satisfied with Robin's explanation.

"What can I say?" added Robin, to fill the silence. "People are unpredictable."

CHAPTER 38

The weather was sympathetically dour as the funeral party of Qamar Liibaan shivered in the drizzle that blew across Waltham Islamic Cemetery. Under faintly buzzing electricity lines that looped between pylons that stood like guardians over the high hillside, a paltry group of mourners lowered the shrouded body of Qamar Liibaan into the ground.

Taifa Liibaan stood with her mother, her father Abdullahi noticeably absent. Evidently his pride was more important than being a compassionate father, thought Elena bitterly as she stood with Ana, respectfully distant. Three or four other mourners Elena did not recognise flanked the grave as Qamar was lowered by four men, clad in surprisingly colourful suits. They had carried her there in a casket, but now lifted her simply swathed body out on elegant golden linen and laid the ends over her prone, surprisingly light body.

Elena wondered about the lack of mourners. She later found out that the rumours that had quickly spread through the clan about Qamar's profession has resulted in many family members deciding not to attend. It made Elena angry, but then she knew little about the culture she was respectfully observing.

Qamar was laid on her side in the open grave, surprising Elena. Facing Mecca? she wondered. She half-regretted coming—no-one had acknowledged her presence yet. That thought immediately made her feel guilty; of course, the mourners had only one thing on their minds—their abused and murdered loved one.

After the simple ceremony, at which Qur'anic verses were recited and simple gestures of mourning made,

Elena was approached by Taifa, who looked quite different in her long, dark blue headscarf and robe. Elena felt guilty about the presupposition that she'd been ignored before.

"Would you like to attend the mosque? We'll have a small ceremony there and some food. You'd be most welcome."

Elena felt a little awkward about it and declined as gracefully as possible. This too was not the time to bring up the subject of the laptop. As it was, the funeral had been delayed by the inquest and the Islamic tradition of burial within 24 hours of death had not been observed. Elena did not want to remind anyone that she was the one responsible for setting off the chain of events that had led to this situation.

Taifa clasped her hand tightly as she made to return to her family.

"Thank you for coming," she said. "It means a lot".

Elena felt a lump rise in her throat.

"Thanks for inviting me."

She was going to leave it at that but then added, "I assure, I'm going to find out who killed Qamar. I promise". It felt vital to make her determination clear.

Taifa murmured a low "thank you" and turned to leave.

Elena would have loved to have asked Taifa about her sister's laptop—maybe she had an idea who'd taken it—but now was very definitely not the time. Perhaps she wasn't made for this sort of thing after all. She wished she'd asked Robin to come with her and wondered why she hadn't even mentioned the funeral to him.

Elena was still getting used to having anyone else to consider but her and her daughter. Things were changing faster than Elena could keep up with.

CHAPTER 39

"He's what?!" shouted Robin, at a volume that surprised even him.

Across the car park, a couple of police constables, loading equipment into the back of a van, stopped and looked over. Robin waved, encouragingly. DCI Purvis was using his most mollifying tone.

"He's been offered, and has accepted, a plea bargain. There's a lot more going on here than we thought. Can you pop in, when you've a moment and I'll take you through it."

"I'll be there in five. I'm right outside."

It was Monday morning, just after 10am. On Sunday Yarmouth had received a text from the duty officer at the station telling him PC Conover was awake and compos mentis. Robin had called the hospital immediately, arranging a visit the following morning.

Robin had just spent an hour with Conover, who was in recovery, still woozy and on painkillers but ambling about. His head was wrapped in bandages, and he sported an eye-patch (he'd detached a retina during his fall) but otherwise in good spirits. The consultant said he could probably be discharged in a couple of days.

Huge relief that had flooded Yarmouth when he'd seen his onetime partner awake and capable again. Along with it came a release of latent guilt, something he'd been irrationally carrying since the attack. He showed Conover his own scar, now pale and insignificant compared to the young officer's own wounds. Conover laughed, displaying the bravado common to both young men and police officers.

Yarmouth had been glad to tell him about their attackers' capture, arrest and likely sentencing. A court date was set for about a week hence, delayed several times once lawyers stepped in. Now Yarmouth faced the onerous task of explaining to his partner that it wasn't going to prove quite so simple as locking the lads up in Feltham Young Offenders for a year or two.

Minutes later, he was climbing the glass stairs to Purvis's office. This time round, the boss was surrounded by files. He peered over the top of a stack of manila folders as Yarmouth knocked and entered.

"Cold case review. Always my favourite task," Purvis muttered, getting up to move yet more folders off a chair so that Yarmouth could sit. Yarmouth had no time for levity as he slumped down.

"The scooter thieves. What's the deal?"

"Well. Turns out the lads weren't of a purely entrepreneurial bent."

Yarmouth signed inwardly. Purvis had a knack of talking this way when it was least helpful.

"They were put up to it," Purvis explained. "Asked to steal McPherson's phone."

"Really? By whom?"

"That's what we're trying to ascertain. We do know that they were approached by two men in a pub and forwarded a photo of McPherson. They'd been stealing phones already but if you look at the report, you'll see the last six phones taken were all from men in their late forties roughly matching McPherson's description..."

"Brick shithouse."

"Well, quite."

"So why the deal?"

"One of the lads alleges that one of the men might have been a police officer."

"Sounds kind of vague. The little fuckers will say whatever they think will keep them out of prison."

"True. But Internal Affairs are already sniffing around the department, following McPherson's arrest, so we do need to get to the bottom of it. One of them won't talk at all but his friend has offered to ID the men who hired him, in exchange for a lighter sentence."

"And CPD okayed this?"

"They'll push for a year, but it won't even be manslaughter. GBH, most likely. ID parade's set for Thursday if we get the go-ahead from CPD."

"Fucksake. Mind my French, sir. But fuck."

Yarmouth couldn't believe it. Then again, if he really tried as hard as he could to empathise with the boys, he supposed they knew they would be in trouble for being caught and it was a brave move to point the finger back at the police. If it was true, the department looked like it had a real problem. As if things weren't already difficult enough, with a broadside of institutional racism and sexism accusations in play.

"I'm meeting IA to brief them at 3pm today," said Purvis. "Hopefully by then, CPD and the boy's lawyer will have firmed up the deal. I'd like you to question the other kid, if you're okay with that? See if we can get a corroboration. Belt and braces sort of thing."

Yarmouth knew Purvis was looking for signs of rage or frustration in him, so he merely shrugged.

"Fine. I'm over it."

"The counselling helped?"

Yarmouth hadn't attended more than the first thirty-minute session with the trauma counsellor. Still, he nodded.

"Just let me know when."

Elena took his hands in hers when Yarmouth recounted the conversation over lunch later. She was grabbing an hour during her working day at Voices Unlimited. A family of Syrian refugees caught hiding in a fishing trawler in Gravesend had been sent her way and Elena was working with the translator to get their story into some short of shape for the immigration authorities. She'd started off doing pure translation work for the Romanians adrift in London but Tony and Aldona appreciated her so much they had her working on some of their 'crisis cases' too. Elena, on a zero hours contract, was just glad for the hours.

As she'd relayed this to Robin, he'd made the appropriate congratulatory noises, but she could see he was pre-occupied. Finally, he came out with it.

"I have a feeling I know who those men in your place were. If Carver was right, they could be the same guys who arranged to have McPherson's phone lifted. I think it might be a blackmail scam."

"And you think they were in my place looking for more material on Qamar's laptop?"

"Well, we probably caught them before they could download the stuff on the phone. And who knows what records she kept."

"With McPherson arrested and his phone back in custody, the blackmailers couldn't get anything from him though. Perhaps there were others."

Elena suddenly squeezed his hand intensely, excitedly.

"Her webcam. Carver linked her into this camgirl site. Maybe she had some sort of app, recording what the webcam saw. She might have left it on, recorded her clients."

Yarmouth paused, fork of linguine halfway to his mouth.

"How do you know that? About the site?"

Elena didn't think it was the right time to reveal her secret visit to Carver.

"Nigel emailed me," she said as casually as possible. "Something came up in his searches. Didn't he copy you?"

"No, he did not. Jesus. We need to track that laptop down before those guys do."

"The dirty cops Carver mentioned?" Elena asked.

"Maybe."

"You could show the kids their photos."

"I could," Robin mused.

Elena loved the way his pupils flicked back and forth when he was thinking intently. It reminded her of an English flautist she'd once seen on TV—John Galway... perhaps James.

"Fuck, I've got it!" Robin cried. "The line-up. Sometimes the plain clothes officers stand-in, when we don't get enough guys turning up from our volunteer lists."

"People volunteer to be in line-ups?"

"Sure—we have a whole database. Thirty quid an appearance, even if you don't get called."

"And why is that better than the photos?"

"Because I can check them out—see how they react. Whether they are hesitant, cocky, nervous..."

"Sounds like a plan."

Elena couldn't resist reaching out across Luca's low, square table and kissing Robin, even though she was generally not one for public displays of affection. Something about this shared experience of detection and investigation was peculiarly stimulating. That thought made her feel immediately guilty, like she was somehow benefitting from Qamar's death.

"How did Ana get on at her new school?"

Elena was grateful Robin had changed the subject. On her way to meeting him, she had dropped her daughter off around the corner from the school, in the time-honoured manner of parents of painfully self-conscious teenagers. Was she imagining it or was Ana simultaneously growing up at an alarming rate and becoming more neurotic? Come to think of it, remembering her own adolescence, those conflicting influences had seemed to run in tandem.

"Fine, I think. At first she was worried about all other girls being in groups or gangs and her being outsider. Not a problem. She texted me at lunchtime to say her accent is already a talking point. Hopefully in good way."

"She'll be fine. Fast forward six months and she'll be the most popular girl in school. She has to be—she has your hair and eyes."

There was something of a catch in Robin's voice as he said this, like he was looking at Elena anew. She felt her pulse accelerate. Uh-oh. That old tugging, yearning sensation was starting—surely it was too soon. She hadn't even hit the three-month mark yet. I can't love him. I just can't, she thought as she mock-batted her eyelashes, deflecting her anxiety.

"You Casanova. Flattery will get you…. Well, whatever you want."

This last bit as a whisper. They finished their coffees and made a hasty exit, Luca waving a folded apron at them as they left.

"See you again soon, my friends!"

CHAPTER 40

Is this it? wondered Yarmouth, eyeing the motley crew of thirtysomething men from the doorway to the public waiting room at the Savile Row Station. The men sat in silence, engrossed in their smartphones, newspapers or, in one case, fast asleep with folded arms and listening to prog rock.

"Best we could pull together at short notice," Fleischer said, seeming to read Yarmouth's mind, as he often did.

They had spent the best part of an hour looking at photo-fits of the man that 17-year-old Sidney Sutton, the scooter recidivist, had described as approaching him in the street. He'd apparently flashed a badge too quickly to read and said his name was DC Leamington (of course, there was no such detective at the station). He'd known about their convictions - the older boy had stolen mopeds and a couple of cars, the younger had been pinched for spraying graffiti and breaking and entering. The stranger had also appeared to know that one was riding a stolen Vespa and he had offered them a deal—arrest or do "a little favour". That favour had been to look out for a man matching McPherson's description in the vicinity of Qamar's flat and steal his phone.

The photo-fit did look a lot like O'Leary but then it was also generic enough to fit a fairly large swathe of late thirties, early forties, slightly overweight white men with closely cropped hair. Fleischer laughed and ran his hair over his own head when he first saw the image emerge from the printer.

"Okay, you got me bang to rights officer, it was me." Fleischer led out his wrists in mock-surrender. "Knew I shouldn't have got that buzz cut. Dead giveaway."

Yarmouth and Fleischer had made sure the identity parade was set for a day when O'Leary and Barnett were in the station doing administration. Helpfully, a memo had been circulated from Purvis's office last week stressing the importance of paperwork. For once, O'Leary was toeing the line.

Yarmouth sent all but two men away, paying them the minimum turn-out rate for their time. The two that remained were both Eastern-European men, one from Serbia, the other from Hungary. They shuffled dutifully into the narrow, brightly lit ID room, facing the one-way glass, and trying their best to look neutral, their hands level at their sides like soldiers 'at ease'. Seasoned pros.

Fleischer called out across the office. "O'Leary! Bob! Come over here, will you?"

O'Leary looked wary as he sauntered over, his partner a little cockier.

"You wouldn't mind filling in, would you? For the beauty contest. We got a right bunch of muppets in this morning. One bloke had just got himself an afro, looked nothing like his picture in the book."

Barnett exchanged an enquiring look with his partner.

"I don't know. The Sarge is breathing down our backs and I'm a bit behind," said O'Leary, avoiding eye contact.

"Won't take a moment," said Yarmouth. "You've not met the scooter lads we picked the other week, have you?"

"What scooter lads?" said Barnett disingenuously.

"Great stuff. One's willing to talk—we just need his thumbs up. Only take a jiffy."

O'Leary gave Yarmouth a look that could either be interpreted as routine cynicism or an attempt to brave it out.

"Whatever you say, friend."

Minutes later, O'Leary and Barnett flanked the paid line-up volunteers, each of them in rumpled suit trousers and plain blue shirt. Barnett especially looked unnerved. O'Leary stood with his arms crossed.

"There should be five, at least," O'Leary muttered.

Robin sighed. He'd anticipated this tactic. Show willing then welch at the last minute. O'Leary wasn't usually a stickler for protocol.

"Fleischer, you wouldn't mind joining the gang, would you?"

For a moment, Fleischer looked taken aback. Yarmouth hadn't mentioned this idea to his colleague, since Fleischer wasn't the most natural of actors and Yarmouth wanted his spontaneity to feel real. Fleischer nodded.

"Sure. I've not met the dozy cunts, either. Take my jacket, will you?"

Fleischer handed his jacket and tie to Yarmouth, who left the room, leaving the five men to sweat in the perpetually overheated little room.

In the office on the other side of the glass, Shah had finished briefing the first of the two lads. He nodded sagely, as if he were DI Shah's colleague, rather than a potential informant. Then he took a wide stance in front of the glass and squinted, head on one side, at the line-up.

"Number four!" he said, pointing directly and confidently at Barnett.

"Are you sure?" Shah prompted. "Take your time."

"Nah, I'm sure. Swear down," the kid said, sucking at his teeth.

"Thank you," Shah said, leading the boy out.

A few minutes later she returned with the other kid, who looked a lot more cowed and bedraggled, and no older than his seventeen years. He too identified Barnett, although with a little less confidence.

A few minutes later, once the volunteers had collected their cash and departed the premises, Robin turned to O'Leary and colleague.

"Guess it wasn't our day. They both fingered Barnett here."

Barnett laughed nervously.

"Bad luck," said O'Leary. "Looks like you're going down, my son."

O'Leary punched his partner's shoulder playfully. Barnett didn't retaliate, looking more baffled than fearful.

"Guess you've just got one of those faces," Fleischer added, letting him off the hook. "Back to square one."

A couple of hours later, Yarmouth sat with Elena and Ana round their new dining table (Freecycle, dismantled and bundled into a £12 Uber), looking at photos of O'Leary and Barnett borrowed from a departmental Christmas photo session (Purvis's initiative and taken far from seriously by his men).

"Well, they look the right size. I mean, body-wise," Ana said. "You know I couldn't see their faces, right?"

"Right," nodded Yarmouth. We're just trying to see if we can rule them out. Take a listen to this."

Yarmouth pressed play on a compact Zoom recorder he'd been hiding in his pocket earlier. The line-up banter crackled around the kitchen. Elena winced at "dozy cunts", instinctively squeezing her daughter's hand. Ana just laughed.

"That sounds like one of them. The sweary one."

"Didn't you get them to repeat what the men who broke in said?" Elena offered.

"We would have done if we'd called Ana in as a witness, but I don't want them to catch on entirely to how much we know. I want them to be nervous, maybe make a mistake."

Fleischer was out shadowing O'Leary. In his first call to report back he noted that the Irishman had headed straight to the Temperance and didn't seem to be doing anything more incriminating than drinking Jameson's and playing pool with colleagues.

"They're not acting guilty," Elena observed as Yarmouth ended the call.

"Give them time."

A couple of hours later, Fleischer called from outside Carver's office. Although it was after office hours, O'Leary had turned up and entered the building. Lights were on in Carver's office.

"That's enough for me," said Yarmouth. "Let's set up a meeting. Don't let on he's a suspect in anything yet. Don't mention it to Shah either. With the ghost squad sniffing around the department due to McPherson, we want to have all our ducks on a row if there's more corruption."

Fleischer sighed his assent and hung up. Tuesday was going to be a challenging day in the office.

CHAPTER 41

O'Leary wandered into interview Room 2 half an hour after the time Fleischer had requested he attend. He looked a little worse for wear, tucking his shirt tail in on one side as he slouched into a metal chair.

"What's up with the meeting room?"

"Heating problem," Yarmouth said. "Thought it'd be cosier in here."

"Fair enough. What can I help you gentlemen with?"

Fleischer had taken up a position by the door, side-on to the Irishman. Robin sat opposite, arms open in a textbook 'inviting' posture.

"Why did you let yourself in to Flat 11, Carlisle Street on the evening of the 3rd May?" Robin asked, without preamble.

There. A definite flinch response. O'Leary turned towards Fleischer, as if looking for the nod or wink that would clarify that this was a joke. It didn't come.

"What is this, lads?"

"Ana Balan, fourteen-year-old daughter of Elena Balan, the resident of number 11 was at home when you called. She hid in the bedroom. She could see you through the keyhole."

O'Leary laughed in comic disbelief. But was there something a little mannered about his response? Almost as if it had been rehearsed.

There was a pause, while O'Leary considered his options.

"I don't know who she thought she saw but it wasn't us."

"Us?" said Robin. "I didn't say anything about anyone else being there."

269

"No, I mean us as in 'give us a fag'. The singular us."

Now it was Robin's time to laugh.

"Oh, the singular us. Of course. So, you didn't go there on that date?"

"I don't think so. You know we attended the suicide?"

"Qamar Liibaan's death. Yes. But this was a long time later, after all the neighbours had been questioned."

"Nah mate, wasn't us? Hey, this is feeling more like an interrogation than a meeting. Maybe I should call my lawyer?"

O'Leary's tone was flippant, yet confrontational.

"Maybe you should," Fleischer chipped in. "And Brendan, didn't I see you pop in to see Mal Carver last night? I was in Soho, and it certainly looked like you."

The cogs turned behind O'Leary's eyes, his eyes searching for a response somewhere on the table before him.

"What the fuck? Have you been following me?"

For a moment, O'Leary's anger almost looked convincing, except his hangover limited his performance to more of a whine than justified outrage.

"We've been following Carver. The old lag's been playing both sides, it appears. You just popped into view," Fleischer added. "Want to tell us why?"

"You know that AC are all over the department," Robin added. "We don't want the whole place to go tits up because of a little moonlighting. So why not set the story straight and we'll see what we can do?"

"Lads, I'm really confused. What the fuck are you talking about?"

This time O'Leary's exasperation felt real.

"Carver sent you in search of something didn't he? Maybe to help out a friend of his?"

Robin frowned a little. Fleischer knew better than to lead an interviewee. That said, they weren't recording this little informal chat, so proper protocol was a little moot.

O'Leary fixed Fleischer with a long stare. Then seemed to slump a little into his suit.

"Fair enough. Carver wanted it. We just said we'd take a look."

"Wanted what?" Robin said. He knew O'Leary was just a functionary, but he still wanted him to admit his complicity.

"The girl's laptop. You know the deal. He's a CI—he scratches our back and we... do him a little favour now and again."

"Like breaking and entering and attempted theft?"

"We had the landlord's keys, and the laptop was already nicked. By your squeeze!"

Here, O'Leary lost his cool and pushed his finger into Yarmouth's chest. Yarmouth fought the momentary impulse to bite it off.

"What did he want with it?"

"Was Carver protecting McPherson?" Fleischer piped up.

Again, Robin wished he'd done this interview alone. His friend had a bit of a problem with impatience.

"McPherson?" O'Leary looked a little confused. "I don't know. Maybe. I didn't ask."

O'Leary now just looked tired. Yarmouth felt a mild pang of guilt for putting him on the spot. Then he remembered how Ana had described the intrusion, how frightened she had felt.

"Then I'd better ask him myself, I guess."

"Why don't you do that. Guys, I'm assuming this is all off the record?"

"For now, O'Leary. Just you keep away from Carlisle Street."

O'Leary was already at the door. Fleischer stepped grudgingly aside to let him pass.

"Maybe you should do the same, Robbo. You should stop dating them exotics and find yourself a nice English girl, eh?"

And with that riposte, he left. Yarmouth let him go. He had the link he needed. Carver would give up McPherson and they could close the loop on the whole sordid affair.

Fleischer was already making the call.

Ninety minutes later, having insisted they pick him up in an unmarked car and bring him in through the back door, Carver sat primly in Interview Room 2, in the seat vacated by O'Leary earlier that morning. Again, Robin led, with Fleischer by the door. On the other side of the glass, Shah and Elena watched. Yarmouth had managed to swing Elena being here for this on the grounds of her last encounter with Carver, which she had admitted to in bed last night. At first he'd been angry at her impetuousness, but he'd grown to appreciate her cunning and accept that she was no shrinking violent and he hadn't a snowball's chance in hell of changing her.

Elena had already given testimony in which she recounted Carver first mentioning O'Leary and Barnett. Shah had made her a cup of tea and Yarmouth was relieved to see her going out of her way to be nice to his girlfriend (gossip travelled fast in the station). He didn't know why he thought the DI would be jealous; San would probably just tell him that was his massive ego talking.

Carver sat picking dirt from under his nails with a key extracted from a very large bunch. The splayed hand of keys lay on the table seemed like a symbol of the man's dubious power and influence.

"This 'aint very polite, Robbo. We had an arrangement that you'd never bring me down here. I'm still a registered CI. If one of my acquaintances was to see..."

"We had an arrangement until you started playing both sides, Mal," interjected Fleischer. "You've given us nothing useful since the Ukrainians and now you're snooping around our crime scenes."

At first, Carver tried his best to convey incredulity but then appeared to give up on it. He pulled his shirt sleeves up and laid both hands flat upon the table like a magician demonstrating he has nothing hidden.

"Listen, Robin," Carver began, with ingratiating familiarity. "It's my place and you know I've always looked after my girls."

"Of the two girls left at Carlisle Street, one's a neurotic junkie and the other's murdered, countered Yarmouth. If that's you looking after them..."

Yarmouth let the thought hang. Carver sat back in his seat with a sigh. If at first he'd thought this was going to be a formality, he now saw was mistaken.

"Come on Carver," Yarmouth prompted. "You know we can ping O'Leary and Barnett's mobiles and we'll get the scooter lads testimony."

A genuine frown this time.

"Don't know about any scooters but I'll admit I gave your boys the keys and suggested they might find the girl's laptop inside. She had a pretty full client list and if it came out, well, your department might find one or two embarrassing names on there."

"You were going to blackmail us?"

Carver shook his head firmly.

"Not at all. At best, it'd have been leverage. Robbo, you threatened me with the Smirnovs and that wasn't sporting. Can you blame me for wanting a little protection of my own?"

"You didn't find it though."

Yarmouth left it hanging as a statement that Carver could choose to interpret as a question.

"They didn't find nothing."

Fleischer and Yarmouth took a brief confab outside with Shah and Elena.

"Is he going to give up McPherson?" Shah said. "Push him guys."

Elena, who had watched the interview in growing disgust, was trying to keep a low profile so as not to embarrass Robin. But she couldn't restrain herself any longer.

"You're being too soft on him. He knows much more than he's letting on. Can't you use the Ukrainian threat again?"

Shah shook her head.

"Sorry Miss Balan. Carver's been a CI for years, he knows the deal. He knows we can't risk him being killed as a direct result of our actions. Even if that was a strategy..." (she looked pointedly at Yarmouth) "that has worked in the past, he's under caution and on record."

Without DI Shah here, Yarmouth and Fleischer might have been inclined to 'accidentally' nudge the microphone off in Interview Room 2, but subtler techniques would have to be employed. They headed back in.

Yarmouth didn't have to feign a world-weary sigh as he resumed his seat in front of the jaded gaze of Malcolm Carver—one slipped out naturally.

"I've talked to my boss. We reckon we can get you for obstruction of justice or even aiding and abetting after the fact since you withheld your thoughts about the whereabouts of the laptop. You also lied to police officers and assisted them with an unwarranted search of Miss Balan's apartment. Your CI contract, needless to say, is hereby void."

"Basically, you're fucked, so you might as well spill the beans and maybe we'll play nice," translated Fleischer into a language Carver might understand.

Carver laughed.

"That the best you've got? Okay, I'll throw you a bone. I'm sure you know already the weird shit your guy McPherson was into. Obviously, he doesn't want that getting out. To be honest, the Somali chick had a fair few clients that nobody, except maybe the Sun and the Daily Mail, wants made public. I've got a reputation to uphold. So, yes, he comes to me, after her death, asking if I've seen her laptop. He knows it's not been admitted into evidence. Of course, I say I haven't a clue what he's on about. But it can't hurt to do a copper a favour now and again, eh Robbo?"

Robin ignored Carver's hint and pressed on.

"So, you gave him the keys?"

"He said he'd send the lads round—couldn't risk showing up there himself. O'Leary was one of the attending officers when the Somali..."

"Qamar Liibaan."

"Yeah, Qamar, whatever. O'Leary had a right to be there."

"Just not in Elena Balan's flat," Fleischer said. "Why did they think she might have it?"

"Girl upstairs—Susan Rae—said the Bulgarian bint had been snooping around."

"Romanian," interjected Yarmouth.

Behind the glass, Elena smiled.

"Whatever. Apparently, she's been sticking her nose in."

"She's been helping our investigation," Fleischer clarified.

"Look, I don't care if you're all fucking her. Just get me my lawyer, or let me out of this shithole. I've told you what you want."

Yarmouth had rarely seen Carver this riled. Then again, the worst offence you could commit, where he'd been brought up, was being a 'grass'. The man apparently could feel shame (or at the very least fear of being shanked in custody).

Later that afternoon Yarmouth took Shah, Elena, and Fleischer into the incident room, where photos of the crime scene were posted, alongside images of the prime suspects and salient pieces of evidence. So far, the major suspects included Qamar's immediate family, all of whom has alibis, McPherson, Carver and a large red X symbolling 'persons unknown' (i.e., one of Qamar's clients).

It was the first time Elena has ever seen a photo of a murder victim and although Yarmouth had primed her before they went in, that only made matters worse. Now she found her eyes inexorably drawn to the bloated, dark blue skin tones, the eerie wide, whiteness of Qamar's eyes, those marks around her neck. She felt tears welling in the corner of her eyes and discreetly wiped them away as Shah took centre stage.

"Let's take stock. What do we have? A murder made to look like suicide, hence premeditated. Not a crime of passion. Could be an honour killing?"

Elena had been trying to avoid that conclusion—it seemed like a knee-jerk reaction to the family's religious beliefs and the way the parents had shunned Qamar. Even Elena's own relatively mild, albeit alcoholic, mother would have had a hard time with the news that Elena was on the game. It was just a bit too pat, too easy. And yet...

"It's more likely to be a John," Shah continued. "McPherson's shame, embarrassment and anger coming out. He knows forensics, he knows what we look for and he's incredibly careful. I still fancy him as our number one, unfortunately. I wish I didn't but there you have it."

Yarmouth nodded.

"Carver's not in the frame," he added. "He sees himself as a businessman now. With a shady past and a few questionable business practices, for sure. But primarily on the straight and narrow. It's still looking like McPherson's our man."

"Must be Christmas for you, Robbo," Shah said, with the hint of a smile.

This annoyed Yarmouth more than it should.

"Not at all, boss. Sure, he's an imbecile, but have you seen his conviction record? And it's never good news when a good officer goes bad."

"With him, O'Leary and Barnett we'll have a severe case of the ACs for months, that's for sure," said Fleischer.

"Anti-Corruption," whispered Yarmouth to Elena.

"I hear you Tom," Shah said. "In conclusion, all eyes on McPherson. The sooner we can put this one to bed, the sooner we can clean house and move on. Find the laptop.

I'll liaise with Nigel about those email addresses and provide a list so we can cross off the other clients."

After the meeting, Elena turned to Yarmouth as they sat in his Mazda and he waited for a double-parked colleague to move his car so they could reverse out.

"I'd like to see her family again."

"The honour-killing angle? You heard Shah. We've got to work through that list."

"Not you, just me."

"I'm not sure that's a brilliant idea. This isn't the Wild West. I can't just deputise you."

"I know that. I just want to be sure. I'll talk to mum and sister. It'll be fine. If I find anything out, you can send someone, make it official. They talk to me precisely because I'm not police officer."

"No, you're not. It's too risky. What does she mean to you, this girl? You only met her, what, twice?"

Robin's tone was curious, rather than accusatory, so Elena gave her reply some thought, as Robin rolled the Mazda out of the yard and onto the little side-street beside the station, throwing puddle water onto London stock brickwork.

"She would have been a friend," Elena said simply, thinking of the bulging eyes of the dead girl in the forensic photos. "I owe it to her."

CHAPTER 42

The discussion with Robin about Elena's role in this investigation had escalated rather quickly into an argument. Elena hadn't seen a problem with how involved she'd become.

"Am I not just 'helping you with your enquiries'? Isn't that right?"

"That's what we say when a person is a suspect," Robin countered. "At best you're a material witness. You didn't see Qamar killed or spot her killer or really have any more idea that me who may have murdered her."

"Except I'm the only one who thought even was murder, remember."

"Look, Elena, I can see you're invested in this. And I'm invested in you. But you won't believe the flak I'm getting from my superiors for letting you get so involved. It's a conflict of interest, for one thing."

"What, am I a suspect?"

"Well, technically, yes. Though we ruled you out pretty quickly. No motive, we know you were at work when it happened. And, as you say, you brought up the murder angle."

"Plus, am not actually a murdering psychopath."

Even as she said this, a familiar little voice inside Elena made itself heard—what about Karl? You killed him, didn't you?

After half an hour, it transpired that what Robin was really bothered by was letting Elena endanger herself or Ana. Once Elena had reassured him that she was only going to pay a courtesy call on Taifa, maybe follow up a couple of things with her, his worry subsided. As did her anger. After all, better to have a man who cared and kept coming back to a woman who vanished after deciding from the kindness of her heart not to pimp Elena out to strangers. How had it come to this? Elena had made much better decisions as a teenager than she had as a supposed adult.

Borrowing Yarmouth's car and struggling a little with the signage, Elena drove north, resolute that she was doing the right thing. Taifa would reveal much more to her than she ever would to a man, even Robin at his most sympathetic.

Then, somewhere between the M6 and the turn-off for the M1 to Birmingham, Elena made an abrupt decision. Seeing the faces of the three surviving Liibaans on DI Shah's suspect board had set a horrible thought process in motion. It was Mr Liibaan she wanted to see, not his daughter. His surgery was just outside of the city centre, a nondescript residential street in Walsall. Elena pulled into the little car park, finding the last available space in front of the whitewashed converted townhouse of the Clifford & Liibaan practice.

Earlier, she had pulled over at a service station—the same one she'd sat in with Robin on her last visit to Birmingham—and had gone online and managed to register with the practice and book an appointment. The NHS, despite seemingly daily news reports about its inadequacies, had impressed Elena so far. Romania's health service was so underfunded and overburdened that filmmaker friends of her cousin had even made an award-winning feature film about it, The Death of Mr Lazarescu. In contrast, Elena had managed to get a same-day appointment at the small NHS surgery, merely by indicating that it was 'urgent'.

Elena felt her heart thumping a little in the waiting room. She remembered Mr Liibaan's enraged reaction to his daughter's death and his wife's insults. Was he really capable of premeditated, cold-blooded murder? Of his own flesh and blood? If so, what might he do to a complete stranger who threatened to pull his whole world down around him? Suddenly, Elena realised she might have made a poor decision in coming here after all.

Bing!

The scrolling LED sign on the wall indicated "Elena to see Dr Liibaan—Room 3" and Elena took a deep breath and walked down the linoleum-floored corridor to the door of Abdullahi Liibaan's room. He didn't seem to recognise her at first, as he beckoned to the chair opposite his desk, and she took a seat. Mr Liibaan's bulk was thrown into even sharper relief by the tiny room and low chair he perched upon, legs crossed at the ankles, leaning forward, professionally inquisitive.

Then his face changed, even as Elena cleared her throat to begin.

"You! The so-called police officer. You lied to us."

"I did and am sorry. I was Qamar's friend."

"And you lied to get this appointment. I don't have to speak to you."

"Is true. And I'm sorry. I had to talk to you away from home. This was only way..."

Mr Liibaan seemed to struggle with something internally.

"Well, you have only ten minutes so you'd better hurry."

Mr Liibaan was looking at his watch as he said this and continued to stare down at his wrist as Elena gathered her thoughts. Was he avoiding eye contact, trying to throw her off or both?

"I don't know how much you know about what Qamar did while she was in London?"

"The bereavement counsellor and the victim liaison officer has made it quite clear, thank you."

"Well, I don't want to re-open old wounds but… Qamar may have recorded detail of some clients and… consultations on a laptop."

Consultations! Why had she used that word? The euphemism embarrassed her.

"There may even have been video. We're not sure."

"Why? Don't they have it in evidence?"

"No. It went missing, somewhere between Qamar's death and when body was found. I thought at first the police must have, but apparently not."

"And what business is this of yours? You're not the police."

"That's true. As I told you, I'm friend. I'm just trying to help."

Elena wasn't sure her 'little girl lost' routine was going to play here. Liibaan looked implacable, sitting with his arms folded, watching the minute hand of his Breitling. Maybe a different tack…

"Did you visit Qamar, after she move to London?"

He shook his head.

"Maybe you sent someone? Did anyone go to check on her? It must have been pretty awful when you learn what she was doing in London. How did you find out?

"From Taifa. She kept in touch, as did her mother. They said very little at first, but then I made them tell me everything."

Elena wondered just how he had "made them", then chastised herself for jumping to conclusions.

"And how did you feel?"

"How do you think I felt! I wanted…"

Elena could see him struggling with the memory of an old shame, half-buried but never forgotten. Was she on to something?

"You wanted her dead? Did you want to kill her?"

He moved much faster than she'd thought him capable, pushing back his chair and leaning forward to throw out a meaty hand. It connected with the side of Elena's face, throwing her off her chair to the floor. As she picked herself up, he was between her and the door. Red-faced, instantly ashamed, he held his hands out in the universal gesture of "please calm down", palms wide, eyes beseeching.

Elena had located the consultation room's panic alarm. It was to the side of Mr Liibaan's desk—a red button mounted into the wall. She considered dashing for it.

"Please, forgive me. I'm sorry. What you said…."

Elena could feel saltwater prickling the corners of her eyes. No—that wouldn't do. She found she was shaking.

"Did your daughter dishonour the family? Did you do something about it?"

Mr Liibaan seemed to come to, apparently realising how much trouble he was in.

"Yes, of course she did. But no, I did nothing of the sort. You must forgive me…"

Elena went for the door and he stepped aside, quietly deflating. He probably expected her to report him. He'd be up in front of the General Medical Council, probably struck off.

"Qamar is the one who could have forgiven you. Except somebody deprived her of that chance. I'm going to find out who."

Elena paused in the open doorway.

"Where is the laptop, Mr Liibaan?"

She stood there, as a young Asian woman walked past and flicked a concerned look in. Mr Liibaan shook his head at the passing colleague, then gave a dumb thumbs-up. The woman moved on. Elena realised she was trembling, her voice breaking.

"Do you have it?"

Again, he simply shook his head. As she closed the door, Elena just made out him saying, almost to himself:

"Taifa. My daughter has it."

In the car-park outside, Elena took some long slow breaths. The side of her face stung and there was a faint ringing in her right ear. Mr Liibaan had given her a hefty wallop.

She felt light-headed and weirdly elated. Given that she had just been assaulted, it was peculiar that her main emotion was one of triumph. She had faced up to a potentially dangerous situation and hadn't crumbled. She wouldn't report him—there would be no point if he was guilty of murdering his daughter, or ordering her killing. He'd be struck off as a matter of course. And if he wasn't guilty?

Frankly, Elena had better things to do.

CHAPTER 43

The first thing Ana noticed about her school was that slim, pale-skinned white girls were very much in a minority. The school, situated in a strange hinterland North of Kings Cross station called Somers Town, was the most racially diverse place she'd ever been. There were Afro-Caribbean kids, Indian and Pakistani kids, children from the Middle-East, West and Central Africa, China and the school's star pupil, featured in the Evening Standard for obtaining nine A* A-levels, was from Venezuela. There were a few Eastern European kids and a few dozen white British-born kids but seemingly nobody from Romania.

Not that it should matter. Ana was proud of her English language abilities and had never been shy. Still, when surrounded by the whirl of races, nationalities, languages, and the inevitable cliques that went with such a social stew, she felt a little overwhelmed. On her first day, after her induction and the first couple of classes were over (English and Geography) she finally gravitated to a group of quieter girls looking at a fashion vlog on an iPad in the corner of the playground. Three were white and one was Asian—probably Indian (although she already knew not to make that assumption). The girls were facing away from Ana as she stood on tiptoes to see what they were looking at.

A perky American girl with pronounced dimples cooed energetically about her "16th Birthday Haul" while showing off a range of clothing and accessories. The video was loud, bright, and heavily branded. Inwardly, Ana asked herself what the hell she was doing. Then she stumbled, fell forward a couple of steps and accidentally jogged the iPad out of the tallest, blondest girl's hands. It hit the tarmac, bounced on its corner, and came to rest face down. Ana's heart stopped as the blonde girl turned it over. There was a small hairline crack in one corner of the device.

"What the fuck! Who the hell are you?" the blonde girl asked, marching up to Ana and holding the iPad in one hand like she was about to slap Ana with it.

"I'm so sorry. Ana. Ana Balan."

Before she knew what she was doing, Ana stuck her hand out, rigidly, for a handshake that never came. Instead, peals of laughter rang out as a small, overweight black boy aged no more than twelve pointed at her.

"You'd better be sorry. Her dad bought her that and he's in Wormwood Scrubs."

The boy looked both pugnacious and in awe of the blonde girl, who patted his head with mock affection.

"My little protector."

The blonde turned her gaze fully upon Ana, stepping close and making the most of the extra four inches of height she had at her disposal.

"You'll pay for that. Foreign bitch."

Then something that had never happened to Ana in her nine years of schooling back home occurred. The girl pushed her, and she fell over, embarrassingly but also fortunately, hitting the back of her head on the soft sports bag of one of the boys who had stopped to watch. As she picked herself up, heart thumping in her ribcage, Ana tried to think of the right response. Her throat felt dry and her face hot and red. It was incredible how quickly a crowd had formed.

Fortunately, Ana was rescued from the thankless 'fight or flight' options by the appearance of a teacher, Mr Edmondson, whom she had met at registration.

"What's going on here?" he shouted, at a volume that silenced the yard.

A tactical silence and then:

"She fell sir," from the blonde girl, who now turned and marched away with her miniature entourage.

"She tripped," said the Indian girl.

Ana couldn't figure out if she was defending her or the blonde.

As quickly as it had formed, the crowd dispersed, and Mr Edmondson administered a warning to the receding back of Ana's blonde tormentor about "using tablets or devices" in the classroom.

"Are you okay?" Mr Edmondson asked, a little peremptorily. Maybe he had other fights to break up elsewhere.

"I'm fine," Ana replied, brusquely, brushing down her skirt.

As the teacher's lanky frame receded, Ana turned to the Indian girl, who was studying her phone intently.

"Jesus. It was just an accident."

The Indian girl looked up from her game.

"Don't talk to me. They'll be sending you back to Poland anyways. My dad says the immigrants are going home."

Ana was dumbfounded.

"I'm Romanian, actually. And anyway, you're...

"I was born here, bitch," said the girl, before turning away.

Things were a little better the rest of the morning, although Ana quickly learned that she had blundered into one of the most dangerous and respected cliques in the whole school.

A small Pakistani girl with bottle-thick spectacles, called Rahmi, told her those girls were the "elite" (then whispered under her breath that half the kids thought they were total cows). Ana had the feeling that Rahmi would become a close friend.

She sent a secretive text under the desk at 11:30am, risking the wrath of French teacher Miss Gardes, whose rules of conduct were many and rigidly applied. The message was to Chris of course and said simply:

RESCUE ME

with a "shocked" emoticon and the address of the school.

At lunch, Ana was delighted to discover Chris lurking against a tree in the small triangle of grass adorned with a bench across the road. Rahmi told her this was the "paedo" bench, where dodgy Polish labourers congregated to drink beer and ogle the girls leaving the school. Ana elected to ignore the implied bigotry—potential friends were a little thin on the ground so far at St Bartholomew's.

"Hi Chuck," said Chris, using his peculiar pet-name for her. She hadn't yet decided if she liked it or not.

They kissed passionately on the bench (Ana checking the seating first for anything unsavoury) and she was gratified to note that a few of the girls from the school were looking through the gate at them both. She'd earn definite cool points for snogging an older boy and a mixed-race one at that. She did stop him when his hand slid down her shoulder to her breast. There were limits.

After eating her packed lunch and sharing Chris's latte (she wasn't much of a coffee drinker, but it felt good to be passing the warm cup back and forth, Ana remembered what she had in her school bag. She fished it out and handed it carefully to Chris.

"You seem to be good with your hands (the innuendo intentional). Can you fix this?"

Chris examined the broken necklace with its intricate design of miniature dice and skulls. One half of the clasp was missing—Ana had tied a knot to stop any more beads from escaping.

"Sweet! Got a friend who designs jewellery. She ought to be able to do something."

Chris had a friend who did anything and everything. It was one of the things she loved about him. With Chris, her world seemed to expand endlessly.

"No thanks. I kind of like it fucked up. I'll manage."

They kissed some more. Ana pushed her body up against Chris as they partially slid down the bench. She could feel a hardness against her thigh, a corresponding heat and wetness between her legs. This was just too much.

Pulling away, she laughed as he made a show of covering his arousal with his retro Adidas shoulder bag. Then he got back on the small bike she only now noticed propped against the tree, gave her a final kiss, a fist-bump and was gone.

Ana walked back into St Bartholomew's, feeling the envious or curious stares burning into her. Fuck the stuck-up elite bitches—she was properly cool.

CHAPTER 44

The phone rang as Yarmouth was halfway through his cardboard container of Pad Thai. As soon as he heard Shah's voice—subdued, monotonous—Yarmouth knew the investigation was in trouble.

They almost had enough to convince the CPD the case against McPherson warranted going to trial. Forensics had come back with hairs that matched McPherson's DNA. Just one or two pieces of physical evidence and the full data report from McPherson's devices would probably cinch it. Plus Qamar's laptop if that ever turned up and confirmed him as a suspect.

The key link in the chain would be the scooter boys' testimony that they had stolen his phone and that they had been specifically contracted to do so by O'Leary and other crooked police officers.

While neither had named McPherson yet, or identified him in a line-up (McPherson's lawyers had stalled them for a few days), the lads had revealed via their lawyer, that they had been approached by a senior officer a few days after O'Leary and Barnett had contracted their services. This officer had threatened them with arrest if they didn't hurry up and carry out their little "favour".

Sutton, the younger boy, had tried to face off against the officer, a foolish decision that had resulted in a knee to the testicles and badly wounded pride. They hadn't mentioned this earlier because the man had scared them much more than O'Leary and Barnett. They had called him "A mean fucker". It had taken two hours of negotiation for either of them to agree (again, via their lawyer) to say anything more. Their testimony would have been recorded officially that Wednesday afternoon.

Well, that was the plan, now suddenly and irretrievably demolished. Minutes after receiving the call, Yarmouth had jumped in a pool car and driven down to a backstreet in Brixton, where a ring of police tape and cordon of constables and panda cars surrounded a depressing discovery.

DI Shah had been the first detective on scene. She waved Tom and Yarmouth under the tape and over to a half-loaded skip. A pair of sneakers and baggy jeans poked out from under a sheet of mouldy MDF. SOCO were already on the scene, carefully lifting each layer of detritus off the body of the young man to reveal...

"Sidney Sutton," sighed Yarmouth.

"Fucking hell. This is getting serious," whistled Fleischer.

Shah filled them in on what they knew and surmised so far.

The skip was located round the corner from Sidney's mother's house. The poor woman was being questioned at home as they spoke but could manage little more meaningful between sobs than "he was a good boy, what them bad ones led astray". She thought it might be a gang killing but others in the locality had a different theory. The area wasn't covered by CCTV but some neighbours had spotted a dark blue or black car with a light on parked around the corner from Sutton's house, a man inside smoking through an open window.

Nobody clearly saw the loiterer's face or the number-plate of his car. All they could agree on was that he was male and white... probably. And in his forties or fifties... most likely. The testimony was only one stage better than the usual big fat zero the Met often drew in tight-knit communities. What was certain was that this didn't look like a hot-blooded revenge killing, nor a random, gang-style hit and run.

Sidney had been stabbed once, quietly from behind, through the ribcage and into the heart. There were no signs of a struggle and the killer had evidently worn gloves. No murder weapon had yet been found and nobody had witnessed the act itself. Constables would be canvassing the community for days and the usual signs had been posted asking passers-by to contact the police with information. Shah didn't look hopeful.

"This was a professional hit, in my opinion. Someone knew about the deal."

"How?" asked Yarmouth. "The ink's barely dried."

"How do you think? We thought we had all the bad eggs. Looks like there's a stinker still out there."

A leak in the department. Not O'Leary or Barnett. The former had no real motive since they had already confessed to their involvement and named McPherson. McPherson was allowed nowhere near the investigation and was under twenty-four-hour surveillance, Purvis's strategic alternative to locking him up. Perhaps he's somehow found a way to get a message out.

"We're looking at the officers we've got guarding Bob," Shah said, as if reading Yarmouth's mind the way she frequently had when they'd dated.

"It just gets worse and worse," said Fleischer.

"You don't know the half of it," said Shah, handing Fleischer a copy of the Daily Mail.

Front page, headline news:

CORRUPT COPS IN DEVIANT SEX COVER-UP.

"Disappointing," murmured Fleischer.

Shah and Yarmouth shot him looks of, respectively, perplexity and amusement.

"No, I mean, I'd have expected something like 'Improper Copper' or 'Defective Detective'" Someone's asleep on the job.

"Okay Tom, we've got a dead teenager here. Focus, will you?"

Fleischer shrugged.

"It's a world of shit, that's what it is," agreed Fleischer. "No harm in trying to lighten the mood."

Shah ignored him and turned to Yarmouth.

"You'd better plan for the other kid clamming up now, obviously. Question is, can we still make a case?"

"We've got the forensic stuff, the video," offered Yarmouth.

"That just shows he was there as a client a few days before. We have no CCTV of him entering on the day of her murder. There are a couple of blokes who fit the bill, physically, but no faces."

"There's the texts?"

"Someone could have got hold of his phone. It could even have been done remotely, Nigel reckons."

"O'Leary and Barrett's testimony. Carver's."

"A couple of bent coppers and a career criminal. You can imagine what a good barrister could do with that."

Yarmouth peered over into the skip. Sidney's face, seen in profile against an empty cement bag, wore a strangely beatific look. Yarmouth knew this was misleading—it spoke only of a kid who didn't see the end coming and had no time to react. There was no happy, heavenly portal awaiting this doomed young boy—just the detritus of some stranger's loft conversion.

"Fucking hell. Could McPherson have got a message to someone?" wondered Yarmouth aloud.

"We've swept his house twice for devices we don't know about, found nothing," Shah replied. "McPherson's popular in the department, he's got a few friends, a brother in Scarborough. New wife clean with an alibi, kids too young. Nobody that strikes me as liable to kill for him. The previous Mrs McPherson hasn't spoken to him for years."

"More likely to cheer from the sidelines," added Fleischer. "Do you remember that time she drove up to the station and emptied a bin bag of his clothes over his car? That was one acrimonious divorce."

Fleischer rolled the word "acrimonious" around his mouth with an evident relish that vanished when he noticed DCI Shah's renowned 'warning face'.

"Well, someone killed the kid," Shah said. "Tom, I want you on this pronto. Robin—concentrate on O'Leary and Barnett. Get them to name the third man. They know they're ruined but they might just escape prison. Sell that angle."

"On it, boss," said Yarmouth, walking away with Fleischer, who shot his friend an incredulous look.

"Boss?"

"Well. Technically, DCI Shah is my superior, Tom. I am under her."

"I'll bet you are."

Yarmouth punched Fleischer playfully in the shoulder.

"Cut it out, Tom. That's old history."

"If you say so. God, she gets hotter with every passing year, that one."

"Did you sign up to that 'professional boundaries' course yet, Tom?"

Fleischer just laughed.

"I'm just yanking your chain, mate. You've done well with Elena. She's a hell of a girl. Takes a strong one to turn down Malcolm Carver."

Yarmouth stopped dead in his tracks.

"What are you talking about?"

"Shit. You didn't know. Look, just forget it. It's an irrelevance, anyway."

"What is?"

Yarmouth's tone had lost all jocularity and Fleischer paled as they got into Tom's car.

"You'd better ask her yourself. Look, it's old history. If she didn't tell you, it's probably because she's on the straight and narrow."

Yarmouth reached over Fleischer and turned the engine off.

"No. You tell me. Now."

It wasn't really a surprise that Fleischer knew more of Elena's background than Yarmouth did. Tom was a good, thorough detective. He'd wanted to know exactly who he was working with, given Yarmouth's insistence on involving Elena in the case. Yarmouth had decided to trust Elena; or perhaps he'd just turned a blind eye to the questions and inconsistencies in her story because he knew it wasn't in his interest to pry.

Fleischer had visited Carver with the name Frances da Costa not long after Yarmouth had first mentioned Elena's London contact. Carver had shrugged and feigned ignorance but, weeks later, Fleischer had gone back to see the gangster to require his presence at the station for questioning and Carver had volunteered a bit of information about their mysterious Romanian. Frances da Costa, it transpired, had worked for him in the past, procuring girls from Romania to work as high-class prostitutes, operating out of Carver's shoebox apartments.

That business model was dead now, but Elena was his last 'find'. Carver had told Frances to drop the girl when he moved his business model away from real-world hookups to camgirls and sold his brothels for residential conversions. The Carlisle place was the last remnant of a dying Soho scene of 'models' and prowling Johns plucking numbers from lurid cards left in phone boxes.

"Elena was a hooker?"

"God no, nothing like that. It's just that Frances had her hooks into her because she did Elena a favour, brought her over here."

"Well, she told me Frances invited her over, sure."

"I think it's a bit more involved than that, mate. You'd better talk to Elena."

Yarmouth sat back in the passenger seat as Fleischer started the engine and began to draw out into mid-morning traffic. He felt stunned and more than a little hurt.

"I will, Tom. I will."

CHAPTER 45

Taifa Liibaan hadn't returned from her job as a legal sec-
retary when Elena pulled up across the street in her
peaceful suburban cul-de-sac. Elena looked at her watch.
Six thirty.

She was just formulating her approach when a Citroen
Saxo drew into the driveway of the small modern-built
block of flats where Taifa lived. Elena got out of the car as
Taifa was manhandling some shopping out of the boot of
the Citroen.

"Taifa. Hello again."

A small frown, then a surprisingly warm smile of recognition as Elena air-kissed the space beside the slender
Somali girl's cheek (at the same time wondering if this had
been a culturally appropriate form of greeting).

"Can I help you with those?"

Taifa nodded her assent. A little later, both women sat
on the plush but slightly old-fashioned sofa (parental
hand-me-down, Elena surmised), with a pot of tea that
Taifa had prepared, and some sweet sesame seed-cov-
ered delicacies Taifa called halwo. Given Taifa's
generosity of spirit, this was going to be difficult.

"I hope you had a good memorial for Qamar," she began. "Thanks for telling me about the funeral."

Taifa nodded and offered a minimal smile. This Liibaan
sister wasn't one for unnecessary words. At least, not at
the moment.

"Taifa, I need to ask something and I need you to know
that you are safe to tell me what you know."

Taifa nodded, gravely. "Okay."

"Now you know I'm not police officer..."

Taifa laughed.

"Really? I just assumed... You sound just like them."

"Thanks... I think," Elena said with a smile. "I'm just helping them out because I knew your sister and I saw her before... I saw her that night."

"Okay. What do you want to ask me?"

"I need to ask if you know where Qamar's laptop might be".

There was a long pause. Taifa seemed to be considering her next words very carefully.

"I had it. But I don't have it now."

"Where is it Taifa? There may be stuff on the computer that could point to person who killed your sister."

The thought seemed to shame Taifa suddenly. She grew defensive.

"I didn't want that... filth getting out. Some of the videos I found..."

Taifa began to cry, softly, into a handkerchief she procured from a sleeve. Elena wanted to touch her but was stifled by her lack of knowledge of what Taifa would consider proper. Did propriety matter?

Then Taifa surprised her by leaning into Elena, their shoulder's touching. Elena felt permitted to put an arm round the young woman's tiny shoulders. Between gasps, Taifa whispered:

"I threw it in the pond in the park. Late at night."

Elena felt simultaneously triumphant that her hunch had been correct but also disappointed that it would probably come to nothing. Then again, data recovery software was supposed to be highly advanced these days, wasn't it? Ana had once spilt cola into her laptop and a small Bucharest firm had managed to rescue most of her data from the short-circuited machine. Qamar's laptop had been in a dank pond for weeks though...

"I have a file I pulled off it. A spreadsheet. It was password-protected but Qamar and I... we always used each other's middle names. Do you want to see it?"

Elena was stunned.

"Yes please. Taifa—why did you save?"

"Because it has names of men. And what they like. Their... tendencies."

Taifa spat the last word out like it was something rotten in her mouth. She got up abruptly and shuffled out of the room in pale yellow house slippers. Elena sat, oddly aware of her own stockinged feet in the plush carpet. This day was getting weirder and weirder.

A moment later, Taifa was back with her own laptop and they opened Qamar's mystery file. As Elena had hoped, it was a client list. Four columns—name (mostly just initials, sometimes a nickname), date and time, payment tendered and 'services.' The last column was the most revealing. LJ was apparently into 'light S&M, submissive, no scarring.' Bunny Boy's preference was for anal sex. PP was simply described as 'vanilla—a sweetie'.

There were three clients listed on the night Qamar was killed. Bunny Boy was a 'no show', someone called BM was listed as 'rockabye'—Elena guessed Bob McPherson. There was also someone simply described as 'Sonny,' the last client of the day. This individual was described as liking AEA and R-fantasy.

"Taifa, when exactly did you take laptop?"

Taifa started crying again. Elena had a shocking thought.

"She dishonoured the family," Elena said, quietly.

Elena let the idea hang, waiting for Taifa to contradict her. Nothing came but more and deeper sobs.

"I used her key to get in. I saw her there, sleeping, half-naked, drunk. Her laptop was still on. There was a man... some website. He was... touching himself."

Taifa didn't need to clarify. Elena saw the scene. Taifa comes round to visit, calling her sister three times (Qamar's mobile phone logs had shown multiple short calls from the same number). There's no answer, so Taifa gets into the stairwell by pressing a neighbour's buzzer (probably Susan upstairs). She lets herself in to flat 10 with the key she knows her sister keeps behind the pipe.

Encountering the sordid scene, Taifa does what any good daughter would do—she calls her father. He drives round. To what extent the daughter is complicit, it's had to say but Elena remembers a detail from the transcript of Taifa's written statement. Eulogising Qamar and the close bond between the sisters, Taifa had admitted that she had once completed a school essay for Qamar, earning her an A*. Presumably their handwriting was sufficiently similar that the teacher didn't notice and if that was true, could she have faked a suicide note?

If so, why the encoded clue that this was 'murder'? Perhaps Taifa had a strange need for confession? It was her, after all, who had told Elena and Robin the secret encoded within Qamar's last words.

Elena's thoughts were now spinning like carousels—noisy and chaotic, making her feel dizzy. Another thought presented itself. Taifa had written 'murder' to implicate her father. He had come to Qamar's flat and, where Taifa had expected tough love, there had been violence—strangulation with whatever piece of cord Abdullahi Liibaan had found closest to hand—the cable from the missing lamp. Then a cover-up, enlisting the daughter to fake the suicide note.

Suddenly Elena felt out of her depth, heart pounding so loudly in her chest, she thought Taifa, who had gone back into the kitchen to make more tea, would know that Elena had figured it out. She had no way of knowing how Taifa would react if Elena were to put her suspicions to her. Perhaps Taifa had changed her mind about confessing and implicating her father. Why then confess to being there at all? Perhaps just to explain why she had the laptop and to get the list of clients to Elena to throw her and the police off the scent? Any kind of subterfuge now suddenly seemed possible.

Elena had to talk to Robin before saying anything else to Taifa. The slender Somali woman was bustling about the kitchen, filling the kettle with water, rinsing cups. Elena leaned against the doorway, announcing her presence with a throat-clearing sound. Taifa turned.

"I'm sorry. I have to go. I'll call you."

"I was going to make more tea..."

There was something chillingly cold in Taifa's eyes in that moment. Elena saw a knife in her hand. A fruit loaf lay cut into slices on an ornate tray, but the blade of the knife was angled towards Elena.

"I'm really sorry. I'll call you later. Something has come up."

Elena smiled thinly and moved as quickly as she could out into the hall and the street. She had Qamar's spreadsheet, which Taifa had emailed. She had the rough location of the discarded laptop. And she had her story. She just hoped Robin would overlook her going off-piste by visiting the father. She was bringing back a lead, after all, a significant piece of the puzzle. And a motive.

Honour.

CHAPTER 46

After Elena called Robin, a SOCO team descended upon Bournville Park, turning the small, manicured space into an industrial excavation. The duckpond didn't stand a chance against the JCBs that dredged its depths. The park's avian inhabitants quacked and strutted in outrage from the tire-tread mutilated banks.

Elena had done as Robin asked and booked them both a room in a nearby Premier Inn. She had expected more praise for their endeavours than the gruff 'well done' he'd uttered over the phone. When he turned up, sharing a car with DI Shah rather than Tom Fleischer for once, he seemed more than usually business-like. No kiss on the cheek, but then there were colleagues watching and propriety had to be observed. Still, Elena couldn't help but surmise that she was in some kind of trouble. Oh well—if so, it wasn't an unprecedented situation for her.

Ana was being looked after by Aldona, who was becoming something of a friend by virtue of all the favours Elena was asking of her at the very least. She'd take Aldona out for dinner when she got back to London. Elena felt the odd pang of worry, thinking of her daughter alone with a stranger in that cramped apartment where so many awful things had happened but then she remembered watching Aldona holding her own in a confrontation with two large and angry Libyan men in the foyer of Voices Unlimited. In any case, Ana was under strict instructions to text her if anything happened or if there was ever the whisper of anything untoward going on in Carlisle Street.

Around five fifteen, Elena sidled over to where Shah and Robin were watching SOCO rake through a slew of mud, half-decomposed leaves and branches, litter, and the corpse of a dead swan. The smell was far from pleasant. Her left foot slipped out from underneath her suddenly as she reached the detectives. Robin caught her elbow, sparing her the indignity of going down in the mud.

"Oops! I'm not really dressed for this, am I?"

Shah looked her up and down and smiled in a slightly uncomfortable manner. Elena remembered that Robin had murmured that they had a 'history' but that it was 'water under the bridge'. He's had to explain the idiom and it had not entirely reassured Elena.

"Miss Balan, can you tell us precisely what Taifa said about the location of the laptop?" asked Shah.

"Please. Call me Elena. She said she threw it in. That's all."

For some reason, Elena found herself miming the act of hurling a laptop, like a giant Frisbee, towards the centre of the murky water. With almost too-perfect timing, a SOCO diver, knee deep in waders in the middle of the pond, pulled out a cracked, discoloured and roughly oblong shape. It had been wedged between two rocks surrounding the small fountain in the pond's centre. The JCB ground to a halt as everyone gathered round the find, like archaeologists of the future.

Half an hour later, the laptop was photographed, tagged, bagged (strands of pondweed included) and on its way to the forensic lab for whatever data recovery method might prove successful, although the SOCO specialist who first examined it did not look hugely hopeful.

Removing her protective gloves and shoe-protectors as the team repaired to the nearby car park, Shah turned to Yarmouth.

"You'd better question Taifa Liibaan formally—we've arranged a room in the local nick. Eight o'clock in the morning, before she heads to work. Get what your friend found out on record. One of the local DIs will attend. Oh, and Robbo?"

Yarmouth knew what was coming before Shah said it.

"Her involvement ends here, okay? I'm already getting grief from upstairs."

Yarmouth nodded. Shah turned to Elena.

"No offence and we do appreciate what you've uncovered but you're a civilian and this is a police matter."

Elena said nothing, a little disappointed that Robin hadn't defended her. He seemed subdued, lost in thought.

Shah and two of the local officers headed off for a local pizzeria, while Robin walked over to Elena with a rueful smile.

"I need a drink. Do I need to ask if you do too?"

Elena shook her head. She suspected whatever Robin had on his mind would go down better over a pint. They walked to the nearest bar, a student-friendly place called Channings, where they ordered pints of IPA from a local brewery and found a dark corner away from most of the speakers.

Robin prefaced whatever he was about to say with a sigh. Elena suspected the worst. Was this the inevitable brush off? Given how her various partners had habitually treated her, it would be par for the course. And as ever, she would bounce back.

"Elena. I love you."

He let it hang, his expression as weary as if he had said 'I'm exhausted'. She sensed a 'but' coming.

"But I can't have you lying to me about something as serious as..."

Here, he leaned close, dropping his voice to a whisper.

"Entering the country on forged papers. Balan isn't your real name is it?"

Elena was terrified. Was this it? Was her boyfriend about to arrest her? That would be a first.

"Elena," Robin said, "Tom Fleischer knows Frances, the woman who brought you to London. He filled me in on her background. You lied to me about her."

Various desperate strategies swum around Elena's head as she struggled to figure out what this implied. The front door was a short dash away and Robin had the table between him and her. The thought of making a run for it almost made her laugh hysterically, however. There was only one sensible course of action.

"I lied, and I'm sorry," Elena began. "I was just too embarrass to admit she'd fool me."

"Elena, you were trafficked."

Elena laughed, bitterly. If only it was that simple.

"Are you joking? Nobody even suggested I do anything. Didn't even cross my mind... Anyway, it was you who put me in that flat, in Carver's sex den."

"I'm going to have a word with him when I get back, Robin said. I suppose Frances had the decency to realise you weren't that sort of girl."

"What sort of girl?"

Elena saw an opportunity to seize the moral high ground.

"You know. Vulnerable."

"You mean likely to sell her body for cash? Well, no, as you correctly identify I'm not that sort. I didn't make you get involved either."

"You asked for my help."

"Which you readily give. If you want out, then go."

Elena gestured to the door. Robin just shook his head.

"Don't be daft. I'm just hurt you couldn't confide in me, after so many weeks. Anyway, I'm confused. You're a European national, so why are you travelling on a fake passport?"

Whatever happened next, Elena knew she absolutely could not answer that.

"I can't tell you. Please don't ask."

"Elena, I'm a police officer. I can't date criminals."

Before she knew what was happening, Elena had pushed the table towards him, splashing beer over the edge of their glasses. She tossed her chair back and stood up.

"If that's what I am to you now, then fine."

Elena thought of sitting down again. Robin's face suddenly looked so forlorn, like a little boy informed that his birthday had been cancelled. She couldn't. The only safe thing to do now would be to push him away. She'd get her stuff from the hotel, get back to the flat, collect Ana and disappear. Robin had to stay in Birmingham overnight for work. London was a big city. Ana might need to start at yet another school and Elena would have to find another job but there were other big cities where they might vanish—Manchester, Liverpool, Glasgow. She'd heard Edinburgh was lovely…

"Elena, don't. Let's talk it out. There might be a way…"

"Why don't you just fucking arrest me? It's much easier."

Elena thrust out her wrists, as if asking for cuffs. Robin just put his hands on her arms, softly. The gesture almost wilted her resolve. She stole herself, turned and walked stiffly out into the fading evening light.

Robin didn't immediately follow her, and Elena couldn't decide how she felt about that. She half-walked, half-jogged back to the Premier Inn, heart thumping with more adrenalin than her exertions required. Packing didn't take long—she'd only got as far as piling clothes from her suitcase onto the bed. Putting them back in took only moment and Elena found herself choking back tears and, even more pathetically, dithering, taking far more time than was necessary.

She had just closed the zip on the small case Robin had packed and brought down for her when there was a familiar knock—tentative but recognisable. Elena had the only pass-card to the room. She went to let him in.

He greeted her only with a hug that was almost painfully tight. They held one another until it became apparent nobody was going anywhere. Tears ran down Elena's cheeks onto Robin's dark grey jacket.

"You'll have to tell me, Elena. But not now. Not just yet. When you're ready, okay?"

Robin pulled back, holding her at arm's length to look at her. Elena quickly wiped away her tears and nodded, mute with a lump in her throat. He wasn't going to turn her in. They could get through this.

He leaned in for a kiss. It began as an apology and ended in hunger. They fell back upon the bed, Elena pushing her suitcase onto the floor. Its thump was accompanied by Robin's laughter. He ran his hand firmly up and down her spine, under her clothes, a movement that always soothed and reassured her. She could feel his growing stiffness against her thigh as he pushed her skirt up her legs. She could smell her own response, a warm and heady scent. This was what she had been missing and wanting all day. To think that moments ago, it had seemed that this intimacy would be lost to Elena forever.

When they had finished, Elena climbed off her exhausted partner and walked naked to the bathroom for a tumbler of water. They shared deep gulps and sat up against the white cushions on the now-rumpled purple coverlet.

"Do you think she killed her own sister?" asked Robin. "With her father?"

"I doubt. Maybe he has it in him, but not her. Family bonds are strong though."

She still hadn't told him about Abdullahi attacking her. That would just cause him to worry even more about her. Elena ran her fingers down the size of Robin's angular face, feeling a three-day stubble prickle against her skin.

"Go easy on her, Robin." She rarely said his name aloud, Elena realised.

He thought for a moment, then nodded.

"I will. She's been through a lot."

Although she didn't tell him, it was that last comment that made her finally respond to the first words he'd said to her in Channings. She rolled the words around her mouth, trying them on for size, but didn't say them.

I love you too.

CHAPTER 47

Digital Forensics worked on Taifa's laptop throughout the night. They carefully dried it out, opened it, removed the drives, cleaned them, electrically tested them, connected them to hardware that gently spun their mechanisms over sensors that read every fragmented bit and byte of data. The resultant stream of billions of ones and zeros was separated into easily readable and unreadable data. Anything that a PC's operating system could not readily decipher was further analysed using proprietary software shared between MI5, the Met, and the ministry of defence. It was a process that, in a heavily encrypted machine, could take days, even weeks.

It took just eight and a half hours to fully read the data left on Qamar Liibaan's laptop. After all, she had nothing to hide (although her clients certainly did). That said, weeks in a filthy duckpond had reduced much of its contents to unsalvageable slurry. What remained was mostly valueless, in law enforcement terms at least. Holiday and family photos, letters to credit card companies, an iTunes folder leaning heavily towards jazz, R&B and, surprisingly, country music.

Then the spreadsheet Elena had already obtained... and something else. Hidden away in Taifa's iTunes media folder under the fictional band name of 'Burao Boys' was a selection of videos. Most were heavily corrupted. The ones that remained seemed to show Qamar's bedroom as she greeted and serviced some of her clients, presumably secretly filmed using her laptop's webcam. The forensics officers got more than they bargained for, with one having to explain to his departmental head that he was not watching internet pornography.

309

Then, a little before 3am, digital forensics wizard Nigel Willard-Tompkins proved himself invaluable once again by managing to retrieve several emails sent out by Taifa that seemed to be directed to clients. Banal stuff—confirming dates and times of appointments—but with the right warrants the email addresses could probably be traced to IP addresses and thence to individuals' computers. It was a red-hot lead; Nigel accepted the high-fives from his colleagues gladly, although they existed purely in his imagination. He dutifully stayed in the office a full hour after his shift ended to Zip up the videos and emails and FTP-them to DI Shah and her team in time for their morning briefing.

Impressed by his digital prowess, the new intern Natalie coyly asked Nigel if he fancied a quick cocktail in a late-night bar she knew round the corner. Remarkably this event occurred in the real world and not in his imagination. Nigel didn't bother disabusing her of the grossly mistaken notion that he drank cocktails. He gladly accepted, pouring out the half pint of cold black coffee he'd forgotten to drink.

Nigel Willoughby-Tompkins loved his job.

Given the nature of the material and the need for secrecy that she insisted was paramount with AC and the press sniffing around this case, DI Shah decided that they would view the video material Nigel has sent them in Yarmouth's room at the Premier Inn.

Elena had panicked a little and gone into frenzied cleaning mode, when she heard that Shah, Nigel and Tom Fleischer were coming round in half an hour. Tom and Nigel had caught an early morning train up from London, the latter looking unusually dishevelled and yawning constantly, until he fell asleep after Bicester.

I don't want everyone knowing our business, Elena said, smoothing down the duvet.

Robin decided it was better not to tell her they'd been the subject of office gossip for weeks. Her helped her tidy away their discarded clothes and hid the used condom under a wad of tissue in the bathroom bin.

It felt weird sitting around in a semi-circle on armchairs and the freshly made bed in which Elena and Yarmouth had made love just hours before, watching the murder victim and her Johns fucking in variously enthusiastic, awkward, and drunken ways. But weird was becoming the norm in Elena's world, she now realised. She did wonder, however, as her mind drifted during one painfully prolonged and dull sequence of anonymous rutting, why Shah seemed suddenly so amenable to her presence having warned her off so clearly the previous evening. Perhaps Robin had spoken to her?

"So, what have we learned?" asked Shah listlessly after they had finished watching the ninth and penultimate video.

"That our victim was a consummate professional," answered Tom Fleischer, prompting uneasy laughter.

So far, they had seen little evidence of a likely killer amongst the lonely and desperate men (and one somewhat butch woman) that had frolicked upon Qamar's divan. There was just one video left. Immediately it started playing, Yarmouth sat bolt upright from his semi-reclining position on the bed (Elena was tactfully standing as far away from it as possible). The indistinct images that played across the screen had piqued his curiosity instantly because it was the only one in which the participant was masked. Elena's own response was an involuntary gasp.

It was a cartoonish fox mask, a parody of vulpine cunning. The well-built yet slim man beneath it was clad from head to foot in tight-flitting black clothing. He prowled towards Qamar holding a length of rope stretched tight between gloved hands. Qamar did a relatively convincing impersonation of a woman in fear for her life, ruined a little by her suddenly laughing when the 'fox-man' tripped over the edge of the rug and did a little hopping dance to recover. Qamar replaced her fake-fear face quickly as he advanced again, hitching up ill-fitting black trousers with a pinkie finger hooked into a belt loop. Qamar crawled backwards onto the bed as he straddled her and put the rope to her neck.

Shah's team had leaned forward intently at this point, half-hoping, half-fearing that they had their man.

Qamar kneed her 'attacker' in the solar plexus and he fell to one side, not entirely convincingly, as she hooked her legs over and around him, grabbing the rope and looping it around his neck, tying it expertly into a slipknot before grabbing the long end with her left hand and unbuttoning his black jeans. She drew a moderate sized erection from his underwear and began stroking him as the rope pulled tighter and tighter.

"Fucking hell mate! You're do yourself an injury right there," exclaimed Fleischer watching this, dispelling the tension in the room.

With a few quick spasms and an unimpressive ejaculation, the fox-man was done. Qamar lovingly untied the rope, saying something to him and kissing his fox mask. The videos had no sound and Shah let them know that they would have a lip-reader on it by the following morning.

As Qamar clambered off the fox-man, she began to wipe her hands on tissues from a nearby box. The man wiped himself down and then walked out of the room, not looking back at Qamar, who flicked an unmistakably furtive look at her laptop before reaching for it. Moments later, the image futzed out in a flicker of distortion.

"Could it be him?" Yarmouth asked. "He grew bored of role-play, came back for the real thing?"

Elena looked thoughtful. Weirdly, she realised that the other three were silently looking at her. Shah cleared her throat.

"You knew Ms Liibaan. Do you think she looked frightened there, just before she switched off the camera?"

Elena clicked the laptop's control pad. Replaying the video. She froze it on the moment Qamar's eyes flicked to the screen. Elena had the eerie impression that Qamar was looking right at her in that petrified moment. Her eyes were slightly narrowed and her mouth tight with concentration. The look of a person with something important to achieve, quickly.

"She's scared, for sure," Elena offered. "But maybe just getting caught. I can't imagine any of her... clients would have been very pleased."

Shah hmm-ed, then turned business-like. "Right folks. This is the strongest lead yet. Follow digital forensics' lead on this one. We want all IP addresses of Qamar's clients, find the men, get them interviewed."

"And woman," Fleischer added. "The bull dyke could certainly have killed 'er."

"Whatever. Just get them on tape. Show them the videos, by all means. We need to know what they know. We

313

need to look into their eyes and let them know they're under scrutiny. The guilty party will make a mistake."

Tom Fleischer rubbed his face like a man dealing with a relentless hangover.

"I still fancy Bob for this. This is blackmail material the victim's collecting. That's my opinion, anyhow."

"She still might have filmed the killer," noted Yarmouth.

"True," said Shah. "We need to get Taifa to talk. Threaten her with her father's imprisonment."

"Really?" asked Elena.

Was threating a suspect's family standard procedure? Elena had said nothing for some time now and felt a little edgy, restless.

"Follow them," she suggested.

Shah was frowning at her with an intensity that could go either way—into outright scorn or grudging appreciation.

"Who? The Liibaans? Why?"

"Let Taifa know we have laptop and have retrieved some material," Elena said. "If she doesn't know killer's identity, let her go. See if she heads for parents or tries to leave the country. Or meets someone that was commissioned to do killing. This guy..."

Elena jabbed her fingers at the shadowy figure frozen in mid-stride away from the camera behind the worried face of Qamar Liibaan.

"He was the last video she made and one of the longest. I have a feeling..."

Shah rolled her eyes.

"We work on facts and evidence, not feelings. I'm afraid I'll have to ask to reiterate that you should have no more to do with this investigation. DC Yarmouth—see that you maintain appropriate boundaries from now on."

Robin looked like he was swallowing a retort. In the end a sigh seemed more appropriate.

"Whatever you say, ma'am."

Fleischer was already getting his coat from a hook behind the door. Yarmouth alone paid any real attention to what Elena said next.

"I think this one knows. Mr Fox."

CHAPTER 48

DI Sanchita Shah found herself in the unenviable position of having to call Elena Balan just a few hours after again warning her off the case. It seemed Ms Balan was considerably more than just Robin Yarmouth's latest squeeze (or a material witness). After sitting in near-total silenced opposite a stony-faced Taifa Liibaan for forty-five minutes while she and her lawyer rebuffed every question and Yarmouth watched from a chair pushed a little back from the interview table, Shah desperately needed a breakthrough. Then, out of the wall of silence came six words that shocked both Mr Anthony Welch, Advocate and DI Shah.

"I'll speak to Elena. Only her."

The interview room at Erdington was noticeably smaller and less well-appointed than the ones at Savile Row, its walls dirtier, its atmosphere dingier. Cold too—the temperature hovering around in that zone between uncomfortable and the legal minimum for a working environment. Shah wondered whether the local police found this worked to their advantage—it was not a place you would want to spend any length of time.

"I'll give her a call," Shah sighed, leaving the room to do the negotiating.

Elena had been driving back to London to see Ana, whom Aldona had seen off to school that morning. She anticipated being back in the capital by about 2pm, in plenty of time to catch up on the housework she'd been putting off for days before Ana got home. DI Shah apparently had other ideas, however. Elena had pulled over into a lay-by behind a couple of parked lorries as soon as she had seen the unknown number appearing on her buzzing phone. Shah's tone was blandly official but was that a hint of something more ingratiating in her voice?

Elena listened, thought quickly about her daughter, managed to go through an arc of worry, guilt, acceptance and excitement before delivering her answer.

"I'm only about forty minutes away. I can be there by 11."

Then she called Ana and managed to catch her during her morning break. Ana's response to her mother asking if it was okay for her to come home to an empty house for a few hours was predictably matter of fact. Elena could almost see the implied shrug.

"Yeah, of course. What's up?"

"There's been a development in the case. They want me to attend."

Ana's laughter cut through the repetitive whooshing of motorway traffic.

"A development in the case? What, are you Sherlock now?"

"Hey, cheeky. I'll be home by five thirty. Help yourself to something if you're hungry."

"Oh, I will. Don't worry about that."

Minutes later, Elena was speeding back the way she had come. She had a strange feeling that they were close to something now—the killer would soon be identified and caught. One thing in her life could finally be laid to rest—her irrational guilt at somehow letting Qamar down —even if other worries and sources of guilt surrounded her like a bad smell.

Taifa looked numb and exhausted through the one-way glass, but as Elena walked into the interview room, her face lit up a little. She thinks I'm a friend, realised Elena.

"May I remind you that Taifa Liibaan is here voluntarily to give her statement and is not under arrest or caution," said Anthony Welch, probably more for his client's reputation than anyone else's.

"We're all aware of that Mr Welch," said Yarmouth. "And we appreciate it."

"It's highly irregular for my client to be questioned by anyone who is not a law enforcement officer."

"Ms Balan is here to listen and observe only. If Miss Liibaan wishes to speak to her, that is her prerogative. Any questioning will be done by our officers."

Okay, thought Elena. This is going to be tricky.

"I believe you asked for me," Elena said, trying to make sure it sounded like a statement, rather than a question.

Taifa nodded.

"Can you please answer with a verbal yes or no, please, Miss Liibaan," reminded Shah.

"Yes, but they must all leave. Even you."

Taifa turned to Mr Welch here and shot him a look of such absolute conviction that he didn't even try to argue.

"Just be aware that you are being recorded on camera and on tape," said Welch.

"On hard disk," Shah clarified, unnecessarily.

"That's okay," said Taifa.

"And we'll still have to observe the interview through the glass," said Yarmouth, gesturing to the dark panel in the long wall behind them.

Elena thought this was a generous touch, although she was also sure Taifa's lawyer would have clued her in to the surveillance.

After a few moments' more silent thought, Taifa concurred with a nod. They all took their places in the interview suite, on either side of the glass. Elena cleared her throat, put her hands flat on the table, the way she'd found effective when dealing with frustrated and sometimes desperate immigrants at Voices Unlimited.

"Taifa. Please tell me what you know. We only want to understand what happened to Qamar. We're here to help."

Elena hoped her request was open enough to prompt something honest and useful from the thin young woman opposite her. At first it seemed unlikely. Taifa's stony silence remained. Then the young Somali closed her eyes and took a deep breath. Taifa made a noise in her throat that sounded something like a sigh and began.

"When I saw her, she was already dead. Hanging there. I climbed on a chair and tried to pull her down, but I couldn't. It didn't matter. I knew she was gone."

At this point, Taifa broke down and Elena passed her a packet of handkerchiefs. Over the rest of the interview, she would use all but one of them, squashing each sodden sheet in turn into a neat ball and lining them up before her before taking another.

Elena thought about the stool positioned oddly behind Qamar, the one that some officers thought she used as a step to reach the higher dining chair (the one she had supposedly kicked over). Now its presence made sense. As did the fibres found on her blouse—threads from the slightly ragged hem of her sister's hijab perhaps?

"I'm sorry I lied. I thought I'd be in trouble. I couldn't stand to leave her there either. I thought I'd call father but before I did, I wanted to remove every trace of what she was doing... The men. I took some items from her room. Including the laptop."

Elena could almost sense the frustration behind the glass as she failed to (decided not to) follow up with the

319

obvious question: what items? Instinctively, Elena knew she had to let Taifa talk.

"I hated seeing her like that, but I couldn't bring her down. Of course, I called my father and he drove down but before he got here Qamar was found and the street was full of police. I threw everything away except the laptop. I didn't tell my dad about it because I was frightened what he would say. I just said she had been seeing a dangerous man. He pushed me but I wouldn't say anything more."

"You took the laptop home?"

"Yes. I broke into it and got that list. And more..."

"Taifa, we recovered the laptop. We saw the videos."

"Then you saw the kind of beasts she was with. Filthy animals. I wanted to kill them all."

At this point, Taifa's lawyer attempted to intercede, opening the interview room door, but she waved him away with a hand gesture that brooked no contradiction.

"Of course, I couldn't do anything of the sort. The Qur'an forbids it. But I did want retribution, so I emailed them, told them about the videos, asked them for money or I would tell the police. It was just a bluff but..."

Outside, an audible groan from Mr Welch, QC.

"Some of them paid up. In fact, I heard from them all except one. I was going to give the money to the mosque. They have a programme for poor kids, to support their education and get them apprenticeships. Something good should come of all this degeneracy."

"That's good, Taifa," Elena said, calming Taifa's rage. "This is all very helpful. Thank you for talking to us."

Robin and Shah re-entered the interview room, sensing a conclusion. There were a few more tentative questions from DI Shah, which Miss Liibaan, surprisingly, chose to answer. Then, with a curt nod and faint smile of appreciation directed at Elena, Taifa left with Mr Welch in tow.

Shah turned to Elena, with a look that somehow mingled resignation and awe.

"She wouldn't say a word to us to begin with. I guess we owe you some thanks."

You definitely do, thought Elena, shaking Shah's hand.

In a local greasy spoon café, a little later (more convivial that the antiseptic environment of the Erdington station), Yarmouth, Shah and Elena sat cradling mugs of tea. Shah gave one of her habitual 'where we are now' summaries of the case and the conversation came around to Taifa's admissions of blackmail.

"CPS can probably be persuaded not to press for Taifa's conviction, given some of Qamar's client list," offered Yarmouth.

Shah snorted. Elena looked concerned.

"If you can spare her from that, so much the better. She's suffered enough."

"I agree," said Shah, surprising Elena. "But let's get her computer to Digital Forensics and chase down those email threads. It might help us isolate the killer."

Something was bothering Elena.

"She said she had responses from all but one of Qamar's clients. Who, when threatened with exposure for regularly visiting a prostitute, doesn't bother to reply?"

"That's a fair point," said Yarmouth. "I reckon we start there. Something else I noted down. Taifa said there were eight videos, corresponding to one for each client but there were nine clients on her spreadsheet and nine people Taifa emailed or texted."

Shah was already dialling. After about eight rings she got through. The music in the background, which sounded like old hardcore punk to Elena, perhaps Hüsker Dü, was suddenly turned down as Shah held the phone a foot from her ear, then put it down onto the table on speakerphone.

"Nigel? You there?"

Sure, sorry, just turning down the Mould.

"The what?"

"Bob Mould... Ex-Hüsker Dü frontman? Never mind. What can I do for you?"

How many video clips did you rescue for the Liibaan case?

"I sent you eight, didn't I?"

"Yes, but you didn't find any more on there?"

"Nope. Well, there was one clip which is basically just an empty room."

"Sorry?"

"There was a static shot of her room. Nothing moving in it."

"Nigel," began Shah, a note of frustration entering her voice. "Did I or did I not ask you to send me everything you found?"

"Yes... but I was just trying to be helpful. There's nothing there, the front of the clip is completely lost."

"Is there a timestamp?"

"Well, yes. I could go and check it if you like."

Shah's annoyance was palpable, but she held it in check.

"Yes please, Nigel. If you would be so kind. And FTP it to me while you're at it, will you?"

Forty minutes later, nearing the end of their second cup of tea (green for Elena) Shah managed to download the clip, which Nigel had confirmed was the last one in the sequence and recorded around the time that Qamar was killed. Shah and the others decided it might be prudent to take their meeting outside to the local park. They found some benches by an empty swing-park and Shah expanded the WMV file to file the screen and hit play on her iPad.

The next 2 minutes and 47 seconds would change everything.

CHAPTER 49

The missing video clip begins with static, which coalesces and cuts abruptly into a view of an empty room.

The shot is a static image of Qamar's bedroom, the laptop evidently having been positioned on the bedside table. The plush red bedspread and crisp white sheets are rumpled and tangled. There are some items on the bed— a large black dildo and a smaller, lipstick-shaped device, presumably a vibrator. A lamp has been knocked over and casts a long yellow oval over the floor towards Qamar's tall vintage wardrobe. The wardrobe has a similarly oval mirror set into each door. The room is dimly lit, but a window must be open because a flicker of lace curtain can be seen blowing back and forth in the reflection of the window behind the laptop.

It is dark in the room and inky black in the street outside, as the occasional glimpses of window reveal. An orange streetlight appears and vanishes behind the net curtain. There is no sound on the clip.

Nothing happens for a minute and five seconds. Watching the image, Elena is reminded of some obscure late-night programme she caught once—a Warhol retrospective. An image of a sleeper, unmoving, just sleeping. Except there is no sign of the room's resident in Qamar's video.

Then—something moves. The breeze in the room picks up and the right-hand wardrobe door, improperly shut, blows gently open. As it does, its mirror catches something out in the hallway. Here Nigel, doing penance for his mistake, had enhanced a part of the image, zooming in, sharpening the lines, brightening, and enlarging the tiny reflection in the glass oval that he had missed first time round.

The figures are dimly lit and only part of them can be seen. A tallish, male figure, lithe, dressed all in black and wearing some sort of mask, reaches out of sight, hands obscured by the doorframe. The wardrobe door creaks further open, revealing a woman's shape, naked, dark-skinned, under this man and writhing.

"Fuck—that's Qamar. And that's him," says Elena, gulping down her instinctive fear response.

The others are too shocked to comment.

Qamar's body, visible only from ribcage to knees, jerks spasmodically under the man who is presumably strangling her. It seems to take an age for her to stop moving and something instinctively in Elena wills her to stop, to submit. The horror of that moment—how the seconds must have stretched out in unimaginable agony—appalled her.

The masked man stands up as Qamar's body finally lies still, some ninety-two seconds later. He turns away from the camera and the image again implodes into static. Nigel had recovered the only usable parts of the image. The rest was just random ones and zeroes and corrupted and unreachable disk sectors. But what is showed was a murder.

"I've seen the aftermath, been to the mortuary. I've never seen it happen before my eyes," Shah said, quietly.

Yarmouth closed the laptop, exhaling a breath he didn't know he was holding.

"It's the guy in the fox mask. As we suspected. We have to track him down."

"I'll bet he's the one who didn't reply to Taifa's threats," adds Shah. "He couldn't risk exposing himself.

He would be the only one to know the threats weren't from Qamar. And he was probably sensible enough to create layers of protection on that email address. I'll see where forensics are with it."

Elena had a thought but didn't choose to express it until Shah had left, in a taxi to the train station for the express back to London.

"Robin, I've got an idea."

"Go on."

His look was more that of a colleague than a lover. For a moment, Elena wondered if their moment might have passed.

"Qamar was doing webcams, putting her stuff on net. I wonder…"

"You think this was a session? Maybe someone recorded it?"

"There's whole websites devoted to clips of these girls. I did research."

Elena gave Robin a wry look.

"They're like… superstars and they have super-fans, who send them gifts and stuff. It's supposed to be just live streaming but maybe, if this was session, someone might have recorded?"

"They would have the whole clip," Robin realised. "It's worth a shot. Thing is this guy knows what he's doing. He's covered up from head to foot."

"Maybe he takes the mask off? Gives himself away some other way," Elena countered.

Robin reached forward, grabbing and kissing her forehead like a proud parent. Not quite the contact Elena found her body longing for, but she'd take what she could get.

"You're really good at this, Elena."

"I know." She smiled warmly, taking the initiative as she took his hand. "Your girlfriend's a better cop than you are."

Robin pinched her. "Oi! I'll have none of that cheek."

Then he kissed her with hunger and relief flooded Elena. When he broke away, Robin suddenly had a plan.

"I'll track down the owner of the camgirl business. I'll also arrange some protection for Taifa. She might be a target if he's getting paranoid."

"And what will I do?" Elena asked, suddenly disappointed to be seemingly off the team.

"You'll come with me of course. You are invaluable."

The word filled her with happiness. It was a sentiment she could get used to.

Tom Fleischer made an appreciative whistling sound when Yarmouth filled him in on the phone, just after dropping Elena off at home. Yarmouth had to raise his voice over the rush-hour Marylebone traffic as he negotiated a route through to his place off the Holloway Road.

"Looks like you're getting close," said Fleischer. "Are you sure it's not just some sick role-play though? Seems she was into some pretty far-out stuff. I mean, her clients were."

"I did consider it but there's something in that clip, something really brutal and sordid. It just feels like murder."

"I hear you. And Nigel can't recover the rest of the clip?"

"Nah. It's gone. But there's just a slim chance there's another copy."

"Taifa Liibaan?"

"No. We've got all we can from her. I'll tell you more when I've looked into it."

"Come on mate, don't keep me in the cold."

"Don't worry, you'll know as soon as I do. It's a long shot. Hey—got to go."

Robin hung up, seeing another call come in. Nigel.

"Nige. What can I do for you?"

Not used to his name being abbreviated, Nigel's tone contained a note of surprise.

"Em. Well, I found out who owns PhantasyGirls. You'll never guess..."

"Malcolm Carver by any chance?"

"How did you know?"

Nigel sounded disappointed. He'd hoped this was a breakthrough that would counter his recent blunder.

"I didn't. Just a hunch. Well done though. Great work."

Robin hung up the call on his car's phone, took a sharp left into a side-street and managed a deft three-point turn. He got the blue light going and switched on the siren. This next hour he would enjoy very much indeed.

Elena looked a little flustered when Robin met her in Carlisle Street just fifteen minutes after he'd dropped her off. Ana had been midway into a rant about the clique-y bitches in her new school when Elena had taken his call and had to cut the mother-daughter time short. Ana was not much impressed. She agreed to double-lock the doors and stay inside while her mother promised, on her life, that it would be a half hour at most.

"It's routine, Elena, but you should be there," said Robin. "You read people really well. I want to know what his reaction tells you."

They walked straight into Carver's office, without more than a nod of acknowledgement to Janice in the reception room. She began a limp protest, but it was lost as Robin slammed the door shut, waking Carver from what appeared to be a late afternoon cat-nap.

"What the fuck? Can't a man grab fifty winks in peace?" Carver groaned, rising from his sofa and throwing the newspaper that had been propped in front of his face onto the floor.

He'd been sleeping with a full-body photograph of Penny Mordaunt across his forehead, Elena noted. Each to his own.

"You'll have all the sleep you could possibly want in the Scrubs," Robin said, feigning indifference. "I need you to give me access to the customer database for Phantasy-Girls. We think one of your pet perverts might have recorded a killing."

This was a telling moment. Robin and Elena knew that Carver's expression would betray one species of surprise or another. The first would just be the surprise of a man who has heard a tall story that indirectly relates to his business. The second might be the shock of a man who has been protecting a murderer and whose world is about to collapse about him.

Carver began to laugh. The noise, though ugly and akin to a water buffalo snorting at a drinking pool, sounded genuine enough.

"You're kidding me? No? Over my dead body will I give you anything like that. The porn business is like the confessional—there's a sacred bond."

"Oh, fuck off. We have warrant."

This was supposed to be Robin's line, but Elena stole it, enjoying the moment as Robin threw down the legal document that would force Carver to divulge business-sensitive information.

Carver reached for it, scanned each page with open mouth.

"How did you get this?"

"It's called due process Malcolm. You should try it sometime."

"And if I refuse?"

Elena held up another document, concealed in a brown paper envelope.

"Then we have this other warrant," explained Robin, "which basically allows my colleagues to tear this place apart. And the secret storage space you've got under the roof."

Fleischer had volunteered this last piece of information a few weeks ago, gleaned from his time as Carver's handler. Carver basically had two sets of books—one for the HMRC and one for his own nefarious purposes.

"There's nothing up there but spiders and piles of old spank mags. You're welcome to it. That said, I would like to co-operate with you lot, if only to get you out of my hair so I can actually do some bloody work."

"Go on then, give," said Elena, holding out a pale hand.

"I don't have it to hand, missy. Call this number, ask for Doberman. He'll give you the address and you can pop round there and collect it. I wouldn't bet on any of the scrotes on our subscriber list helping you though. And mind who you shake hands with, if you know what I mean."

Carver mimed sticky palms. It was Robin's turn to laugh now. Some part of him really did rather like Carver.

"Where there's a will, there's a warrant."

Carver was already scribbling the eleven-digit number on the corner of page 34 of The Sun. Elena folded it into her pocket. They left with a shared sense of triumph and Robin didn't wait until they had even left the building before he took her hand, pulled her to him and kissed her.

"You, my dear, were magnificent."

Tearing up the manila envelope containing a copy of The Big Issue and dropping it into the bin, Elena smiled an inner smile. I was, wasn't I?

CHAPTER 50

The main office of PhantasyGirls turned out to be the only completely enclosed corner of a warehouse in Brixton owned by Carver. The rest of the 1000-square foot space was crudely partitioned into 'rooms' containing artfully styled but cheap furniture and questionably 'glamorous' backdrops of big city skylines, sunset beaches and, in one case, rather ironically, a gloomy-looking dungeon. Variously bored or excitable young women trooped in and out of these rooms, strutting down the corridor between the two rows in six-inch heels, making themselves tea in the tiny kitchen attached to the office or popping to the bathroom that still displayed traces of the factory-setting the company had taken over—an enormous urinal trough, largely unused, faced by a eight toilet cubicles and four showers. The bathroom was also the only space in which there were no mirrors.

The warehouse echoed with a heady throb of R'n'B and pop music, not all of it in English. It was brightly lit, the two-dozen cubicles roofless, although some were draped with gauzy fabrics to give a more 'Bedouin' feel. There was a pungent cocktail of skin-lotion, hairspray and perfume in the air. As 'Chief Executive' Madeline Parsons showed Elena and Yarmouth round, it felt a little like she'd forgotten they were from the police and were perhaps interesting in franchising this innovative outsourcing of the sexual urge.

"The girls rent the spaces in eight-hour shifts. We charge a little more for the prime-time shift, which runs from 8pm until 4am. Other than that, they keep every penny."

If Miss Parsons was feigning professional pride, she was doing it very well. Elena had to admit to herself that the set-up did seem very efficient.

"I'll show you one of the rooms if you like."

Elena and Yarmouth exchanged a look. They knew one another well enough to know that curiosity must be satisfied.

"Sure," Yarmouth said, letting the women lead the way.

"Melody called in sick today so her room will be free."

Miss Parsons opened a partition that Elena was amused to note was a repurposed toilet door, complete with "vacant" indicator. The interior of the space was about the size of Ana's room back home. The inadvertent comparison made Elena shudder. If she ever found out Ana was doing something like this for money...

"We supply a double bed, a small wardrobe plus the laptop. Everything else belongs to the girls," said Miss Parsons, her tone still proprietorial.

Elena looked at the smartly-made bed, wider than her own. As if reading her mind, Miss Parsons shot back:

"This one's actually King-size. Melody, Charm and Destiny are three of our most popular girls. They sometimes like to bring friends along."

Yarmouth cleared his throat.

"Other girls I mean. Purely softcore. We're fastidious about our license and about the law, officers."

"I'm not actually..." Elena began but stopped when she saw Yarmouth's surreptitious head-shake.

Yarmouth examined the laptop, wireless mouse, and webcam remote. There was also a strange pink device with a tail.

"That allows customers to… interact with the girls remotely. Bluetooth.

Yarmouth dropped the device as if electrocuted.

"The girls can control the view that customers get. Some of them get a bit creative with mirrors."

Elena opened a drawer of the small bedside cabinet. It contained a selection of surprising large sex toys. She shut it and nodded sagely as if taking a library tour. This was so weird.

"A popular girl can make around three hundred pounds a shift, sometimes more. Not bad for eight hours work, is it? Some work pretty much full-time at it. You can earn over two grand a week, before tax."

"They pay tax?" asked Yarmouth.

"Of course. We insist. This is a proper business, officers."

Yarmouth suddenly looked bored.

"Okay, okay. Thanks for the guided tour. Can we ask you some questions, in private now?"

Miss Parsons' smile slipped a little at his brusqueness. Elena recognised the strategy—he was reminding her of her status, of the risk of not co-operating. As respectable as this business purported to be, Elena was sure it had some shady corners.

They repaired to the office which was as functional but comfortable as the boudoirs beyond. Elena and Yarmouth sank into a plush leopard-skin sofa, while Miss Parsons sat on a high stool, long legs crossed at the ankles. Elena could tell that her swelling bosom was partially manufactured.

"Did you once work as a Cam Girl?" Elena began, surprising the others with her directness. Their hostess took the question in her stride.

"For a couple of years, I did. In a seedy room in Shoreditch, along with other... transactions I'm less proud of. The problem was I could see how to make a proper business of it, but my employers were rather more short-sighted. They didn't take kindly to my criticism."

Here Miss Parsons rolled up her right sleeve to display an undulating welt of fused skin running from her elbow up and over her shoulder. A burn, as healed as it ever would be.

"Some of the clients pay more for scarred girls, oddly enough."

An edge of bitterness crept into Miss Parsons' veneer. She smoothed it over, but Elena saw the fragility still lurking beneath the pristine surface.

"Then I met Carver and pitched my idea to him. Fortunately, he can spot a real opportunity when he sees it. Two years on, we have over three hundred girls... and a few boys. And over ninety thousand subscribers and climbing."

Yarmouth gave a whistle of mock appreciation. Elena wanted clarification.

"You said three hundred? There's only maybe thirty here."

"Most of our girls work from home. Here it's just the transients and those who want to separate home and work life. Some have boyfriends and hubbies who wouldn't really approve, although we find they seldom question their girlfriend's income, interestingly enough."

Yarmouth shifted in his seat. Elena knew that tell—he was impatient.

"I can see you run a legitimate, albeit rather sleazy business Miss Parsons. It's actually those subscribers we're here about. Now we have a warrant so..."

"It's no problem. Carver phoned ahead, told me exactly what you need."

Miss Parsons' immaculately manicured nails deftly plucked a piece of paper from a folder on her desk.

There are the subscribers who were known fans of Miss Liibaan, or Black Cherry as we knew her. We can't record the guests who hover without registering but the metadata on these is tabulated for you on the right.

Elena flicked through the seven stapled pages with Yarmouth. It was double-sided and there were 914 names. The spreadsheet contained inscrutably-named columns—"hover time", "click-through rate" et cetera. How were they going to make head or tail of this? With comic turning, both turned to the other and said:

"Nigel."

As they were leaving, Yarmouth turned to Elena, a disbelieving smile on his face. Elena took his hand as they walked up the alleyway outside the PhantasyGirls warehouse. Robin's palm felt a little sweaty. Proximity to all those underdressed lovelies?

"Don't take this the wrong way," he began. "But she kind of reminds me of you."

"Ha! Do I seem like brothel madame now?" Said Elena with mock indignation.

"No, no. I mean, she's just so... composed. Steely."

Robin leaned away from her a few inches, squinting against s shaft of early evening sunlight to look at Elena's expression. Fortunately for him, she was smiling.

"She knows what she wants and gets it. Is a good business model too."

"Really?" Robin sounded surprised.

"It's clean, there's no contact, girls earn good money and is regular work," clarified Elena. "I can't see the harm."

Robin stopped in his tracks, span on his heels dramatically.

"Shall we go back and sign you up?"

"God no." Elena left a dramatic pause. "I'll work from home. I'll be called Nosferata and dress entirely in black with spider web underwear."

"Is it wrong that I'm becoming strangely aroused?"

What they both weren't saying, of course, was how close that destiny had been to a reality for Elena, had she been less fortunate and just a little more desperate.

With his newfound zeal for impressing both new girlfriend Natalie and his employers, Nigel ran the figures Miss Parsons had presented (she had even followed up with an emailed CSV file, making it easier to ingest the data) and within the hour had a report for them. He presented it over a pint of Wizard's Sleeve in the Temperance.

"I cross-referenced the subscribers who spent the most time on Miss Liibaan's profile with uploader profiles on the top five user-generated porn sites. I used a little hack there... don't tell the cybercrime boys."

Nigel's weirdly shrill laugh was offset nicely by a new habit he seemed to have formed for blinking a lot and rubbing his eyes. Elena wondered if there was an IT geek handbook of behavioural tics somewhere.

"Sorry," Nigel explained, "new contact lenses. I've never worn them before. Might have put one in back to front."

Elena felt a little ashamed for her cliched assumptions as Nigel continued.

"There were nineteen users who had uploaded clips ripped from PhantasyGirls and nine of those were of Black Cherry. Just one clip was removed and then deleted by site moderators. I've got a contact there. I mean, I found one."

Nigel blushed lightly at the implication. Yarmouth looked at the list of subscribers. One was highlighted—Morbidity666. Date of birth 11.03.07. Living in Stratford.

"I'm sure he's a charming kid," Yarmouth sighed. "Shall we go and talk to him?"

Elena knew the offer was more of a rhetorical question. She was in this to the bitter end.

"Of course. Stratford," she said. "Lay on, MacDuff."

Yarmouth and Nigel laughed far more than Elena's enthusiasm required, she thought. But then she'd never been to Shakespeare's birthplace.

CHAPTER 51

It had been Fleischer's idea, apparently, to maintain the illusion that they were headed for the Midlands. Robin had called in to keep his friend and DI Shah up to speed and Fleischer, ever the joker, had even sent through some tourist links for Robin to forward on to Elena to keep her preoccupied while the Jubilee line whooshed east instead of north-west.

It was only when they exited the station to a place that seemed to combine the most alienating aspects of large-scale housing development and shopping centre that Elena twigged that they weren't in Stratford-upon-Avon but just plain old Stratford. That Robin and Fleischer had conspired against her irked Elena more than she let show. She had to make do with a shoulder punch, administered to Robin a little more forcefully than usual.

Elena told herself she was right to have been distracted on the unexpectedly short journey here. They were zoning in on Qamar's killer. Justice would be done; the promise she'd made at Qamar's funeral would be kept.

"Sorry!" cried Robin, rubbing his shoulder, where her knuckles had hit bone. "That was mean."

"Yes, it was," Elena replied. "But I'm sure you'll find way to make it up to me."

They followed the directions Robin's iPhone indicated, short-cutting through the vast emporium of commerce that was Westfield to find what fragments of old Stratford remained. They crossed Liberty Bridge over the railway line and passed from the Olympic redevelopment zone into the more mundanely suburban part of town. There, halfway up Chobham Road, they found the house of serial school offender Morbid666, otherwise known as Hugo Bremner.

The name 'Hugo' might have alerted Elena as to what to expect had she known more about English nomenclature and class. She had expected a surly troublemaker who probably played angry bass guitar in a thrash-metal band. Again, her expectations were confounded.

On the second ring, the yellow-painted front door was opened by a rather elderly lady who, after some confusion and a good minute poring over Robin's police ID, let them into a small hallway that smelled of macaroni cheese. After she was satisfied as to Robin's identity, Mrs Bremner confirmed that their witness was home.

"I'd better go check on the supper," Sheila Bremner said. "My grandson Hugo's upstairs. You'd better knock. He gets a bit uppity if you barge in."

With that, the blue-haired and tiny lady of the house vanished into the kitchen. Robin and Elena tramped up the carpeted stairs and Robin rapped with professional vigour.

"I'll be out in ten!"

The muffled voice, accented midway between Hampshire and East London youth culture, sounded peevish. Robin knocked again.

"Hugo Bremner? This is Detective Constable Yarmouth of Scotland Yard."

There was a pregnant pause. The door opened six inches and a pale, thin and worried teenager appeared in the gap. He was wearing a Tinie Tempah t-shirt.

"If this is about the Blu Rays, those films are out of print. I mean, you can't get them anywhere, especially Cannibal Ferox. I didn't see any harm..."

Robin sighed. Elena recognised this as part of his professional performance.

"I couldn't care less about video piracy right now, son. This is about something else. Can we come in?"

Floppy-fringed and blonde Hugo looked around behind him, as if assessing the room for embarrassing detritus. Evidently the coast was clear; Hugo swung the door open wide.

The first thing Elena noticed was the smell. This was evidently a room in which a teenage boy spent a considerable amount of time masturbating. The curtains were drawn, and Hugo's laptop was closed but his large external drive's LED was winking guiltily.

Hugo walked over to the curtains, threw them open and pulled open a window.

"I was working out," he explained, indicating two dust-covered dumbbells in the corner of the room. The sixteen-year old's naivety was almost endearing.

"Morbid666?" Elena rolled the avatar name round her mouth, dramatically emphasising the demonic digits. "Bit of a weird name to choose for internet, isn't it?" she added.

Hugo's face didn't know whether to front confidence or betray insecurity. It settled on a kind of dopey gaucheness. Robin said nothing—he was watching Elena. He had evidently decided to let her lead this one. The thought filled Elena with a strange pride.

Hugo hovered awkwardly by the window. She wondered whether he planned to jump out. She decided to be kind.

"We're here because you may have witnessed a crime. You uploaded a video to the internet, to a site called Filthstore…"

"I was doing research... for a school project."

Hugo's accent slipped and the patois gave way to a Home Counties whine. Elena put a protective hand on his shoulder. She had no idea if it breached some sort of protocol, but she didn't care. The boy looked like he was about to explode with shame.

"We don't care, Hugo. You can be into whatever you like. We just want to see clip you uploaded."

Hugo took a moment to calm down. Then his skinny frame stiffened once more.

"You're not saying...? It's not real, is it? It looked really well made but..."

Elena looked at Robin for guidance. He stepped in.

"It's fake, but we have concerns about how the director treats his actors. Can we see the clip?"

Hugo finally relaxed when he realised that, in his case, 'helping the police with their enquiries' wasn't a euphemism. He fired up his laptop and nervously filled in the background of how the clip came into his possession.

"I got it off a website. I guess you know which one. The girl sometimes has this really weird bloke come round and they... do stuff. It's all, like, consensual and legal. At least I think so. I thought it was amazing... really vivid. I had to upload it. I'm sorry."

Elena felt torn. The kid was obviously into some dark and sexually deviant material. Then again, here he was, aged sixteen, living with his grandmother. A bit of research had unearthed how this came to happen. Hugo's parents had been killed in a road traffic accident at Christmas three years earlier. His father had been drinking heavily. His mother was pregnant. It was reported in the local press under the headline 'Couple Killed in Drink-Driving Smash' and the piece had carried a picture of the Audi, concertinaed against a motorway bridge. How that might affect a thirteen-year-old boy, Elena could only imagine.

Hugo had queued up the clip, after shielding the laptop first with his body. Did Elena want to know what he was hiding? Not really. The QuickTime file opened up, and Hugo hit play.

Surprisingly, the clip had audio. Something had evidently happened to corrupt the files they had recovered from Qamar's laptop. African-sounding pop music rang out; Elena thought perhaps Malian or Senegalese. Qamar's body moved into frame, draped in a shimmering silk bathrobe featuring Japanese dragon patterns, as bold and dynamic as Qamar herself. Qamar looked at the screen.

"I'm back!" She coo-ed, to her unseen admirers. "Don't keep me waiting though—let's go private."

Qamar propped one foot up on the bed and began to paint her toenails. Elena and Robin exchanged a look.

Elena whispered, "the coroner noticed she didn't finish."

Robin nodded, offering a grim little smile.

The video clip looked cropped and at one point an arrowhead cursor flicked across the screen, a tell-tale sign that this was ripped and clipped from Hugo's laptop screen. Hugo resumed his 'safe place' by the window as Elena and Robin watched the clip.

Qamar's bathrobe fell open a little at the front and she coyly did it up again, but not before a swelling curve of breast revealed itself, the hint of a dark nipple promising more to subscribers who "went private".

Moments later, the mood changed dramatically. A sound from behind Qamar evidently startled her. She drew the robe tighter and double-knotted the cord as the fox-faced intruder came in, marching straight into the bedroom from the unseen doorway and throwing something down on the bed. Keys. He had evidently let himself in.

Qamar immediately stood up, put her nail varnish bottle and brush to one side, and stepped away from the microphone. The argument that followed was scarcely audible over the sinuous, rhythmic music. Qamar turned her back to the laptop, as if deliberately covering it. Elena thought she caught the word 'funny' from Qamar. Was she saying "this isn't funny?' What happened next was far from amusing.

Fox-face slapped her, knocking her back onto the bed. She bounced immediately back to her feet, defiant but there was something a little performative too. Qamar raised her voice.

"Not the face. You're not my only regular, you know."

At this, Fox-face pulled a large knife from his inside pocket. Even though both Robin and Elena knew that Qamar had not been stabbed to death, this was a frightening sight. The intruder reached into the back-pocket of his trousers, retrieving a folded piece of paper with some difficulty in the gloves he was wearing. He shouted at her.

"Write what I say. And no funny business."

The line was hammy, the delivery given in a self-evidently faux-American accent. Elena almost wanted to laugh. Almost.

They watched Qamar grab a magazine and a pen from a drawer and write the suicide note that now lay in an evidence locker in central London. Elena took a mental note as Qamar hesitated over the signature. This was the moment she perhaps knew that something had changed. As soon as she lifted the pen from the paper, Fox-face made his move.

Fox-face grabbed her robe, tearing it from her shoulders. Elena wondered what was wrong with young Hugo's mind that he'd found this arousing. She found it overwhelmingly awful to see this proud Somali woman abused in this way in her own home.

Qamar, to her credit, fought back, for real this time, dislodging the knife from Foxface's hand with a kick. He must have retrieved it later, since it was never found. Elena surmised that by the time Foxface returned to the room, Qamar's screensaver had gone dark, hiding PhantasyGirls from view. The killer never suspected he was being watched, or if he did, didn't care.

Fortunately for Robin and Elena, although not for Qamar, Fox-face next pulled Qamar out of shot and presumably out into the hallway. The room stood empty for a few moments, the net curtain blowing into shot and leading them into the segment they already knew. To spare Hugo, and Elena, who was holding back a sob, Yarmouth fast forwarded the clip to where the wardrobe mirror revealed the murdered sex-worker's inert torso. The Fox-Face man then left the shot for a full minute before the body of Qamar Liibaan was dragged unceremoniously out of frame.

The clip ended.

"I stopped recording then," said Hugo. "I thought it was really well shot, that's all."

Elena knew he was lying. Suddenly she no longer had the urge to be kind to Hugo. She straightened and shouted in his face.

"You knew this was real and you did nothing! That makes you an accessory as well as a fucking freak!"

345

"Elena!" Robin held her back with an arm.

Unsteady footsteps were heard coming up the carpeted stairs outside. A frail voice.

"Hugo? Is everything all right."

Hugo looked utterly panic-stricken. "Please don't tell her. Gran's all I have left."

Minutes later, they were walking back up Chobham Road, Elena fuming and a little way ahead of Yarmouth, who was struggling to fit Hugo's laptop in his leather bag.

"I was right, wasn't I? He knew what he seen and he upload it because it was horrible and lots of disgusting, depraved blokes getting off on this stuff!"

"I don't think he knew for sure," Robin countered. "He may have suspected..."

"Don't be so fucking pedantic. Will you have him arrest?"

"Elena," Yarmouth began and Elena already knew the answer. "The kid is a juvenile, plus it would be almost impossible to prove. Plus—what's the point?"

"The point is... The point is that it's not okay! It's just not."

Elena felt the floodwaters breaking and the tears came. They came for her own culpability as much as Hugo's. She too had stood by while someone died, admittedly a man she despised. An abusive paedophile. But at least it had not aroused her in any way. Karl's death had been squalid and disgusting and so had Qamar's.

Robin kept his distance for a moment then cautiously walked forward. He reached out for a placatory hug. Not this time.

"No! you don't get it. You just don't. Death isn't a turn-on. I know."

Robin looked frustrated... then confused. "What do you mean you know?"

Before she had any time to reflect on what she was saying, the story of Karl's death poured out. The real reason why she had fled Romania, the significance of the false identities and Frances's part in all this. Elena didn't look at him as she recounted her story. Instead, she spat the memories out onto the chewing-gum spotted pavement. When she looked up, Robin was shaking his head, silently. He couldn't make eye contact with her.

"Well?" was all she could utter.

Robin just turned and walked away. Elena considered running after him. But then she didn't. She wasn't entirely sure why, but this felt important enough not to compromise with pleadings for understanding. He'd either get it or he wouldn't.

It wasn't until Robin's slim, loping form turned out of sight at the end of the street that Elena realised that she had just admitted involuntary manslaughter to a police officer she had only met a few weeks ago.

CHAPTER 52

Back at Savile Row, the Anti-Corruption rumblings were gathering pace. O'Leary and Barnett had been suspended pending the conclusion of the investigation. They had already admitted working for Carver on the side and O'Leary confessed to helping McPherson obtain his stolen phone; their careers looked shaky at best. McPherson was likewise suspended for tampering with evidence and obstructing an investigation, although as a more senior officer, it was possible he'd worm his way out of the indignity of being fired. Demotion and/or transfer looked likely.

There was an atmosphere of suspicion and mistrust about the department, with detectives and street police eying one another with doubt—who were the bad eggs and how far did the corruption reach? If AC were combing through the whole building, what else might they find? As everyone got their heads down and played it straight, there was a consequent lack of laughter and a feeling of permanently being watched.

Without the big personality of McPherson booming around the department, CID felt considerably quieter than usual as Yarmouth, Shah and Fleischer set up their presentation for DCI Purvis. Purvis brought in two AC investigators, a sharply suited officer called DI Bruncliffe and the equally power-dressed female DI Calton. Bruncliffe bore more than a little resemblance to the actor Idris Elba, which excited a couple of the female front desk staff until they discovered he was both gay and Anti-Corruption. Nobody liked a snoop, even if they brooded in a powerfully manly way. Calton was tall, blonde, and willowy. She had enjoyed long, geeky conversations about ultra-running with the department's own weekend athlete, DI Kevin Fletcher, who had had to defend himself when other officers had noticed his flirting. She might be AC but she's still human, he had protested. It was a minority opinion.

"DIs Calton and Bruncliffe are here just to observe," explained Purvis. "You can put your crucifixes and holy water away."

Uneasy laughter all round. Purvis stood flanked by the AC officers as Shah outlined the state of the Qamar Liibaan investigation so far. On the now redrawn suspect board, a still of the fox-masked man took centre-stage. Underneath, Shah had written the letter "M" with a question-mark. Even with the forensic and circumstantial evidence mounting, nobody could quite bring themselves to write out in full the name of their colleague for the whole department to see. After a few moments' silence, Purvis took the bait.

"We're all thinking it, Shah. Let's not be so coy. Is McPherson the killer?"

DI Shah looked considerably younger and less confident that Yarmouth had ever seen her. He thought it interesting that Purvis had dropped the "DI" in addressing her—familiarity or everyday bigotry?

"There's growing evidence to suggest that. However, forensics have yet to find anything that would definitively link him to the act of murder. The fibres and hair belonged to the victim's sister, whom we now know was in the flat the afternoon after Qamar Liibaan's murder and handled the body. We have found plenty of traces of Bob McPherson being there but then we already know that Bob..."

"DI McPherson," corrected Purvis.

"Sorry, sir. We know that DI McPherson was a client of Qamar Liibaan. What we need is skin under fingernails, a murder weapon..."

"Or that mask," added Yarmouth. "There would be traces of sweat, maybe a hair."

"Absolutely," said Shah. "I don't think the CPS would prosecute with just the texts, the limited forensics we have and the CCTV footage. We have no confession, nothing even close."

"I don't actually think it's him."

The voice was Yarmouth's and it sounded almost like he was talking to himself. The room seemed to relax, however, once someone else had offered the ray of hope they wanted, especially given Yarmouth's history with the suspect.

"Sure, McPherson's hot-headed and a sexist bastard but I have difficulty seeing him as some sort of psychopath."

"Tommy Blunt," said Shah. Everybody in the room knew the name, even the two AC bookends.

A former colleague, DI Blunt had had a drinking problem and had been on disciplinary warnings several times before he had been finally suspended following a fracas with his wife in, of all places, a garden centre. With the prospect of being pensioned-off early (the kind way out his bosses had suggested), Tommy had returned home one night to find his sixteen-year-old son helping his wife pack their bags. Tommy had flipped. An incandescent rage that several colleagues had witnessed in arguments before boiled over into physical violence.

Fuelled by a half-bottle of Jack Daniels, Tommy had beaten and kicked Kevin until he stopped breathing. His regret had evidently surfaced as suddenly and fatally as his anger. His wife Chloe returned from her night out to find him hanging in the garden shed. Tommy's name was now a watchword for the inscrutability of human nature. And sometimes rhyming slang, for officers in a particularly vicious mood.

"Tommy was different," Yarmouth said, scarcely believing he was defending McPherson. "He was a nutter in the making, and a drunk. McPherson is just pathetic."

"I disagree," piped up Fleischer. "We can all suddenly lose it and do something stupid. You of all people know that, Robbo."

"What do you mean?" asked Yarmouth.

"Well, you've been there yourself."

"What?" Yarmouth looked baffled, staring at his friend in incomprehension.

"Gentlemen," warned Shah.

"I just mean we can all lash out," explained Fleischer.

Yarmouth laughed, although the sound seemed decidedly forced.

"You think I have sympathy for McPherson because I once lamped him one?"

"I don't know Robbo. We build up this picture, this growing mountain of evidence and all of sudden you're his best buddy or something. He's a rotten egg, mate."

Yarmouth felt his anger subside. Fleischer was just frustrated. He probably knew the case against McPherson wouldn't stand.

"Okay guys, take it down a notch," Shah said. "Where are we with fox-face?"

"Nigel's team is on the case," said Yarmouth. "We should have his IP address by the end of play. My guess is it's not his home computer, so we might still have a hunt on our hands."

"Forensics? Anything new to report there?" Purvis interjected.

"We found a few fabric fragments in the carpet beside Qamar's bed," said Shah. "The fibres have been narrowed down to a particular type of glove. Men's, black, leather—could be a thousand manufacturers, unfortunately. No sweat or fluids identifiable on the bedclothes either."

Purvis looked frustrated. "He left no traces? We've seen the video. The struggle that girl put up..."

"He was protected head to foot. This was very well planned," said Yarmouth.

"Could the killer be one of her existing clients, adopting a new masked persona? I assume we've interviewed everyone?" asked Shah.

"Thoroughly," admitted Yarmouth. "I doubt it though. They were all run of the mill Johns, ashamed and deeply lonely. This was a premeditated and surprise visit by someone very sure of themselves. Whoever he is, we don't know this guy yet."

"Whatever," Fleischer said. "I'm going to re-check McPherson's place. I don't know if we combed the attic space properly."

"You do that," Shah said. "If only to finally put this line of enquiry to bed."

"And the lad in the skip?" Purvis asked.

Yarmouth realised with shame that he had almost forgotten Sidney Sutton.

"We can't prove it's related," he replied. "He had gang connections. But his mate, Bradley Lennox, is convinced he's in danger now, although he won't say why. He's completely clammed up. We won't get an ID from him. Not before we have the killer banged up."

"Fuck," said Fleischer, sighing. "He's a pro, this guy."

352

Shah shook her head. "Professional criminals don't murder prostitutes. Nor do they get themselves recorded doing so, she" countered. "His time will come, sir."

Purvis smiled grimly. "Good to hear it DI Shah. Carry on."

The meeting subsided, with Purvis satisfied that the net was closing in on the murderer, even if there was controversy about who the prime suspect might be. Shah and the other officers she had suborned in the search for the fox-faced killer were crossing the T's and dotting the I's on the paperwork and the witness transcriptions, including those of Hugo and his mother. These would be especially vital in establishing the provenance of the video clip in court.

Yarmouth found himself at something of a loose end. Digital forensics had reported that they still needed a couple of hours to identify the computer terminal that the pervert with the fox fixation had used. What could he do?

Perhaps repair some damage.

CHAPTER 53

Ana had spent most of the week hiding from Lisa Bennington, her blonder persecutor, and was in no mood to fight with her mother, yet it seemed inevitable.

The campaign of petty bullying against her had developed from name-calling to pushing and hair-pulling, together with the usual ostracization that Ana found easier to handle. Covert ankle kicks and spitting seemed to be Lisa's main MO. Ana couldn't figure out why the blond girl hated her so much. She had already given her £30 to have her iPad screen repaired, the money snatched out of Ana's hand, but the device noticeably still cracked a week later. Ana had apologised, made good and avoided Lisa and her little gang of acolytes ever since, but she still got the scowls and petty punishments whenever encountering her persecutors proved inescapable. Just what was Lisa's problem?

Ana had already bunked off a couple of classes and knew she'd be pulled up for it eventually. The worst one was art, which Lisa interpreted as an intense victimisation opportunity for some of the weaker students. Mrs Blume, the art teacher, was entirely too much of a hippy to be effective in disciplining Lisa. Ana wasn't very good at art anyway and didn't need the stress of battling "bitchface" (Ana's secret nickname for her tormentor). Today she had texted Chris and had got lucky—he had no classes and wasn't working at the cinema. He cycled round to meet her at the school gate. They walked slowly down the canal towpath together, Chris wheeling his bike along with one foot on the pedals like a scooter.

About ten minutes into their walk, Ana started telling him about the bullying. He stopped his bike abruptly with a scritch of gravel.

"That's not all right Ana. You have to say something."

"Yeah, like the teachers care or can do anything. A teacher touches a pupil, and the parents sue. The mums play the system and are just as shitty as their horrible kids."

"Tell your mum?"

Ana rolled her eyes. "She's too busy playing detective or having some drama with her boyfriend."

Ana said this last word with a sarcastic drawl. Then she had a thought that made her immediately happy.

"She's working until 5pm today. Want to come round to mine?"

Chris folded her in his arms, her had resting against his warm chest. He kissed her passionately and, as ever, she could feel his penis stiffen against her. Maybe today was the day?

An hour later, they lay down together in Ana's room, Chris's phone blaring out Green Day's latest album (he was into that old shit). Chris had removed Ana's bra, not without some comic difficulty, had had spent the last few minutes kissing her face, neck, and nipples. It was kind of weird but kind of pleasant too. Ana had decided she'd let him do anything he wanted. Sofia had told her how amazing sex was—why was she still hesitating?

His face suddenly deadly serious, Chris ran his arms down Ana's slender thighs and up under her skirt. He found the waistband of her panties and began to pull them down. Ana lifted her bottom off the bed to let him, thankful she'd worn the pretty pink ones. Breathing heavily in his excitement, Chris was about to unbuckle his own belt when the front door crashed open.

"Fuck!" Ana hissed in a stage whisper, grabbing her blouse as Chris adjusted his penis into a less visible protuberance inside his jeans.

There was a sharp rap on the door and Elena's voice, agitated. Chris switched off the music.

"Ana, is that you in there?"

The door opened as Chris comically dodged behind it and then realised he was visible in Ana's full-length mirror from the doorway. A harried looking Elena stepped in as Ana just managed to do up an errant button. Her bra and panties still lay on the floor, partly obscured by Ana's feet. Chris stepped away from the wall, pretending to be looking at something on his phone.

"Hi Mrs Balan. I was just helping Ana with some homework," Chris said, entirely unconvincingly.

Elena's face wore an expression of exasperation.

"Whatever, Chris. Can you both come through to the lounge for a moment?"

There then followed a lengthy discussion about boundaries which Ana found cringeworthy and which Chris must have found just as excruciating. Ana ached to hold and squeeze his hand, but it seemed poor timing. As she sat there wringing her own hands, the clasp of the bracelet she'd found under the floorboards came open again, as it had been doing for days. She'd really have to get it fixed at some point.

Elena finished her speech:

"...I don't know what you do outside, but I won't have underage sex happening in my house."

"Is that because your boyfriend's a police officer? Do you think he'll arrest us?" Ana challenged.

"No, is not. It's just not something I approve. I'm your mother and I pay the rent."

"That's fine, Mrs Balan. I'm so sorry," began Chris, eyes downcast.

"Will you call me Elena, Chris, I've told you already. Look, I trust you to be... safe and sensible. Both. But please, not here. Not yet. Can't you wait?"

"Why should I?" Ana countered, "when you're at it with Robin night after night. These walls are thin, mum, remember that."

For a moment, Elena looked chastened, then she reasserted herself.

"I'm an adult and you are still a child, though you may wish otherwise. You do as I tell you."

"And what if I don't? What if I decide to have... to rule over my own body?"

Like her mother, Ana's English slipped when she got angry. Her hot brain began to jump to expletives, always in Romanian. They just seemed so much more expressive.

"Ana, I am your mother!"

"Yes, and you're showing such a fucking good example. Come on Chris."

Ana stood up and offered her hand, as if to an errant child. Chris looked up from under the curly bit of fringe that stood out from his closely-cropped head. He looked from Ana to Elena, whose arms were crossed in the universal sign of a mother waiting for the response to an ultimatum.

"Ana, I really don't think..."

"Well, fuck you then Chris!"

Ana felt hot tears swelling and her hurried exit from the room, grabbing a jacket on the way out, was designed as much to avoid showing this emotion as to express any real anger or frustration. She took a little longer than necessary to leave, hoping Chris would rush after her. He didn't. She slammed the door as loudly as it's rusty hinges would allow.

Elena sat in the vacuum of silence left by Ana, looking at the awkward 18-year-old before her. Was Chris waiting to be dismissed?

"Well go after her, will you?" Ana said, exasperated. "You're supposed to be adult one."

Chris nodded and mumbled something, then headed off, loping at the odd angle that was his signature. This time Elena heard the door shut with almost deferential calm. She smiled to herself. There was something undeniably funny about the whole scene she'd just concocted. I didn't handle that well, she thought, but then what parent would? Ana would get over it. Her pattern was to rant, smoulder, reconsider and eventually apologise. It was a pattern Elena recognised, since it was often hers too. Chris was so placid and accepting that he was probably perfect for Ana.

As she made herself some tea, Elena's mood darkened. She started thinking about Robin, about what she had confessed to him and about what he might be forced to do in his role as police officer. Should she call him? Elena was worried she'd say the wrong thing and spark a fight. She got halfway through a convoluted text, made more complicated by the fact that her phone's predictive text was still set to Romanian, when Robin called her. The stupid, early morning face she'd snapped and saved as his avatar grinned up at her. She took a deep breath and answered on the fourth ring.

"Hi Elena. Can we meet?"

For once, Elena couldn't read Robin's tone of voice. It seemed a little flat. Was he about to end it with her? She decided to play it as neutrally as he had and agreed to meet him in a local park. She would try Ana again later, once her daughter had had a chance to cool down a little.

They sat at the café in front of the lake in St James' park, watching the squawking, strutting birdlife and the endless phalanx of tourists that circled the water, adding their many languages to the background hum. Robin looked almost impossibly handsome as he appeared suddenly before Elena, haloed in sunlight. He smiled and relief suffused Elena.

"Well, I won't be reporting you to Interpol," he whispered, putting her even more at ease.

"Thank you," she said, quietly.

They ordered coffees and shared a piece of carrot cake. Elena had to be at the Voices Unlimited office for noon. She wouldn't have time for lunch—these empty calories would have to do.

"As far as I'm concerned," Robin said, sotto voce, "what happened to you was an accident. I'm not going to ask you any more questions about it because if I learn anything more, I might have to conclude otherwise."

"I'm sorry," Elena said. "It really was just unfortunate accident. I should have told you sooner."

"That's right," Robin said. "I can see why you didn't though. You've put me in a bit of an awkward situation."

Elena nodded. Was this going to escalate after all. Robin seemed to sense her mood, taking her hands in his.

"I have some good news, though. I did a little digging. The death isn't filed as suspicious. I guess local police did their forensic work properly."

Elena was surprised. If that were true, why had Frances been so adamant that she must flee? She suspected he saw it as an opportunity to fleece her of her savings.

"So, I'm in the clear?"

"Not exactly. They'll still want your testimony on file I expect, since it happened in your house. But I don't think you're a suspect and you're certainly not listed as a fugitive."

This seemed too good to be true. However, Elena decided not to press the matter.

"Any news on the case?"

Robin took a moment, as if switching gear. He was about to answer when his phone rang. It was DI Shah. Elena couldn't help but note that the image that came up on Robin's phone was of a noticeably more off-duty and glamorous Sanchita Shah than the one she'd met. Perhaps embarrassed by this, Robin put the phone on speaker.

"Hi San. What's the score?"

"Nigel just got in touch. Digital Forensics have isolated the IP address our Foxy suspect used most often. It's an internet café in Kilburn."

"Those still exist?"

"They do in Kilburn. Can you get down there pronto?"

"I'm on it. I'll be there within the hour."

Elena felt the new kind of thrill she'd enjoyed ever since she first took it upon herself to investigate Qamar's death. It was the excitement of closing in on a suspect. She imagined this must be the adrenalin that police detectives seek. Robin had told her it what helped them put up with the abusive and uncooperative witnesses, endless bureaucracy, and tedious legwork of the job.

"Go then!" Elena encouraged Robin. "I guess I'm off the case."

She made inverted commas with her fingers around the last three words. Robin grinned and kissed her forehead as he took one final swig of coffee and stood up.

"I do sometimes forget you're not an actual detective. I'd better go alone."

He made a pained face. Elena kissed him in reassurance.

"I've got work in half an hour. Plus an angry teenager to deal with. Again."

They parted after a long hug.

CHAPTER 54

Yarmouth got picked up by Tom Fleischer at The Mall and they plotted a route through late morning traffic. Just as they were about to drive off, someone slapped the window, making Yarmouth jump. It was a grizzled, homeless man—black and dressed in a khaki suit with a lot of badges adorning both lapels. He held a damaged paper cup containing a few coppers out as Fleischer lowered the windows.

"Sonny Jim!" said the homeless man. "Thought that was you. Got anything for an old friend in need?"

The homeless man jingled his paper cup. Fleischer reached into a pocket and retrieved a two-pound coin from a pocket.

"You do remember I'm a police officer Lionel?"

Lionel muttered something incomprehensible and then, with a gap-toothed smile and a kind of salute, wheeled on his heels and headed off down the Mall, roughly in the direction of Buckingham Palace.

"Say hi to her majesty for me!" called Fleischer as they drove off.

Receding in the rear-view mirror, Lionel threw a lazy wave. Yarmouth turned to his friend, seeing him in a new light.

"Never took you for a soft touch."

"Me? Never. Lionel's one of my best informants. He sees everything and nobody sees him. Plus, if I'm honest, he's a bargain."

Yarmouth shook his head, typing a postcode into the sat nav. Fleischer turned on the blue light and they were off, destination Digital Eden on Kilburn High Road. Yarmouth was enjoying Fleischer's creative way with the steering wheel even more than usual, sensing they were zeroing in on something important. Then the radio buzzed into life. Control patched DI Shah through.

"DC Fleischer, have you got DC Yarmouth with you?"

Shah's formality was unusual. Something was up.

"Gripping the hand-rests beside me as we speak," said Fleischer. "We're chasing down a lead."

"Well, forget that for the moment. O'Leary's been attacked. He's in ICU."

"Seriously?" said Yarmouth. "Jesus. What happened?"

"I'll explain when I see you. Whittington Hospital. How far away are you?"

Yarmouth felt an inner conflict. They were just five minutes away from the cybercafé. And perhaps even closer to uncovering the identity of fox-face.

"Maybe twenty minutes," Fleischer estimated. "Did he say anything about his attacker?"

"He's on life support. Found unconscious in his flat. A neighbour had seen him lying there through the window."

"Thank Christ for nosey neighbours," said Fleischer. "We'll be there in a jiffy."

Fleischer signed off, changing lanes to redirect them towards Highgate.

"Tom, can you just drop me off first?" Asked Yarmouth.

Fleischer switched on the siren, gesticulating aggressively at a driver for whom pulling over for the police just seemed a little too demanding.

"Not really Robbo. You heard Shah. O'Leary needs us."

"O'Leary is unconscious. Plus, Shah's no doubt got officers with him. We're only a couple of minutes from the café."

Fleischer looked awkward, as if struggling with an impulse that didn't come naturally.

"Look mate, I don't want to be a stickler, but we have our orders."

"Yes, and I'll be there right after you. I'll get the tube. Just let me out, will you?"

Fleischer was slaloming down Kilburn High Street, cars pulling over as he negotiated the narrow and busy road. "I can't exactly stop in the middle of traffic..."

"You're a fucking police officer Tom, you can do what you like. Brake, will you."

Before he knew quite what he was doing, Yarmouth grabbed the handbrake and pulled it on, stalling the engine.

"For fucksake Robbo! Fuck off then! One of our own's in hospital but you go avenge some prostitute who got in too deep because your current shag bonded with her over a glass of vino."

"Tom, don't be a twat," was all Yarmouth could muster in response.

With a strange mixture of embarrassment and anger, Yarmouth popped his seat-belt, and jumped out of the car, a scooter wobbling uneasily around him, driver cursing. He held his hand up to stop traffic, flashing his badge and made the pavement in time to see Fleisher's car shooting across the junction ahead, tyres squealing as it tore away along the bus lane.

Why was he in such a hurry? Hadn't Fleischer recently called O'Leary a "knobhead who deserved whatever they threw at him"? This sudden display of procedural adherence and loyalty was perplexing. Maybe Shah had given his friend a bollocking lately, or the AC officers had him rattled because of some of his trademark 'shortcuts'.

Yarmouth shook the bafflement from his mind as he used an app on his phone to find the quickest walking route to Digital Eden. Suddenly he was a bobby back on the beat again, this time in plain clothes and with a solid lead to chase down.

After memorising his route, Yarmouth dialled down his police radio. He needed to think clearly now and avoid distractions. He'd deal with the fall-out from disobeying Shah and pissing off his friend later.

CHAPTER 55

By the time Chris finished and rolled gently off Ana, she had entirely forgotten the argument she'd just had with her mother. The experience had been not quite as revelatory as Sophia had led her to believe it would be but sex with Chris had still changed things forever. Weirdly, as her boyfriend lay breathing heavily, head upon her rising and falling chest, tears prickled in the corner of Ana's eyes. She was grateful that the angle of Chris's head meant that he couldn't see this as she surreptitiously wiped them away.

Ana ached down below but with that ache came a feeling of pride as well as a subtler note of something like loss. Not loss of innocence—that was such a cliché and anyhow, Ana had felt more transgressive and adult when she had smoked her first joint at thirteen in a shabby Bucharest backstreet. This was more like a loss of possibility. Chris was her first and there would be no going back if things went wrong between them. She didn't think they would though—she loved him, and he seemed to love her. He had certainly told her so, as she rose to her orgasm.

Chris's room was illuminated with low autumn afternoon light, which crept in through an inch-wide gap in his dark red curtains. The shaft of light fell across their entangled bodies, highlighting the bracelet on Ana's wrist, which was all she was wearing. Chris had the radiator on full, drying some t-shirts and underwear and the heat of their exertions was only now fading away.

Finally, a guilty thought about school crept in to spoil the idyll. Ana wouldn't have been much missed at art class—she had only attended three sessions so far. But it was 4pm and the Thursday double maths nightmare would have begun. Ana could picture Mr Graveley ringing her name in red pen in his register. Fuck it—she'd take the detention or extra homework for an escape like this. No Bitchface to face off with or hide from either. In half an hour Ana would walk home along the funny little lane behind the houses to the bus stop where the number 3 would take her home. She'd forgive her mother, maybe do something nice like make dinner for her. That would buy Ana some goodwill when the shit hit the fan regarding her bunking off.

Plan made, Ana lay back and Chris tilted his head up to meet hers. The kiss was long and slow and loving. It made Ana feel like she could face anything.

The small, half-blind Romanian man pushed something into Elena's hand. It was a postcard of Margate beach, seemingly a pretty seaside resort.

"Please read you," he said, in faltering English.

Mr Popescu had been coming to see her at Voices Unlimited for three weeks now, mostly to get job specification documents translated for his small team of plumbers and plasterers. Most of his workers spoke good English but some of them had a little more trouble reading it, so Elena would painstakingly translate the pedantic technical jargon into readable Romanian. She had to look up a few of the terms herself— 'ball-cock' had entertained her for a full minute. It was easy enough work.

This though would be harder. Elena cleared her throat and flipped over the postcard, where a spidery scrawl had written a few brief lines in pidgin English. Elena started to formulate a Romanian sentence in her head that captured the simple and direct sentiment.

My darling Peter. I write to you to tell you my sister is poorly, and I won't be home for some more weeks, maybe

a month. The sea air here is invigorating [bracing? rejuve-
nating?] but Liliane is getting weaker by the day. I miss
you so much. I hope you will come and visit soon. You are
in my prayers nightly. Love, Roxanna.

Cu dragoste, Roxanna. Elena finished, satisfied to look up from the page and see Peter's tiny walnut face break into a grin that took at least a decade from his eighty-odd years. He reached into his pocket and Elena found herself hoping there was another postcard in there.

Instead, Peter extracted something wrapped in tissue. He presented it with the care and ceremony with which one might offer a tiny animal for petting. Elena opened the thin pink paper and found inside a beautifully ornate carved rosewood bangle.

Is for you. I make, Peter beamed.

Elena felt a lump forming in her throat. Somehow, Peter's gnarled, arthritic hands had made something exceptionally beautiful. Of course, Elena protested that she couldn't possibly accept it and, of course, Peter was just as forceful in his old-fashioned and gentlemanly Romanian as he pressed it onto her hands. Elena wondered if he had a crush on her. What would Roxanna say?

A little later, as 4pm rolled around, Elena sat in the small staff-rooming drinking an instant coffee. She found herself playing with the bracelet and thinking about her daughter and what she would say to Ana when she came home as Elena was convinced she would soon. A text message pinged in. Ana.

Be home in 5 mins. I'm cooking din. X

That was unexpected. Ana, cooking? Elena guessed she had a remorseful rather than resentful teenager to deal with later. That was progress at least. Elena rotated the bracelet on her wrist, looking at its designs. Fishes and something stranger—lizards? Tails entwined with open mouths. It was actually quite sinister...

Something clicked into place in Elena's memory. Ana's bracelet. She'd been walking around with a peculiar skull-patterned bracelet that didn't look like anything you could pick up in a branch of Accessorise. Camden Market, maybe. Where had she got it from? Had Chris given it to her? Had she found it? That triggered another thought. If Ana had found the bracelet somewhere, where would that have been? Could it have been Qamar's?

Elena had a hazier memory image now—had Qamar ever worn something similar? She didn't have access to the evidence locker containing Qamar's possessions, but she had followed her Instagram page, where her neighbour had sometimes posted new looks and hairstyles. Elena logged on using her phone and flicked through a saddening array of images of the pretty, smiling Somali girl with her perpetual optimism in the face of overwhelming isolation and pain.

There! An image dated three months ago. Qamar wore a daringly low-cut black top and draped across her shapely bosom was the very same skull and dice-patterned jewellery. Except this was a necklace. There must have either been matching bracelets or...

Ana had found the necklace and adapted it to a bracelet. Elena's mind was racing with possibilities now. Was there a chance that Qamar had been strangled with this necklace? Would that explain the strange ligature marks on her neck that didn't quite tie-in with the cable she'd supposedly been hanged with? Was her daughter walking around wearing the murder weapon?

Another thought, and this more worrying—when O'Leary and Barnett came calling at number 10 Carlisle

Street, were they only looking for Qamar's laptop for McPherson? Could they also have been looking for the murder weapon? Ana could be in danger. Elena would never forget the photo Robin had shown her of the murdered Sutton boy in the skip. His body had been tossed there like refuse.

Elena called her child, frantic with worry now, but the phone rang five times and went straight to voicemail. She guessed that Ana was still in class and couldn't answer it. Still, she'd be safe there. She'd try a couple more times as she made her way home. Ana would probably get back to the flat before her.

Making excuses about a poorly daughter to Tony and Aldona, Elena hurried home, frustrated by the downstairs keypad, which always took an age to respond to her passcode. Her key was also infuriatingly unwilling to turn, until Elena jiggled the door so hard that a passing neighbour turned and stared. Elena smiled rigidly at the woman and pushed the door open. Her heart thumped furiously in her chest.

"Ana!"

She didn't know quite why she was calling her daughter's name. In any case, nobody was home. Elena called Robin next and went straight though to his voicemail. He'd be working of course, but couldn't anyone just answer for once? Elena left a slightly garbled message, trying to sound more excited than afraid and insisting he call her back.

It was only when Elena had sat down on the living room sofa with a cup of tea that she remembered her hiding space under the floorboards. Pushing back the armchair and prising open the boards with a kitchen knife, Elena checked that her money was still safe (what was left of it). She used her phone's light to peer further into the musty darkness. Something white reflected back, nestling in a layer of dust—a tooth?

Elena reached deep into the space beneath her floor, feeling around with the knife and drawing the mysterious object closer. She brought it up into the light.

It was a tiny, miniature dice, with a hole running through the middle of it, where it had once been strung onto a chain.

Elena's phone rang, startling her. She dropped the tiny bead and was gratified when she managed to catch it under her foot and answer the phone at the same time. It wasn't a number she recognised.

"Is this Miss Elena Balan?" asked a slightly prim female voice.

"Yes, it is. Who's calling?"

"This is Mrs Gohil, calling from St Batholomew's. I need to inform you that unfortunately, Ana hasn't been seen at school since lunchtime."

Elena quickly brushed past Gohil's officious manner and got to the point. Ana had been missing for three hours and nobody had called her until now? Gohil began a stammering response, but Elena had already hung up and called DI Shah.

To her credit, Shah acted quickly and efficiently. She said she'd send a couple of cars out to scour the area between Ana's school and her house. Elena also asked if someone could visit Chris Ngoro's house. Shah thought this was a good idea—they'd get his address from Ana's school.

"Are you certain this is the murder weapon she's wearing?" Shah asked, tentatively.

"Well, no, but it's a strong possibility. The killer is doing everything he can to cover traces. Please help us!"

Elena could feel tears building and angrily gulped them down. She didn't want to show weakness to Shah, of all people.

"Don't worry, Elena. We'll send someone round to yours. And I'll contact Robin on his police radio. We'll find her."

CHAPTER 56

Walking into Digital Eden was like walking back into the late nineties for Yarmouth. The place smelled strongly of shisha smoke, which wafted back into the room from a cramped yard outside. Tea, coffee, and pastry-based Middle Eastern snacks were available at a small counter where London's transients and travellers queued for internet passcodes so that they could log on and Skype with relatives, wire money home, book flights or just check Facebook. Nobody here was working—this was not some Wi-Fi-friendly, chichi, Shoreditch coffee shop.

The only visible concession to the café's odd name was a flock wallpaper featuring an actual flock—of parakeets—flying over a tropical island, in endless monomaniacal repetition.

The café's owner was called Ahmed Ali and he was roused with some difficulty from a downstairs room by the Eastern European girl behind the counter (Slovakian? Polish?—perhaps Elena would know). Having called ahead to say he was coming, Yarmouth had no time for any nonsense.

"Did I wake you Mr Ali? DC Robin Yarmouth. I need to see your customer records and I have a warrant."

Administration had emailed over a digital copy of the warrant they had hastily obtained. Yarmouth showed Mr Ali the document on his smartphone, half expecting the usual half-hearted reluctance and protestations regarding confidentiality and sensitivity of data. Ahmed Ali just shrugged.

"Sure. I print out the credit card details like you ask. They're downstairs. Come."

Yawning as if he had indeed been napping, Mr Ali led Robin down a flight of spiral stairs in the corner of the room and into a low-ceilinged basement that was cold and dark. A caged-off area held a rack of winking servers, processing terabytes of data.

"We haven't put CCTV in yet, but I do keep all receipts. I'm a bit of a hoarder, if I'm truthful," admitted Mr Ali.

He wasn't exaggerating. They turned a corner into the toe of the L-shaped room to find a small fridge, a desk loaded with folders, ledgers and boxes and boxes of till receipts. Mr Ali ferreted amongst them for a while before retrieving one from halfway down the pile.

"These are receipts from period in question. Feel free. I'll be upstairs—shout if you need."

Without further ceremony, Mr Ali left Yarmouth there to unpick roll after tightly fastened roll of credit and debit card machine receipts, each tied with a red rubber band. It took almost an hour to find what he needed. Yarmouth carefully correlated the list of email times from his note-pad against the customer payments and Mr Ali's careful log of email addresses (it was a condition of using the café that you provided one—Mr Ali was a canny businessman).

There was a strong chance that the fox-faced man had taken the precaution of paying only in cash. This would have potentially saved him, were it not for the invention of the contactless payment card. Cash had once been the simplest way to pay for anything. Now with a wave of the hand, small payments could be made instantaneously. Most customers now paid with such cards as well as the slightly more painstaking chip and pin method; cash payments stood out. Yarmouth was not so much looking for a specific result as for a pattern. One hour into his search, he found it.

A customer with the email address sonny0874@ fidgit.com had appeared in the café at times that correlated with each of the threatening emails. So had four other customers, but they had all paid with cards and that's what ruled them out, Yarmouth thought. The email address was almost certainly a fake one and would probably bounce if anyone tried to use it, but it was a start. Yarmouth had another idea to try.

If 'sonny' was the fox-faced man, he might be caught on camera outside the café. There were three Barclays bank cash-machines nearby, all of whom had built-in cameras, as well as a CCTV dimple in the corner of the little park opposite the café. If he could correlate a passing pedestrian or car with the times of the emails, Yarmouth might just have the lead they'd need to crack the case.

It was only when Yarmouth had bagged the evidence and returned upstairs to thank Mr Ali that his mobile phone bleeped several times, indicating several missed calls. There had been no reception in the dingy basement and Elena had apparently called three times. He'd call her back in a short while. First, he had a contact to call at Barclays security division. Now, where in his notebook had he listed the number?

Yarmouth was halfway through dialling the digits, when he stopped dead still. He'd just had a terrifying and awful thought. It made perfect sense. The location of the café, the strangely familiar way the killer had hitched up his trousers in Qamar's video, his choice of email address, the word Qamar had shouted that they'd taken for "funny".

With a horrible strength of certainty, Yarmouth knew the identity of the fox-faced man.

CHAPTER 57

Ana was listening to a band called Led Zeppelin and it was both a strange and incredible experience. Strange because Ana had never heard anything quite like the propulsive energy of 'Immigrant Song' before. Incredible because she was listening to a band from before her mother was born, playing off a first-generation iPod, of all things. While Robert Plant wailed ecstatically about Vikings, Ana enjoyed a feeling of symbolic closeness with the boy with which she had just lost her virginity. Chris had gifted her a special compilation of his favourite music and instructed her to listen to it on the way home. It must have taken him some time to put together and was filled with a mixture of the relatively recent—Billie Eilish and Chvrches—and a bunch of ancient music Ana had never even heard of.

She couldn't say in all honesty that she loved all of it, but Ana at least appreciated the effort that Chris had put into his selection. She couldn't help but read something into the title selection too—Thank You for Sending me an Angel, Love Hurts, The First Time Ever I Saw Your Face. Ana was loved – she felt sure of it. The feeling warmed her inside even as she shivered on the outside (she wore only a tiny leather jacket) as she walked to catch the number 3 home.

She made it to the bus stop, which was empty, and used an app on her phone to check the time of the next bus. Eighteen minutes! Ana pulled her hands back into her sleeves and gripped her cuffs like gloves before digging her arms under her armpits. She leaned against the angled plastic bench and tried to focus on Jimmy Page's angular riffs and John Whatever's thunderous drumming.

She'd tried to remember all the information that Chris had told her about this band, but all she could think of was the intense sensation of him inside her and her swelling desire to have that happen again as soon as humanly possible...

"Hey, Ana!"

Ana took a moment to identify the source of the voice, before seeing the car sidle up alongside her, window rolled down. A middle-aged face leaned over from the driver's side. Ana felt she recognised the kerb-crawler. Clearly he thought he knew her...

"Ana, it's Tom Fleischer, Robin Yarmouth's friend. DC Fleischer, if you want to get all formal about it."

Fleischer flashed his police ID. Ana relaxed. Of course. She recognised his booming, confident tone from the discussions that had taken place round her house with her mum, Robin, and this man. She'd always been asked to stay in her room during their meetings, but Tom's voice travelled.

"Fancy a lift?"

Ana shook her head. Something told her she'd be better off waiting for the bus, although she couldn't really say what it was. Shyness? Perhaps just the weirdness of being picked up in a police car, albeit one whose only indicator was a blue light behind the windscreen, currently deactivated.

"It's fine, the bus will be here soon."

Fleischer rubbed his stubbled chin in mock-frustration.

"You see, that'll land me in a heap of trouble. I'm under strict instructions to offer you a police escort home."

"Why? Is mum looking for me?"

"And a bunch of other people, Ana. The school called."

Shit. Ana had been trying to push her worries about her truancy to the back of her mind, onto a high shelf in a cupboard marked 'deal with later'. Fleischer had just opened that cupboard and sent its contents tumbling to the floor.

"Crap. Are you here to arrest me?"

She was only half-joking. Ana didn't have a clue how strict the police were here on truancy. Back home you were lucky if the school even noticed.

"Don't worry, lass. I used to work a truancy beat when I was a street cop. There were some kids the teachers wouldn't even recognise if they did turn up. You're a beginner, believe me. You might be up for a bit of a slapped wrist from mum, though."

Ana still hesitated before finally picking up her back and getting into the car. She felt like there was something Fleischer wasn't telling her.

"Sounds about right. Better get it over with."

Ana slung her bag at her feet and made sure she fastened the seatbelt, although she noticed that Fleischer didn't bother to do his. As they drove, Fleischer turned on the radio. She immediately recognised the passionate yawp of the singer. Led Zeppelin. Weird coincidence.

What's happening at school then? Fleischer asked, as casually as he could, eyes on the road ahead.

Ana considered not answering, but it seemed rude to say nothing.

"Just some trouble with a stupid bitch called Lisa."

"Is she bullying you?"

The question was too direct to avoid. Maybe this was a solution—tell a police officer and get bitchface expelled? Perhaps that was overkill though.

"She's just a stupid little slut, with a fan club who think the sun shines out of her ass."

Ana's vehemence shocked even her. Fleischer nodded, turning to her conspiratorially.

"I know the type. I've had bosses like that. Women mostly, I have to say."

"Girls are the worst," Ana admitted. "I know I shouldn't say that. Feminism and everything. But... Boys just hit you or pull your hair or something. Girls get inside your mind and fuck you up from the inside."

"They certainly do," Fleischer agreed.

Ana was warming to him. He was kind of weirdly handsome too.

"I like your bracelet," he said, suddenly, turning to face her.

Ana pulled back her sleeve to look at the loop of skulls and dice.

"This? Found it under the floorboards. It's a broken necklace. I tried to make it into a bracelet but it's still a bit loose."

"I could do something about that, if you like."

Ana looked over at Fleischer, whose eyes were firmly back on the road ahead.

"I think it needs a new clasp", Ana demurred. "Probably a jeweller could do it."

"That's what I mean. Friend of mine makes necklaces and whatnot. He has a shop not too far from your place. We could swing by?"

"I don't want to put you to any trouble."

"It's no trouble, Ana. Plus, anything that delays your talking to your mum can't be bad, can it?"

She had to admit, having a bit more time to prepare what she was going to say to Elena would be handy.

"Yeah. Why not."

Fleischer turned off Vauxhall Bridge Road about five minutes later and drove down a cobbled lane, past a row of lock-up garages. Ana looked around her, a little surprised. There were no shops in sight.

"It's really more of a workshop, Fleischer said, as if reading her mind. He makes and repairs jewellery."

Fleischer stopped the car and turned off the engine. He turned to Ana, one hand held out.

"Give us a squint then?"

Ana slipped the bracelet off her wrist. Fleischer gave it the once over.

"Yep, should be a piece of cake for Marcus. Come on. We'll have that fixed in a jiffy."

With an energetic motion, Fleischer leapt out of the driver's seat and popped open the door for Ana in a show of old-school chivalry.

"Follow me, mademoiselle."

Ana slipped out of her chair and stepped out onto the cobbles. She wobbled on her heels and Fleischer caught her lightly at the shoulder.

"Sorry, should have warned you. Best take your handbag. There's nutters round here that would even steal from a cop car."

As Ana reached down to grab her bag, she heard Fleischer take a deep breath and then he grabbed her. One hand around her chest, pinning her arms to her side, the other holding a damp cloth to her face. A strange, chemical smell. Ana felt suddenly weak. Within moments, her legs crumpled under her, and she fell. She was unconscious when she hit the ground.

CHAPTER 58

Clutching a torn scrap of envelope with Chris Ngoro's address, Elena dashed up the steps at Kennington tube station into bright sunlight which momentarily blinded her. Her head swam with panic, a feeling that seemed to expand within her, pushing all other thoughts out.

She grabbed her phone from her shoulder bag and flipped open the case. She could use a mapping app to plot the quickest route to Chris's house. Ana had left there just over an hour ago. She'd try and retrace her footsteps. Plus, Chris might know something more he'd be willing to share with her but not the police. Who could say? Elena was clutching at straws.

Before she could flick through her apps, her phone, able to pick up a 4G signal once more, began to bleep and vibrate with missed calls and messages. There were so many, Elena had no idea which to respond to first. A missed call from Shah, two texts from her too. Three missed calls from Robin—finally he had replied to her messages. One text from Tom Fleischer. She clicked on that first, since it was at the top of the heap.

I HAVE HER. CALL ME. Tx

That was weird. The melodramatic capitals. The kiss at the end. The sheer terseness of the message too. Mind you, she'd never had a text message from Tom Fleischer. Perhaps he was just one of those people who just didn't get the medium. She hit the 'call' icon. Tom answered immediately.

"Elena. At last. I was thinking maybe you just didn't care."

"That's not funny Tom. Is Ana with you?"

"I have her, yes."

381

"You have her? Can you put her on?"

Why was he being so annoyingly oblique? With a strangely teasing tone in his voice. Had DI Shah not conveyed how worried Elena was about Ana?

"Well, that would be a little difficult," replied Fleischer. "She's not with me at the moment."

"What do you mean not with you? Can you stop being so fucking cryptic, Tom, I've been worried sick. Can you just put her on?"

"You're still missing the point. But fair enough."

Why was he acting so strangely? There was a metallic click and a tearing sound. Distortion on the line from wind, perhaps. Then Ana's voice broke through the white noise.

"Mum, it's me. Help me..."

The voice cut off, as if smothered with a hand. Ana had been tearful, distressed. Elena's heart began to beat faster, her anxiety levels rising. Now she knew who had killed Qamar. The fox-faced killer was Tom Fleischer.

There was a metallic bang and his voice, steelier now and less playful, replaced Ana's.

"Do you have the drive?"

"The what? Tom, if you've hurt her..."

"She's perfectly fine. For now. Did you copy anything off the drive? The one with the little home movies Qamar made."

"No. We didn't know who to trust so I kept it on me. It's still on my bag. Is that all you want?"

Of course, this was a lie. Elena had passed the drive to Robin, who'd given it straight to Nigel in Digital Forensics. He'd probably already uploaded its contents to the evidence files and backed it up multiple times, just in case. Nigel was nothing if not paranoid about data loss.

"Bring it. And don't take forever. Ana doesn't have long."

"What do you mean?"

"You'll find out. Tell nobody, not Rob, not Shah, not nobody, and come here alone. Right now. I'll text the address."

"Okay. I'm coming. Please don't hurt her."

"Whatever you think, I'm not a monster. I'm a pragmatist. Believe me though—I will do whatever it takes. The question is—will you?"

He hung up, leaving Elena shaking. She sat down on a bench to gather her thoughts. She didn't have the drive, but Tom was convinced it contained enough to convict him. She could go to Nigel and get the original back. Who knows how long that would take? She could call Robin or Shah. Tom had expressly forbidden that. Who knows if he had another accomplice in the police they'd not identified yet. She could think of only one viable course of action.

The text from Fleischer came in. It contained the photo of a map—an arrow indicating a canalside road junction and the instruction to "walk half a mile up the towpath towards Broadwater Locks".

If all went according to plan, Elena could be there in about forty minutes.

The nineteen-year-old PC World employee Qasim had been infuriatingly laid-back as Elena ducked though the double doors he was in the process of closing.

"Sorry, we're shut now. We open at eight am tomorrow."

"This is life and death. I need a portable drive."

"Sorry, what did you say?"

Elena was in such a state, she's spoken in Romanian. She reiterated the urgency in English.

"Please. I know exactly which. Take me to external drives."

Perplexed but finally catching the urgency in Elena's manner, Qasim marched her over to a bewildering array of portable storage options and began talking her through them, as if she were a casual Sunday shopper.

"That one! Give me that one."

"Are you sure?" said Qasim. "The Seagate has 8TB storage and is more reliable."

Elena flashed Qasim a murderous look.

Five minutes later, drive in hand, Elena had grabbed an Uber and had been delighted to see the driver's name was named Ioan Petrescu. A fellow Romanian. That would make things considerably easier.

When the lean, pock-marked Ioan arrived, she quickly made him see how urgent her mission was, in determined yet polite Romanian, without quite telling her driver that a murderer had her fourteen-year-old daughter locked up somewhere. She couldn't risk anyone tipping off the police until she'd got Ana back, especially if there was a co-conspirator in their ranks.

As the Toyota raced away, Elena almost called Robin. She got as far as dialling half the digits and then closed her phone. He'd try and stop her or call for back-up, which Fleischer had also forbidden. She couldn't risk it. Elena swiped the phone completely off and buried it in her bag. She'd have to do the handover alone.

The taxi made impressive speed through the side streets of Haggerston, but still it wasn't fast enough for Elena.

"Please go faster. It's super-urgent."

"Okay, okay. Everyone so impatient these days."

"I'm sorry—just do what you can."

He did, running a light that changed red just moment before they crossed the junction, taking a one-way street the wrong way for fifty yards and stopping on a double red line by the tiny bridge over the canal. Just like the drivers in Bucharest, Elena thought.

"Be quick. I lose my license they see me stopping here."

"I'm so grateful. Thanks."

Elena blew him a kiss, a bizarre gesture that made her driver smile but baffled Elena. She was behaving erratically, a kind of terrified nervous energy and adrenalin high controlling her now. Trotting down the steps which curved down to the industrial and forbidding stretch of the Grand Union Canal, Elena tried to calm herself. If she looked worried, Tom might see through the subterfuge.

She took several deep breaths as she hurried up the towpath past corrugated iron-walled factories, the murky strip of canal mirroring idyllically fluffy white clouds against a background of iridescent blue.

A figure stepped out from the trees ahead. Tom Fleischer, the fox-faced man unmasked.

"Not bad. You're only ten minutes late."

"Tom, where is she?" Elena said, fury filling her. Fury and fear.

"Somewhere close. Don't worry." Fleischer looked at his wristwatch. "We have enough time. The drive."

Elena walked up towards Fleischer. Where previously he had seemed avuncular, harmless, perhaps even a little slow and overweight, he now looked coiled and ready. The fox-faced man's posture. Was this man's whole life a cover for something evil surging underneath? Was something that profoundly mendacious even possible?

"Hand it over," Fleischer said impatiently.

Elena did so, making a show of rummaging in her bag as if she didn't know exactly where it was. She had even scuffed it slightly on the pavement outside PC World, baffling Qasim, as he finished lowering the shutters. It looked used and identical to the drive on which Nigel had sent the clips.

"Righty-ho. I'll just check the contents."

Fuck. Elena hadn't planned for that.

"It's password protected," she bluffed.

Fleischer, turning back towards the bridge and steps, stopped.

"Well give me the password then."

"I need to see Ana first." Elena stood, arms crossed in front of her, trying to control the shaking, the fight or flight response that was demanding violence or escape.

"Are you fucking joking?"

Elena took several steps back towards the bridge. "Where is my daughter?"

She tried to say it calmly, but it came out as a harsh and guttural sound. A mother in distress. Elena already feared the worst.

"Let's just see about this password then. Follow me."

Fleischer pushed past her, and Elena caught a whiff of sweat and desperation. He was scared. Elena knew what a frightened man was capable of. She followed him to the car, running through her options. They seemed to be narrowing with every footstep.

Fleischer jogged up the steps and led Elena along the small side street past lock-ups and graffiti-scrawled brick walls. His Audi was parked at the end of the street, a dead end by the wall of a giant roofing factory, closed and silent now as the sun sank towards the horizon.

He opened the passenger seat and clicked open a laptop. It hummed into life. Fleischer connected the drive as Elena tried to think of anything she could do to prevent this gambit from failing. She stuck her hand surreptitiously into her handbag and clicked on her phone. Maybe she could text Robin or Shah.

"Phone. Now!"

Fleischer had her around the throat quickly, pushing her back against the car bonnet as he took her phone and tossed it over a wall. A dim splash sealed the iPhone's fate. He looked at the laptop—a helpful pop-up box had appeared, asking if the drive should be initialised. Fleischer released Elena and a couple of clicks later, knew the truth.

"This isn't the drive. There's nothing on it. Fucking bitch!"

From his half-crouch, leaning over the open door of the Audi, Fleischer started to turn. Seizing her opportunity, Elena threw herself at the car door moments before Fleischer removed his hand. There was a sickening crunch and Fleischer screamed.

"Where is Ana?" Elena shouted in his face.

For a moment Fleischer looked frightened. He had lost control of the situation. Then he seemed to re-group in an instant and grabbed for something at his waist with his undamaged hand. Something flashed in the evening light and Elena felt a click and a pressure against her wrist. He had handcuffed them together—his shattered left wrist to her right one.

Fleisher rolled to his feet, pulling Elena off-balance. Elena heard a dull thump from somewhere as she struggled to follow Fleischer, as he dragged her inexorably back towards the canal. Again, came the muffled thud—and then an equally muffled voice. A young girl's voice.

Ana was locked in the boot of Fleisher's car. Elena turned back to shout, but Fleischer had his good hand around her throat, squeezing her voice box. His grip was remarkable. Qamar must have felt that pressure in her last moments, as he tightened the skull and dice necklace around her throat.

Elena felt herself losing consciousness and struggled to make a sound, to kick, to bite. But nothing seemed to connect and in moments she found herself kneeling by the filthy water of the canal, Fleischer's furious, red face spraying spittle into hers as he shouted:

"Where is the hard drive, you cunt?"

Elena jabbed an elbow into his ribs, but Fleischer pulled away and the blow didn't fully land. She felt herself descending over the lip of the canal, pulling him with her. They struggled in the water until Fleischer managed to straddle her from behind and push her head down under the surface.

It took an age for Elena to drown—and she was certain that she would die here. Panic fountained in her head as she held her breath, the last shards of golden daylight shattering against a darkening blue above the water's surface. She twisted round, her free arm and hand floundering.

A flicker moved amongst dark green and a thick, gimlet-eyed carp swam into sight, watching her struggle before wriggling away into weed again.

Elena's outstretched finger probed over gritty soil, beds of reed, pebbles, seeking purchase. The light was fading now, and a dangerous sense of calm was filling her. Perhaps she could let go? She gulped slightly, almost gratefully, and a half pint of foul water surged into her mouth and throat.

In that moment, her hand finally found what she was looking for—something hard, gritty, and square. Elena flexed her body one more time, unbalancing her killer. He went down on one knee as Elena's head and arm broke the surface and she slammed the half-brick home.

It made a sound a lot softer and wetter than she imagined as it connected with Fleischer's skull. He writhed beneath her still, so she hit him again, then one more time to arrest his movements completely. Fleischer's spasms ebbed away as warm blood seeped between Elena's fingers for the second time in her life. She knelt in the water stunned, turning at the sight of a flashing blue light and sirens.

Then she had a simple thought. Not again. Elena stood up, dragging the body of Tom Fleischer over to the canal's walled bank. She turned to the officers racing down the steps, gratified that Robin was there first. He hoisted the limp body of Fleischer onto the compacted gravel of the towpath, the impact making him reflexively vomit up water as he came to, groggy and moaning. Blood was streaming from a deep wound in his head.

"Robin—she's in the car," Elena gasped. "She's in the car!"

Robin dragged her out of the water, fumbling amongst Fleischer's pockets for the key to the cuffs as he barked instructions to the paramedics who descended the steps, stretcher, and defibrillator in hand.

"Fucking listen, will you!" Elena shouted. "Ana's in his car."

CHAPTER 59

Finally, Yarmouth realised what Elena was saying, releasing her to the care of the paramedics and other officers as he raced back up the steps.

There was a metallic thumping sound coming from the car at the end of the dead-end lane. Robin grabbed a crowbar from DI Shah's car and ran with her to prise open the Audi's boot. It popped open on the third attempt, Robin straining with everything he had. The girl and her mother meant more to him than anyone ever had. They were more than a lover and her daughter; they had become family.

Ana lay curled up, hands gaffer-taped behind her back, feet tied at the ankles, mouth taped shut. Robin realised with a shock that Ana must have been using her head to beat on the metal of the car's boot. He gently removed the spittle-moistened gaffer tape from her mouth, and she collapsed sobbing into her arms. Then, moments later, they were joined by Elena, wrapped in a blanket like a refugee from a terrible trauma, which of course she was and in more than one way. Ana held onto them both as she cried out her fear and relief.

Robin looked over Elena's shoulder to see DI Shah striding up the lane. She made a 'cut-throat' gesture and Robin knew that his friend Fleischer was dead. The man had evidently hidden a whole inner life from him, a dark and evil emptiness that had found succour in degradation and death. Robin would miss the illusion of a man he'd thought his friend was but that was all.

Elena hugged her child with all her might, neither daughter nor mother minding that Elena was still dripping wet. Elena felt only the raw pleasure of sudden relief from a living nightmare. There was no room yet in her head for anything else.

The truth was pieced together painstakingly in the weeks to come. Without the testimony of the killer, much was still speculation but what Shah presented to Purvis was as thorough a picture as they'd ever have.

Tom Fleischer had, together with O'Leary, Barnett, and others, been on the take from Malcolm Carver for several years. In exchange for intelligence about what and who the police were investigating, Fleischer had received payments and favours, including 'on the house' trysts with Qamar Liibaan. Because his fantasies were a little more deviant than most, he'd grabbed an animal mask from the cupboard where he stored remnants of his son and daughter's childhoods. There were several masks in the box; Fleischer could just have easily have become the Panda- or Lion-faced man. He'd always worn this mask with Qamar, perhaps to hide his real identity from her and perhaps for more disturbingly psychological reasons. It was one of the things they'd never know for certain.

What they did know is that, on the night of Qamar's murder, a man matching Fleischer's description had been seen entering the Carlisle Street building not long after McPherson had left, although the latter had never known that Fleischer was a client of the murdered Somali too. Forensics had found traces of food on the paper on which Qamar had written her suicide note and Qamar had eaten a meal matching those traces an hour before she was killed. Fleischer had visited her and played one final, deadly sex game. Someway through writing the mock-suicide note to indulge Fleischer's murderous fantasies,

Qamar must have sensed something was different this time. She had signed it with the word 'murder'.

Later that evening, as Qamar was busy on Phantasy-Girls, Fleischer had taken Qamar's hidden spare key and let himself back into her place, having either decided to take his perversions one stage further or, Elena suspected, because Qamar had told him her plans to leave the sex trade and Fleischer had become enraged at losing his outlet for depravity. He had killed her with the skull and dice necklace, used Carver's keys to hide the necklace under Elena's floorboards while she was out (and before she lifted the same loose board to hide her money). If found, Fleischer must have reasoned, the necklace would only implicate Carver or Elena.

Fleischer had used the cord from an old telephone to hang Qamar's body from the ceiling rose while it was still warm. He had left the chair in what he thought was a believable position and placed the suicide note on the counter. He had painstakingly removed his prints but made sure he was seen visiting the crime scene (hence his surprise presence there when Robin and Elena 'broke in', so that any trace DNA from him would be discounted. Qamar must have showered after their session and before he killed her, wiping off vital evidence of her own killer.

Fleischer's cover-up had worked remarkably well to begin with, until Elena started investigating and turned the case from a suicide procedural to a fully-fledged murder investigation. Fleischer had volunteered to assist and brought Robin in as a way of getting close to Elena and finding out what, if anything, she knew. He'd quickly realised they needed a suspect and had bribed Sutton and Lennox into stealing McPherson's phone. He might have played a similar trick to the swap con he'd run with Robin and Elena later, to seed the murderous messages onto McPherson's phone. Temporarily changing the date and time on McPherson's phone had allowed him to back-date the messages to the days preceding the killing. The embarrassing videos of McPherson's infantilism fetish had just been the icing on the cake.

Fleischer had murdered Sutton when it seemed like the boy might talk and had beaten O'Leary to warn him off talking to McPherson and Anti-Corruption about the link to Carver. By then, Fleischer had crossed the line beyond which violence and even murder seemed like justifiable acts of self-preservation. He had also grown increasingly desperate and, when he'd seen Ana on Elena's Facebook feed wearing the murder weapon and then failed to locate the laptop that might have filmed the killing, his meticulous schemes had begun to unravel. The laptop had surfaced, the incriminating files salvaged from it.

Fleischer himself had leaked information to the press and to Carver to make Yarmouth, Shah and Elena paranoid enough to keep the data on one drive so that he could get hold of it. Fortunately, Shah had insisted on sending it straight to the evidence store and hiding it under a false case number. Elena had instructed Nigel to make back-ups. Yarmouth guessed Fleischer hadn't been in on those discussions, fortunately.

The killer must have known by then that things were spinning out of his control. Snatching Ana had been a last desperate ploy. Could he ever have believed that it might have worked? Yarmouth half-thought that Fleischer had known that it would probably end with his death. Certainly, that might have seemed preferable to a life in prison amongst many of the hardened criminals Fleischer had put away. Cops don't do well in jail.

When Fleischer had discovered that Sidney Sutton was close to talking, he had killed him in cold blood. Yarmouth had never imagined his friend could be so callous. His blindness worried him—did he himself lack even the basic level of insight needed to know that one of his drinking buddies was a sociopath?

Shah had tried to reassure him that all the literature indicated that such people were very good at hiding. When it came right down to it, what do we ever really know about what is going on in the minds of our nearest and dearest? Shah had added, ruefully. This notion gave Yarmouth only a modicum of comfort.

As he sat in Bar Italia a week later, drinking Luca's famous coffee and holding Elena's soft hands, Yarmouth wondered if Shah's world-weary cynicism was nothing more than a self-preserving posture. He had no time for cynicism himself, for always expecting the worst in human nature. Not if he wanted to make this unexpected new relationship work.

Robin Yarmouth wanted to know the two crazy, unpredictable, Eastern European women with sincerity and hope. It was the purest, simplest, and most certain truth he possessed.

Elena's worries were of a different order altogether. They were numerous and they had no easy solutions. She was in the UK illegally, a country that, post-Brexit, might well decide to kick her out, even if her catastrophic mistakes never came to light. The trauma of what Tom Fleischer had put her and Ana through was a vivid wound than she feared might never heal. She had run from Romania to protect her daughter, not endanger her life. In that primary principle of any parent, Elena felt she had failed.

In addition, there remained the background hum of worry that was Frances da Costa. What if she decided to turn their fugitive status to her advantage? Could Frances re-emerge to blackmail them both? Elena thought it unlikely, but it remained a possibility. Even as the nightmares of drowning and drifting away from Ana and all that she knew and loved began to recede, Elena had much to keep her awake at night. And yet...

As she wiped a smear of cappuccino froth from Ana's top lip and stole a bite of cantucci from Robin's plate, whilst the bustle and noise of Soho reminded her that life went on all around her, constantly, in all its teeming multitudes, Elena Balan held onto a consolation and an idea.

The consolation: she had not failed Qamar. Justice had been done.

The idea: that she might have finally found something she was really good at.

Elena finished the last swallow of her coffee and looked up at Robin, as he smiled warmly at her. Ana was showing him a funny clip on her phone and Robin was humouring her, doing a pretty good impression of a man engrossed.

This was worth preserving—this, quiet, simple moment. Elena wanted to linger. She raised a hand and attracted Luca's eye as the proprietor stepped back in from the street tables and heavy raindrops began to plop down on the pavement outside.

"Can I have another coffee, Luca?", she said. "Guys, what do you want?"

Like that, they whiled away a gentle hour, there amongst the hidden violence of a Soho afternoon.

Acknowledgements

Thanks are due to my father for his wonderful design work, and to Detective Michelle Sanna, of Kent Police for her invaluable and encouraging feedback on matters procedural as well as the overall story. Many thanks to writer and activist Elisa Hategan for her moving translation of the frontispiece folk song, and for permission to use it. Appreciation is also due to my ex-employers, the Practitioner Health Programme, who tolerated me tapping away in the staff kitchen during my lunch breaks.

About the Author

Gavin Boyter is a Scottish writer who has been living in London and Margate since 1999. Having previously worked in advertising and healthcare, he is now concentrating on creative writing and freelance copywriting. In 2018, he ran from Paris to Istanbul, as described in his 2020 book *Running the Orient*. Boyter is also a screenwriter with two optioned projects in development, including the psychological thrillers *Nitrate* (co-written with Guy Ducker) and *20 Questions*. He loves running long distances and will almost certainly never learn to play the guitar properly. This is his first novel.

Books by Gavin Boyter

Short Fiction:

Running Coyote and Fallen Star, and other Stories.

Non-Fiction:

Downhill from Here
Running the Orient
Run for the Hell of It

www.gavinboyter.com

Visit *Gavin Boyter's Unforeseen Tales* on YouTube.

If you enjoyed this book, please consider giving it a short review on Amazon or Goodreads. Every review helps defeat the algorithm.

Printed in Great Britain
by Amazon